DEDICATION

For the women who want everything and never settle.

I hope you find a love like Jay.

A best friend like Sophie.

And breakfast for dinner when it all becomes too much.

Extra DIRTY

BOSTON BILLIONAIRES

BRITTANÉE NICOLE

This is a work of fiction.

Names, characters, places, and incidents either are the product of the author's imagination or are used fictitiously. Any resemblance to actual persons, living or dead, events, or locales is entirely coincidental.

Cover Design Mary of Books and Moods

Formatting by Cover to Cover Author Services

Editing by Beth at VB Edits

Beta Editing and Proofreading by Brittni Van of Overbooked Editing

www.brittaneenicole.net

"I defy you, stars."
William Shakespeare
<u>Romeo and Juliet</u>

PROLOGUE

THE SCIENTIST BY COLDPLAY

Jay

"And you're sure he's dead?"

The man sitting across from my desk looks at me blankly for a beat, as if bored with the conversation. "He's not in charge of the Mob anymore. It's been handled."

"And the debt is paid?" I ask again.

He flicks his wrist, checking the time on his watch. "So long as you keep your end of the deal, the debt is paid."

I smile genuinely for the first time in over a decade.

Men like Evan McCabe understand two things: money and power. I have both. Now he does too. I hold out my hand across my desk. "It's been a pleasure doing business with you."

He shakes my hand and stands. Before he leaves, he spins back to me. "There's only one thing I haven't figured out."

I cock a brow. "What's that?"

"Out of all the things you could have asked for with this deal, why a women's magazine?"

I laugh at the question. For thirteen years, I've kept the truth about why I paid someone else's debt from those who sought to collect it, and there's not a chance that I'll ever let anyone have that kind of power over me again.

I shrug. "I love women."

He laughs as if it's a joke. And to an extent, it is. I may be known as the playboy of Boston, but I've only ever loved one woman. And I still do.

Once he's gone, I settle back into my office chair and open up the account I've logged into over and over for the last thirteen years and pick a song.

It's time to take back what's mine. It's been thirteen long and lonely fucking years, but it's time to go back to the start.

I click on the link and upload the song. "The Scientist" by Coldplay.

1

YOU'RE ON YOUR OWN, KID BY TAYLOR SWIFT

Cat

"**Y**ou've done all your homework?" I ask as I tap my nails against my desk and absently watch the people congregating on the sand outside my office window. It's only May, and yet Bostonians are already flocking to the beach in their shorts and sunglasses, sporting smiles while they toss frisbees and scan the shoreline for treasures.

Chloe sighs on the other end of the phone. "Yes, and I did extra math."

I laugh. I hate math. "And your mother said it's okay?"

"Cynthia is fine with it. Come on, please," she whines, for once sounding like the eleven-year-old she is. It's surprisingly heartening. Usually, she acts like she's my mother.

"It's weird that you call her that."

"You call her that," she volleys back.

"She's not my mother," I say, focusing on my screensaver. Cynthia, Chloe, and me in front of the Eiffel Tower for her eleventh birthday. My heart aches for them both.

"She's not my mother either." It's not said in a bratty way. Rather, it's a statement of fact.

With a sigh, I ignore the comment. "I'll be there tomorrow. And yes, if your mother says it's fine, I'll take you to the fashion show."

"And to L'Etoile?"

This one is always scheming. Last time I took her to her favorite restaurant, the server assumed she was older than she is and poured us each a glass of champagne. I let her have a sip, and I swear the entire experience went to her head.

Smiling, I reply, "And L'Etoile."

Chloe cheers on the other end of the phone, the sound buoying me like it always does.

"Tu me manques," I say, closing my eyes and wishing away the hours between now and when my flight to Paris leaves so I can spend all my time with them.

"Miss you too," she says quietly, though she holds back the additional word I know she wants to include along with that sentiment.

"Put your mom on the phone, 'kay? I'll see you soon, Love Bug."

I slide my mouse back and forth to wake up my computer and pull up my flight information while I wait for Cynthia to take the phone.

"You hear anything more?" I ask once she's on the line. Ownership of the magazine has changed hands, but we've heard almost nothing about the identity of the investor or what their plans are.

For years, we've operated as if we run the place. Well, Cynthia did anyway. She's been the editor in chief since long before I started working at *Jolie*.

But since the beginning, she's had faith in me. When she traveled back and forth to Paris, she left me to run the Boston office. Then she met Peter, and because he lives in Paris, she and Chloe now live there too. It isn't exactly the greatest thing in the world, but I deal with it.

Cynthia hums, as if she's not concerned. "We'll know soon enough. The announcement is scheduled for next week. They'll fill me in before then."

"Right," I admit, sounding a lot more sure than I feel. The mystery

14

behind this investor and the way things have gone down eat at me. But if she isn't worried, then I'll do my best not to be either. "My flight says it's on time, so I'm going to get ready. I'll see you in the morning."

"I still think you should stay at the apartment," Cynthia says, her tone full of concern.

I smile, but it's forced. "It's important that you guys have your own space."

"We don't need space from you," she murmurs.

I can imagine Peter doesn't share the sentiment. For years, I stayed with Cynthia and Chloe when I traveled to Paris, but once Peter came into the picture, I quickly became the proverbial third wheel. An outsider. Peter is trying to be a father to Chloe, and I can't be anything but appreciative of that. She deserves it. Having me around confuses the situation.

I'm not her mom. I'm just...*me*.

"It's fine. I'm getting in late, and I don't want you to have to wait up. I'll be by in the morning with breakfast."

"If you insist," she says with a sigh. "Have a safe flight." Then she hangs up before I can reply.

I laugh to myself. She definitely fits in with the Parisian crowd. She has little time for emotions and is incredibly focused on work and what brings her pleasure. But when it comes to Chloe, there is no one she loves more.

My phone vibrates before I have time to spiral about Chloe, the acquisition, or any of the millions of files and projects for *Jolie* that need attention. "Hey, Irish," I say as I pick up the phone.

"Almost ready?" my brother's best friend Frank asks, always all business.

"Nope. I have a few more things to do. You mind coming up?"

He laughs. It comes out gruff, scratching at that part of me that demands attention every once in a while. "You need to come, Princess?" he says in a teasing voice, never one to beat around the bush.

I bite my lip, already feeling the ghost of his fingers wrapped around my throat while he takes me from behind. "Yes."

"Take off your panties and be bent over that desk when I walk in. Quick and dirty, Cat. We don't have much time."

I smile as I shimmy my panties down my thighs. "Ticktock, Mr. McCabe. I'm waiting."

2

IN MY PLACE BY COLDPLAY

Jay

The only time my brain shuts down and allows me a reprieve from the guilt and planning and scheming I've been consumed with for years is when I'm gliding across the ice. As my stick connects with the puck and sends it flying into the net, I can't stop the cocky smile that spreads across my face. "Take that, motherfuckers!"

My brother Hayden grumbles from the net, "Next time, it's Hansons against the rest of you. I'm tired of having Kevin on my team."

Kevin skates up next to me and glares. "That was a cheap shot you took back there."

I laugh it off as Gavin Langfield, the owner of this rink, skates up and claps me on the back. "No way, Hanson. We're keeping this one. Maybe if you stayed on this side of the pond more often, you wouldn't be out of practice, and you could block your brother's shots."

Hayden grumbles again. To be fair, he's running on only a few hours of sleep. He flew in from London late last night. He runs the European operation of Hanson Liquors, while Garreth and I handle business here in Boston.

Garreth, being the grumpy bastard he is, didn't show up this morning. He rarely joins us for our Thursday morning skates, but I don't miss a single one. My time with the guys on the ice is the only thing that's helped me get through the past decade.

Beckett Langfield, Gavin's brother, offers me a fist bump. "This has been fun, but I have to get to the office. Drinks tonight?"

"Can't. I'm heading to Bristol this afternoon. Not sure what time I'll be back," I reply, skating back to the bench.

Gavin whistles in surprise behind me. "It's time, then, huh?"

"Time for what?" Kevin asks, as if I haven't been counting down to this moment for the last few years.

Hayden laughs as he drops to the bench and snags his water bottle. "Time for my baby brother to get his girl back."

KITTEN'S SONGS

The drive to Bristol doesn't bother me as much as it normally does. My phone is connected to Bluetooth and shuffling through Kitten's Songs, and for once, I find myself smiling as I listen to the soundtrack of the early part of our relationship.

For years, I beat myself up over how we met. Stewed in the what-ifs.

What if I'd been open with Cat when she first told me who she was? Would things have gone differently? Would she have accepted my truth? That I had started out hating her family. That her father and my mother had an affair that cost my mother her life. That because of their indiscretions, I set out for revenge. But that when I met her, I was willing to give all that up.

No. She probably wouldn't have believed me. Would have hated me. Even if she hadn't, keeping that secret from her family, from her brothers, would have eaten at her.

Instead, I've watched her from a distance for years. Pined for the woman whose heart I broke. But I had to keep my distance. The Mob knew I wasn't responsible for the stolen money. They knew I was protecting someone. I couldn't let them see me even talking to Cat. There was no way I'd be able to hide my love for her if we were face to face, and the men who were watching me wouldn't hesitate to dig into our relationship if they knew one existed.

She was my weakness. *Is* my weakness. The only person I've ever truly cared about. The one person I'd give up everything for.

By staying away from her—*by hurting her*—I protected her.

And now that the last of the two men who were present when my father uttered her name is dead and the debt is paid in full, I'm taking back what's mine.

I pull into the circular driveway and turn off my music, allowing the car to settle, along with my heart rate. I've been coming to meet with Theo James in secret for the last thirteen years. He's like the father I never had. Or maybe who my father was before my mother cheated and his sole purpose in life became revenge. With a long exhale, I let go of the comparison.

Theo stands on the front porch waiting for me. Just like he did all those years ago when he finally told me the dirty truths that changed everything.

I step out of the car and suck in the warm spring air. Birds chirp, and the sun beams down on me. Even though Bristol is just over an hour from the city skyscrapers in Boston, it's like a completely different world.

"Jay," the old man says as he strolls up to greet me with his hand extended. When I put my hand in his, he pulls me in for a hug. I don't get the feeling that Theo James is a big hugger. I think he just knows that I'm starved for affection. "It's good to see you," he says in his gruff tone as he pulls away and leads me toward the house.

"Is Carolyn home?" I ask.

He shakes his head. His wife is never home when I'm here. We've always kept our meetings between the two of us. But after today, that will change. "She's in Nashville visiting with Cash. I swear that woman has more energy than any of her grandkids. She's been like a mother hen worrying over Carter and Chase these last few weeks, wishing she could get Carter to settle down. Flew straight to Nashville from Boston, since she made a stop to visit with Cat too." He winces as he says her name. But it's not a sore subject anymore. In fact, all I want is to know more. How is she? Is she happy?

Is she…seeing anyone?

I have no right to the twisting that occurs in my stomach when I imagine Cat with someone else, but I can't change my body's reaction to the idea of another man touching her.

Or a woman.

There have been no signs of a serious relationship in the time we've been apart. That's one blessing, I suppose. Although a better man would hope that she'd found someone to make her happy. That she has had love in her life for all these years. Someone to comfort her when I couldn't be the one to hold her at night.

But I never claimed to be a better man.

I'm selfish. And selfishly, I'm glad that the evidence points to there being no one else. At least as far as I know. Theo would tell me if that wasn't the case. He'd prepare me.

I think.

"He's dead," I offer, getting right to the point.

Theo nods like he isn't surprised by the information. Of course he knows. The man posed a threat to his family. Obviously, keeping tabs on his whereabouts would make sense.

"I've done my part for the last decade," I remind him.

He squeezes my shoulder and watches me silently.

"It's time, Theo. You owe me. You *promised*."

He sighs. "And I don't intend to break that promise. But we need a minute to process this, to plan it. You can't just barge into Cat's office and tell her everything and expect her to forgive you. *Us.* We need to be thoughtful about this. Approach it in the right way."

Despite my utter misery for more than a decade, I can't fight the smile that spreads across my face. I know exactly how to get Cat to forgive me. It starts with the man before me telling her everything. "Don't worry, I have the perfect plan. Just do exactly what I say, and we can make your granddaughter one very happy woman."

3

WHAT A TIME BY JULIA MICHAELS

Cat

Chloe hits my chest with a thump as she crashes into me and wraps her arms around my waist. Most of the time, she acts older than she is. It guts me because our time together is so limited, and it's moving way too quickly. But right now, she's every bit the little girl who hangs on my every word. The one who lights up when she talks about music, who knows more about fashion than anyone I know—other than Cynthia, of course—and who has been stealing sips of my coffee since she could walk.

The little girl with chestnut hair the exact color of mine and eyes the color of the sky.

She's a conundrum in the greatest sense of the word. The best thing I ever did and the one thing I'd give up everything for.

I squeeze her tightly and press a kiss to her forehead, taking in a long drag of her sweet scent. "Missed you, Bug," I whisper, emotion stealing my voice.

It's so damn hard not having her and Cynthia in the apartment down the street in Boston. I hate missing out on daily hugs. That she can't barge into my office after school like she used to. That I'm not part of her everyday life. All I get is short visits every other month if we're lucky.

Cynthia's eyes meet mine above Chloe's head, and she smiles warmly. "She missed you too." The sentiment and the obvious love she has for both Chloe and me sets my heart at ease, but only momentarily.

At the sight of Peter behind her, my body goes rigid. I loosen my grip on Chloe and take a step back as he eyes me, but she's literally attached to my hip. "Come on, Chlo." I go for lighthearted as I hand off the coffees I brought to Cynthia. But she doesn't budge. I have to fight back a grin as I waddle farther into their apartment. "Let's have breakfast."

"How was your flight?" Peter asks as we settle at the round table in their kitchen. Apartments in Paris, especially in this area, aren't cheap, and so it isn't nearly as spacious as Cynthia's place in Boston.

"It was quick," I say, squeezing Chloe's hand.

She's watching me with big doe eyes, like she senses the tension, and I hate that for her. I want her to be comfortable with Peter. I want her to be happy. That's all I've ever wanted.

Cynthia tilts her head and shoots him a look. It's a warning shot. Thankfully, she's on the same page as me. Chloe's page. That's all that matters.

"I'll let you girls catch up," he says, scooting away from the table. Without looking at any of us again, he takes one of the croissants I brought with him and disappears down the hall.

The second he's out of the room, the tension in the air dissipates, and for the next hour, Chloe talks a mile a minute about everything she wants to do this weekend. Once she's stopped long enough to take a breath, I send her off to get changed, and when she's finally out of earshot, I turn my attention to Cynthia and wait for her to open up about what's clearly weighing on her.

Her shoulders are tight, and worry is etched in every line of her face. She's been like this since I walked in. If I'm honest, she's been tense during my last few visits. But this feels different. The other instances could have been chalked up to work or other stressors. But the way she's been studying me makes it clear that this time, whatever she's got on her mind is something she wants to tell me. Something she *needs* to tell me. I don't do well living in the dark, so I fold my arms over my chest and stare her down. "Hit me."

She laughs, but there isn't a hint of humor in it. She pulls out a cigarette from the pack beside her and lights it. She takes a long drag and holds it for several seconds before she lets it out and looks at me. "Peter wants me to retire."

"Excuse me?" I practically choke on the information.

Cynthia closes her eyes, as if she's trying to garner the courage she needs for this conversation. "He wants to travel. We're in our fifties, Cat. We no longer have our whole lives ahead of us. We're in the middle of them."

All I can do is gape at her.

She puts the cigarette out before leaning across the table and tugging on my arm. I stand my ground for a moment, processing the implications of her retirement, but eventually, I relax and let her pull my hand from where I have it tucked against my chest.

She sits silently until I look at her. "I'm sorry. I know...I know this isn't easy, Cat, but you're ready."

"Ready?" I huff. "I can't run the magazine without you. Who'll be editor in chief? We have the new acquisition to deal with, and now you want me to deal with a new boss too? And what about Chloe? She can't just quit school to go gallivanting around the world with you. This is *selfish,* Cyn."

Giving up Chloe was the hardest decision I've ever made, but knowing she would always be part of my life took a fraction of the sting out of it. For almost twelve years, I've been the cool older sister, the aunt figure, Chloe's person. And Cynthia has been so much more than my boss for all these years. She's been like a mom to me too. It was hard enough being left behind when they moved to Paris last year, but at least we still speak daily. And she visits Boston for work often and brings Chloe with her.

Now when will I see them?

I wish I could cry. I wish I could feel anything other than rage and fear, but those are the only emotions left inside me. Sadness, defeat, and heartbreak all left me when I gave birth to my daughter by myself. After that night, I swore I would never shed another tear. And I haven't.

Right now, I'm regretting that oath. Because honestly, who couldn't use a good fucking cry? But try as I might, the tears won't come. That promise has been etched on my heart, the scars permanent.

Cynthia peeks over her shoulder, then in a hushed tone, says, "Chloe's not happy." Her entire being deflates, and she blows out a breath as she pulls her hand back from mine. "I'm trying here, Cat, but since we moved to Paris, she's been miserable."

Frowning, I try to wrap my brain around this comment. My daughter isn't happy. That can't be right. Obviously, she misses Boston and me, but…not happy? She hasn't mentioned a word about it to me.

"She's eleven." I sit straighter, not giving into this idea. Cynthia and Peter may not want to parent her right now, but it isn't right for them to put this on her. She shouldn't be made to feel like a burden.

"And she misses her mother," Cynthia says, cocking her head to the side and studying me. "You can't be this obtuse."

I roll my eyes. "How am I being obtuse?"

"Cat, she wants us both. But if she can't have us both…" She presses her lips together, probably fighting back the tears welling in her eyes. "If she can't have both of us, she wants you. She wants *her mother*."

I shake my head. "That's not fair. You made me promise I would never ask you to give her up."

"I know I did, sweetheart. But she's not happy," she says softly. "And I love her enough to recognize that."

At a loss, I turn to the window. I can't look at her while I process

28

what she's saying. The air in the room is suffocating. My daughter isn't happy.

That…that just won't do.

I blow out a long breath, then shift in my chair, finding Cynthia still watching me closely. "What can I do?"

"Chloe will finish out the school year here…and then…if you're willing, she'll move back to Boston with you."

I shake my head, but not in rejection of her suggestion. No, my reaction is more along the lines of *what the fuck is going on in this conversation*? It's everything I've wanted for months—since the moment they moved to Paris—and nothing I ever thought I could have. But that doesn't solve the one problem that has been staring us all in the face. "I need to get the test done, then."

Cynthia nods. "You need to get the test done."

"And if it comes back positive?" I choke out, nervous about the future. Or the lack thereof.

My mother was thirty-four when she was diagnosed with cancer. She was dead by thirty-six. When I hit thirty, Cynthia started pushing me to get the test to find out if I carry the gene responsible for my mother's death.

"Fuck," I mutter under my breath.

Cynthia is on her feet and by my side in two strides. She lowers herself to the chair beside me and takes my face in her hands. "We will handle it once we know what the results are. But you need to get the tests. You need answers. Chloe needs you. *We* need you."

I suck in a breath and nod. "Why does it feel like I'm walking through quicksand?" I whisper.

Cynthia gives a dry laugh. "Welcome to life, darling. Just know that I'll always be here to pull you out."

KITTEN'S SONGS

My phone rings as I let myself into my hotel room later that week. Despite the way my trip started, I've had the best few days with Chloe. We agreed not to tell her the plan, not to get her hopes up, until we know how everything will fall into place. And as she's done since we've been so far apart, the girl has clung to me all week. We loitered in cafés and had chocolate-stuffed croissants with espressos. She ordered crème brûlée from a different restaurant every night, then gave a detailed critique of each one, her comparisons becoming more in-depth and elaborate as the days went on. She accompanied me to the fashion show and proudly told me what she thought the up-and-coming trends would be. I couldn't fight back a smile at her theories and supporting arguments. The girl has an eye for it. Although Cynthia has a lot to do with that, I can't help the bubble of pride welling in me, because I do too.

But it's been a long week, and I'm exhausted.

When Frank's name flashes across the screen, I know it can only be for one thing.

"I didn't realize we'd gotten to the phone sex stage, but I can get behind it," I tease as I slip my shoes off and balance the phone between my ear and my shoulder.

Truth be told, I could use an orgasm or two after this week. As much as I relish the time with my daughter, the knowledge of what I'll face when I get home has weighed heavily on me. So has the constant voice in my head reminding me that I'll have to leave Chloe for months before we can get her moved back to the States.

If anyone can get my mind to go completely blank, it's Frank. Fucking my brother's best friend on the regular takes expert-level mind-numbing capabilities. The first time, I felt bad about it. But now? Now I don't think at all.

"Cat, where are you?" he says in his no-nonsense tone.

"'Bout to take off my clothes and get into bed. Give me five minutes and I'll call you back."

Frank sighs. "Thank fuck. You need to get a flight home."

"What?"

"It's your grandfather. He's had a stroke."

4

DÉJÀ VU BY OLIVIA RODRIGO

Cat

"**Y**our brother is flying in tonight," Frank says as we stand side by side clutching cups of coffee and looking out at the view from my office. It's been three weeks since I threw everything I had with me into my suitcase and hustled to the airport. Three weeks of sitting by his hospital bed, getting him set up in a rehabilitation facility, dealing with my overbearing grandmother and her comments on my attire, on my lack of a husband, basically anything she could say to me that would distract herself from the seriousness of my grandfather's situation. I'm *exhausted*.

Now Cash is flying home for good. *Someone* has to take over the family company since Carter isn't interested, Chase is too young, and I don't have any experience when it comes to James Liquors, the whiskey company my family is known for.

Thank God my father hasn't shown up. I wouldn't put it past him to do something insane with my grandfather laid up in the hospital.

Cash can't get here fast enough. Even if it means that this thing between Frank and me has to end.

I turn and study him. His face is stoic. The light freckles that pepper his skin do nothing to soften his expression. His green eyes are hard and focused on the view in front of us. As is his scruff-covered jaw.

I'm a tall woman with plenty of curves, but Frank makes me feel small. He's built to protect, and he's always done that. Since he left the military last year and returned to Boston, he's been by my side. I think in part because Cash was in Nashville, and other than my brother, I'm the only family he has. Had. Because now we've gone and screwed that up.

"I know. I told him I'd meet him for dinner."

Frank turns to face me. "We can't…" He doesn't finish the sentence. He doesn't need to.

I slip the cup of coffee from his hand and set mine beside his on my desk. "We absolutely can't," I agree. "Not after today," I whisper.

His lips curl, and before I know it, his hand is on my neck. He presses me against the window and slides his knee between my legs, drawing them apart. "Last time," he grits out, and then his lips hit my clavicle.

I moan as his hot tongue works circles against my skin. "Last time."

Frank slips a hand up my skirt and finds my clit, circling gently while blowing hot breath on my neck, just the way I like it. By the time he slides two fingers inside me, I'm writhing against his palm, already chasing my impending orgasm. "That's it, Princess. Fuck my hand, and then I'm going to fuck that ass one last time."

I pulse from his words alone and have to bite my bottom lip to hold back my sounds.

Frank doesn't ease up. He continues working me until I can't hold back any longer and I sink my teeth into his shoulder to keep from screaming. I'm so lost in my orgasm I don't hear the door, but when I open my eyes, a set of cold blue irises I haven't seen in over a decade are locked on me. A set of lips I haven't felt on my skin since college are parted, as if their owner is at a complete loss for words. I push against Frank, but he doesn't get the message. Instead, he says, "One more, Princess. Give me one more, and then I'll take that ass."

"The fuck you will," Jay snarls from across the room, his anger a

34

force I can feel like a chill setting into my bones. One so frigid I don't think I'll ever shake the cold that just swept through my body.

Thirteen fucking years, and this is how I run into him for the first time. What the actual fuck?

Frank, God bless him, doesn't embarrass easily. Nor does he take directions lightly. He presses me against the glass to block my body from being exposed, and then he slips his hand out of my panties, smooths down my skirt and dips his chin so our faces are inches apart. "You okay?" he asks, his voice low.

I can barely swallow, let alone reply. At my lack of response and frozen stature, Frank presses even closer and spins cautiously, making sure I'm hidden behind his body. "Hanson, to what do we owe the pleasure?" he says casually.

As if my ex didn't just walk into my office while my brother's best friend was getting me off.

I repeat. What the actual fuck?

I can't see Jay over Frank's back, but the tremor in his voice is hard to miss. "I-I came to see Cat."

Closing my eyes, I fight off the wave of emotion that just hearing his voice conjures. Thirteen years. One little girl. He doesn't get my tears. *Fuck him.*

Three deep breaths, and my armor is back in place. I step around Frank, and with my chin raised, I stare down Jay. "Come to gloat?"

His face falls, and what looks like confusion swims in his eyes. "What? No, why would I gloat? I came to see how you were holding up."

I don't believe a word out of his mouth, but I take the opportunity to study him before answering his question. His hair has gone a little more dirty blond. Or maybe those are grays mixed in with his fair hair. Unlike Frank, there's no scruff on his face. He wears a blue Tom Ford suit that highlights his physique. While he was in good shape when we were younger, it's clear he's harder now. His shirt strains against his muscular chest, and although he's still lean, he's filled out.

Though there are lines around his eyes now, the color is just as bright. And right now, his irises are as frozen as an icicle as he stares back at me. There's a hint of the boy I used to love within that body, yet he also looks like someone I've never met. Then again, the boy he claimed to be was nothing but a mirage. A person who convinced me he loved me completely and then disappeared from my life without a backward glance.

I sigh. "Why do you care how my grandfather is doing? My brother is taking over. So you can fuck right off. Whatever you think you can do to our company isn't going to happen."

Jay closes his eyes and lets out a pained breath. "Didn't your grandfather talk to you?"

I settle myself against the corner of my desk and fold my arms across my chest. "My grandfather can't exactly talk right now."

Jay lets out a choked sound and runs his hands through his hair, tugging on the strands so hard it looks painful. He looks at the floor and then back at me again before flicking his gaze to Frank. "Could you give us a minute?"

I laugh. I don't actually mean to, but I can't help it. "You walk in on us, and then you have the nerve to ask if he can leave?" I shake my head. "You're unbelievable."

Jay rubs his thumb against his lip, and my heart clangs. It's what he always did when he was looking at me years ago. "You two a thing now?" he asks in a gruff tone.

Since I have no interest in being embarrassed by whatever will come out of Frank's mouth, I hop up before he can respond. "That's none of your business. However, we were *in the middle of something*."

He winces. "Fine, come upstairs and find me when you're done, then."

"Upstairs?" Fuck. I just want this conversation to end, but every time I think I've almost gotten out of it, he says something else that leaves me asking for more.

For the first time since Jay walked in, I see a hint of the boy I remember. His lips curl like he knows he's caught me. "Yes, upstairs. I'm your new boss."

5

MAYBE BY MATTHEW NOLAN

Jay

I'm shaking when I get back to my office. Clenching my teeth so hard I'll likely break one.

"Mr. Hanson," my secretary says, swallowing hard when she sees my face, "can I get you something?"

"Unless you have a time machine or a shotgun, Elyse, you can't help me," I reply without thinking.

She blanches.

"Just get my brother on the phone," I say, flicking my wrist in her direction.

She nods without asking for clarification. She knows which brother I want. Elyse has been with me since I graduated from college. When I transferred my office to *Jolie's* headquarters for the foreseeable future, I asked her to make the move too. I didn't demand it—although I could have—because, for the most part, I'm a good boss. And Elyse would probably smack me on the back of the head. She's in her early sixties and treats me more like a grandson than her boss, which is exactly what I need. I've got legions of people who will bend over backward to do my bidding, but she's one of very few who will stand up to me and tell me things I don't want to hear but often need to.

"And a whiskey," I add.

In the doorway, she turns around and looks at me with fire in her eyes, like she's ready to scold me, but in an instant, her expression softens, and she simply nods.

Fuck, I must look bad if she's not giving me lip.

I slide my hands into my pockets to keep myself from throwing something and take in the view of the ocean. "Fuck," I scream as I finally let the last hour replay in my mind. Cat's soft moans as she came. Her teeth digging into Frank's shoulder, her body going limp for him. My own personal nightmare come to life. Witnessing Cat moving on. Seeing her with someone else. Until that moment, I truly believed we had a shot. That her grandfather had talked to her, and I'd waltz in there and get my girl back. But once again, fate isn't on my side. He clearly had the fucking stroke before he could talk to her. Though that doesn't even matter, because she's already moved on. She wouldn't be fooling around with her brother's best friend unless it was serious.

And what the hell did I expect? It's been thirteen fucking years.

I slam my fist against the glass and wince when it doesn't give. When I look down, I'm not surprised in the least to see blood already seeping from my knuckles.

Elyse walks in with my whiskey. "Your brother is on line one," she says as she steps up to my desk. When I turn at the sound of her voice, she sucks in a breath. "Mr. Hanson! You're bleeding!"

I close my eyes in defeat. "I'm fine, Elyse."

"You most certainly are not. Sit down." She points to my office chair, then hands the rocks glass to me. "I'll get something to get that cleaned up."

I throw back the drink in one go and focus on how the whiskey burns on the way down, then slump in my chair. My hand throbs, and I feel the slight pulse of the blood seeping out, but aside from that, nothing. Physically, I'm numb. Broken. Like I've been since I walked away from Cat thirteen years ago. It's like ice filled my veins and froze me in time, protecting me from the anguish of losing the most important person in my life. And while that detachment is what's allowed me to survive these last several years, right now, I want to feel what I just experienced. I need to know that I *can* still feel.

When the memory of Cat writhing against Frank enters my mind, my blood burns hot, and a stabbing pain slices through my chest.

"Your brother," Elyse reminds me, pointing to the phone while she takes an antiseptic wipe to my cuts.

I curse at the sting and pick up the phone to distract myself.

"Hi," I say. That's all I've got. Unless I count the defeat and depression and desperation threatening to drown me.

"Shit, I take it things didn't go well?" Hayden asks.

Growing up, I was never close with my brothers. I considered them the competition for my father's affection and for control of this company. But when my father died and I was beaten to within an inch of my life, Hayden and Garreth stayed by my side. For a long time, I still believed it was because they wanted the company, but Garreth assuaged those concerns when he promised that as soon as I was well, I'd be the head of Hanson Liquors. He swore to me that they were only there to help. And they kept their word.

Now, though, we're closer than ever, and we run our family business together. Our different talents have been pivotal to our success in the last decade or so. Garreth has a keen eye and can spot problems before they happen. Hayden, on the other hand, is better with people, which is why I called him. Right now, I need someone with a heart. If I called Garreth about this, he'd probably hire a hitman to take out Frank.

I cough out a laugh and pull my hand away from Elyse. "It's fine," I mutter to her.

She rolls her eyes but leaves me to sulk in private.

"Doesn't sound fine," Hayden counters.

"I wasn't talking to you," I grumble.

"Oh, I'm sorry, considering I was pulled from a meeting with Clinton to take this call, I figured you actually *wanted* to talk to me."

With a groan, I drop my head back against my chair and search my office for something to focus on. Something that will calm my nerves while I get out the next few sentences. Instead, my mind conjures up Cat's face. The way her lips parted as Frank touched her. How her cheeks flushed. The soft moans she made, even though it was obvious she was trying to hold them back. It's probably sick that I'll be jacking off to that image tonight while simultaneously fuming over it.

"I do want to talk to you," I grate out, scrubbing a hand over my face, hoping like hell to gain some clarity. "And no, it didn't go well at all."

Hayden's voice softens. "What happened?"

"She doesn't know." My voice cracks. "He didn't tell her. He had the stroke before he could tell her."

Fuck. Cat needs to hear the truth from someone she trusts, and it kills me that she might never get to hear it from him. And I'm fucking devastated that the man who's been by my side for the last thirteen years is in the shape he's in. I can't even visit him, because his family thinks we hate one another.

Hayden hisses a curse on the other end of the line. "Then you have to tell her."

I shake my head, even though he can't see me. "She'll never believe me, Hayden. And even if she does…there are parts even I don't fully understand. I'm not sure how to navigate them. Chase's birth mother, our parents' affair. Theo was supposed to take the lead. Now it looks like I've been hiding these secrets for years. But they aren't mine to tell. If I tell Cat the truth, I'm betraying Theo's trust and taking away his opportunity to tell his family in the way he thinks is best."

"But Jay, you've sacrificed enough over the last decade. You deserve your life back. And Cat deserves to know that she meant something to you."

"She didn't mean something. She meant *everything*." I growl in aggravation.

"And that's not the worst of it." I close my eyes. "She's dating someone…and it looks serious."

"Fuck."

"Yeah, fuck. I walked in on them. *Together*." I stagger a breath. It feels like a knife is being twisted into my lungs as I choke out the words.

"Oh shit," Hayden mutters.

I grind my teeth. "Maybe she's better off with him. Better off not knowing. What the fuck good is the truth to her now anyway?"

"The truth is worth everything, Jay. Don't rob her of that too." Hayden sucks in a breath. "There isn't a single person in this world who could love her the way you do. You gave up everything for her.

"And from what you told me about how fucked up her childhood was, and how she'd never truly been loved before? If she knew there was someone out there who'd never given up, who loved her completely…who would do anything for her, don't you think it would mean everything to her to know that?"

He hits me where it hurts. Because he's right. Frank may be a good guy—I truly have no fucking idea—but there isn't a person in this world who loves her as much as I do. And if nothing else, Cat needs to know that I've been fighting for over a decade to come back to her. Even if she chooses to walk away—to be with someone else—I love her enough to let her do that.

"So what do I do? She fucking hates me. She thought I was going in there to gloat about her grandfather's stroke."

Hayden laughs, making my skin prickle. What the fuck is funny about this? Of all the reactions I could have anticipated, this was the last.

"Jay, you aren't exactly known for being everyone's favorite," he says.

"Fuck, I woulda called Garreth if I wanted my balls handed to me," I grumble, scrubbing a hand over my face.

"My point," Hayden says with a chuckle, "is that she hated you the first time, but you still won her over. And you've won over plenty of people since. Be yourself. Your cocky but charming self. She'll remember who you are. Who she fell in love with. Just be *you*."

Be me. That's his advice. "I should have called Garreth."

"Garreth would put a hit out on anyone he thought hurt you," my brother reminds me, his voice full of far too much humor for that kind of comment. "So unless you have a death wish for whoever she's dating, I'd suggest you keep him out of it."

"I wouldn't hate that..." I grouse.

Hayden laughs again. "No, I'm sure you wouldn't. But don't you want a level playing field? Can't exactly compete with a dead guy."

He's right, even if the idea of Frank dead after he touched Cat isn't the least appealing thought. I lean my head back and stare at the ceiling. "Be myself."

"Yes. I'll see you at dinner. I have to finish this meeting. You going to be okay?"

"I'll be fine." I close my eyes and let out a breath. "Hayden?"

"Yeah?"

"Thanks."

"It's what brothers are for," he says, and then he disconnects the call. That response seals the deal. I walked away so she would never have to choose between her future and her family's. So that she would always have her brothers. And in doing that, I found mine.

6

I MISS YOU, I'M SORRY BY GRACIE ABRAMS

Cat

I walk into Sophie's house to the sound of her children screaming about things I can't quite make out. Daphne has escaped from the madness in the kitchen and waddles toward me with her arms extended. I scoop her up and snuggle into her soft skin. With each stroke of her hair, my heart rate settles a little more. And for the first time since Jay walked into my office and upended my life today, I feel like I can take a full breath. I've tried calling Cynthia at least a dozen times, but she has yet to call me back. I need to know what the fuck Jay was talking about when he said he's my new boss.

I enter the chaotic kitchen and bite my lip to keep from laughing. Sophie is covered in some type of—sauce? Gravy? Baby puke? What is that?

Her son Declan is talking to an audience that is not listening to anything he's saying. Her oldest daughter Delilah is holding baby Dara, and Dexter is trying like hell to keep from laughing while he wipes at the substance dripping down Sophie's chest and arms.

"What's that smell?" I mutter.

Every head in the room turns in my direction, and Delilah's eyes light up.

"Aunt Cat! Thank God you're here. Switch!" she says as she sidles up to me and holds Dara out. It's at that moment that I realize the smell is her baby sister—the child she's about to hand me. I pull Daphne back to my chest and hold on tight. After the day I've had, the last thing I'm doing is changing a shitty diaper.

Delilah's eyes narrow as we square off. For an eleven-year-old, she's surprisingly good at the resting bitch face.

Across the room, Sophie blows out a breath like she's fighting back tears. Immediately, I regret being a brat and snag Dara from Delilah. "I got this, Soph," I say with a child on each hip. "Go take a shower."

Dexter saunters over to me, his eyes bright and his perma-smile in place. The man always looks like he hit the jackpot. And he truly did. He married the greatest woman I know and has four beautiful children. He hated every minute they were apart while we were in Paris for our internship, so he showed up unannounced and proposed to Sophie. They were married three months later, and she was pregnant almost immediately. The first year with Delilah and Chloe at the office still feels like a dream. One that I'm grateful we got to live together, because without these people, I'd have been a wreck. Sadly, no one but Cynthia, Dexter, and Sophie knows that Chloe is my daughter.

I never confided in my family. I hid the pregnancy, stayed in Paris, gave birth, and then gave her up.

To the world, Chloe is Cynthia's adopted daughter. And since it was a well-known fact that I worshipped the ground Cynthia walked on, no one batted an eye about how much time I spent with her.

With a shake of my head, I clear my mind of the memories and focus on the present. The really loud present.

"How about I change Dara? You can hang with Del, Declan, and Daphne while Soph showers. Dinner in twenty?"

This man is damn near perfect. I want to throw my arms around him and sob. After today, I'm so damn glad that I have my people.

Sophie takes one look in my direction and shakes her head. "Change of plans. Del, watch your sister and brother. Babe, take care of the baby. Cat and I have some drinking to do."

God bless my best friend. She grabs a bottle of wine and two glasses and tilts her head, silently motioning for me to follow her. I hand the kids off, and Dexter leans in to plop a kiss on my cheek.

"Take your time," he says in that soothing tone of his. He's now full-on gray and has beautiful laugh lines around his eyes and mouth. My friends did good. They are the one and only example of true love in my life. Just watching them reminds me that not everyone has to suffer through the kind of heartache I was unlucky enough to experience.

When I enter Sophie's bedroom, she's stripping off her clothes. There's no modesty left between us. I was witness to each of her children's births. I've seen everything there is to see of this woman. "Wine's over there," she says, pointing to her nightstand.

I grab for it and take a sip before I've spoken a single word to her. Once the shower in the bathroom turns on, I take the opportunity to check my phone again.

Still no response from Cynthia. *Where the hell is she?*

"You going to bring me a glass of wine and tell me what the hell is going on?" Sophie yells from the shower.

Though my day has felt like a scene from a horror movie, I can't help but laugh as I grab her glass. No matter what shit comes my way, I know exactly what to expect from my best friend.

She snatches her glass from me with a sudsy hand, takes a sip, and hands it back. She leans her head out, her hair lathered with shampoo, and looks at me. "Start talking."

I place both of our glasses on the counter and lean against it, summoning the words to start. "I've been sleeping with Frank." That's as good a place as any.

The water stops, and Sophie opens the fogged-over shower door, exposing her nude body as she stares me down. "Excuse me?"

I grab for a towel and toss it at her. "Geez, Soph, a little modesty wouldn't be terrible."

"Oh, that's rich coming from the woman who just legit gave me the shock of my life. You haven't touched a man since—" She cuts herself off. We don't ever speak his name.

I sigh. "I know. And I'm getting there."

With a furrowed brow and her eyes still locked on me, she dries her body. "Well, get there quicker. You're sleeping with Frank…is it serious?"

I throw my head back and laugh. "God, no. He's…*Frank*."

She wraps her towel around her torso and cocks a hip. "Right, hot younger guy with tattoos and a possessive alpha attitude. Sign me up."

"Says the woman who married the first *daddy* she met and has been singing the praises of older men since."

"I'm an equal opportunist when it comes to hot men." She shrugs. "Believe me, age doesn't matter. Frank could be a daddy any day of the week. But I have a feeling that is *not* the point of this story."

"Right. It's not." I pick up my wine and take a healthy gulp. The sound it makes when I set it down a little too aggressively echoes around us while I work up the nerve to keep going. "Jay walked in on Frank and me…well, ya know."

"Girl, if you can't say the words, you aren't old enough to do it," she teases.

"Did you not hear what I said? *Jay Fucking Hanson* walked into my office while Frank had his hands up my skirt."

Sophie smiles. "Much better. Now, tell me, did you finish, or did he interrupt that? Because if so, I can understand why your panties are in a wad. You have lady blue balls."

I twist my lips to the side. "Is that a thing?"

"Of course it's a thing. Did you not read my article last month? It causes stomach aches." She shakes her head. "Wait, has no one ever stopped before getting you off?"

Honestly? No, that's never been an issue for me. "I guess I'm just lucky?"

She laughs. "No, it's because you normally fuck women. Fewer selfish assholes in your dating pool."

I groan. "We're getting off track."

She smiles. "I know, but I couldn't handle that sad face. Come sit on my bed and tell Mommy what happened."

I huff out a laugh. "You have problems."

"But you love me. Now come on. Out with it."

"That's just it," I say once I'm cuddled on her red duvet. "I'm not really sure what the hell happened. One moment, I was sharing a hot, forbidden moment with my brother's best friend, and the next, as I'm coming, my ex is staring at me."

A wicked smile splits Sophie's face. "I mean, he more than deserves it."

I laugh and put my head in my hands. "I know." I take a deep breath. "It just doesn't make sense. Why is he here? Why now?"

Sophie taps on her chin. "Yes, why now?"

"That's not even the worst part," I add quietly.

"Don't hold out on me now." Sophie grabs the wine bottle from the nightstand and pours us each another glass.

"He said he's my new boss...*our* new boss."

Sophie scrunches her face in confusion. "*What*? What did Cynthia say?"

"I can't get her on the phone." I blow out a breath. "But Soph, the acquisition...you don't think..." I shake my head, afraid to put words to what I'm thinking.

"That Jonathan Hanson purchased the magazine—one you happen to be an editor for—so he could win you back?" Sophie asks with a straight face.

I flinch. "No. That he bought the magazine to, ya know, fuck with me or something…"

"But why, Cat? It's been thirteen years. Why would he do it just to screw with you now? It makes no sense."

"That's just it. Nothing with Jay has ever made sense. And now, right when we're making plans to move Chloe here, when I'll finally have her with me all the time…*now* he's back in the picture?"

"Fuck," Soph mutters. Then she tips back the rest of her wine.

"Yeah. Fuck."

7

ABOUT DAMN TIME BY LIZZO

Cat

With my red lipstick in place, a killer black dress hugging my curves, and my phone in my hand, I stride to my office. "Call me, Cynthia," I whisper down at my phone.

But the damn thing remains silent.

As soon as I settle at my desk, Sophie appears in the doorway. "Any word?"

I shake my head and hold my hand out to the chair across from my desk. "Nope. Just waiting for Cynthia to call me back. I still have to go see my brother since I canceled on dinner last night."

"Oh, will his best friend be for dessert?" she teases as she makes herself comfortable.

I roll my eyes and turn on my computer without bothering to respond.

"You never told me how that happened, by the way," she says.

I lean back in my chair, aware that she won't let me get any work done until I tell her. "I met up with him when he returned from his last deployment. Cash was busy in Nashville, Chase and Carter were traveling, and you know how his family hasn't been in the picture for years. Cash asked me to be there, and we love Frank, so of course I was happy to welcome him home."

Sophie's eyes flash and she steeples her fingers. "Oh, we do love Frank. The question is just how much?"

"It's not like that," I sigh. "We just…I don't know…I brought him to his apartment and we ordered takeout and we drank too much. The guy hadn't been with anyone for a long time because of the service…"

Sophie squeals. "So you serviced him!"

"Oh my God, you are a child. How are you managing to raise four of your own?"

She laughs. "Keep going."

"That's it." I frown. "It doesn't mean anything. He's really hot, gives amazing orgasms, and doesn't expect anything more. Which, as we both know—"

"Is all you can offer. Blah, blah, blah. Keep saying that."

I glare at her. "I have good reason for feeling this way."

"Right, because our new boss broke your heart thirteen years ago."

Pinching the bridge of my nose, I huff. "It's not that simple and you know it."

Sophie softens her approach. "Of course it isn't, Cat. But refusing to acknowledge that you have feelings does not make them any less real."

"I don't have feelings for Frank," I bite out.

A growl steals my focus. "Well, that's good to hear," Jay says, his frame taking up the entire doorway.

For a moment, the sight of him makes me forget to breathe. He's wearing a gray suit—just like the first time I laid eyes on him. Fuck me for remembering that moment in such vivid detail. His hair is a mess, as if he's been outside in the wind, or like a woman had her hands in it, gripping it while he went down on her—that thought sends a surprising zing of jealousy through me; one I refuse to analyze—and he's carrying a cup of coffee.

"Mr. Hanson…" I mutter and leave it at that, because every other greeting I come up with wouldn't be suitable for the workplace. *Fuck you, Get the hell out of my office,* and *Why the hell are you here?* are all vying for first place.

"Oh, you do remember my name. Maybe we can start over," he says, the smile never leaving his face.

Why the fuck is he smiling? Maybe it's like when a psychopath cracks and smiles at his victim before going in for the kill. Because there is no reasonable explanation for the charming look he's directing at me. We aren't friends. He didn't have the decency to return my phone calls thirteen years ago. Even after I caved and told him *over voice mail* that we were having a child.

Sophie, who knows me better than anyone and can surely sense my impending loss of composure, props herself against my desk so she's blocking his view of me. I've never been so excited to stare at a woman's ass, and that's saying something. "Let's not. Instead of starting over, how 'bout you tell us why you're here? Then we can move on with our day."

I blow out a breath. Thank you, Sophie.

"I told Cat yesterday. I'm your new boss. Lucky for you both, we'll be spending plenty of time together going forward." He stalks into my office and sits in the chair next to the one Sophie just vacated, leaving him with a side view of me.

I huff, ready to let loose all the names I've come up with for him over the years, but before I can unload on him, my phone rings on the desk in front of me. Cynthia's name flashes across the screen. "Finally," I grunt out. "Where the hell have you been?"

"I'm so sorry. We were traveling. I didn't get the news until we got back. I was going to call you, but then Jonathan Hanson called, and I had to talk to him first."

My gaze slides to Jay. He's watching me with a relaxed smile, coffee cup still in hand, and one leg crossed over the other casually.

"Did he now?" I reply.

Cynthia sighs into the phone, making the line crackle. "He bought the magazine."

A sardonic laugh escapes my lips. "You don't say."

"And since word of my retirement is already out…Cat, he gets to pick the new editor in chief. You're going to have to play nice."

This time my laugh is more of a bark. I spin so I'm facing the window and not Jay's smug face. As quietly as I can, I snap, "I'd rather quit."

"Don't say that, Kitten," Jay says, suddenly appearing in front of me. "Here, I brought you a coffee. I know you need caffeine before the day starts."

I glare at him. He knows nothing about me. He assumes I'm the same person as I was thirteen years ago. Damn, is he in for a surprise.

"Cat, just give it a few days. I'll make sure all the editors will back my recommendation of you," she says, unaware that I'm staring at the man who holds all the cards. It'd be humorous if life wasn't so cruel. Once again, the man is controlling my future.

Fuck. That. Shit.

"I've got it covered, Cyn." Without waiting for a response, I pull the phone from my ear and hit End.

Jay smiles that rage-inducing smile at me, as if he's won this round. "Your coffee," he says, holding it out.

Because I could use a moment to think, I take it and bring it to my lips. Of course, I underestimate just how well Jay used to know me. When the hazelnut hits my tongue, I moan involuntarily. His crystal blue eyes flare. It's like I've waved the red flag in front of the bull. Game on.

"Cat," Sophie says from behind me.

I spin away from Jay and look at her.

"I have to go. You going to be okay?" She looks back and forth between us.

I wave my hand like it's no big deal. "I'll be fine."

"Lunch?"

"Can't." I shake my head. "I have lunch with Cash and then a doctor's appointment."

Sophie nods. "Right. I forgot. Keep me posted, okay?" She holds up her hand to her ear in the universal *call me* signal.

"Of course." I smile at her and take another sip of my coffee, avoiding the person hovering to my right.

"Doctor's appointment?" Jay asks, as if he's entitled to an answer.

"I've got work to do." Without looking at him, I point to the door, making it clear it's time for him to go.

Instead, he leans against the window, studying me while I focus on my computer screen and prepare to get my day started. Eventually, the hole he's boring into the side of my face begins to burn, forcing me to turn to him.

"Why are you here, Jay?" I finally ask, curiosity getting the best of me.

Jay smiles. "You look good, Kitten."

I huff out an annoyed breath. "Stop with the Kittens, the compliments, the comments, the stares...*just stop*."

He smirks. "Am I allowed to breathe the same air as you?"

"I'd prefer you not."

He laughs. "Right. I guess that's enough for day one." He pushes off the window and stands tall.

"Day one?" I ask before I can stop myself.

Why do I keep doing this? Let the man leave. It doesn't matter what he says. You don't need answers; you need him gone.

Jay pulls a small object from his pocket and tosses it in my direction. On instinct, I catch it. The cold metal is a shock when it lands in my cupped hands. At first, I don't recognize it, but when I turn it over, I catch sight of a familiar inscription.

Happy Birthday, Kit Cat

Love, Cash Money

My iPod.

Why the hell does Jay have this?

When I look up, he's standing in the doorway again. "I left you a song, Kitten. Make sure you listen to it. Consider it your first assignment from your new boss."

I give him the finger, but he just laughs as he walks out the door.

"Asshole."

I spin the cool metallic device in my hand, begging myself not to give in to his little games. That's all I ever was to him. A game.

Convince the girl who only dates girls to kiss you. Take the virginity of the girl whose father you despise. Tell her you love her and then ghost her and break her heart.

I grind my teeth as an ocean of memories washes over me. Of the countless nights I dialed his number over and over again, allowing it to ring out until my phone would die in my hands.

I'll drown in the memories if I continue down this path.

In the end, though I hate myself a little for it, curiosity gets the best of me. The need to know, to keep him from holding one more thing over me, eats at me. So I take the headphones he dropped on my desk, press them to my ears, and hit Play.

When Eminem sings "Guess who's back," I actually cough out a laugh. Well played, Mr. Hanson. Well fucking played.

From: <JHanson@jolie.com>
To: <CJames@jolie.com>
Subject: Coffee?
June 3, 2022

Morning Kitten,

Hope you enjoyed your song. Have coffee with me today.

Thinking of you always.

Love,

Jay

From <CJames@jolie.com>
To: <JHanson@jolie.com>
Re: Coffee?
June 3, 2022

Please do not contact me unless it's about work.

And if you don't understand that…maybe you'll understand this.

Britney Spears "Toxic."

Regards,

Catherine James

8

PUSH BY MATCHBOX TWENTY

Cat

As I approach the table where my brother and Frank are seated, I can't help but squeal. "Gah, I missed you so much, Cash Money."

He's up and has his arms wrapped around me in under five seconds. "Not as much as I missed you, Kit Cat." He squeezes me tight and presses a kiss to my forehead before turning to his best friend. "How good does my sister look, Frank?"

Over the rim of his glass, Frank watches me, his gaze searing. His lips curl up as he replies, "She always looks good."

I roll my eyes. "I'm not a prize pig, Cash. No need to force your friends to compliment me."

The seat next to Frank is set with an additional place setting, so I slide in next to him and smile a little hesitantly. I'm not really sure how to act. In the past, I wouldn't kiss him on the cheek in greeting—I don't think I did, anyway—but how did we greet one another before we started sleeping together? We rarely even kiss. He normally goes straight to his knees. Where I prefer him.

"Ah, my two best friends. This is great," Cash says, drawing my attention back to him. Despite the joy he infused into that statement, there are dark circles under his eyes, and he's obviously lost weight since the last time I saw him. It's clear the stress of taking over the company is getting to him, and so is our grandfather's condition. We all knew Cash would take over one day. Have known it since he was young. But this isn't how he wanted it to happen.

"You should go away," I suggest.

Cash laughs, but there's no humor behind it. "I just got here, and you're already trying to get rid of me?"

Beside me, Frank leans back and settles his arm against the back of my chair. He's just getting comfortable, but the action leaves me wondering if he would have done this before we slept together. What is normal? What's not? I don't know. "I agree with Cat," he says casually.

Cash narrows his eyes. "What are the two of you going on about?"

"You're about to become the CEO of a billion-dollar company, Cash." Frank clears his throat. "It's a lot. Not to mention your grandmother's comments…"

I frown at Frank. "What comments?" This is the first I've heard of them.

Cash's dark chuckle returns. "Oh, you haven't heard grandmother's latest plan?" He props his elbows on the table and tilts closer. "She wants me to get married. Says the CEO needs a wife. That if I'm to take over, I need someone by my side."

I roll my eyes. Of course. My grandmother has no hope for Carter or me. She acts like we won't be there to encourage him every step of the way.

"I hate to say it, but if grandmother is plotting your marriage, you better take the vacation while you can."

Cash blows out a breath and looks around the restaurant. After a long moment, he slides a hand through his hair and turns back to face us. "Maybe. So what's new with you, Kit Cat?"

"Nothing as exciting as you. New CEO. Next up, marriage," I tease, doing my best to keep the conversation focused on him rather than my train wreck of a life.

He closes his eyes and shakes his head, but then he finally smiles that smile I love so much. "How was Paris?"

Memories of the days I spent with Chloe instantly brighten my mood. "It was great. Chloe has become her own little person. It's crazy."

"Oh, yeah? I miss her. It's been years since I've seen her. She's probably huge."

I take out my phone and slide it across to him. The lock screen is set with a picture of Chloe at one of the restaurants we visited. The cornflower blue of her dress makes her eyes shine brightly. Just like her father's.

I gulp down the fear that rattles through me at that thought. Now that I have to face him daily, the likelihood that she may actually meet him one day has multiplied significantly.

Chloe has always known the truth. That I'm her mother. That I gave Cynthia full custody when she was a baby. That I'll always be in her life, but for the world, she is Cynthia's.

But I love her fiercely, and she knows no piece of paper will change that.

She also knows about her father. She knows he was a boy I loved, and that things didn't work out.

I promised I'd never lie to her, and now that Jay has popped back into my life, I'm scared to death that she'll ask more questions. That she'll be forced to deal with the fact that he chose not to be part of her life. That knowledge would devastate her.

Guilt gnaws at me for having smiled over Jay's antics this morning. He doesn't deserve even one smile.

"She's beautiful, Cat," Cash says, sliding the phone back to me.

I don't say thanks. That would be acknowledging that I had something to do with it. I wonder sometimes if my brother knows the truth but allows me to hide behind it. Or is it possible he really doesn't know that Chloe is my daughter?

"So where do you think you'll go?" I change the subject.

Frank chuckles beside me.

"What are you laughing at?" Cash asks with a tip of his chin.

Next to me, Frank shakes his head. "When Cat gets a thought in her head, you might as well just go with it. She's like a dog with a bone."

I nudge him in the ribs, and in response, he squeezes my shoulder with the hand he's still got propped on the back of my chair.

Opposite us, Cash hisses. "What's going on here?"

Frank and I both stiffen. "What?" I ask.

Cash narrows his eyes and then shakes his head. "Never mind. I'll make ya a deal," he says to Frank.

Pressing his lips together, Frank watches my brother silently.

"You agree to work for me, and I'll take the damn trip."

Scoffing, Frank shakes his head and crosses his arms over his chest. "Not a chance."

Cash sighs and stares him down, his expression surprisingly hurt. "Why won't you work for me?"

"I don't need a pity job," he says gruffly.

"It's not a pity job," Cash argues.

"What are we talking about?" I turn from my brother to Frank and then back again.

"Your brother," Franks says in an annoyed tone, "wants me to be his driver."

Cocking my head, I regard Cash, taken aback by the ridiculousness of that request.

"That is not what I want," Cash replies, sitting a little straighter. "I want you to be my second hand. Yes, I need someone to drive me, but not like that. I need protection, Frank. And I need someone I can trust. Someone on the inside of the company who can listen and watch and do all the things you know how to do. And the pay is really fucking good."

He glares at his best friend.

I take a deep breath, wanting nothing more than to stay out of this argument.

Frank drops his elbows to the table. "You should use who your grandfather used."

"I don't trust him," he counters. "Not because he's not good. But because he's not *my* best friend. I need you, Frank." He runs his hands through his hair. "There is no one I trust more than you. And I have no one there right now."

I rest my palm on Frank's thigh and squeeze, willing him to hear my brother out. Cash never asks for anything. If he thinks he needs Frank, then it's for good reason. And I hope he listens.

Frank tucks his chin and glares at my hand as if it's on fire but says nothing. Then he blows out a breath and leans back. "Whatever you were going to offer me, take fifty thousand off it, and we've got a deal."

Cash laughs. "You realize you're negotiating in the wrong direction, right?"

Frank shrugs. "Take it or leave it."

Cash smiles. "So where should I go on vacation?"

9

I WANT YOU BACK BY NSYNC

Cat

My legs moving with precision, I hit the pavement and settle into my run. For reasons I refuse to examine, I slipped my old iPod into the pocket of my leggings before I left my apartment. I'll blame it on nostalgia. This week is weird. First, Jay shows up as my new boss. Now my brother is actually considering my grandmother's request that he find a wife. And Frank agreed to work for him.

In a matter of days, everything in my life has changed.

And summer is here, which means I'll be raising Chloe here in Boston in a few short months. That reminds me—I have to look into schools and activities to keep her busy in the afternoons. And forget dating or going out. Not that I have much of a life outside of work these days. I visit Sophie and her family every weekend. Then brunch with my brothers on Sundays. I don't exactly have a social life. And dating? Ha. What Frank and I have been doing definitely doesn't qualify as dating.

And that's over now anyway.

So I have a few months to live it up. I might as well make the best of them. I hit play on the iPod and roll my eyes, knowing Jay is to blame as "I Want You Back" by NSYNC plays in my ears.

KITTEN'S SONGS

Three hours later, I'm sitting at my desk, editing a post for our Instagram page, when Rose steps into my office. She plops into the seat in front of my desk without an invitation and smiles. "Jonathan Hanson is our new boss."

I give her a bored expression.

"Didn't the two of you—"

I hold up my hand to stop her. "Rose, we've been over this before. I don't do office gossip."

She looks down at her nails with a smile. They're a pale yellow with a white strip across the top. Then her green eyes are on me again. "I'm not talking about you, Cat. I'm talking *to* you." She tilts her head toward my office door. "*They* will be talking about you, though, when they get wind that your ex-boyfriend is the one deciding who our next editor in chief will be."

I groan, but not because I'm concerned about the gossip. I've earned my spot in this company. Nepotism has nothing to do with where I am today. While Cynthia and I may be close, no one would believe for a second that she would promote someone she didn't deem worthy.

No, I groan because I'm once again being reminded that Jay is the boss now. And he decides my future.

Again.

"*Anyway*," Rose drawls, "I came down to tell you he's called an office meeting at ten." She stands and watches me, surely waiting for a reaction she can dissect.

I've grown accustomed to her games over the years, and I've spent

70

that time perfecting my poker face. I plaster on a fake smile and shrug. "See ya there."

As soon as she's gone, I hit the intercom. "Looks like it's starting..." I say ominously when Sophie picks up.

The bitch has the nerve to laugh. "Oh, it's like the Hunger Games—are we on team Katniss or team—"

"We're on team *Jolie*," I snap. "And my team, dammit."

Sophie's teasing vanishes. "I know, babe. We have to make the best of this, though. And I still believe he's doing this to win you back, not to hurt you."

"I don't want to be won back," I say, anger getting the best of me.

"So you admit that's what he's doing?"

I sigh as I inspect the stupid iPod that I've been carrying with me everywhere. What is wrong with me? I'm not ready to share details about what Jay's been doing with the godforsaken device. Probably because Sophie would be reasonable and tell me to throw it out, or ya know, not turn it on, if I didn't want to hear the songs Jay sends daily.

That's what a normal person would do. He doesn't have some special ability to force the songs into my ears. I'm *doing* this to myself.

"He's obviously here for several reasons. And I'll admit that maybe one of his motives is to weasel his way back into my life, okay? But it's just a game to him, Soph. I was only ever a game to him." My throat clogs with uncharacteristic emotion, and behind my eyes, I feel a pressure that hasn't existed for me in years. One that used to be followed by tears. Is it possible that I could cry? After all this time?

"Babe, *no*. Do not cry over that asshole. I'm sorry. I was teasing. You wanna skip the meeting? Let's go eat cake at Dexter's photoshoot instead. You know how mad he gets when the models get hungry."

I guffaw. "You're an asshole."

"But I'm *your* asshole. Seriously, let's skip the meeting."

With a sigh, I scan the beach outside my window, taking in the people on the sand. The families. The couples. "I'll be fine. We need to be there. I've given thirteen years to this magazine; I'm not letting him take it from me."

"That's my girl," she replies. "Hey, how did yesterday go, by the way?"

I bite my lip. "I didn't go."

"Catherine James," she reprimands in a hushed tone.

"I don't need bad news on top of everything else right now, Soph. I'll do it for Chlo, I promise. But just…I can't stand the idea of feeling weak right now."

"You aren't weak, Cat. No matter what the news is, you are the strongest woman I've ever met. And you've met my mother…"

"Thanks," I whisper. Then I straighten my back and blink away the emotions threatening to rear their ugly heads. "I'll meet you in the conference room in ten minutes."

"You got this, babe," she reminds me.

But do I?

10

I'M GONNA BE (500 MILES) BY SLEEPING AT LAST

Jay

"Elyse, where are the waffles?" I ask in a panic. The meeting is starting in five minutes, and everything needs to be perfect.

Elyse doesn't even try to hide her laughter. "I've never seen you so disheveled, Mr. Hanson."

"The waffles," I grunt.

The ridiculous woman only smiles serenely, not bothered by my tantrum in the least. "The owner said he'd have them here by 9:55." She flicks her wrist to check her watch just as a man walks in.

I recognize him immediately, and for the first time this morning, I feel like I can take a full breath.

"Jay," he says. His soft voice is one I've grown accustomed to over the years. He places the bag of food on the table and moves toward me, offering me his hand.

I grab for it, and he pulls me toward his chest and claps me on the back in a manly hug. When we pull apart, he smiles. "I take it the plan is in motion?"

I breathe out a sigh and look around the room. "Appears so."

"Let's not waste another minute, then," he says, heading toward the bag and helping Elyse set up breakfast.

Years ago, after losing Cat, I spent months in a fog. The only time I felt remotely at peace was on Sundays at the farmers' market. She was living in Paris, her life a world away from mine. As it needed to be. I didn't dare go anywhere that would lead them to linking her to me, but the farmers' market was a safe place to get lost in our memories. On Sundays, I'd have a waffle at Ivan's stall and pretend for a few moments that Cat was there with me. That the laughter from a woman passing by or stopping at the stall next to me belonged to her. After my fourth or fifth visit, Ivan asked if he could join me on his break, and after that, he sat with me each week. At the time, he was the only person I could talk to so openly. And even then, I guarded a lot of what I said, certain they had someone following me.

Thirteen years of Sundays spent together means Ivan is like family. He and Theo and my brothers are all I have left. And now I've lost Theo.

He isn't gone, but the steady contact I once had with him is. I can't just waltz into the James Estate and demand they let me see him. So though he's still alive, the relationship between us has all but ended.

People trickle into the conference room wearing surprised looks. Filled with pride, I take in the table in front of me. There are jugs filled with water, orange juice, and coffee. Pastries and bagels are piled high in wicker baskets. Napkins, plates, and silverware are set up in front of every place setting, and Ivan is setting up the waffle bar on a side table, being sure to include the fresh strawberries and homemade whipped cream I requested—Cat's favorite.

Sophie and Cat arrive together, chatting with their heads down as they step inside the conference room. Cat almost walks straight into Ivan, but before she can slam into him, he gently clasps her arms. At the contact, she looks up at him with wide eyes. "I'm so sorry," she says.

He smiles and takes her in. It's obvious by his warm smile that he recognizes her from the pictures I've shared over the years. Filled with pride that I was able to call her mine, even for a few short months, I couldn't not show him the most beautiful woman I've ever seen.

"Catherine," he says reverently.

I shake my head with a smile. He's spent half a second with her, and he's already giving away my secrets.

"I'm sorry, do I know you?" she asks with a frown.

He shakes his head and then looks to me for help.

"Kitten"—I turn on my most charming smile as I approach—"this is Ivan. He makes the waffles you love," I say, nodding to the table.

Her face scrunches in confusion as she stares at the breakfast food. Then she turns back to Ivan. "Have we met before?" she asks, still lost.

He looks at me again. Like he doesn't know which way I want him to spin things. But all anyone is going to get from me is the truth. I'm tired of secrets and lies. I press closer to her so the employees mingling around us can't hear and whisper, "He owns the waffle stall we went to the day I first kissed that perfect fucking mouth."

She stiffens next to me.

"To this day, it's the best thing I've ever put in my mouth," I say with a sly grin and a wink as I pull back.

She's still silent, but her breathing is more erratic, and her chest rises and falls quickly.

"Your mouth; not the waffles," I clarify. Then I spin on my heel and stride to my spot at the front of the conference table. "Okay, everyone," I call, "grab some breakfast and take your seats."

Across the room, Cat's frozen, but she's watching me with an intensity I haven't seen from her in years. Sophie squeezes her arm, and finally, she comes back to the room, suddenly very aware of her surroundings. Once she's got her bearings, she narrows her eyes and glares at me.

I can't help it. I have to laugh at her reaction. It may take some time, but it's obvious after that small exchange that I still affect her just as she affects me. And until she's mine again, at least I can tease her as if she is. She's always been my favorite thing to play with. And God, is this fucking fun.

11

IT AIN'T ME BY SELENA GOMEZ

Cat

Eyeing Jay over my coffee, I lean back in my chair and listen to him formally introduce himself to the staff. His attempt to ingratiate them with his breakfast spread missed the mark by a mile. Almost no one has taken a pastry. Even the fruit remains mostly untouched.

This is a fashion magazine. We may tout that we focus on real women, but in the end, we still work in an industry that expects us to look a certain way. No one in this room would dare to entertain the calories laid out before them in front of others.

As he speaks, Jay looks at the pastries every few seconds, as if willing someone to take one. If it were anyone but him, I'd feel bad, and I'd probably take one for the team and dig in.

In all honesty, my mouth is watering over the damn waffles. Unlike when I was younger, I don't allow my grandmother's comments to sway my feelings on food. I have curves and cellulite and I don't give a shit. I also have a c-section scar that takes creativity to hide, since no one knows I had a child.

Speaking of—when I break free from the thoughts swirling in my mind and look to the front of the room, her father is watching me. What exactly is his game? Bringing the waffles from our "first date," the iPod, the songs…I can't figure him out.

"I'm sure you're all wondering who will be taking over as editor in chief with the news that Cynthia is retiring."

At that comment, every person in the room sits up a little straighter. Except Sophie and me, of course. She's the only one at the table who's dared to take a pastry, and instead of focusing on Jay, she's humming over how good her donut is.

Though she has no idea she's missing out. The waffles are delicious. I glance in their direction longingly, but I refuse to give Jay the satisfaction.

"The decision has been left to me as the new owner of *Jolie*, and I have a plan in place that I think you'll all find fair."

Sophie snorts beside me, and I have to press my lips together to hide my own laughter at her outburst.

"Something funny?" Jay asks.

With an innocent tilt of her head, Sophie goes in for the kill. It's always fun watching her take people apart. I'm downright giddy to have a front-row seat when her victim is Jay. "Just trying to figure out what qualifies you to make the decision about who should run a *women's* magazine."

Jay licks his lips. "I happen to love women."

This time, I don't even try to hold back my laughter. "That's for damn sure," I mutter under my breath. Every person in this room has seen Jay with a different woman on his arm in every one of our issues. He was the worst type of ghost over the years, appearing everywhere, making it so he haunted me when all I wanted was to live in the present and ignore the ghosts of my past.

Jay shoots me a look, and in return, all I give him is a shrug. If he wants respect, he needs to earn it from his new employees. Mine isn't up for grabs.

He clears his throat. "I understand that some of you may have your concerns about me taking over, seeing as how, until now, I haven't worked in the magazine industry. But I assure you my experience is in management and in helping those who are good at something succeed. And the resources at my disposal will allow us to make this the best magazine on the market."

Sophie sighs and tosses her balled-up napkin onto the table. "We already outsell every magazine on the market, Mr. Hanson."

"Yes. Under Cynthia, you did. But she's leaving, and now it's time for you all to prove your worth." With that, he looks around the room again. "As I was saying before. We need a new editor in chief. And since Mrs. Sullivan has so aptly pointed out that I'm new here, I will base my decision on how each of you produces over the next few months. I'm not looking backward. I don't care if you were Cynthia's favorite editor." He glances in my direction. "And I don't care if you were her right hand." He glances at Rose.

Apparently, he knows more than I gave him credit for.

"I'm making my decision based on what I see. For the summer edition, I want each of you to pitch me a story. Something different. Something no one has done. The best idea will get the feature in August's edition, and the author of such will be promoted to editor in chief. Any questions?"

Whispers abound around the room. An open playing field. I don't miss the glances in my direction. They all know I was Cynthia's pick. Suddenly, every person at this table is wondering whether they have a shot at what is supposed to be *my* job.

He stole my heart a long time ago. But I'll be damned if he takes this from me too.

KITTEN'S SONGS

Scrolling through my inbox, I curse again at Cynthia's sudden inability to return calls and emails. I'm still stewing over Jay's grand plan for picking an editor in chief. If she thinks I'll let her retire without the guarantee that I'll step into her position, she's lost her damn mind.

When my cell phone rings, I say a silent prayer that she's finally crawled out from wherever she's been hiding and that she's got a plan. But when I pick it up, my brother's name flashes across the screen. At least a chat with him is sure to lift my spirits.

"Hey, Cash Money. How's vacation?"

"Pretty good, Kit Cat. Everything okay at home?"

No. Everything is a complete disaster. But that's not what he's asking, so I take a deep breath and focus on remaining upbeat. "Yes, everything is under control. Pa looks better than he did last week, and Grandmother isn't letting the nurses out of his room. I feel bad for the poor guy; he probably hasn't had a moment of peace with her staring at him every minute of the day."

Cash asked Frank to stay at our grandparents' house while he's gone. Frank is keeping me up to date.

"She's just worried about him," my brother replies in his easy tone.

I can't help the laugh that comes out of my mouth. He *would* defend her. He's the favorite. The one who never disappoints our grandmother. "She's unbearable, and she's all wound up. Be ready for her to focus all that energy on you as soon as you're home."

"Be good to her. I'll see you when I get back to Boston."

"Wait a second. How's your last big hurrah? How come you didn't have Carter and Chase meet you? I'm sure they could take the plane if you're bored."

My brother's reply is quick and murmured, like he's making sure he isn't overheard. "Promise I'm not bored. I have to go, though. Later, Kit Cat."

He disconnects the call before I can say goodbye, and I stare at the blank screen for a moment, shocked. *He hung up on me.* Maybe that means my brother has found someone to entertain him for the weekend. I hope she deserves him.

Truth be told, I could really use a woman of my own. I think Frank will be the last of the men for me.

"What has you smiling?" Jay says as he raps on my office door. Why he bothers with the formality is beyond me since he doesn't wait for me to grant him entrance before he saunters in.

When I don't reply, he holds up a platter. "Brought you a waffle, Kitten," he says, wearing a stupid smile.

Tipping my chin, I focus my attention on him, ensuring my expression is hard in hopes that he'll take the hint and move along. "If I wanted one, I would've had one while they were still hot."

"Don't be difficult, Kitten. I had Ivan deliver this one fresh for you." He steps around my desk and holds the tray lower, bringing a waffle with fresh strawberries and a bowl of whipped cream into view.

I eye them for a moment, then peer up at him. Difficult? I'll show him fucking difficult.

Without breaking eye contact, I swipe a strawberry from the plate and plop it into the whipped cream, all while Jay still holds the platter. His eyes flare as I bring it to my lips. Slowly, my tongue darts out and sweeps along the edge of the whipped cream–coated strawberry, and then I close my eyes and moan as I slip the piece of fruit between my lips. When I look up at him again, still sucking on the strawberry, the fucker is smiling.

With a huff, I toss the strawberry into the bin next to my desk and turn back to my computer.

He ruined my fun.

"It's cute that you think you're screwing with me, Catherine." He places the plate on my desk, and with one hand on the armrest of my chair, he spins me so I'm facing him again. Just as slowly as I did it, he takes a strawberry and mimics my actions. He dips it into the whipped cream and then presses it to my mouth.

When I don't open for him, he runs it against my lips, sending a full-body shiver coursing through me. Jay leans in until his face is inches from mine, but I don't back away. Letting him get this close is undoubtedly the stupidest thing I could do in this moment, but I refuse to let him see how he affects me.

Before I can stop him, his tongue darts out, and he licks across my lips, cleaning up the mess of whipped cream he just left. Then he runs his thumb against his lips and sucks the excess whipped cream into his mouth. "Fucking delicious," he says, holding my gaze. His lips are still dangerously close to mine. "Enjoy the waffle, Kitten. By the way, it still holds true. Best thing I've ever had in my mouth."

When he winks, it's like my entire body comes back online. My palm finally connects with my brain, whipping back and slapping Jay straight across his smug face.

"What the hell is wrong with you?" I hiss, blood pulsing through my veins wildly.

Jay's jaw falls slack as a red mark in the shape of my hand appears on his cheek.

"You think after thirteen years you can waltz in here and fucking *lick* me? *After what you did to us*? This isn't a game. I'm not interested in your motives, your songs, or you damn treats. Keep your tongue and everything else of yours away from me."

"Cat, I—"

I cut off his apology with a glare.

"Save it. You've had years to reach out to us. *Years*! Like I told you the last time I called, we don't need you. So please, just leave me the hell alone."

Jay's brow pinches, and he studies me. Whatever he sees has him shaking his head and stepping back.

EXTRA DIRTY

Spinning to face the window, I don't give him the opportunity to see me break. Once he's gone, I stare down at the waffle he's left behind and let out a slow breath. Screw it. I rip off a hunk of it, dip it in the syrup, and shove it into my mouth.

The first bite leaves me groaning.

Fucking hell. The waffle is just as freaking good as I remember.

If only I could erase all the memories that came after that.

12

DEMONS BY IMAGINE DRAGONS

Jay

The sting of Cat's handprint burns, even hours later. The fuck is wrong with me? Why the hell did I bother listening to Hayden's absurd suggestion that I be myself?

Be myself. Fuck. Worst advice ever. The woman hates me. I need to be someone else. Someone less cocky. Less…me.

The look on her face said it all. And if that wasn't clear enough, I can't get her damn words out of my head.

You've had years to reach out to us. Years! Like I told you the last time I called, we don't need you. So please, just leave me the hell alone.

The last time she called? When was that? And what did she say? How long did she wait before moving on?

I shake the questions from my head. I'll likely never get the answers I seek, so I push them aside and wander into my brother's office at Hanson Liquors and plop into the chair opposite him.

He looks up with a scowl. Garreth's face is permanently set that way, so it's of no concern to me. For all I know, today could be a good day for him. His steely blue eyes meet mine, and he points to the whiskey bottle on his desk.

With a shrug, I reach for it. "It's a little early and I don't normally drink James Whiskey, but if you insist."

"Your fucking girlfriend's brother sent that."

I grimace. "Now that's just cruel. You know she's not my girlfriend, and you know I'd do anything in the world to change that."

"Even give up your family company?" he asks with a bite.

Rubbing at my bottom lip, I lock eyes with him. "If she'd agree to be my wife, I'd give up everything."

My brother huffs out a sigh. "A damn romantic. How did I end up with a damn romantic for a brother?"

I run my hand through my hair. "Stop acting like our father. It suits you too well."

"The James brothers sent us that bottle to gloat." He points at it again and sneers, like the bottle walked in here itself.

"So what?" I honestly don't understand why he's losing his mind. From what I've gleaned from my sources, Theo is stable. Eventually, he'll wake up and tell them our plans. It will all be fine.

"Jay." Garreth levels me with one of his patented glares. "I get that Catherine James is your focus right now, and I sincerely hope things work out for the two of you. You deserve it. But don't forget that we've been with you along the way. *We've* invested like you asked. We've given you the money you needed for your project. *We bailed her out.*"

Yeah, but our father and my actions are what put her in the position to begin with.

I sit up straighter, hating myself. "And for that, I'll always be grateful. What can I do?"

Garreth sighs. "All our money is tied up in this deal. In the investment we made into Theo's plan to open the damn distillery in Bristol. But if the James brothers don't know about it—and it's clear they don't"—he points at the whiskey bottle on his desk—"then we need to go straight to Sintac ourselves."

I shake my head. "We aren't cutting Theo out of the deal. Sintac wouldn't allow it, even if we tried."

Garreth looks out the window and blows out a breath. "Jay, this isn't a request." He snatches up the piece of paper propped against the bottle and hands it to me.

Watch your back. There's a new CEO in charge, and I know what you did to my sister.

There's no signature, but there doesn't need to be. Cash is taking over James Liquors, so I have to imagine it's from him.

You think after thirteen years you can waltz in here and fucking lick *me? After what you did to us?* Cat's words taunt me. Us. It wasn't just her that I screwed over. It was her brothers. My supposed best friend too.

And apparently, she told them what I did all those years ago. She told them about *us*.

There's a part of me that feels a swell of pride at that. I meant enough to her that even after I disappeared, she shared her feelings with Cash. She was always closest with him.

But defeat seeps into my bones as I realize what else that means.

If she told them, then the wall I'm scaling is a hell of a lot higher than I imagined it would be. Because not only do I have to convince her that I'm not the man she believes me to be, I also have to convince her brothers.

"What can I do?" I ask, slumping back in my seat.

13

NEVER BE THE SAME BY CAMILLA CABELLO

Cat

Sliding into Frank's brand-new car, I can't help but smile and squeeze his thigh. "The new whip is nice. You found her, right?"

My brother called last night. He went on and on about his weekend away and how he'd met the most incredible woman, only for her to slip through his fingers before he could get her number. He asked Frank to find her, and since I could use the distraction, I'm tagging along when he breaks the good news to Cash.

Frank darts a look my way, then merges into traffic. "Princess, you're going to get us into trouble."

I laugh. "Yeah, I probably will, but I deserve this fun."

"You want to talk about what happened between you and Hanson?"

"Not really."

"You'd rather just butt into your brother's love life?" he teases.

"As a matter of fact, yes."

He chuckles, but his face sobers quickly. "I'm not an idiot. I know you two were something all those years ago."

I blink at him, my poker face perfectly in place. "Hmm." I don't want to lie, but I'm not ready to tell the truth either. I'm not sure I ever will be.

"And Chloe…"

"What about her?" I ask quickly. *Too quickly*. It's obvious I'm hiding something. Or maybe it's the secret that eats at me and makes me believe it's obvious.

Secrets do that, though. They eat and eat and eat, chipping away little by little until the person in the mirror is unrecognizable. It's been a long time since I've seen the girl I once was, and it's in big part due to the truths I've kept hidden.

"You can be honest with me, you know?" he says softly, gently, far too kindly for what we are. Friends, I suppose, but really, he belongs to my brother. We may fool around, but I'm wise enough to know I don't come first.

I've never come first for anyone.

Looking out the window, I avoid his scrutiny and his questions. "Let's focus on Cash," I whisper.

Maybe Frank really is my friend, because in that moment he puts me first and drops the subject. He pulls into the garage below the James building, and I turn my focus to Frank's tattoos in hopes of avoiding the onslaught of memories this place evokes.

Late nights sneaking around. Kissing on the sidewalk. Making love on the rooftop.

There's a reason I don't come here often. It's the same reason that keeps me from visiting another handful of places in Boston, that forces my shields just about any time the radio is on. And once again, that reason's name is Jonathan Hanson. Is there a single area of my life he hasn't infected? A corner I can turn where the ghost of our past won't haunt me?

Of course not. Even days later, the taste of his tongue still lingers on my lips.

The man should come with a warning label.

"Cat," Frank says, as if it's not the first time he's tried to catch my attention.

I turn his way and shake the thoughts of the past, and the present—really any thoughts in general—out of my head. "Sorry, lead the way," I say, trailing behind.

Frank chuckles, and his warm palm finds the small of my back as he presses us toward the elevator.

A woman walks past us quickly, and for a moment, her gaze meets Frank's. Beside me, his entire body stiffens, and at the same time, she stumbles.

In an instant, his hand has left my back and he's catching her elbow and steadying her.

"Thank you," she murmurs, her words soft and quick. But then her attention shifts to me, and she shakes off his hand and rushes out the door.

Frank spins and watches her until she disappears from view.

"You know her?" I ask.

He's clearly reeling from their interaction—struck by her. If he doesn't know her, he wants to.

Oddly, the thought doesn't bother me in the least.

See? It's just sex.

And Sophie thought I was falling for him. Can't wait to share this tidbit with her.

"Her eyes," he says. The words are rough, like it hurts to say them. "She reminded me of someone I used to know."

"Oh, like your telenovelas," I tease. "Is this the start of a long-lost love affair?"

Frank clears his throat and straightens, finally coming back to planet Earth, and ushers me into the elevators. He chuckles. "No long-lost loves for me."

"Not buying it," I tease.

He arches a brow and I swear mischief glints in his eye, like he's about to turn the tables back on me, so I slump against the elevator wall. "Fine, I'll drop it. Let's both go live vicariously through my little brother, okay?"

He smiles. "Whatever you say, Princess."

KITTEN'S SONGS

Frank sends me in to see my brother first so that he doesn't know we came together.

"So, good news," I say, walking into Cash's office without knocking. I plop down in the seat opposite his and wait for him to give me his full attention.

"What's that?" he asks, his voice devoid of emotion and so very un-Cashlike.

Oh, he's going to turn that frown upside down once he hears what we have to say.

"I found her!" I exclaim, too excited to beat around the bush and wait for Frank.

Cash sighs and heaves himself out of his chair, ignoring my excited words completely and heading for the bar. He pours brown liquid into two glasses.

"What are you doing?"

Without a response, he simply walks back over and hands me one drink, then takes a sip from the other.

"Why are we drinking? I found her! Your mystery woman! Your Grace!"

With zero excitement, he sneers, "How?"

Frank walks in, and I point in his direction as he takes a seat beside me. "Okay, well, Frank found her."

"Really, Frank?" my brother asks, like he's annoyed.

"What? I found her like you asked. Don't look at me like that."

Cash tightens his grip on his drink and glares at his best friend. "Yeah, I asked you to give me the information. Not involve my sister."

Frank smirks. "She's better looking than you."

"Cash, why don't you seem more excited? We found her!" I fling the piece of paper Frank gave me in the elevator toward my brother. It has all of Grace's information on it.

My brother doesn't even look at it. "I found her too. Unfortunately, I also discovered she's married. So, that ends that."

My stomach drops. It appears all of us Jameses are unlucky when it comes to love.

14

IF I CAN'T HAVE YOU BY SHAWN MENDES

Cat

"**W**hy do you look miserable?" Sophie strides into my office and plants both hands on her hips, eyeing the plate on my desk.

I'm not proud of the scene she's just stumbled upon. Me stress eating another one of Ivan's waffles. Damn Jay for reminding me of how much I enjoy these things.

Around a huge bite, I reply, "I'm not."

She laughs. "Yeah, okay. Considering we both know you only eat sugar when you're stressed, I'm not buying it."

Once I've swallowed the last bite, I rinse it down with a sip of coffee. I wish it was vodka.

"My brother fell for a married woman and Jay is my boss and I don't get to have orgasms anymore because I was getting them from my brother's best friend, but now my brother's back. And he's bitchy, by the way—which is so not Cash—so the orgasms had to stop, and I can't even have orgasms." I slump back in my chair. Fuck my life. Then I remember another kicker. "And to top it all off, I still can't think of a damn story to win the position that should already be mine!"

Sophie's eyes soften. "The position is yours, honey. Not just because Jay is trying to win you back and will undoubtedly give it to you as part of whatever his plan is, but because you deserve it. But what is this about Cash?"

I roll my eyes like a teenager. I'm so annoyed by my little brother it's not even funny. "Cash met a woman when he was on that vacation last week," I start, pushing the take-out tray away. "She ghosted him, and he asked us to find her."

"Who's us?" Sophie interjects.

"Well," I hedge and bite my lip, "he asked Frank."

"Okay, keep going."

"Anyway, we found her. Turns out she's married."

Sophie blows out a breath. "Ah, shit. Poor Cash."

My skin heats just thinking of what I'll do to this Grace woman if I ever come face to face with her. "Yeah, he didn't take it well. But it gets worst. She's a matchmaker—that's how he found out she's married—my grandmother hired her to set Cash up with his future wife."

"Shut up!" Sophie says like a sixteen-year-old girl, her eyes wide and locked on me.

I laugh at the absurdity of it all. I've never seen my brother so torn up over a woman. And when he's finally ready for something serious, she's got to go and be toxic. "Apparently, when it comes to picking 'em, Jameses aren't too smooth."

Sophie shakes her head. "I'm so sorry, babe. I feel like you need a night out."

I perk up at the prospect. "Really? Do you think Dexter would watch the kids so we could go out tonight?" I ask, way too excited.

Sophie frowns. "Shit, I wish I could, but tonight is sex night."

Disappointment over not having a girls' night doesn't even register, because my mind goes straight to the last part of her response. "Sex night?"

"God, it was a good run," she mutters to herself. "Ten years…"

"Why are you talking to yourself, woman?" I tease.

Sophie shrugs and sits straighter, apparently already over the guilt she was harboring. Crossing her legs, she leans forward and grins wickedly. "Don't tell Dex I told you this. He swore me to secrecy. But really, I think it's incredible I lasted this long."

I roll my eyes. "Sex night. Details. Now."

She laughs. "Once a month, we go to a sex club and play..."

I swear my eyes bug out of my head. "With other people? You guys are swingers? What the—"

Throwing out a hand, she stops my spiral. "No." She huffs in annoyance. "Not that I wouldn't mind getting boned by two dicks at the same time." She bites her lip and stares vacantly at something over my shoulder.

I snap my fingers. "Focus, woman!"

She shrugs and brings her attention back to me. "We go to play with each other. Sometimes we watch others, but no we've never..." she sighs. Like now that the thought is in her head, she knows she won't be able to shake the idea of a threesome. And all it took was one damn conversation with me. I know how Sophie's mind works. No wonder Dex wanted to keep this part of their marriage private. "Have you ever?" she asks.

"Had two men at the same time?" I laugh. "Sophie, I've been with two men my entire life! And well..." I cringe, afraid to admit the next part.

Sophie leans in. "Well, what?"

Twisting my fingers in front of me, I study a spot on my desk to avoid looking at her. "I've only ever had sex with Jay."

Sophie practically falls over in a coughing fit. "But what about Frank?"

Sucking in a deep breath, I finally tilt my chin up and meet her intense gaze. "We've only done oral..." I swallow thickly, then add, "and...anal."

Sophie laughs so loud I'm sure the people on the beach outside my window can hear her.

"This isn't funny!" I grate out through my teeth.

She schools her expression, trying like hell to hold in her laughter. "Oh, babe, come on. It kind of is. You've avoided sleeping with men for thirteen years! Don't you miss it?"

I shrug. "My battery-operated friends keep me company. I'm fine," I lie.

I've been miserable. But the idea of allowing anyone to get as close to me emotionally as I let Jay get is too harrowing. Long ago, I vowed that no one would ever have that kind of control over my heart again. I can't guarantee that sex won't make me fall for someone else.

Sex with Frank would be too messy if it was any more intimate. We've successfully left the emotion out of it. I don't even look at him when it's happening. It's the perfect way for me, an emotionally stunted woman, to be in a completely unhealthy relationship with her brother's best friend. And if I didn't trust Frank with my life, if I didn't know him so well, none of what we were doing would have happened, period.

Sophie groans. "You are so not fine. You need to step out of your comfort zone, babe. Sex can just be for pleasure. It's possible to leave the emotion out of it. That's why Dex and I go to the club. At home, in our bed, with our kids down the hall, it's about us. Just us. About the marriage and all that. But at the club?" She smiles devilishly. "There, I can be Sophie, the hot young thing with the older man who can't get enough of her. Dex can fuck me ten different ways. He can unravel me, call me his whore, spank me…do all the things I *need* as a woman. He does it all for me. I get to be selfish for one night and it's…" She sighs. "It's freeing."

I'm hit with a twinge of jealousy. Not only does Sophie have the kids, the house, the incredible marriage…she has true freedom to be herself. Dex has given her that.

"Why are you making that face?" Sophie says, panicked.

"It's just…that's beautiful, Soph. You're happy." I stand and round my desk so I can hug her.

She looks at me oddly when I loop my arms around her and then laughs as she squeezes me tight. "You're a nutjob, you know that?"

I laugh against her shoulder. "And you're the whore who likes to get spanked by your daddy."

The sound of a throat clearing comes from the door, and there stands a red-faced Jay. "I heard nothing," he mumbles.

Sophie bites her lip and grins at me. "Aw, don't be jealous, Jay. One day you'll find someone who calls you a whore and lets you call him Daddy too!" She laughs as she saunters past him.

Since his reappearance in my life, I've done all I can to avoid showing anything but apathy in his presence, but I can't hold in my giggles as he stares at her with his jaw dropped in horror.

"Can I help you with something, Mr. Hanson?" I say sweetly, fluttering my lashes in his direction.

Jay pulls on the tie around his neck, drawing my attention to the way his Adam's apple rises as he swallows. Even when he's flustered, he's hot as fuck. Simply swallowing is sexy when he's the one doing it.

Life isn't fair.

Jay clears his throat and finally looks at me, blinking a few times before he speaks. "Meeting. Conference room. Ten minutes," he manages to sputter before hustling out of my office.

15

ELASTIC HEART BY SIA

Jay

"By now, you all should have chosen a topic for your articles," I say, scanning the room of editors. It's been fun playing boss of a magazine. The day-to-day is far more enjoyable than the time I spend sitting with the board that oversees my family's company. The people here know little about me, and so far, they treat me with more respect than I ever received at Hanson Liquors. There, it has always been assumed that my position was based on nepotism rather than merit. That I hadn't actually earned it. Rather, it was handed to me by my father. Or my brother.

After the attack, when I was out of the picture for months, Garreth took over as CEO. When I was well enough to come back, he insisted I lead the company, and to this day, it's clear the board believes that was a mistake. I'm sure most of them were thrilled when we announced Garreth would be taking over day-to-day operations while I deal with our newest acquisition.

It's a better fit, if I'm honest. Here, I'm just Jonathan Hanson, owner of *Jolie*. And I look the part. I'm fucking good-looking, I wear designer suits, and the editors sitting around this table look at me like I belong.

Everyone except Cat, Sophie, and Dexter, that is.

I don't even want to know what the fuck Sophie was talking about twenty minutes ago. After I left Cat's office, I went to the bathroom, splashed cold water on my face, and shook her haughty laugh and ridicule from my day. For my sanity, I tried to erase the way Cat looked at me. How her eyes darted to my throat, how her cheeks flushed. Because every time I picture her expression, all I want to do is go back to her office, bend her over her desk, and take her like I know she wants me to.

She's being stubborn. Understandably so, but we both know how this is going to end—with me inside her. The two of us together. If only I could skip this part of the journey. I want the fucking happily ever after. I've earned it, dammit.

Rose is the first to respond. She makes a show of licking her lips, trying to draw my attention. She's a gorgeous woman. Tall, dark hair, small curves. She's dainty. And obviously interested. Not that it matters. "I'm going to do a piece on women in small-town politics—from PTO to the governor's office," she says, pulling her shoulders back and resting her clasped hands in front of her primly.

I study the faces around the room, gauging the climate and searching for reactions that convey agreement or dissension. Most look bored, but it's Cat's reaction that I zero in on. She's smiling at Sophie.

"Have something to say, Ms. Bouvier?"

"It's James," she replies, eyes narrowed.

I shrug. "My mistake. Please, Ms. *James,* do share your thoughts."

Every set of eyes in the room ping-pongs between Cat and me. Mine, however, don't stray from my favorite subject. The source of the only joy I've ever had in my life. When she's fighting with me—when those eyes that are the color of my favorite drink flare—my blood ignites into flames. My body buzzes and I feel alive. Like I can take on the world— like I could possibly *win* her back.

"It feels like the story we've been telling since Hillary Clinton stood beside Bill all those years ago. Women can do everything men can do. Bravo." She slow claps.

"That's cruel," I choke out. When the malevolence is directed at me, that's one thing. I deserve it. But in front of her peers—toward her peers? Cat has never been a cruel person. Is my presence so uncomfortable that it's causing her to lash out in this way? The thought guts me.

She stares at Rose, completely ignoring me. "What did Cynthia say when you presented that idea two years ago?"

Rose clears her throat. "She said it'd been done before. That the story needed more."

Cat prods, "A human aspect. Or a twist, correct?"

Rose nods.

"You need a face for the article. A woman who's gone from staying at home with her kids to the governor's office—or something along those lines. But more than that, you need a reason. A Why. What will make women want to read her story?

"Politics don't interest people anymore. The topic is tiring…but humanity? The stories behind why people do things, why they tick. Why a person would walk away from one life without a glance"—her eyes find mine—"those are the stories our readers want. *Truths.* And the dirtier the better. It's what sells magazines," she adds, leaning back in her chair.

The entire room is rivetted, and all eyes are on her. It's clear Cynthia groomed her for this position. And she revels in it.

"And how will you sell magazines, Ms. James?" I press. My attention never wavers. I pick up my coffee cup and take a sip, reminding her that I'm the one in charge. These people may eat up her words, but they answer to me, and until I say she's their leader, she needs to remember that.

Cat smirks as she purrs, "Sex club."

I choke on my coffee. Trying to cover up my reaction, I clap a hand against my chest and shake my head. "You want to write an article about a sex club?"

She remains unflappable, watching me with indifference, as if I'm boring her, and then inspects her nails. "Yes."

"But…this is a women's magazine."

"And women don't like going to sex clubs, Mr. Hanson?" She raises a brow in challenge.

She's got me there.

I loosen my tie. The temperature has suddenly spiked. "Can you open a window?" I ask the guy sitting nearest to it.

"The AC is on," Cat teases with a smirk on her face.

"I want *fresh* air; I didn't realize that was a crime."

Her answering smile is smug. She knows exactly why I fucking need air. "As I was saying, my article will be about a sex club."

I take another sip of coffee to give myself time to formulate a response. "And what, pray tell, do you plan to write about?"

Cat leans back in her chair and taps her pen against her plump red lips. Lips I've imagined around my cock more times than I can count. Lips that moaned my name at a sex club oh so many years ago.

What the hell was wrong with us back then?

And how do I get us back to those people?

"Oh, I've got a story idea," Sophie perks up.

Cat's lips fold in on themselves, like she knows she has to prepare for the words Sophie is about to utter.

"Men in the workplace who overcompensate for their small dicks by being huge ones…and other *me too* things…"

KITTEN'S SONGS

As soon as the meeting is over, I stalk into Cat's office and slam the door. She jumps in surprise, and her expression immediately turns cold.

"What the hell was that little show you put on back there?" I demand, my heart pounding.

"Show?" she scoffs.

"Yeah. You aren't going to write about a damn sex club. You should be taking this assignment seriously, Cat. I can't hand you the editor in chief position just because I love you."

At my confession, the apathetic mask she wears slips, and she looks stunned, but only for a second.

The woman is good, I'll give her that. But I've always been able to see past her poker face.

Fucking finally, she gets it. I'm not fucking with her. I'm here because I'm head over heels in love with her. I'm here *for her.*

Behind her desk, she tucks her chin and takes a few deep breaths. Cautiously, I shuffle closer, ready to be there for the moment it finally clicks, desperate to be close when she's finally ready to give in.

With her palms pressed flat against the desk, she pushes herself to standing, as if she's getting her strength from the piece of furniture itself. Then she lifts her head and her eyes meet mine. They're full of nothing but darkness. Coldness. The mask is firmly back in place.

"For the record, Mr. Hanson," she grits out, "I don't put on shows. I choreograph them. I'm the puppeteer, standing in the back, ensuring all my plans come to fruition. I don't say things flippantly. I'm not looking for a reaction from you. Truly, I could give two shits what you think.

"For the last thirteen years, I have put my blood and sweat into this business. I have worked myself to the bone so I could one day take over as editor in chief. I have missed out on dinners with my family, dates, time with Chl—" She clamps her mouth shut before she can finish that sentence, piquing my curiosity. "*Time with people who matter.* This job was meant to be mine. You want to know what my story is, you'll see it when it's ready. Just like any other owner of a magazine. You don't dictate what goes in the magazine, Mr. Hanson, *I do.*"

"What about tears?" I ask.

Faint lines around her eyes appear as she frowns in confusion. "Tears?"

"The saying is blood, sweat, and tears."

She huffs. "I haven't cried in almost twelve years. No one gets my tears. Not even *Jolie*."

I swallow thickly, afraid to make a sound. Afraid to move. This is what my lies have cost her. She doesn't even *feel* anymore. She's like stone before me. With a heart encased in armor. It's kept her from crying, for fuck's sake.

I did this.

I step closer and reach out for her. "*Cat*—"

Pulling back, she shakes her head and glowers. "No. You don't get to pity me. I'm fucking fantastic, Jay. You didn't break me. And what you witnessed in that meeting wasn't a show. Your concern is unnecessary. I have a story, I'm going to tell it, and then you're going to give me the position I've *earned* over the last thirteen years."

I close my eyes and nod. "Whatever you want."

She huffs out a sarcastic laugh and turns toward the window. "You're not Santa Claus. Stop making promises we both know you'll never keep."

16

SWAY BY THE PERISHERS

Jay

Sitting at home and obsessing about Cat's words would only send me spiraling into a depression I may never crawl out of. So instead, I called the guys and forced them to meet me for drinks.

"You don't understand. Watching her…seeing her break…maybe I should just give her the magazine." Defeated, I down my drink in one go.

Garreth glares at me. "You think she'd accept your handouts, brother?"

Tired of the weight I've been carrying for so long, I drop my head back and close my eyes. "Of course she wouldn't. But it's not a handout. She's earned the position. Fuck, she's earned the right to everything. I destroyed her." I drag a hand down my face and groan. "Watching her day in and day out fight me? I thought…Fuck, man, I don't know what I thought. That I could walk back into her life and convince her to forgive me? Now, though? I see the damage I did. I really think I lost her. And the right thing to do would be to give the woman I love her freedom. Give her the one thing she does have control over—her job."

Garreth shakes his head. "She won't accept it like that, and you know it. Let her earn it."

Growling, I ball my hands into fists in my lap. "Let her go do a story on a sex club? That's your suggestion? Have you lost your damn mind?"

This time it's Gavin who jumps in. "She's fucking her brother's friend, right? So it's not like she's at home pining after you. She's not yours, and what she does is out of your control."

I bring my fist to my mouth to keep myself from punching the table or my friend. "Sex clubs are dangerous. Who knows what kind of skeevy fucks could get their hands on her there."

Garreth shrugs. "So buy it."

A disbelieving laugh skates up my throat. "Buy it? I don't even know which fucking club she's going to."

Beckett runs his finger over the rim of his glass as he studies me. "So buy them all."

God, we sound like a bunch of rich pricks. Which is exactly what we are. Beckett owns Boston's baseball team. Gavin, hockey.

And my brother and me? Well, we aren't exactly hurting for money.

I shake my head at the absurdity, and then I let Beckett's words settle. It *is* an option, I suppose. I have an inkling about which club she'll go to—actually, I have a pretty fucking good idea—but on the off chance she chooses somewhere new, I've got to do my research about other clubs in the area. "Yeah, that could work."

With one side of his mouth lifted slightly, almost like he's smiling, Garreth leans back in his chair.

Moments like this—moments where I can all but see the wheels turning, feel him manipulating a situation—he reminds me of my father. But unlike my father, Garreth cares. He may not say it, but he shows it. He listens and he shows up. He's British, so he's not overly emotional. Hell, he's damn near a robot. But his presence here tonight tells me all I need to know. I matter to him.

Beckett huffs out a laugh and forces his chin up. "Look who's over there."

I follow his gaze and spot Cash James sitting at a table with a beautiful woman. They're deep in conversation. At first, I can only see her profile, but then she shifts, and her full face comes into view.

"Grace Kensington," I mutter, almost as a curse.

"Didn't you date her?" Garreth asks.

I laugh. *Date.* Whatever the fuck that means. Grace and I had a fling during undergrad that only lasted a few weeks. I bumped into her again when I was in my angry phase. I suppose I'm still in that phase almost thirteen years later, but at that time—maybe six months after I ghosted Cat—her grandfather told me that she was considering returning to Boston. She was going to give up her internship.

He and I both knew I had to keep Cat from coming back to the States. I had to give her a reason to avoid finding me. Because if she came anywhere near me, the men who'd put me into the coma would discover who she was to me. They'd use my one and only weakness against me. They'd use my love for her to force me to divulge information about where the funds went. Then they'd track it to Cat's bank account, and she'd be their target.

So I did the only thing I could think of. I dated publicly. I made sure all the papers got wind of it. I made sure it looked like I was in love. Though it killed me, I flaunted it. So she'd think that if she came back to Boston, she'd be bombarded with news of my love life. That she'd risk running into me with another woman. I made sure to hurt her in a way that would keep her from looking for me again.

And Grace Kensington, formerly Grace Winters, was the woman I used to do that.

We'd ended things in college amicably, so when I asked her out again, she was open to it. I was up front with her about my state of mind. I was broken, and I had little to give. But she was kind and funny and a good friend at a time when I needed it the most.

Shortly after the magazine articles ran, I introduced her to the man she went on to marry. I'd always thought he was a good guy, but I'd recently heard he was having an affair.

And now it appears she's on a date of her own—with Cat's brother. Talk about a small world.

"I'm just going to say hi," I say to the guys.

Before I can get too far, my brother grabs my arm. "Remember, Cassius James just sent over that bottle of whiskey. He's made his point clear. He's coming after our company. I know you want Cat, but that family—James Liquors—until Theo is healthy again and back on board with our deal, they're the enemy, Jay. It's us or them."

I close my eyes in resignation and give a quick nod.

Just another role for me to play.

From: <JHanson@jolie.com>

CC: All employees

Subject: New Procedure

July 1, 2022

Effective immediately, any charges for research purposes must be approved by me in advance. Please submit a formal request that includes the location of such research. I must sign off on the venue in advance.

Sincerely,

Jonathan Hanson

From <CJames@jolie.com>

To: <JHanson@jolie.com>

Subject: Re: New Procedure

July 1, 2022

I don't need you *or* Jolie to pay for my outings, Mr. Hanson. Nice try.

Sincerely,

Catherine James

Editor

Jolie Magazine

From: \<JHanson@jolie.com\>

To: \<CJames@jolie.com\>

Subject: Re: Re: New Procedure

July 1, 2022

Kitten,

I don't need to come up with silly procedures to find out where you're going. I've been following your every move for years.

Always yours,

Jay

From CJames@jolie.com

To: JHanson@jolie.com

Subject: Re: Re: Re: Procedure

July 2, 2022

Need I remind you this is a company email? You are my boss, and the actions you referenced could be considered stalking.

Catherine James

Editor

Jolie Magazine

From: JHanson@jolie.com

To: CJames@jolie.com

Subject: Re: Re: Re: Re: Procedure

July 2, 2022

Very aware of our titles, Kitten. And I wear my title as your stalker proudly. Feel free to turn these over and sue me. The company is yours if you'll be mine.

Give in already. I miss your taste.

Forever thinking of you,

Jay

17

DON'T BLAME ME BY TAYLOR SWIFT

Cat

Pictures of Jay, Cash, and Grace Kensington, one after another, hit me like a whip. They slice at my skin, tearing at the last semblance of control I've managed to hold on to over the last few weeks.

Grace Kensington. How did I miss it when Frank found her for Cash?

Before today, I'd only seen her once. But it only took that one picture for her to be seared into my brain. The picture from the article *Jolie* ran about the happy new couple, Jonathan Hanson and his new girlfriend. Back then, she was Grace Winters.

That name has been seared into my brain for years.

My lungs burn as I try to suck in more air, willing myself not to return to that moment all those years ago when I stood at the table of my Paris apartment, cradling my baby bump, and read a story about how the man who'd told me he loved me completely had, without a single word to me, moved on with another woman.

The woman who is now married yet has somehow turned my brother into a fucking forlorn puppy chasing after her scraps.

And Jay too.

Unlike that photo, this one is candid. It's my brother and Jay fawning—

no, fighting—over Grace Kensington, the married matchmaker.

They were taken last week. My brother, idiot that he's become since meeting Grace, was on a date with her. And Jay? According to the photographic evidence and the story that ran with it, he interrupted their cozy evening, and the way he's looking at Grace makes it clear he's interested in her. God, how many times did he look at me like that? Like I was his whole world. And I fell for it again and again.

Hell, I almost fell for his lies this time too. I actually thought he wanted me back. Not that I'd take him back, but God, did he have me fooled.

Bile worms its way up my throat, but I choke it back and shake my head.

"They get worse," Enzo warns. He's the lucky photographer I asked to do the story about the hot new restaurant. As luck would have it, he spotted my brother just as another photographer did. Angel that he is, he promised the photographer an interview with the magazine if the man agreed not to sell the damning pictures. But the one of Jay and Cash fighting over Grace was too valuable, apparently, and Enzo wasn't able to finagle an agreement where that one was concerned.

Grace has yet to be publicly identified in any of the articles, thank God. The last thing my family needs is scrutiny over how my brother is dating a married woman.

What a fucking nightmare.

I fixate on the pictures that Enzo warned are worse. My brother—who swears he's not dating Grace, who told me over and over again that he was disgusted, that he'd never entangle himself with a married woman—is grabbing her in a pretty freaking desperate kiss. I flip the pictures over, unable to stomach the lies and betrayal. "Thanks, Enzo. I owe you one."

My heart breaks over Cash's lies. I can't *not* take this personally. We're best friends. We always have been. And he knows how I feel about cheaters. I thought he felt the same.

We grew up hearing stories about the affairs our father had. Of how, while my mother was dying of cancer, he was bedding every woman who walked by. And then he went and got our nanny pregnant. She was only seventeen at the time. Our family has somehow miraculously kept that story out of the press—and from Chase—for years.

For all of those reasons, I despise cheaters.

And that feeling only compounded when Mia cheated on me…and then Jay.

No one other than Sophie and Cynthia knows how broken I was after I found out that Jay had slept with Mia while we were together. That she has a child Chloe's age. *Chloe's half sibling.*

I close my eyes as hurt crawls its way through my body. It scratches at my inner psyche like it did for so many years when I thought of how two people I trusted more than just about anyone shattered that faith so tremendously.

Every relationship in my life has been tainted by their actions.

And now my brother is sleeping with the woman Jay moved on from me with.

And according to this article and the photos, Jay is unhappy about it.

I squeeze my eyes shut, blocking out the images flicking, one after another, inside my head. It's like a horrible movie. I'm mentally reliving every interaction with Jay, frame by frame, up until that awful moment when I realized it had all been a lie.

Never again.

I would never let him hurt me again.

The one flicker of light in this mess is that I don't have time to wallow in my sadness. I have a brother to put in his place.

I can't change my past, but I can sure as hell keep him from repeating it.

KITTEN'S SONGS

⤮ ⏮ ⏸ ⏭ ⇄

My brother isn't in his office when I arrive. His receptionist isn't at her desk either, so I sneak into his office and settle on the couch, preparing myself for this confrontation. I wish I could tell him why I'm so upset about Grace. I wish I could confide in him about what happened all those years ago with Jay. How he moved on with her, dated her. But it's been too many years. And none of that matters now. The woman's marital status alone should be reason enough for my brother to stay away.

I thumb through a magazine while I wait for him, choking back my hurt over the entire situation. But every time I think of the way Jay was holding Grace in the photo, my heart rate skyrockets.

The door swings open, and my brother barrels in, grimacing when he spots me.

I fake a smile. "Don't blame Lucy. I snuck in here while she was in the bathroom."

At exactly that moment, Lucy scurries in with a coffee and practically falls over when she spots me. "Oh, Mr. James, I'm so sorry."

My brother sighs before shooing her toward the door. "Hold my calls, please."

With a glare fixed firmly on me, Cash settles behind his desk. "Why are you here?"

"Is that any way to address your favorite sister?"

"Cat, I have a busy day. What's up?"

Trying to keep my demeanor calm, I slip on a smile and stand from the couch. "Can't a girl visit her baby brother?"

He doesn't bite. "No. Out with it. You are here for a reason."

I drop the cheerful act and let my animosity take over. If he's going to be a dick, I'll treat him like one. "Fine. I love how you are acting like

I'm the one that did something wrong, when *you* are the one who was doing *this*." I don't bother saying anything else, choosing instead to toss the photographs onto his desk.

He doesn't bother looking down. Instead, he maintains a bored expression and keeps his attention firmly locked on me. "Nothing happened. Just had a little fun with the boys. Can a single man not go out and have a good time?"

"Nothing happened? Seriously? Then why are you making out with a married woman for all of the damn world to see?"

Cash's face falls, and he drops his gaze to the evidence I tossed his way. Picture after picture of Cash kissing Grace in public. What a damn fool.

"Are these in any magazines?" he grits.

Balling my hands into fists at my sides to keep from screaming, I shake my head. "Not for your benefit, though. The one who quashed it was looking out for Grace. What were you thinking, Cash?"

"I wasn't. That damn woman takes all reasonable thought from my mind. It's like I see her, and my body controls my every move."

"That's not real life, Cash. You need to take responsibility for your actions."

"*I am*. I left that night. And I was a dick about it. Ran into her again last night. Once again, we fought. We can't seem to make it through a conversation without bringing out the worst in one another."

I narrow my eyes at him. "Or groping one another, apparently."

He smirks. "Yeah, that too."

"I don't have to tell you that this needs to stop."

He eyes me sheepishly, then mutters, "No, you don't. I am very aware."

"Okay, good. My work here is done. Dinner this weekend?"

"I think I'm going out with the boys again Saturday. Sunday brunch?"

I round his desk and drop a kiss to his cheek. "Like always. See you then, little brother."

When I exit his office, I feel a little lighter. One cocky asshole handled; too bad I still have to deal with the other one.

KITTEN'S SONGS

Back at the office, I'm more determined than ever to focus on earning my position as editor in chief. And it's been an exhausting day. After taking a stroll down memory lane and arguing with my brother, I need to direct my focus on something constructive.

I drop into my chair and smile at the picture of Chloe on my screen saver. She's why I'm doing this. In a few months, she'll be living with me. I need to get my shit together. I want to be someone she would be proud of—someone who can take care of both of us.

Just the sight of her sweet face reminds me that none of this matters. Not Jay, and not my brother's stupid mistakes. Those are only distractions from my true focus in life.

Everything I've done over the last thirteen years has been for her. I've worked every day to be the mother my own would be proud of. Even if I had to do it from a distance. Even if I had to do it silently.

Chin wobbling, I close my eyes for a moment to center myself, then open them again and push myself to work.

> No waffle today, Kitten?

The message pops up on my computer screen while I'm researching female doms. It's a fascinating thing, really. Women who put men in their places. Who have all the control. I don't know that it's something I'd ever have interest in—although I wouldn't be opposed to punishing a certain cocky billionaire.

I groan at his interruption and ignore him, closing the chat box and returning to my research. The whips are certainly interesting, and the one with the spikes on it would be quite fun to paddle Jay with.

"Uh, stop thinking about him," I whisper in anger.

> Never stop, kitten.

I startle and scan the room, but I'm alone, and my office door is shut.

> You look beautiful today.
> Have dinner with me.

Scanning the ceiling, I get the sinking feeling that he's watching me on some type of video device.

With a growl, I type back:

> Watching me now, Mr. Hanson? You have crossed the damn line. I'll own the company when I'm done with you.

His response is immediate.

> It's yours.

A sarcastic laugh rips through my chest. What the hell is wrong with this guy? He makes me want to order all the toys I was perusing so I can punish him with them.

I drag my hands down my face. He's making me insane. This isn't me. I don't obsess over people. I'm focused, unaffected by emotions. I don't cry or get worked up.

No. I get even.

With Jay, I've been deprived of that satisfaction for thirteen years. But now…

I smile as the perfect punishment formulates in my brain. He wants to watch? Fuck with my mind? I'll give him something to stare at.

18

STUBBORN LOVE BY THE LUMINEERS

Jay

I've never been good at playing hard to get. Never bothered trying with Cat. Then or now. Since I started at *Jolie*, I've worn my heart on my damn sleeve. No matter how hard I try, I can't keep the words from tumbling out of my mouth.

She wants the company? She can have it.

She wants every dime I have? They're hers.

When she accepts the fact that I belong to her, that everything I have belongs to her, that nothing else holds meaning to me, *then* maybe we'll get somewhere.

I'm preparing to leave for the day, to head down to ask her to dinner. We need to get everything out in the open. I can't wait for Theo to tell her.

She needs to know that I didn't willingly walk away all those years ago. That even though I wasn't with her physically, my soul never left. I have belonged to that girl since the day I met her in the coffee shop. Since the moment she refused to tell me her name.

I glance down at the computer screen to make sure she's still in her office, and that's when I spot him.

Frank fucking McCabe.

He's stalks toward Cat and presses her up against the window. Unable to stop myself, I watch as his hands skate over her hips and she arches into him. Then his lips are on her neck and he's peppering kisses down to her chest. Cat's unbuttoning her top and pushing her chest toward his mouth.

When he slides his hands over her shoulders, her top falls to the floor, and she's left in nothing but a bra and a skirt.

Fuck.

She puts her hands behind her back and unhooks her bra, and his mouth is instantly latched to her nipple.

"What the fuck, Cat!"

I rub my forehead and tug at my hair, at a loss for what to do. Do I storm into the office and demand he stop? Do I fall to my knees and beg for forgiveness? Because I'm not above that when it comes to her. I'll do anything for her, no matter how outrageous or pathetic.

Do I let her go?

If she's happy with him—if this is what she really wants—then yes. There's no other choice.

Closing my eyes, I pinch the bridge of my nose, forcing myself to come to terms with what's happening. Trying to convince myself that it's really over. But when I focus on the screen again, Cat's looking up into the camera. There's a hint of a smile on her face as she stares straight at me. Even while Frank presses her onto her desk.

She's not focused on him or what he's doing to her. She's looking for my reaction. Thinking of me while he touches her.

The opposite of love isn't hate; it's indifference. And there is nothing but hate in Cat's eyes right now. Anger. She cares.

Hate I can work with. Revenge happens to be my specialty.

She's not over this. Us. *Me.*

She doesn't want me to leave her alone.

My little kitten wants to play.

EXTRA DIRTY

She thinks she's playing a game with me.

She should know better than to hop into the lion's den, though. I'm going to devour her.

19

DON'T START NOW BY DUA LIPA

Cat

Convincing Frank to play along with my little game was easy. Sure, we both agreed that this thing between us was over, but with my brother acting like a fool over Grace, I can't muster the guilt I should probably feel over sleeping with his best friend.

And Frank? He knows exactly what this is.

Revenge. Pure and simple.

And if there's anyone who understands revenge, it's this man.

"Fuck, Princess, you're dripping. Does the idea of him watching get you this turned on?" he teases as his fingers skate over my underwear, which are, in fact, drenched.

I won't lie. I like being watched.

But the idea of Jay watching me? Knowing that I'm punishing him? It makes it almost impossible to breathe.

When the phone on my desk rings, I can't help but giggle. I know *exactly* who's calling. I glare up at the ceiling and ignore it.

Frank peers up at me wearing a smirk. "You're enjoying this entirely too much."

"Am I not supposed to enjoy when you get down on your knees for me?"

He chuckles against my thigh, then slides my panties down my legs just as the intercom beeps. "Pick up the goddamn phone, Cat, before I send someone in there to pick it up for you."

I have to press my lips together to keep from laughing too loud. He's such a fucking baby. The cell phone on my desk rings, and this time I accept his FaceTime request. The timing couldn't be more perfect, because at that moment, Frank flattens his tongue against my sensitive lips, making me moan, despite my best efforts to stay quiet.

"Fuck, Kitten…" Jay says, his eyes flaring on the screen.

I lay the phone flat on my desk, refusing to stare at him.

"Pick up the phone," he growls.

"I answered like you demanded, Mr. Hanson. What can I do for you?" My eyes roll back as Frank sucks me long and hard. Another moan escapes.

"You're doing this to hurt me. I get it…I-I understand."

Fuck. I pick up the phone and glare at him. He's ruining this for me. I don't want his sadness or defeat.

I want anger. I want fire. I want him to be enraged like I am. *Jealous. Seething.*

I want him unhinged, because clearly that's my default setting these days.

I'm sprawled across my desk with my brother's best friend's face between my legs while he watches. All I want is a damn reaction.

Seeing the photographs of him with Grace has made me lose my mind.

I don't bother to respond. Instead, I flip the camera to face Frank. He's on his knees between my legs, and he doesn't let up. Ensuring the camera captures every move, I grasp his hair with one hand and press him closer.

"Fuck," Jay grits out.

"Yup," I laugh, "he's doing an excellent job of that. Now, if you'll excuse me…"

"Use two fingers. She likes that," Jay instructs.

With a gasp, I stare down at Frank, dumbfounded. Frank smirks up at me as he works his tongue on my clit. He only pauses momentarily to acknowledge Jay. "I know what she likes. She's come on my tongue quite a few times, Hanson."

Jay growls, "Tell him, Kitten."

I squeeze my eyes shut, hating that he's right. "Please," I whisper.

Frank smiles. "Whatever you want, Princess."

When he adds the second finger, I moan loudly.

"Bite that lip, Kitten. Don't let anyone but us hear your cries."

"I'm trying," I pant.

"Try harder, or I'm gonna come down there and stick my cock in your mouth to keep you quiet."

I turn the phone back to face me and glare. "You wish."

His expression softens as soon as he sees me, and I squeeze my eyes shut to cut the connection.

"Open your eyes," he rasps. When I don't, he says it again. "Please, open your eyes."

When I finally steal a glance at the phone, he's got his turned to face down. I watch in fascination as he strokes his hard, throbbing cock.

Fuck, that's hot.

"I know you want it, Kitten. I know you miss the feel of me sliding inside you."

Frank laughs against my clit, snagging my attention. The sight of him between my legs, the feel of his tongue moving in circles while Jay's dirty words fill the air and he strokes his cock, all of it, elicits a growing wave of hot, intense desire that crashes through my body. I bite down hard on my bottom lip to keep my sounds from escaping.

As I come apart, Jay curses, and spurts of cum shoot out onto his hand. I can't help but watch in fascination.

"Bend over, Princess, and hang up the fucking phone," Frank grits out.

My eyes go wide at the desperation in his voice. "I thought we weren't—"

He places his hand against my lips, silencing me. "You two aren't the only ones getting off. Now bend over so I can fuck the shit out of you."

I smile at him, thrilled that he's giving in. God, I need this.

"Cat, if you hang up that phone…" Jay warns.

I laugh as I take in his beet-red face. "Why don't you give Grace a call? I'm sure she could help you." I hit End before he can reply. Then I laugh as Frank spins me around, knowing Jay is still watching.

20

MERCY BY SHAWN MENDES

Cat

Avoiding thoughts of the shit show that is my life, I head to James Liquors to visit my brother a few days after my little stunt with Frank. Cash has a date tonight, and I want to make sure his married matchmaker hasn't talked him into canceling it.

I don't trust that woman, and I don't want her anywhere near my brother.

Voices carry through the corridor as the elevator doors open at reception. The receptionists look at one another nervously but don't try to stop me when I stride straight to my brother's office.

"Well, they should be nervous. We have contractors backing out left and right. I'm telling you; Hanson is behind this," Chase urges as I throw the door open.

"Hanson is behind what?" I ask, plopping onto the couch beside him.

All three of my brothers are here, and each one's face is redder than the last. Obviously, I walked in on one hell of a disagreement.

"Cat, what are you doing here? You have a job, and it isn't in this company," Carter says, though there's no heat behind his words.

Going for aloof rather than letting on that I'm losing my mind over the possibilities of what Jay has done now, I pull a nail file from my bag and focus on my nails. "Well, I'm starting to think that I should be working here. What are the rumors I'm hearing about Forester?"

I haven't actually heard any rumors. But one of my brothers said the man's name moments before I walked in, so it's as good a place as any to start.

I look up at Cash and raise my brows, waiting for his response.

"I've got it under control," he mutters.

Beside me, Chase sits up straight, the movement shifting the cushion beneath me. "No, he doesn't. Until he agrees to show his face in Bristol and prove that the company is continuing in Gramps's stead, our suppliers and contractors are going to fear that we're going under."

Caught off guard, I stop filing my nails and gape at Cash. "You're thinking of going back to Bristol?"

His eyes go soft, and he presses his lips together as he studies me. "You don't have to come. But yes, we are going to spend some time there. Landry likes to do business with local companies, and while we used to be one, we haven't made our presence known there in quite some time."

I don't know a lot about the family business—my ignorance on the subject being 100 percent intentional—but my brothers have mentioned a deal with a man named Charles Landry before. He lives in Bristol, the town where we grew up, and the boys have been working to gain his favor so they can expand the business by partnering with him.

While I try to spend as little time in Bristol as I can, this expansion is huge for my brothers, and I'd do anything for them. "If you guys can do it, so can I."

Cash moves from his position behind his desk and sits next to me on the couch. "But you don't have to, Kit Cat." He pulls me close. "This isn't your problem."

"I'm a James too, ya know. Just because I'm not a man doesn't mean I can't be of use in this company," I argue. The idea that they don't see me as an equal has my blood going hot.

"Cat, you've never expressed interest in the company," Cash says.

140

He's focused solely on me, his expression genuine. He's never judged me for that choice. "If you want a seat at the table, I'll grab you a chair. Hell, I'll build a bigger table. Whatever you want, it's yours." He holds out his hands, motioning around the room. "You tell us what you want, and we'll go along with it."

Chase and Carter both nod in agreement. They're willing to let me in. Let me work alongside them in our family business. Relieved, all I can do is sigh. While the business has never interested me, it is nice to be wanted.

"When?"

Carter pipes up with the details. "The party is in a month. But we should start showing up around there before then. I'll start next week. Cash, you handle the party since you are who needs to be the face of all of this. Chase can handle another one of the weeks, and, Cat, you just tell us when you want to join."

"Thanks. I'll try for the event." I drop my nail file back into my bag and check my watch. "Don't you have a date?" I ask Cash. "That's why I'm here. I wanted to make sure you were dressed appropriately."

Chase guffaws, and Carter brings a hand to his mouth to hold back his own laughter.

Cash glares at all of us. "I've dated women before, Cat. I'm pretty sure I can handle this."

With a smirk, I drop all pretenses. Whether he likes it or not, he needs me to give it to him straight. "Yes, it's not so much *women* that concern me. It's the *woman* that is arranging the date. I want to make sure she isn't the one showing up. Ya know, another setup."

"You act like Grace is this conniving person. She's not like that."

"I did hear she showed up here the other day out of the blue," Carter mutters.

Ha. I knew that woman wouldn't give up. It's a good thing I came today.

Cash massages the back of his neck, avoiding my gaze. "She delivered the list of women. That was all."

"And she couldn't do that via email?" I ask. There's no point in hiding my incredulity. He knows she could. He's just being a damn fool about her.

"Listen, I can't control her actions. I can only control mine. I took the list, and she left. I'm moving on. I'm going out with someone new tonight. I know how to date. I think I'm dressed all right." He waves a hand up and down, motioning to his outfit.

I must admit, he looks fine. My brothers are all stupidly good-looking. They really don't need help in the women department. If I didn't loath the woman he's fallen for, I wouldn't be concerned about his dating life at all.

"You look fine," Chase grunts.

"Okay, well, now that we have resolved the company's crisis and my dating crisis, can we adjourn this family meeting?" Cash asks with a roll of his eyes.

"Yeah, I'm out." Chase stands from his spot on the other end of the couch. "Good luck, bro," he says, then he's gone.

Cash breathes out a sigh of relief. "Geez, that was a close one."

Carter laughs. "He gets overly worked up. Have fun tonight." He lifts his chin in Cash's direction, then stops in front of me and offers me his hand. "Want to grab dinner, sis?"

Tossing my arm around Cash's shoulder, I give him a hug goodbye. "I know I'm hard on you about Grace, but I just want you to be happy."

He kisses the top of my head. "I know. And I am. I'm completely fine. Promise."

I follow Carter out of Cash's office. "Sushi?" he asks as he slows so we're walking side by side.

"Yeah, that works. So what's the deal with Hanson?" I hedge.

Carter quirks a brow in my direction as we pass the reception desk. "Don't worry about it. The less you have to do with that bastard, the better."

I laugh, but there's no humor behind it. "He's my boss these days, Carter. I'm kinda forced to deal with him on a daily basis."

"No fucking way," he grumbles as we step into the elevator. "Dickhead. Has he been bothering you?"

I keep my head down as I press the button for the ground floor, making sure to avoid even looking at the button for the penthouse. But even without looking, memories of years past flood my brain, just like I knew they would. Will there ever come a time when I forget that man and all the things we did?

What will it take for me to really move on?

"I can handle Jay," I say coolly.

I affect an unbothered expression as my brother studies me. He doesn't need to know that I'm, in fact, not handling Jay well at all. I'm playing stupid games with the man, and there's no way I'll win a single one.

"Be careful. I'm pretty sure he's making a play for our company with Pa out of commission. He thinks Cash is an easy target. He's trying to exploit what he sees as our weaknesses right now, and I don't want him using you to do it."

Biting the inside of my cheek, I keep my emotions at bay. "Got it. Don't trust Jonathan Hanson. That's easy enough."

Now if only I could stop thinking about him too.

21

SOMEONE TO STAY BY VANCOUVER SLEEP CLINIC

Cat

Last night, Cynthia sat Chloe down and talked to her about moving back to Boston with me. She was apparently cautiously optimistic. So when my phone rings and Cynthia's name lights up on the screen, I feel a whoosh of excitement. It's the end of the day in Paris, which means this is likely Chloe.

"Hi," I answer, holding my breath just a bit, nerves dancing in my belly.

"Hi, Cat." Chloe sounds equally nervous, her voice softer than normal.

"How was your day?" I ask, trying to warm up to the conversation I think we're about to have.

"It was good. Mom took me shopping for summer clothes."

"Nice, heard you guys are going to Greece next week. I'm super jealous."

The question apparently settles her, because suddenly the girl is telling me everything they plan to do in Greece. But when she finishes, there's an awkward pause, and I know it's my turn to talk.

"So your mom mentioned she talked to you about maybe coming to Boston to live with me?"

There's a long silence, and then some movement and what sounds like a door shutting. "Um, yeah."

I bite my lip and twirl the pen in my hand, trying to ease my nerves. "And how do you feel about that?"

"Good," she says quickly.

Good, good? Or…

God, this is hard.

"You don't have to—"

Chloe interrupts me. "I want to." She lets out a long breath that crackles down the line. "If you want me there, that is."

I blow out a relieved breath. "Nothing would make me happier."

"Cool," she says. "So we go to Greece next week, then it's only a month until I move back."

Wow. In six weeks, she'll be living here…with me.

My smile spreads. "Yeah, Chlo. The countdown is on. I can't wait."

I can hear her smile when she replies, "Me too."

"Tu me manques," I whisper.

"Miss you too. Love you, Cat. I'll talk to you tomorrow."

"Love you too," I reply and then set down the phone, my heart feeling lighter than it has in ages.

Chloe is really moving here. I can't believe how easy that conversation was. Sliding the mouse, I wake my computer monitor, then navigate to google, ready to search for something to send to Chloe for her trip to Greece. A notification pops up in the corner, letting me know that I have a new email from one of my photographers.

When I click on it, I'm confronted by yet another photograph of Jay sitting in a restaurant with Grace. Fuck, it hurts. More than it probably should.

Jay really wants to piss me off. There is no other explanation.

Or maybe he likes her, my traitorous mind taunts.

This is all a game to him. It always has been.

And my brother trusts this woman to set him up with his future

146

wife? The entire thing is insane. Although, any of her choices would be better for my brother than herself—the married woman who used to fuck my ex. And might currently be.

My stomach twists at the thought.

It's a sick game we're playing. I flaunted Frank, and now Jay is parading around with Grace. And for what? I don't want to think about him anymore. I don't want to live like this.

For years, I pushed thoughts of him to the back of my mind, only falling victim to his memory during moments of utter weakness. Yes, he owned my midnights and space in my psyche during sex, when I'd retreat into those memories and envision the one thing that could always bring me to orgasm—Jay sliding in and out of me. Like that first time. When he took my virginity. Images of the way his ice-blue eyes melted for me when he sank into me that first time have always been my undoing.

I want him in a way that makes no sense. I can't stand to look at him. Can't stand to talk to him. And certainly can't stand to fucking work for him.

Yet right now, I'm doing just that. Watching the prick of a man as he waltzes past my office door. He offers me his signature smirk when he catches sight of me and stops at the threshold. "Morning, Kitten," he says, rapping on the doorframe twice, "how was your night?"

I glower at him. "Not as good as yours."

His brows draw together, like he's working out a puzzle and can't quite figure out the last piece. Good. That's how I like him to feel. Confused. Thrown off. I don't like when he can read me...when he knows my thoughts before I voice them.

"Frank leave you dissatisfied?" he teases with a smirk. "I'm happy to take over going forward."

I grunt out a sigh. Why do I engage with him? "Go away. Better yet, go bother Grace if you're looking for someone to entertain you."

"Why are you mad at me? You're the one who doesn't want her with Cash. I'm doing you a favor."

What? How the hell does he know I don't want her with Cash? Ah, that fucking man has been listening to my conversations. It's bad enough he's been watching me on video. I didn't realize he also had sound.

I huff out a sigh. "Very funny, Jay."

He smiles, *fucking smiles*, in response to my frustration. "Thanks. I've been told I make people laugh."

"At you, Jay. They're laughing at you."

He shoots me a cool glare. "You're the one who said you don't want to be with me."

A bitter laugh escapes my throat. "I don't."

"So what do you care if I'm with Grace?" He tilts his head and scrutinizes me, as if he's genuinely curious.

I spin in my chair and look out the window. He really has no idea what seeing her again has done to me. Each photo sends me back to that apartment in Paris. Where I stood, my hand resting on my stomach, and read that article about Jonathan Hanson and his new girlfriend.

The woman my brother is now infatuated with. The woman who took my place in Jay's heart. No, that's not possible, because I never held that spot to begin with. And the sight of her is like salt in that wound.

"I don't," I bite back, keeping my attention trained on the horizon.

"Can we talk?" he murmurs. He's closer now.

Finally, I turn back to him and steel my spine. "No" is all I can choke out. I stand and grab my purse from my desk, but Jay grabs for me before I can get by him. With one hand on my arm, he holds me in place.

He angles close so his breath is warm against my ear. "I'm not sure what you want from me. Do you want me to leave you alone? Are you— are you happy with Frank?" he grits out. "Because fuck, Cat, right now, it seems like you're jealous of something you say you don't want."

I huff out an annoyed laugh and pull back. "I'm not jealous."

He scowls and shakes his head like he doesn't believe me. "Give me one hour to explain everything. In one hour, I can clear everything up."

"In an hour," I scoff.

"It's not what you think, Cat."

Piercing blue eyes the same color as our daughter's implore me to listen. Beg me to give him the time to make us right. Something itches at my brain, scratching until I can't ignore it. The way my grandfather looked at me all those years ago, as if he was trying to convey a message. Just like Jay is now.

The way he spoke, as if he didn't really believe the words he was saying when he said Jay had betrayed me. And for a moment, I second-guess everything over the last thirteen years.

It never felt right.

But just as quickly, those devastating blue eyes bring me back to reality.

And the ice settles back around my heart.

Chloe.

Even if things aren't exactly as they seemed, even if Jay could somehow explain himself, would it matter?

No.

My main focus has to be Chloe. No matter what. Jay doesn't matter. The past doesn't matter. My feelings *don't* matter.

"I'm not jealous. Date Grace, don't date Grace. Do whatever the fuck you want. None of it matters to me," I say as forcefully as I can. "Now, if you'll excuse me, I have some research to get to."

"Research?" he says softly, his brows pulling together.

Why do I always do this? Just as I get a conversation all but wrapped up, I give him one more tidbit to grasp on to. I sigh. "Yes, I'm going to the club tonight."

Jay growls, and his irises go a steely blue. "That's not safe."

"Frank is coming with me." I lift my chin in defiance. It's not true, but it's enough to keep him from following me.

Lightning quick, Jay's hand drops from my arm. The twinge of desperation I feel to reach out to him makes me want to stab myself in the eye.

Looking past me, he straightens and turns to the door. "Right," he says over his shoulder. "I hope you two have a good night."

Like a fool, all I want to do is holler that I'm kidding. That I didn't mean it. Tell him that nothing but a series of meaningless hookups connects me to Frank, but why do I care what Jay believes? And why would I want to console him with that truth?

KITTEN'S SONGS

"It's been a while since the last time I did this kind of thing. What exactly does one wear to a sex club?" I ask Sophie as we sort through a rack of clothes in Dex's workroom.

Dex shakes his head and cocks a brow at his wife. "You told her," he mutters.

She shrugs. "Ten years, Dex. I kept a secret from my best friend for ten years. You should be proud."

Thankfully, he responds with a chuckle.

"God, why can't I find a Dex!" I whine.

He slides behind me and gives me a hug. "There's plenty of me to share," he teases.

Sophie grins and bounces on her toes. "Can we go with her tonight?"

Dex straightens behind me, and I spin, catching sight of one of his infamous glares. It takes a lot for him to get angry. The man is always smiling, so it's obvious that idea isn't sitting well with him. That's *their* thing. And I totally get it. I actually love it about him. That he's so possessive of her that he wants to be the only one experiencing that with her.

"No," I say so he doesn't have to. "I want to do this on my own. It'd be weird being there with my old married friends."

Sophie's eyes grow wide. "Did you just call me old?"

I laugh. "We're the same age."

"She called *me* old," Dex says, squeezing me again and plopping a kiss on my cheek.

"I need to take it all in, really sit back and watch. And if you're there, I'll be too busy wanting to point things out, and you know we'll end up off topic."

She laughs. "True, there's so much to gawk at."

A whoosh of excitement tumbles through my belly. I've been to a sex club a total of one time in my life, and that was years ago. I don't know what to expect tonight.

Once I'm dressed in the outfit Sophie insisted I wear, she hollers after me, "Oh, I left something on your desk. For the story."

I turn back and smile. "I'll grab it on my way out. Wish me luck."

Downstairs, the office is empty. It's after eight, and everyone is long gone for the day. My day, on the other hand, is far from over. I only have a few weeks until Chloe moves back to the states. In that time, I need to get this promotion. Then I pray that Jay will stay out of my day-to-day life.

I need to work on an explanation my family will buy about why Chloe is moving in with me.

I need to…

Grow up.

Because moms don't belong in sex clubs on weeknights. Moms belong at home with their kids.

My life is going to look very different, very soon.

I really need to get my shit in order.

With a hand on the light switch, I turn back to make sure I haven't forgotten anything. That's when I catch sight of the small black box on my desk. Sophie's gift. The small piece of cardstock on top reads:

For tonight. Enjoy.

I laugh to myself. What did she do?

I slide the top of the box open and press my lips together as I study the two gold balls. I *think* I know what to do with them. *But...should I?*

Fuck it. My life *is* changing in the near future. Six weeks, to be exact. I'm going to enjoy myself while I can.

22

ALREADY GONE BY SLEEPING AT LAST

Jay

I didn't have to buy every club in the city like Beckett suggested. Somehow, I knew she'd walk into this one.

The previous owners had done plenty of updates in the years since I was last here, but the name remained the same. I'll change that next week. For tonight, I'm sitting in the owner's suite at Rebel, watching the camera trained on the front door, waiting for my kitten to make an appearance. The whiskey in my hand is a must—its effects will hopefully temper the feelings I'll no doubt experience when she walks in with Frank.

And Gavin is sitting by my side to make sure I don't kill the man when he does step inside with her.

It fucking stings that she's with Frank. He's known her longer than I have. They mean something to each other.

The women I've been seen with, photographed with, linked to, since we broke up, have meant nothing to me. Each one was a means to an end.

But Frank…he's her brother's best friend…that has to mean something.

"Do you think I should trade Vaughn?" Gavin asks without looking up from his phone.

"No idea."

"What about Rivers? He wasn't great last year."

With my eyes still locked on the monitor, I shrug. "If you want."

"You aren't even paying attention to me. Rivers was fucking phenomenal last year! He's my best player." Gavin laughs.

I take another sip of my drink, unable to muster even an ounce of the humor he's using. "Sorry. Can't focus on anything but what I'm going to do when she walks in here."

"Which is why I'm talking about hockey. It's been a while since we played. You need it."

Finally, I glance in his direction. My friend's face is etched with worry as he scrutinizes me. I run my hand across my forehead. "Ain't that the fucking truth."

"If she shows up with the best friend, we're leaving," he deadpans.

"Not happening."

"Why are you doing this?" he grits out. It's the same thing he and all my other friends have asked me for years. None of them have settled down. None have been in love. Maybe one day they'll understand, but for now, there's no point in even justifying my reasoning.

It's like explaining division to a toddler. The guys would have to understand the basics first. Comprehend what it feels like to love a person so wholeheartedly. See how much easier, brighter, more enjoyable life is because that person is in the world.

Then they'd have to suffer. Lose it all and live in darkness. Exist in a place where they'd do anything to claw their way out. But my friends, they've always lived in the shadows. They've never experienced the true warmth of the sun. And without that, how could they fathom the lengths a person would go to in order to get it back?

Anything. I'd do fucking anything to get back to how I felt when Cat was mine.

Even sit and wait for her to walk in with another man. One she'll likely go home with at the end of the night.

I suck in a breath when she finally walks in. And my heart races when no one follows her.

My cock twitches at the memory of the last time she walked into this club.

The chase. The rush. The taste of her on my fingers.

"That." I point to the screen. "That's why I'm doing this. Because for that woman, I'd do just about anything."

Gavin quirks a brow. "There's something you *wouldn't* do?"

I laugh bitterly. "Yeah, let her go. You can leave now. I'll be good."

Gavin stands and buttons his jacket. "You sure?"

I don't bother with a response. My attention is focused solely on the woman on the screen. "Oh Kitten," I growl, rubbing a thumb along the smooth edge of the remote in my hand. "I've got you all to myself tonight."

It's playtime.

23

WAR OF HEARTS BY RUELLE

Cat

The club is not what I remembered at all.

The lights are low, but it lacks the red glow that gave the place a sexier vibe when I was here years ago. The dance floor is to the side rather than in the center. The couches in the corners are tired and sagging.

But I didn't come to explore this room—the club space. No, I'm headed to the second floor.

As I turn toward the elevator, my body jolts, and I have to slap a palm against the wall to steady myself. What the hell? It's barely noticeable, but the balls I slid inside myself an hour ago are vibrating lightly, and the sensation is making it hard to breathe.

"Shit," I mutter, biting down on my lip hard. I can't believe Sophie would do this to me. Strike that. Actually, I can. That sick bitch. And yet…

It feels so fucking good.

Blowing out a breath and trying to focus on my surroundings, I press the button to go upstairs. I want to explore what's up there more than I did five minutes ago. That hint of sensation vibrating through me

My phone buzzes as I slide into the elevator. Once the doors close in front of me, I take it from my bag, expecting to see a text from Sophie.

> **Unknown:** Ready to play a game?

I frown but jolt again when the intensity of the vibrations increases a notch or two. Practically panting, I blink a few times before leaning against the cool stainless-steel wall of the elevator.

> Who is this?

The door opens, and the buzzing inside my body stops. Before me, a man stands at a velvet rope. He takes one look at me and moves it aside. "Ms. Bouvier?"

I jolt in surprise. I haven't used that name in years. As a fuck-you to Jay, though I'd never admit that aloud, I started using James again after Chloe was born.

I'd finally found someone I hated more than my father, and I could no longer stand to be referred to by a name he'd murmured to me too many times to count.

"Um, sure, yes," I stammer.

"See or be seen?" he asks.

Confused by the question, I stare at him for a long second. Finally, the implication hits me. I have no intention of participating. I'm here to do research. Though I don't know that this is the right answer, I respond in the way that makes the most sense. "See."

"Plenty of options down the hall, then," he says, holding an arm out and motioning behind him. "There's a bar at the end. The door is on the right if you're not quite ready for anything else."

Obviously, he sees something in me that justifies his suggestion. And he'd be right. I'm in so far over my damn head it's not even funny. Why didn't I ask Frank to come with me? Or beg Dex to let me borrow Sophie?

Instead of focusing on things I can't change, I blow out a breath, smooth my hands down the soft silk fabric of my dress, and stride forward.

The low music that floats down the darkened hallway gets louder as I reach the magical door to the right, where I'll find booze that will hopefully take the edge off.

The bar is small, despite the large space. Once again, my mind takes over categorizing ways to make women feel more comfortable here. Rather than the single white light that hangs above the bartender, red lighting would set the mood and allow for shadows that could be used to one's advantage. Whether that be to hide in or to bring out inner courage. A woman occupies one of the three barstools. When I step beside her, she looks up at me with gorgeous blue eyes. She has creamy skin, high cheekbones, and berry lips that she licks as she returns my perusal.

"Can I get you a drink?" the bartender asks. He's wearing all black and has his sleeves rolled up, exposing tattoos that snake down his arms. I don't mind the eye candy in the least. His gruff appearance reminds me a bit of Frank.

Before I can reply, my phone buzzes again. In my haste to find the safety of the bar, I'd forgotten about the mystery message. I ignore it and order a drink instead. "Vodka martini…*Extra Dirty*," I instruct.

"No other way to have it," the woman beside me murmurs.

I give her an agreeable smile, but the expression slips from my face when a zap between my legs has my tongue going to the top of my mouth to hold in a moan.

Fuck, Sophie is killing me here.

Trying not to pant, I focus on the way the bartender pours the vodka into the silver mixer, followed by the olive juice—using a perfect ratio, I might add—and then I study the muscles that strain against his shirt as he shakes it.

The vibration inside me goes up another notch.

My body is stretched taut, and I'm afraid to remain standing. I'm so drenched, I worry the balls will slip from my body.

I clench tighter, working my inner muscles to ensure that doesn't happen. Dropping my head to the side, I lose myself, just a little, in the pleasure.

I finally give in and pull my phone from my bag again, needing a distraction from the desire that's threatening to drown me. Fortunately, at that moment, the vibrations return to a dull ache.

> Unknown: I'm sad you deleted my number.

> Unknown: Stop staring at him.

> Unknown: Don't stare at her either.

> Unknown: Fuck, Kitten, you're making me jealous.

Kitten.

Fucking Jay.

Determined not to let him get in my head, I slide my phone back into my purse, aware that he's somehow watching me actively ignoring him, and turn my attention back to the gorgeous woman beside me.

He has no right to make demands of me. I'll do whatever the hell I please, and right about now, I think it's her.

"I'm Catherine," I say, holding out my hand.

Those plump lips curve into a smile, and she takes another swipe across her bottom one. "Ari."

"Here alone?" I ask as the bartender slides the drink in front of me.

I mouth a *thank you*, and he winks back.

She drops her gaze to the floor for a second, then peeks up at me through her lashes. "No, actually, my girlfriend is in the other room."

There goes that idea. I lift my drink in the air and dip my chin. "Enjoy your night."

She scrapes her teeth along her bottom lip and trails gentle fingers across her breastbone. It's intentional. She wants me to look. But I don't do cheaters.

"You could enjoy the night with us," she murmurs.

My lungs seize, and I lose my train of thought. Only a few minutes into this excursion, and already I'm being invited to be part of a threesome. I involuntarily clench again as the vibrations ricochet inside me.

"Actually, um, I'm just here to watch—"

Her eyes light up at that comment.

Shit. I tuck a strand of hair behind my ear and correct myself. "Observe, I mean. For…research." I finally stutter out an explanation, all the while squeezing my thighs together as tight as I can. The edging from the damn balls inside me is getting to me. I need to get off. Fuck. No. This is pathetic. What I need is to take these things out of me so I can focus on why I'm really here. Focus on getting the damn promotion I'm owed.

With a shy smile, she drops her chin. When she looks back up at me with those incredible blue irises, I'm mesmerized. She exudes a genuine innocence, even as she continues talking about things that are nowhere near virtuous. "Watch with me, then. My girlfriend…she's in with someone else. Just…if you're here to learn, come…*learn*."

I suck in a breath as heat and desire pool in my belly. Her voice is raspy, like she's been screaming and her throat has yet to recover. I look back to the bartender, who's wearing a knowing smirk. He knows exactly what I'll say, even before I've made the decision.

His cocksure stance reminds me of Jay, and that alone sets me off. The fucker is watching me. Might as well give him a show.

"Okay." I lift my drink to my lips once more and down the contents. "I'm game."

She slides off her chair, and I follow. Her navy jumper clings to her ass as she leads me out of the bar. That's when I decide to stop thinking. The purpose of tonight is to investigate what a woman would experience during her first visit to a place like this. To understand what it would be like to explore this lifestyle for the first time. I'm here to see it not from my nervous, judgmental eyes, but from the perspective of someone who is curious and open to the activities they may encounter.

And I *am* curious, so perhaps I'm overthinking this either way.

She turns back, giving me her side profile. Her brown hair acts as a curtain, hiding most of her face as she talks. "I was nervous my first time too."

"How often do you come?"

She looks back at me and smirks. Yeah, I suppose that was a double entendre. Running her hands through her hair slowly and holding my attention as she no doubt intended with that move, she replies, "Once a month. It's more my girlfriend than me. She likes to explore."

"And you don't mind?" I ask. If I were in a relationship, I can't imagine being okay with my partner touching someone else. My stomach twists at the mere thought of it. And then, for some godforsaken reason, I picture faceless women touching Jay. I grimace. It's a painful image, and it wasn't hard to conjure. It's one I've seen plastered in magazines for years.

I hate this feeling.

The truth is, I've never felt that way about anyone but him. Not even when Frank looks at other women. However, the mere *thought* of another woman touching Jay makes me murderous.

Lost in my head, I'm caught off guard when Ari stops and grasps my hand.

"Look up," she whispers, drawing my attention to where she's pointing with her free hand. In front of us is a floor-to-ceiling window with a view of the room beyond it. Inside, a woman is sprawled out on a bed—naked, legs spread—as a man eats her.

Holy shit.

"This—that's your girlfriend?" I whisper, unable to tear my attention from the sight before me.

With both palms, the man pushes the woman's legs farther apart, then dives between her thighs. She arches back and tips her head to one side. As she does so, she spots us and props herself up on her elbows, training her gaze on Ari.

"Yes, she's beautiful, right?" she murmurs. But she's not looking for a response from me. Her entire focus is on that room. Not that I blame her. Mine is too.

Crooking one finger in a come-hither motion, the woman on the bed summons Ari and then falls back, moaning in ecstasy and pressing her pelvis into her partner's face.

The shudder that racks through me as Ari's breath hits my ear forces me to lean against the glass. With gentle fingers, she pushes the hair away from my neck and kisses me softly, eliciting a whimper I can't hold back.

"Sure you only want to watch?" she asks against my skin as her fingers circle my exposed shoulder and slide down to my swelling breasts.

My breath catches in my lungs, and goose bumps erupt along every inch of my skin. "Um—no, I'm good," I pant.

Her soft hand finds my cheek, and she turns me so I'm looking at her. She's leaning in close, her lips only a whisper from my own. "I hope you change your mind," she says before pressing her mouth to mine. It's just a gentle brush, and then she's smiling and stepping inside the room. On the other side of the glass wall, she turns and locks gazes with me as she brings a hand to the back of her neck and tugs at the halter strap of her jumper, allowing the silky garment to fall to the floor. The move exposes her creamy white skin, her hard pink nipples, and her bare pussy. She nibbles at her lip, then saunters to the bed, crawls over her girlfriend's face, and sits.

"Oh my God," I can't help but murmur aloud.

The space between my legs pulses with a need so strong all I can think about is touching myself. I peek over my shoulder, thankful I'm alone in the hallway, but I don't dare do anything to ease the ache just yet. I need to get out of here and go home, then my battery-operated toys can finish the job.

Just as I resolve to leave, a large hand palms the glass beside my head. A hard body presses against my back, and warm breath teases against my neck. Of their own volition, my eyes flutter closed. I know precisely who it is. I suppose I knew from the moment I pitched the sex club idea that he would make an appearance.

Part of me craved him.

"It's not safe for you to be alone in a place like this," he teases in a low rasp against my shoulder. My entire body shudders as the vibrations between my legs amplify and I finally lose the battle and let out an audible moan.

"I-I'm fine." My argument is somewhat nullified by the way I stutter through it.

In response, Jay presses his other hand to my waist. "I could be anyone. Anyone could take advantage of you right now."

"Will you?" I ask. Immediately, I realize my mistake and clarify, "I mean, is that what you're doing right now...taking advantage?"

His gruff laugh hits my skin. "I would never," he says softly. "All I want—all I've ever wanted—is to give you everything. I'll take nothing from you..."

Another whimper escapes me as his hand slides down my hip and falls away. I want those hands on me. I don't want to want it, but God, I do. And then the vibrations build again, and I bow backward into Jay. He rests his chin on my shoulder, and I give in and let my head fall to the side so it rests against his.

I no longer see the sex acts happening in front of me. No, Jay's body against mine has become my entire focus. I need him inside me more than I've ever needed anything in my life.

"I need you to fuck me," I rush out, keeping my voice low, embarrassed by how desperate I sound.

His body stiffens against mine. "Say it again," he growls as he grasps my arm roughly and spins me to face him. His eyes search mine, but I turn away. It's too hard to look at him. To see those beautiful blue-gray eyes fill with hope. To let myself wonder why he's looking at me like that when he's the one who walked away. When he's the one who kept us apart.

"Look at me and say it, Catherine," he says with an edge, his tether about to snap.

Focusing on a spot on his shoulder, I shake my head and turn back to the scene playing out before me. Ari is now riding the man, and her girlfriend is watching with hungry eyes. The elicit act, combined with the heavy vibrations inside me, sends heat ricocheting through my body as my orgasm starts to crest.

Jay draws the hair from my neck and kisses up my bare shoulder to my ear. "You want my cock inside you, Kitten?"

I drop my head back to his shoulder again, giving him more access to my neck. "Please," I beg.

"I need your eyes, then."

"You said you wouldn't take anything from me."

He sucks in a breath.

I got him there. He wants my orgasm. He wants my eyes. He promised he'd take nothing, but the second I look at him, he'll know

I've got nothing left to take. He already has it all. He's had it since the day I met him. I have nothing to give, because Jay took my heart and never gave it back.

He owns me, and all I own is anger. For just a few minutes, I'd like to forget that.

"Fine," he says. It's a soft breath against my clavicle. "But not here."

He drags me away from the spectacle, out of the light, and leads me to the darkness. Under the protection of the shadows, he presses me into a room and pushes me against the door. I can't see a thing, but he's everywhere. His mouth on my collarbone, one hand on my breast, the other skirting up my leg.

"Fuck, Kitten, I've missed the feel of you."

Me too.

"Make me come," I say instead.

Jay licks up my neck and tilts my head, angling me so I can't move. "I've waited thirteen years for this mouth. Give me two damn minutes, please," he says softly, his breath mixing with mine.

Petrified by the idea and yet paralyzed by indecision, I do nothing but wait for the moment his lips ghost against mine. When they do, he hums as if I'm an old song he's just recognized playing on the radio. His favorite one. And then he grinds his hips against me so I feel every inch of his want. Every ounce of his need. And then his tongue hits the slit of my mouth, begging for entrance, and for the first time in thirteen years, I taste him.

His lips are soft, his kiss pure passion. Surprise and salvation nip at my lips. Unable to experience this as a passive participant, I drag both hands up his chest and shoulders and around to the back of his head. Raking my fingers through his hair, I pull him closer, needing him every bit as much as he needs me. "Tu me manques," I whisper against his lips, unable to stop the words from tumbling out.

Jay's brows pinch together, but I cover his lips with mine before he can question me. As we kiss, his thick cock rubs against my aching clit, the friction almost amplifying the vibrations inside me. That's all it takes to trigger my orgasm, but it takes on an almost dangerous level of heat from his lips on mine. From the way his fingers sear me, even through layers of clothing, as he simply holds me. From the feel of our bodies melded so close together.

There's a reason the French call it le petit morte. The feel of him is like dying and going to heaven. But it's not enough. It's never enough when it comes to Jay.

Even as my orgasm subsides, I beg for his touch. "I need more," I pant as he kisses me softly. "I need you inside me."

His mouth ghosts against mine as he shakes his head. "Not until you're mine, Kitten."

With a groan, I drop my head back against the door. That was surface level. It barely touched the ache within my body, even if it was the best orgasm I've had in a very long time.

Because it's him.

Always him.

Only him.

His fingers ghost up my legs and between my thighs, and we both groan when he slips inside my panties and coats one finger in my desire. "Oh Catherine, it'd be so easy to have you right here. You'd let me, wouldn't you? You'd let me fuck you silly. Probably bare," he says like the cocky asshole he is.

And yet he's not wrong.

I've only ever had one man inside me there…and I want him so badly. I've missed him so intensely.

"Fuck you," I respond, but there's no bite.

Two fingers slip inside, causing me to buck against him.

He chuckles. "Wouldn't you like that?" He kisses me again.

I deepen the connection, trying to keep him in place, but he's got an agenda.

He stretches his fingers deeper and pulls out each little ball, and I die a little in embarrassment. "Did you enjoy your play toy?"

My cheeks heat at his comment. It's then I realize that it wasn't Sophie who left me the toys. I push against him, but he holds me in place as he laughs.

"Stop. You know you enjoyed it. And now I have a mess to clean up," he says, kissing me ferociously and leaving me breathless.

Then he drops to his knees and slides his hands up my legs. With a squeeze to both hips, he finds the waistband of my panties and drags them down, helping me out of them. He presses a soft kiss to my knee, then another to the inside of my thigh. Then he nuzzles against my heated flesh, using his head to push my legs apart. With one hand, he pulls one calf up to his shoulder, then he presses his lips against my entrance.

I hiss and squeeze my eyes shut when his tongue slides between my lips.

"Fuck," he says in what almost sounds like wonder. Then he brings one hand to my ass and digs his fingers into the flesh there, tugging me closer. His other hand glides up and down my leg, as if he's grounding himself to this moment. Like he needs the feel of my skin beneath his fingers to know that this is real. Like he can't believe he's really on his knees before me, eating me lazily. Like we've been doing this forever. Like we never stopped.

I'd almost forgotten how much Jay loves the act of pleasuring me. His moans tell me he's exactly where he wants to be. Turned on from my taste alone.

It isn't long before he takes me over the edge, and I cry out his name without any thought of the consequences.

He growls as he continues to suck. His strokes are long and easy as he hums against me, the echo of it vibrating inside me. "I love the sound of my name on your tongue, Kitten. Almost as much as I love doing this."

I push against him, suddenly aware of how vulnerable I am in this position. How close I've let him come.

He smirks up at me. "Done with me already?"

I'm sure he's hard as steel, and it's only fair that I return the favor. "No, I'll take care of you," I reply softly.

Jay shakes his head against my legs, then moves up my body until he's cupping my face in both hands and pressing a kiss against my lips. "Have dinner with me."

"What?"

"Dinner. With me. Let's go get something to eat. I missed you."

Oh my God. He's insane. He got me off, yes, but that doesn't reset things between us. "Jay," I scold.

He kisses me again, then pulls back. "I love when you use that tone with me. Fuck, there isn't a thing I don't love about you. Yell at me all you want. Just have dinner with me."

I huff out a breath. "Wouldn't you rather I suck your dick?"

He laughs. "Shockingly, no." He moves one hand under my chin and pulls me in for another kiss. This one is sweet and slow.

It's insane how much I want his lips on mine. That I'm not pushing him away. Already, I'm addicted again. I *can't* push him away.

I absolutely hate myself.

"I want more than a few minutes of pleasure, even if I've been dreaming of your lips around my cock for…well, a *long* time." He kisses me again. In the darkened room, he's a shadow that looms over me, but those eyes of his, they sparkle with mischief.

"Why do you always sound like you're in a freaking Hallmark movie?" I groan and press my forehead to his shoulder.

He kisses the crown of my head. "Baby, I say cock and fuck too much. I know that. But *fuck*, I just want to have a meal with you. Please, just…give me an hour. Talk to me about what you saw tonight. What you think of the place. Your article. Talk to me about the weather, I don't give a shit. Just *talk* to me."

I roll my eyes, but I can't hide the small smile that teases at my lips. "You'd really prefer I talk to you than drop to my knees right now?"

His hot breath warms my skin as he hisses, "*Yes.*"

I sigh in resignation. I really am dying to taste him again, but whatever. "Fine. Give me my panties." I huff and hold out a hand.

Jay chuckles as he snags my wrist, then laces our fingers. "Nah, they're mine."

24

ANOTHER LOVE BY TOM ODELL

Jay

"I can't believe you bought a sex club." Cat's curled up on the couch in my new office, with her feet under her thighs and a carton of chicken and broccoli in her hand.

"Three," I say with a smirk, then take a bite of my sesame chicken.

"Three?" She shoves her chopsticks into the container and gapes.

"Didn't know which one you'd go to, so I bought the ones that are close to our office."

She rolls her eyes. "And how did you know I'd come to this one tonight?"

Cocking a brow, I give her a knowing look. "I took a calculated risk, I guess."

"Just assumed I'd go back to the place you and I first went?"

I laugh. "You did, didn't you?"

She groans. "You're annoying."

"You're adorable."

She blows out a breath and looks away. "So, you going to sell this place now?"

I take one more bite, then set the food on the small table beside me and take a sip of water. "Actually, I think I'll keep it."

Her loud laugh fills the space, and everything inside my body feels lighter. "Why?"

"You don't like it here? You seemed to be enjoying yourself when I found you," I tease.

She ducks her head and blows out a breath. "I'm not normally like this." She motions toward me. "You have me acting like a crazy person, calling Frank to service me at work, coming to a sex club…letting you touch me again."

A groan rumbles through my chest at the mention of Frank. He's the last thing I want to talk about right now.

I run my tongue against my teeth, trying to regain control. "You can hardly blame me for the way you're acting. If I remember correctly, the first time I came into your office, Frank was there *servicing you*, as you put it."

She grunts. "Yeah, that wasn't my finest moment." With a shake of her head, she pulls her shoulders back. "I just don't know what you want from me."

You.

But she's not ready for that yet.

"Like I said, I just wanted to have a meal with you. That's all." I pick up my take-out container and point to her food with my chopsticks.

It's after eleven p.m. Neither of us needed dinner, but I want the hour she promised.

She smiles and takes another bite. "You bought a sex club so you could have dinner with me?" she teases.

"Oh Kitten," I say with a sigh, "you have no idea the things I've done and would do for just a moment of your time."

She tips her face to the ceiling and blows out a breath. "I don't understand you. You're the one who walked away. Why are you rewriting history?"

I set down my food again and drop my elbows to my knees, giving her my full attention. "I'm happy to clear everything up, but I don't think you're ready. Or are you? We can talk about what went wrong thirteen years ago if you want. I'm happy to discuss."

She scoffs, but then her gaze shifts away, and she changes the subject—*she knows I'm right.* "If you're going to keep this place, you should change a few things."

My lips tip up in a smile. "Oh yeah? Like what?"

Cat ticks off the things she noted as she walked in. Lighting she would change, furniture, ambiance. All things I've already considered, but her ideas are far better than what I've come up with thus far. When she's done talking and we've both abandoned our food, I watch her every move, wondering what comes next.

"This wasn't so bad, was it?" I ask, rubbing the back of my neck to ease the anxiety I feel. The food's gone, and she's given me more than the hour I requested. I don't have any excuse to keep her here.

She closes her eyes and hums. "No, it wasn't."

I place my hand on her thigh to get her attention, and her lids fly open. Her whiskey-colored irises burn, practically begging for relief. She wants to move forward just as much as I do, but she's not over the past. That battle is clearly written all over her face. In her body language. But she's growing tired of fighting. Tonight, that wall she's built around herself has crumbled just a bit.

"Have dinner with me again?"

She tuts. "Jay, my brothers hate you."

If that's the only hurdle we have, then my efforts tonight were nothing short of miraculous. "I can deal with that."

She barks out a laugh. "Yeah, because it's so easy to win them over."

I squeeze her thigh. "Have dinner with me."

She closes her eyes again, and when she opens them, her expression has cooled. I've lost her for the night. "You asked for an hour, and you got it. Thank you for dinner, Jay…and the orgasms."

She scans the room, preparing to get up and go, but I need one more taste. One more minute. "Come sit in my lap, and I'll give you one more."

Her eyes go wide, and her breath falters. "I—"

"Shh, Kitten. Just let me take care of you."

When she hesitates, I grab her waist and hoist her onto my lap. My heart damn near soars when, instead of the fight I expect, she only laughs. As I cradle her, she studies me, her black lashes fluttering. There's a hint of confusion and a decent dose of concern there, but I don't give her a moment to think. Quickly, I kiss her. She moans, and after only a second of hesitation, she mimics my movement, her tongue tangling with mine. And then I take her over the edge again.

25

APOLOGIZE BY ONE REPUBLIC

Cat

Though Sophie asks for details about the club, I leave out the part where I ended up on Jay's couch, making out with him like I was in college again. I don't mention that his hands worked me over so well that I came twice more in his office before he cleaned me up with his tongue. I don't tell her how he refused to fuck me, even after I practically gave him a lap dance.

He said not until I'm his. Not until I agree to another dinner. Things that will never happen.

And since I don't tell Sophie, I don't tell anyone.

And that means it didn't really happen.

At least that's what I'm telling myself as I sit across from the cocky bastard. Who, by the way, is wearing glasses—*glasses*!—at today's meeting. As if the guy wasn't already disgustingly good-looking, he's now got the smart, sophisticated daddy thing going. I hate him.

"I'd like updates on each of your stories," he says, his attention landing on me from behind the black-rimmed glasses, even as he says Rose's name.

As she prattles off her newest story idea, I clench my jaw to fight back a smile and try to ignore the way he's running his fingers up and down his pen. How he licks his lips every few seconds. How fucking hot he looks just sitting at the head of the table. His unbuttoned suit jacket hugs his broad shoulders perfectly as he fucking owns the room like he owned my body last night. Damn him. He's all I see. And when all eyes are on me, waiting for my story update, Sophie squeezes my thigh below the table and stares at me, wide-eyed, silently telling me that all my secrets are written on my face.

I bolt from the conference room as soon as the meeting is over, but Sophie is hot on my heels. In a loud whisper, she bellows, "You fucked him, didn't you?"

Turning quickly, I shush her and pull her into the first office I see, which happens to be Jay's office. *Shit.* "Shut up!"

She tries, unsuccessfully, to smother her smile. "Oh my God, you totally did!"

"I said shut up!" Stomping a foot, I heave a breath, then another.

I don't know what else to say. So we just stare at one another while her eyes dance with glee and I telepathically beg her not to make me say it.

We both jump when there's a knock on the doorframe.

"Ladies," Jay says, wearing a knowing smirk.

At least he's taken off the godforsaken glasses.

To my complete horror, Sophie turns to him, pulls her shoulders back, and says, "We were just discussing the two of you."

"We *were not*," I hiss.

Jay chuckles as he folds his arms across his chest and props himself against the doorway. "I love talking about the two of us. It's actually my favorite topic. What were you saying, Kitten?"

With my hands on my hips, I look at the ceiling and suck in a deep breath to keep myself from screaming at both my best friend and my boss.

Also known as the man I loathe, the orgasm man, Satan.

Sophie laughs and Jay smirks.

"I prefer orgasm man," he says, "but I'll answer to any name that crosses those perfect lips."

Fuck. My face goes hot when I realize my thoughts weren't as internal as I intended them to be.

"Come on," Sophie says, "let's go get coffee before you burst."

She grabs my arm and drags me past Jay and his Cheshire grin. I hate him.

"Tell me more about the orgasm man," she says far louder than is necessary as we walk out of the office.

As we stride down the hallway, my phone rings in my hand. I ignore my bestie and answer without looking at the display.

"Hi, Cat. This is Vanessa Simpson. Not sure if you remember me, but we met in college."

I come to a halt in the middle of the hall as I'm catapulted to years earlier. Vanessa was a friend of Mia's. I haven't heard from either of them in over a decade.

"Oh, yes. Hi, how are you?"

Sophie's eyes narrow, probably at my weird tone. Over the years, I've worked hard not to let thoughts of Mia invade my mind, but when they do, I can't help but stiffen.

"I'm good. I'm actually calling because I was set up on a date with your brother, believe it or not."

"Carter?" I ask with a frown. I prefer not to think about what my older brother does, but dating isn't it.

"Oh, um, no," she says with a nervous laugh. "Your younger brother."

"Cash?" I question.

"Yes! We met through a matchmaking thing, and honestly, I think we hit it off. Has he said anything? Never mind. Obviously, he hasn't if you don't know about me."

Interesting. Now this is something to smile about. *Finally.* "No, but I haven't really seen him in a few days. That's amazing. Have you heard from him?"

I can practically feel her nervous energy through the phone. My brother is a catch. He's good-looking, kind, funny, and the head of one of the most successful liquor companies in the world. He's a ten on anyone's scale.

"Not yet. I think he has a few other dates lined up."

Right. With his damn matchmaker. Who used to date the man I'm currently fooling around with.

And there goes that glimmer of excitement. I don't know what Jay and I are doing, but the idea of him having slept with the same woman my brother is sleeping with is a bit too much for me. There's no doubt I'd die if Grace and Cash actually turned into a long-term thing.

Tiny shivers skate up my body at just the thought of spending holidays with the awful woman.

"I have an idea," I singsong into the phone.

Sophie studies me with one brow raised, probably wondering what kind of chipper demon has possessed me, since I'm not one to sing song anything.

"Yeah?" Vanessa says, her pitch rising with hope.

"What do you have planned for tomorrow? Any chance you and a few friends would want to meet me and my brothers for drinks?"

"I've got two sisters who I'm sure could be free," she croons.

"Awesome. I'll text you the details."

"Thank you so much!"

"No, seriously, thank you. See you tomorrow," I say, no doubt wearing a huge smile.

"What did you do?" Sophie asks after I hit End.

I let out a deep breath, telling myself that I did the right thing. That I'm *doing* the right thing. "I made things better," I say tentatively.

That phone call was a sign. A reminder of why what happened last night can never happen again. And a way to hopefully move on completely from the past.

I glance back toward Jay's office. He's sitting at his desk with his head down as he works. Almost as if he can feel my gaze, he looks up, and a genuine smile crosses his face. Ignoring the way his smile makes me want to run toward him instead of away, I grab Sophie's arm and guide us in the opposite direction.

There are certain things that can't be undone, some things that are insurmountable, and my past with Jay is one of them.

It's time to finally move on.

SOMEONE TO YOU BY BANNERS

Cat

From: <JHanson@jolie.com>
To: <CJames@jolie.com>
Subject: Club opening
July 25, 2022

Ms. James,

You are cordially invited to the opening of Black Label.

Date: Thursday, July 28th

Attire: The fuck-me heels you wore to the club Saturday night

Nothing else.

XOXO,

Jay

From: <CJames@jolie.com>
To: <JHanson@jolie.com>
Subject: Re: Club opening
July 25, 2022

You're supposed to be paying attention to the meeting right now, not sexually harassing your employees.

XOXO,

The woman you can't have again.

From: <JHanson@jolie.com>
To: <CJames@jolie.com>
Subject: Re: Re: Club opening
July 25, 2022

Ms. James,

I can't focus on the meeting when you're looking at me that way. And biting your lip.

Fine, you can wear whatever you want on Thursday night. Just tell me you'll come.

All over my face.

XOXO,

Jay

From: <CJames@jolie.com>
To: <JHanson@jolie.com>
Subject: Re: Re: Re: Club opening
July 25, 2022

Mr. Hanson,

Considering you and my brother are fighting over the same woman, I'll pass.

Link: <u>Woman Cassius James and Jay Hanson Fighting over Identified as Matchmaker Grace Kensington.</u>

"Fuck," Jay mutters across the table, his eyes trained on the phone in his hand.

Fuck is right. I'm going to *kill* my brother.

27

ROSES BY THE CHAINSMOKERS

Cat

"You're playing a dangerous game," Sophie says as we sit across from one another at the bar on the first floor of Black Label. Now that Rebel has reopened under its new name—and Jay has installed all of my suggestions—Dexter was okay with Sophie meeting me here for a drink after work so I could show her.

In two weeks, Chloe will be moving in with me for good. Nights like these will be few and far between.

Holding the olive skewer above my martini glass, I shrug and give her my best wide-eyed expression. "Whatever do you mean?"

She lets out a loud, raucous laugh. "Girl, you aren't fooling me. You can sit there all cool and pretend you aren't dancing with the devil, but the flames are burning in your eyes. You want Jay. And choosing to only give him your body is a bad idea."

"I'm not giving him my body. I'm just here for a drink with a friend."

Sophie's obnoxious laugh tells me she isn't buying what I'm selling.

I groan. "Whatever. Honestly, after the last two weeks, I deserve an orgasm or two. I can't believe my plan with Vanessa backfired."

With a scrunch of her nose, she sips her pink drink. In a red dress and heels, my best friend is one hot mom. And I've missed being out with her like this. "I never liked that girl."

"Anyone is better than Grace." I mime sticking my finger down my throat. "God, you should have seen the two of them. One look in Grace's direction, and my brother was like a forlorn puppy chasing his favorite toy around the club. He ditched all of us—*and Vanessa*—and then I heard him call her Angel as they were leaving."

Sophie shakes her head. "He always seemed like such a smart guy. I'm surprised by him. Then again, you James siblings tend to lose your minds when it comes to falling in love."

"I'm not in love!" I scoff.

A devilish grin crosses her lips. "Whatever you say."

"Fine, I'm going to prove you wrong." I sit up straight and survey the bar. I'm not sure what exactly I'm looking for, but I'll know when I see it.

Sophie tsks in disapproval, but that only ratchets up the challenge. "You can't have casual sex. You're not wired like that."

"May I remind you that I was having casual no-feelings sex with Frank?"

Sophie eyes me, unimpressed. "Frank isn't just anyone. You've known him forever and trust him more than just about anyone else. Not to mention you only allowed him to fuck you from behind—in the ass. I'm sorry. You don't get brownie points for that one. You avoided feelings by avoiding looking at him. It's what you do. You avoid."

"Fuck you," I say and then slide one olive into my mouth. My words may be harsh, but there's no bite to them.

She smiles as she bounces to the low beat of the music that thrums through the space. The red lights and new couches, combined with the women weaving between tables and groups of patrons serving drinks while wearing nothing but tassels covering their nipples and black booty shorts, set an erotic mood.

"This place is going to be epic," she says as she scans the dance floor and bar area.

Pride fills me at her comment. Before, it was a little seedy, but now the ambiance is heightened, even with the women barely dressed. It's sexy. I wonder if he considered my suggested changes upstairs.

Not that I'll find out.

Licking my lips, I spot a group of men sprawled out on the couches in the corner. Each man owns the space, broad suit-covered shoulders, legs spread wide, drinks in hand, laughing at one another and not giving the almost topless women even a moment's glance. Twirling my toothpick in the air, I point in their direction. "Him. The one with the brown hair and scruff on his face."

The growl from behind me has us both turning. Behind me, Jay wears a scowl, and I have to press my lips together to keep from laughing. The man is nothing if not predictable.

"Hey, boss," I croon, shimmying my hips on my stool.

Jay grunts a hello to Sophie and then turns his scowl back to me. "What are you doing?"

I down the rest of my drink and search for the server to order another. Jay holds up his hand to get the bartender's attention, and within seconds, I see our drinks being made.

Perks of being the boss.

"Just checking out the new club," Sophie replies since I've yet to answer Jay's question.

"And the gorgeous men over there." I point toward the group who are now glancing over, smirks on their faces. Clearly, they can read the room.

"They're not interested," Jay deadpans.

"Rude!"

"Considering they're my brothers and my best friends, they know you're off-limits."

Well, so much for that plan.

The bartender appears with our drinks, and I take a moment to appreciate the dark-haired beauty.

Jay's hard body crowds my space, and his lips ghost the shell of my ear. "Dirty martini?"

"*Extra Dirty*," I reply. With a lick of my lips, I take a sip, humming when the vodka coats my throat and trying, though failing miserably, to ignore just how close Jay stands.

"Some things never change." His hot breath hits my neck.

"Oh, but so much does," I reply.

"Not my obsession with the way you taste." His voice is so low the gravelly rasp makes my thighs clench. "Not the way you sound when you come, and obviously not your drink of choice," he whispers in my ear, tilting his head toward my martini glass.

He's moved impossibly close, but when Sophie's eyes bug out and she squeezes her lips shut, I know she heard what he said.

I plant my hands on his chest and, ignoring the hot, hard muscles beneath my palms, push against him. "Jay, people can hear you."

He presses closer, forcing me to feel every inch of his body. His warmth, his solidness, and the way he smells…it all goes straight to my head. "I could sincerely not give two fucks," he rasps, his mouth grazing my neck.

I squirm beside him. "Jay, please."

"Yes, Kitten, I love when you beg." He runs his teeth up my jaw, sending sparks of desire shooting through me. "Now say goodnight to Sophie." Before I know it, he's got an arm under my thighs and one looped behind my back.

"My drink!" I whine, trying to keep from spilling it as he pulls me into his arms and cradles me like a freaking baby.

Jay merely eyes me and stalks away from the bar. Unstable, I slide my arm around his neck to balance, aware that my cheeks are probably bright red over the spectacle he's making.

"Jay, what are you doing?" I hiss. "I came here to have a drink with Sophie. Put me down."

When I turn back, she's waving, wearing a huge smile. Her purse is already in hand, and she's ready to head for the door.

Bitch. She's just going to let him kidnap me!

"Sophie!"

"Call me later." She holds her hand to her ear.

"You're insane," I hiss. "Your friends are staring at us!"

His hard stare burns into me as he stops abruptly. "I'm insane because of you, Cat. I'm fucking gone for you. So don't push me," he warns.

The tone. The words. The hardness in his gaze. None of it should turn me on. It should make me want to run.

But it doesn't.

The blood traveling through my veins heats to boiling, and the fire inside my belly grows. Sophie's right. I'm playing a dangerous game. We're combustible. No good can come from this.

But I can't get myself to walk away.

Not tonight.

I'm an addict. I had one taste of him, and now I'm itching for more. Just one more night…

"Do we have a deal?" he grits out, his eyes hard.

"Mind-numbing casual sex?" I offer with a grin.

Jay's jaw ticks.

"Frenemies with benefits?" I tease.

Growling, he pushes forward again. "I'm going to turn your ass so red you won't be able to sit tomorrow."

I down the rest of my drink and hold it out to the bouncer as we wait for the elevator to take us upstairs. Then I turn to Jay and loop my other arm around his neck. "Promise?"

KITTEN'S SONGS

"What did you do?" I whisper in awe as Jay carries me into one of the newly redecorated bedrooms.

He stands in the center of the space, but he doesn't let me go as we take in the details of the room. Against one wall, there's a bed with a black leather headboard equipped with hooks. There is no bedspread, just white sheets. And the pillows aren't meant for sleeping. No, each is a different shape, perfect for positioning in a variety of ways.

The walls are a slate gray, and the lighting is low. Against the opposite wall is a dresser I can only assume is filled with all sorts of toys.

It's an adult dream. And a replica of the one I described to him.

"How do you always find places for us to hide, Mr. Hanson?" I say, trying to lighten the mood.

He keeps a firm grip on my ass with one hand while he uses the other to push the hair out of my face. "I'd do anything to not have to hide. I dream of the day when you'll be proud to walk down the street with your hand in mine."

I shake my head and squirm, suddenly needing to extricate myself from his grip. "Don't say things like that."

Narrowing his eyes, he squeezes me tighter in response. "Why? It's true. I know you aren't ready for that, so I won't push, but Catherine, make no mistake, I came back for you, and I always get what I want." He nips at my bottom lip.

I whimper in defeat and rub against him. "What I want is for you to make me come right now."

"I never could deny you." Jay chuckles, his chest vibrating against mine. "So tell me, how do you want it?"

I bite my lip and survey him. What I want is for him to fuck me until I can't think. No sweet words. No soft touches. I need hard and quick. "You know what I want," I dare.

With a smile, he looks away from me. "I told you what you need to do to get that, Kitten. You want my cock, I want your future. I think it's a fair trade."

I laugh. "You think pretty highly of your cock, don't you, Mr. Hanson?"

"Keep calling me that, and I'll bend you over your desk tomorrow and treat you like the dirty employee you're trying to be."

At his promise, heat gushes between my thighs. "Please."

He drops me onto the bed and stalks over the dresser. "Clothes off, on your stomach, ass in the air," he commands.

A surprised breathy laugh escapes my throat, but when he turns around holding a red silk ribbon, he isn't smiling.

"Clothes off."

Okay. He's serious. I undress quickly, keeping my chin tucked and my focus locked on the floor. I don't look like I did thirteen years ago. I've got cellulite and stretch marks, and a jagged line runs across my belly from my c-section. If he asks me to turn over, I'll leave.

No one has seen me naked since I gave birth to Chloe. Sophie's right, I've kept myself guarded. Kept any kind of sexual act impersonal. I've allowed Frank to touch me plenty, but to never really have me. Not completely.

The last man who did is standing in this room, breathing so heavily I think he may hyperventilate. The air is charged. Our chemistry is palpable—an electric undercurrent that threatens to set fire to my carefully constructed walls, to burn down every defense I've built up over the years.

In its aftermath, there could be beauty. Life would grow. I could start again.

Not with him. *Never with him.* Not after what he did. And that's the problem. It's the circle I continue to go in. I'll never be able to move past what happened, so instead, I retreat into my body, choosing to ignore my emotions and do nothing but feel.

"Do you know how fucking beautiful you are?" Jay whispers, closer now, his voice a low gravel vibrating through the room.

I squeeze my eyes shut and whimper. "Please."

His responding laugh is mirthless. It's dangerous. Heady. Filled with anger. "Only ten minutes, ago you looked ready to beg one of my friends to touch you. Now you want me?"

I wiggle my ass, relishing the tingles that run through my body at his tone. "I don't want you, Jay," I say desperately. "I *need* you."

I'd do just about anything for those words to not be true. But it's useless to fight against the desire. He's the only person I've ever needed. No matter how badly I want to deny it.

He chuckles against my bare skin, his mouth ghosting up my back and his hands sliding from my waist, up my torso, and to my arms. His body encases me in warmth, but the sensation of his clothes against my skin is wrong. I want to feel his muscles, to count the heartbeats that drum against my back, to be stitched back together as he slides into me. Even if it's only for a slice of time.

"Tell me, Kitten, how badly do you need me?"

"*So badly*," I pant.

He loops one silk ribbon around my right wrist. Fascinated, I watch as he ties it to the hook on the headboard. He then repeats the action with my left wrist.

Tied to the bed, at his complete mercy, I've never felt more free.

Wiggling my ass against his rock-hard erection, I urge him to continue.

"You want to come?" he murmurs, his mouth next to my ear.

"Oh God, yes."

He pulls back quickly, and the first slap is so jarring I barely register it. "Say my name."

"Fuck," I rasp under my breath.

His palm meets the flesh of the opposite cheek, and I screech.

"Jay," I babble in compliance, so turned on my knees wobble.

In response, he smacks me again.

Harder.

Desire pools between my thighs and has me bucking against him, searching for relief. He doesn't give it, though. No, instead, he continues his punishment. In rapid succession, he slaps my ass— left, right, left, right.

Red-hot searing pleasure scorches me. Eviscerates every last thought in my brain. Leaving me a puddle of need.

Whimpering, I beg him to make me come. The man hasn't even touched my clit, but here I am, a blubbering mess, with tears streaming down my face as I plead with him. "Please, please…"

"You want my cock?" He smooths his palm over my ass, running circles over the stinging skin.

"Yes," I cry.

"Say you're mine, Kitten. Admit what we both know. Say you've always been mine. That you'll only ever be mine. Then I'll give you everything you've ever wanted."

Even delirious with lust, I can't do it. I can't admit it.

Shaking my head against the now moist sheets, I mutter, "No. But my body is yours. Please, Jay, my body has only ever been yours."

His hand stops its circling, and he pulls it away. Is he ready to give in? Did he catch the meaning behind my admission? That he's the only man I've ever been with in that way? Will that be enough for him?

But the crack of his hand on my skin gives me the answer. With a grunt, he unbuckles his pants, the sound of the zipper sending a surge of desire through me. The bed dips as he repositions himself in front of me, with his back against the headboard and my head level with his hips. "Your pussy doesn't get this cock until you admit you're mine," he grits out as he looms over me. Fisting his shaft, he strokes himself only inches from my face.

Fuck. I can't help but lick my lips in anticipation.

"Open," he instructs, tapping his head against my lips.

Obediently, I stare up at him from under my lashes and lick at his slit, making us both groan. The taste of his arousal coats my tongue, and I close my eyes in appreciation.

God, this man. The things he makes me want.

He slides in slowly, and I let him. He pulses his hips forward, then pulls back a fraction. I have zero control of our movements since my hands are tied to the bedposts, and even when I try to adjust my hips, I'm left with little movement.

The taste of him makes my core pulse, and a fresh wave of desire coats my inner thighs. Every movement, every noise, only amplifies my need to come. But I continue to lick, to suck, to work him over. When I peek up at him again, desperate to see the desire I feel reflected back, his steel-blue gaze is focused on me. Except lust isn't the only thing I see written on the unfamiliar lines on his face. There is so much love in his expression I have to look away.

This man is in love with me. That much is clear. But in time, he'll learn that I'm no longer capable of such emotion in return.

Rubbing my thighs together, I moan around him again.

He chuckles. "Give me a second," he says, his voice warm like honey now. So different from the authoritative tone from moments ago.

The bed dips again, and for a moment, I'm alone on the mattress while he strides to the dresser. Once he's returned and positioned himself behind me, I shift, trying to see what he's doing. If he leaves me without release, I'll sob. I'm not too proud to beg.

"Please, Jay, please."

Buzzing sounds, and my hips buck in excitement. "Yes," I chant as the first vibrations press against my clit. "Oh, fuck yes," I mutter again.

He runs the vibrator from my clit, between my lips, to my opening. Gently—almost too gently—he presses in. I shift again so I can watch.

Behind me, he has his bottom lip clamped between his teeth as he watches the vibrator enter me. "Fuck, baby, your pussy wants this so bad, doesn't it?"

With his other hand, he fists his cock and works himself without taking his eyes off me, fucking his hand while the vibrator fucks me.

I'd do just about anything to get him to switch places with the damn silicone toy. But I know the price, and I'm not willing to pay it. So instead, I focus on the way he moves his hand over himself, and within minutes, my orgasm rips through my body. As I cry out his name, his body convulses. His cock twitches, and warmth coats my ass, easing the lingering sting from his punishment, as he comes with a guttural groan.

For several long moments, neither of us moves, and the only sound in the room is our breathing as we work to compose ourselves. And as the high wanes, Jay unties me and wipes me down with a warm cloth. The second he's finished, I reach for my dress, but he puts his hand on my arm to stop me.

"Please, just lie with me for a second."

The need in his voice makes me pause. I can't lie naked with him, not with the light on, even if it's dim, but I'm also not ready to leave. I nod and slip under the sheets. "Sorry, just cold," I lie.

The temperature is obviously kept comfortable in these rooms for this exact reason.

He quirks a brow as he slides in next to me, but he doesn't say anything. "C'mere," he murmurs as he pulls me against his chest.

When I'm tucked into his side, he plants a gentle kiss on my forehead. I close my eyes and try to ignore the butterflies that awaken at just that little touch.

He shouldn't stir these emotions in me. It's a betrayal of everything I am to feel so at home in these arms.

"What do you know about Forester?" I ask, grasping for anything that will keep me from focusing on how right this moment feels.

Jay's brows are pinched together when he looks down at me. "The bottling company?"

I bite my lip and nod.

He shrugs. "Nothing. It's who your family has used for years. Why?"

I hum, flipping through memories of the conversation I overheard when I showed up at Cash's office. They said it was Hanson's fault. What did they mean, exactly?

"Are you going after my family's company now that my grandfather isn't in the picture?"

He pulls back and lets out an annoyed laugh. "Fuck, Cat. Is that really what you think of me? That I'd take advantage of the situation with your grandfather? That I'd want to benefit from his illness?"

My lips twist along with the nervousness in my stomach. "I don't know what to think," I admit. "I don't know you at all."

Squeezing my arm, he pulls me in closer again and murmurs, "You know me."

"Tell me something, then," I say, keeping my gaze fixed on the new lighting hanging from the ceiling. "Explain to me why you're suddenly back in my life so soon after my grandfather's stroke and while things are going wrong with our family business. Add in how your ex is now shacking up with my brother, and it's all too convenient. I don't *trust* it." My voice breaks on a whisper as my fears get the best of me.

Jay blows out a long breath and runs soothing circles over my arm with his fingers. "Remember how I told you Hanson Whiskey tastes better than James Whiskey?"

I scoff and pull away, but he holds me in place.

"Your grandfather happened to agree."

I suck in a shocked breath and turn to look at him. "What?"

He's staring up at the ceiling, lost in thought. "It's the grains." He chuckles. "Your grandfather didn't want to believe me." He sighs and gives me a nudge. "I see where you get your stubbornness from. But when faced with facts, he didn't shy away from them. We had plans…" He trails off. And just when I think he's run out of things to say or he's not ready to get into this with me, he continues. "Your brother will figure it out."

Jay tilts his chin down and regards me. His expression is soft, open. So I take the time to study him, really look at him, and in my heart, I believe he's telling me the truth.

Color me shocked. He and my grandfather were, what, friends? Seems crazy after everything Pa told me all those years before.

But even then, I knew he was hiding something.

The truth is that none of it matters now. I'm thankful for this time, this summer, to finally get what's eluded me for so long. *Closure.*

That's all we can have. Chloe is coming to live with me, and despite how at home I feel with this man, he turned his back on us, and I'll never force her to endure that.

"Thank you," I sigh.

His brows are pinched as he scrutinizes me, but I force myself to get the words out.

"I don't know why you left or why you came back, but I'm choosing to let that go. It doesn't matter. I'm just thankful we've had this time."

Jay scans my face silently, the intensity in his expression making it hard not to squirm under his scrutiny. "Why does it feel like you're saying goodbye?"

"Because I am."

He jackknifes to a sitting position on the mattress. "Cat, *no*. Please."

"You promised me anything," I remind him, tugging the sheet up to cover my breasts and propping myself up.

He sags in defeat. "I did."

"This is what I need."

Licking his lips, he glowers at me. "You and I both know that what you need is me."

"No. What I *want* is you. What I *need*—what I've needed all this time—is closure. And now I have it. So please, if you love me as much as you say you do, let me go."

With Chloe's move closing in, that is truly what I need. Even if I die a little inside knowing this is the last time I'll ever feel at home again.

Jay closes his eyes, and a look of anguish crosses his face. I take the opportunity to kiss his jaw one last time. Then I slip out of bed, toss on my dress, and run.

28

CIRCLES BY POST MALONE

Jay

"**I** need you to do this for me, Jay," my brother says over the phone. With a grunt, I run my hand across my chin. I'm tired. It's been a week since Cat left me in the club, shattering any hope I had that I'd win her back.

To top it off, we're officially competing with James Whiskey for a deal that Theo and I put in place before he got sick. It was supposed to be the union of our two companies. A new beginning so that Cat would never have to choose between her brothers and me.

But since Cash isn't privy to the plan, he's now going after the deal by himself. He's trying to win over Charles Landry, a businessman from his hometown, and if I don't counteract the situation, it could cost both my brothers a lot of money.

I don't want to be the one fighting with the Jameses, though. We're supposed to be brokering this deal together. It feels like a betrayal to do this while Theo can't protect his company. And if I could find a way to sit down with Cash—to fill him in on the plans his grandfather and I made—maybe we could work it out.

But at this moment, as the woman who owns my heart strides toward me, I know I have no choice. The only reason I had a shot at Catherine was because of what my brothers have done for me. And as hotheaded as Cash is these days, there's no doubt in my mind that he will destroy my family company before I can even get a word in. He won't take my word about the plans Theo and I made. And since Theo is still in a fucking coma, I have no one to corroborate my story.

But when he does wake up, we can make this right. Hopefully, he can get through to Cat, because I sure as fuck can't.

I don't know whether it's because of the past or the present. I thought we were moving forward, and then the fucking media had to go and make up another lie about me battling it out with Cash over Grace.

I couldn't care less what Grace and Cash do.

The only perk of bumping into my old friend was that the media speculation left Cat jealous enough to actually recognize she had feelings for me. That's why I said yes to dinner with Grace weeks ago. Not because I have any interest in rekindling some love affair that never existed in the first place. I seized the opportunity because it made Cat jealous. Petty? Sure, but jealousy was an emotion I was afraid I'd never evoke from her again.

I blow out a breath while I follow Cat's movements. Maybe I can talk to her. Convince her to tell her brothers I'm not the scum they believe me to be. We can tell them we're together. Then we can figure out a way to work on the Sintac deal as a cohesive unit.

Cat stops at the door, her eyes narrowing and her lips pursed. Something has my kitten ready to scratch. "I gotta go, Garreth. But I'll do what I can."

"The event is next Friday, Jay. You need to be there."

I curl my finger in Catherine's direction, summoning her as I push back from my desk and spread my legs wide in invitation.

"Fine. I'll talk to you later," I say to my brother, then tap End to disconnect the call.

Cat remains standing, her arms crossed and her expression shuttered. "What happened now?"

She finally stalks into my office and tosses her phone onto my lap. I take a deep breath to keep myself from losing it, but it isn't easy. This last week has been an exercise in restraint for me. I've had to watch the woman I'm in love with day in and day out ignore me because she refuses to move forward, punishing not only me, but herself as well.

"It's an article. They say you and Grace are moving in together," she seethes.

I laugh, which only makes her expression darken and her scowl practically vibrate through the room. "What? You and I know it isn't true. It's absurd, Cat. Obviously, we aren't moving in together."

"Are you going to set the record straight?"

"Are you ready to tell your brothers we're together?"

She scoffs. "We're not together!"

My jaw tics. This is fucking exhausting. "I have an event, Cat. Come with me. Give me a chance to show you how good we could be together."

"No."

"Cat," I warn.

"No," she snaps.

On my desk, my phone rings, and I can't help but laugh in aggravation at the name that flashes on the screen. *Grace.*

Cat glares at me. "Answer it," she dictates.

I roll my eyes, then pick it up without dragging my attention from her. "Gracie, I figured I'd be hearing from you soon. I'm actually surprised it took you so long."

"Sorry. I know I should have called sooner. I'm sure you're not loving the press."

A dark laugh rumbles from my chest, and I keep my eyes on Cat as I reply. "Being considered one of the men lucky enough to be dating you is not a hardship."

Crossing her arms over her chest, Cat mouths, "Put it on speaker."

I turn away from her. She's acting like a child, but maybe if she hears the conversation, she'll realize that Grace means nothing to me.

Grace's laughter fills my office as I hit the Speaker icon. "You are ridiculous. Anyway, as you can imagine, this has caused quite a conundrum. People don't know that I'm getting divorced, so it appears that I'm currently sleeping with both my client and you. Not a great look for me."

Behind me, Cat mutters, "Now she suddenly cares about how she looks."

"Cash hasn't released something to set everyone straight?" I ask, ignoring the jealous woman behind me.

"Um, no. I asked him to let me handle this. He's a client of the firm. It's my job."

I sigh. What is wrong with the damn Jameses? Are they all incapable of admitting the truth about their love lives? "He's also the one you are actually dating. He should be protecting you."

"It's not the right way to go about this. No matter what we say, people are going to assume that I cheated, since no one knows about Steven's affair. And I really don't want to get into a mudslinging contest. The most important thing is my business. I can't have people thinking I sleep with my clients."

I turn around and pin Cat with a look. Hopefully, she's actually listening to Grace's words and coming to the realization that she's misjudged the entire situation.

"I know I'm asking a lot, but would you consider going out with me a few times and letting the media think it's you I'm dating?"

I mute the call and rake a hand through my hair. "Let's end this charade," I say to Cat. "Tell your brothers we're together, and I'll tell her no."

She shakes her head and takes a step closer. "No. Say yes. Date her." She taps her finger against her lips. "This is good," she whispers, almost as if she's trying to convince herself.

She sure as fuck isn't convincing me. "No," I say, a bored expression marring my face.

"Jay, I can't watch her with my brother. It takes me back…" Her voice catches, and she looks away. It's that look, the stormy expression, the brokenness, that kills me. Then she pulls her shoulders back and drags her attention back to me, pinning me to my seat. "You say you love me. Prove it. Help me break them up. Don't worry about Grace's feelings. *Choose me.*"

As if it's ever even been a competition.

Unmuting the phone, I hold Cat's gaze. "Gracie, I would do anything to protect you. If you think this is the right thing to do, I'd be happy to take you out to dinner."

Across from me, my girl sags in relief as she mouths a thank you. When I end the call, I roll back in my chair again and pat the top of my desk, summoning her.

"This is good," Cat hedges as she leans against the edge.

Unable to stop myself, I settle my hands on her hips and stare up at her.

Her golden eyes soften, and she pushes my hair out of my face, then settles her hand against my cheek. "Thank you," she whispers.

"I would do anything for you. *Anything.* But you're playing with fire here. Your brother has real feelings for her. And she has them for him."

Her look of relief crumbles. "She's married." Her voice is tortured. Exhausted.

"Was," I say pointedly. "Her husband cheated on her. Not the other way around. She's not a bad person, Kitten."

Cat drops her hand from my face and focuses on something outside the window behind me. "I can't go back to that time, Jay. And seeing her with my brother…I just can't do it."

Fuck.

I close my eyes and rest my head against her abdomen. I don't know how to take away her pain, and seeing her this way kills me. There's nothing I can say to make it better. Nothing I can do to convince her. Until she hears the truth about what happened all those years ago from her grandfather, she won't understand. And I have too much respect for Theodore James to take that opportunity away from him. The information I have on his family could destroy them, and he deserves the chance to explain.

"I can't lose you, Cat." In quiet desperation, I plead with her to find a way to see the truth, even if I can't give it to her yet.

She bites her lip and shrugs. "You can't keep me either."

29

DON'T GIVE UP ON ME BY ANDY GRAMMER

Cat

"**B**ug!" I grunt as Chloe launches herself into my arms and wraps her legs around my waist.

"I'm here!" she shouts.

I'm closer to tears than I have been since she was an infant. But this time, they're the happy kind. My daughter is finally back in the United States. And it's because she's coming to live with me.

Work has been insanely busy. My brothers are driving me nuts over the merger with Landry. Jay is holding up his end of the deal, gallivanting around town on fake dates with Grace, hopefully driving my brother crazy enough to ditch her once and for all. And I've been avoiding the office because I told Jay I was out of town, when in reality, I was preparing my apartment for Chloe's arrival.

My world may be unraveling, but right now, with this little girl in my arms, I'm the happiest I've ever been.

Kissing her forehead, I look up and spot Cynthia sauntering toward us, wearing a bright smile. "Missed you," I whisper to my daughter, then ease her to the floor.

Once we've collected all their luggage, we step out into the warm air and make our way to where Frank is waiting to take us home.

"Can I come to work with you tomorrow?" Chloe asks, turning from me to Cynthia and back again.

I suck in a breath. The idea of Chloe and Jay being in the same place terrifies me. Eventually, Jay and I will have to discuss the past. Even if the conversation is short and one-sided. He probably needs to know that Chloe will be living with me so he can stay away.

I've mulled over his words a dozen times since we lay in bed together the other night, and each time, I'm more sure that what happened all those years ago that kept him away is more complicated than I realized. I wasn't lying when I said I forgave him. Harboring that resentment, that animosity, did me no good. However, no matter his reasons, he turned his back on his daughter, and despite all our recent interactions, he hasn't once asked what happened to her. That alone is all I need to know that we can never truly be more. Because she's the most important person in the world to me. She will always come first, and I'll never allow him to hurt her the way he hurt me.

"Not tomorrow, Bug," I say over her head, giving Cynthia a look. "Why don't we go to the beach instead?"

She bounces in her seat. "Really?"

I run my fingers through her hair and drop a kiss to the crown of her head. "Yeah, really. I'm sure your mom has stuff to do in the office, but I'm all yours."

The smile my girl graces me with is worth every bit of stress that's weighed me down since Jay returned to my life.

KITTEN'S SONGS

For the next week, I spend every day with my girl. After our beach day, we spend the weekend decorating her room. Not surprisingly, she opts for a yellow wall to match the necklace I gave her years ago. The same one her father gave me. It's the only thing she has of Jay—other than his eyes.

While my focus has returned to its proper place, my brother's focus has, unfortunately, turned solely to Grace Kensington. The idea of them together makes my skin crawl. The woman isn't even divorced, but it's obvious my brother's mind is spinning. And if something doesn't change soon, I'll have to endure a future of holidays with her.

I'm not sure how I'll ever stomach that.

When I walk into the coffee shop on Thursday morning, an alternative option is finally presented to me. One last ditch effort to make my brother see that Grace Kensington isn't the one for him.

Vanessa Simpson stands in front of me, perusing the chalkboard behind the barista.

Here goes nothing. Taking a deep breath, I tap her shoulder. When she spins around, her eyes light up. "Cat, it's good to see you."

"You too. My brother and I were *just* talking about you," I lie.

It's wrong to meddle in Cash's life, but I truly believe my brother will be happier with Vanessa. In the end, he'll forgive me.

Her eyes gleam in surprise. "Really? I haven't heard from him since that night at the club. I figured he met someone else."

"Can I buy you a coffee? I have a proposition for you."

Then, over the next forty-five minutes, we sit in the corner of the busy coffee shop while I sell her on my plan.

30

LET IT ALL GO BY RHODES AND BIRDY

Jay

I suppose this is the point in my life where it's time to come to terms with the idea that there is no going back.

The script of my life was written long before I met Cat. Our destinies were intertwined in a tragic way, and it's time I accept that our story will never pan out the way I want. I'm not the author, and neither is she. All we can do is play the parts we were born into.

In my heart, I believe Cat wants to move past what I did to her. She may not say the words, but her body always speaks the truth. She's drawn to me in the same way I'm drawn to her. But I realize now that she'll never give up her heart again.

She hides herself from the world. And I'm the lucky bastard who's been given the chance to see the real her. The beautiful woman who lives just beneath the surface. The one I've dedicated my life to.

And it's because of that dedication that I'm standing on the lawn outside a lavish outdoor banquet with my arms wrapped around another woman.

"This place is so beautiful," Grace says, her violet eyes dancing as she soaks in every detail of the event before us. For the past few weeks, I've taken Grace out to work events, just as Cat asked. It's a win-win.

Garreth wants the contract with Sintac, and Grace is flawless when it comes to dealing with wealthy donors.

But something has changed with Cat since I last held her in my arms. The fire in her eyes is gone. She's stopped fighting with me. She's stopped fighting in general. Maybe it's because Cash is still hung up on Grace.

I get that.

The woman at my side is a reminder of a time she'd like to forget. Hell, I'd love to forget it as well.

But since I can't erase the past, the only thing I can do is break up Cash and Grace like Cat asked so that this reminder of our past isn't thrust in her face for the rest of her life.

Which is why we're here. In about ten seconds, Cash James is going to walk into the event, and when he sees Grace here with me, when he sees her helping me win over the contract he's been after for months, he's going to lose his mind.

Do I want to hurt the two of them? Absolutely not. But the only person I've ever cared for matters more. Everything I do is for Cat, even if she'll never let me back into her life.

"Not as beautiful as you." I give Grace a cheeky smile.

She rolls her eyes and smacks my chest. It's not a lie. Grace is gorgeous. She's wearing a purple dress that accentuates the color of her eyes. The high slit in the fabric could make a grown man cry. Just not *this* grown man.

Jazz music floats around the garden, and the moon reflecting off the surface of the ocean behind the lavish tent creates a perfect backdrop. Men are dressed in tuxes, myself included, and the women are all trying to avoid sinking into the grass while wearing their stilettos and long gowns.

The things people with money do for a good time.

A server stops by with a tray of champagne, and while I offer one to

Grace, I request a glass of whiskey for myself.

"What's the purpose of tonight's event?" Grace asks, surveying the garden.

"We've been working to partner with Mr. Landry. He owns a business here in Bristol, and this event raises money for the local schools. Seemed appropriate to support it."

She nods and brings her drink to her lips. It's at that moment that she spots Cash. She gasps, then coughs as the champagne goes down the wrong way. As the niggle of guilt I've been carrying with me grows a little, I grab her glass and rub her back.

Fuck, this is hard.

I look up, expecting to find Cash's hard eyes on me, but instead, I practically mimic Grace and suck in a sharp breath when my attention lands on Catherine. She's a dream in black chiffon that swirls around her. Our eyes lock the moment she steps onto the grass. Then her focus drops to where my arm is locked around Grace, and she pulls her plump red lip between her teeth.

Fuck.

The pain that flashes through her eyes hits me like a knife to the chest. She shouldn't have to witness this. But, as usual, I'm not in control of the script. Surely, whoever is pulling our strings is laughing from above.

KITTEN'S SONGS

Cash and Catherine aren't the only Jameses here, and it looks as though Cat is the only one who didn't bring a date. Chase is working the crowd with a blonde at his side, and Carter holds on to Grace's best friend Tessa possessively. I always liked her. All five feet two inches of her is hilarious.

Cash arrived with a woman I recognize on his arm. Beside me, Grace has gone rigid at the sight. Seeing her boyfriend with another woman has the knot in my gut loosening a bit. At least I know I was right to interfere in their relationship.

I was the one who introduced Grace to her husband, and since I learned of the asshole's cheating, I've felt terrible. I should have known better. He was an ass back in college, but I thought he'd outgrown it. Guess I was wrong. She deserves better than men who find her easily replaceable.

What Grace deserves, what every woman deserves, is to have the love of someone whose world stops turning each and every time they see her.

That's what Cat does to me.

The party is lively, and I fake one conversation after the next, chat with my brothers, and schmooze Mr. Landry, all while thinking of nothing and no one but her.

When Mr. Landry asks Grace to dance, I take the opportunity to try to get Cat's attention. I just need five minutes alone with her to remind her of why we're doing this. Why I'm even here with Grace. *Because of her*. Because she asked me to help.

Five minutes to remind her that she's all that matters to me.

I'm under no illusion that this will change things for us, but hurting her is the last fucking thing I wanted to do.

But Carter doesn't leave Cat's side. He and Tessa remain sitting at the table with Cat, and she keeps her attention trained anywhere but at my table.

Growing frustrated, I head to the dance floor and interrupt Mr. Landry and Grace. Vanessa has her arms draped around Cash's neck while they sway to the music, but Grace is missing it. She's so wrapped up in her conversation with Landry that she doesn't see what's right in front of her. I'm ending this once and for all. I'll show Grace that Cash is not the man for her, I'll return Cat's brother to her, and then I'll leave this damn party.

"May I cut in?" I ask as I approach Mr. Landry and Grace.

He gives me a nod in understanding and whispers something in Grace's ear. Then he hands her off to me.

I pull her close and sway to the music. "You're doing a fantastic job, Gracie. Thank you."

"Did you know Cash was going to be here?"

I chuckle softly. "I imagined he would."

She pulls back a fraction of an inch and glares at me. "Jay, you've put me in an impossible situation."

"Grace, I keep trying to show you that he's not who you think he is." I spin her so she can finally see how close her darling Cash has gotten with his date. "I may not be the man for you, but someone who shows up with another woman on his arm and holds her as close as he's holding that woman? He's not the man for you either. We are made of the same cloth, Cash and me. Neither of us are good enough for you."

With pain swimming in her eyes, Grace watches Cash, obviously warring with herself over what to think. Without warning, she pops up onto her toes, kisses me on the cheek, and apologizes. "I'm sorry, Jay, but you couldn't be more wrong. Excuse me."

And then she slips out of my arms and exits the dance floor with her head held high and her shoulders back.

Blowing out a breath, I head toward the bar. So far, I haven't accomplished a single thing I set out to do. Maybe another glass of whiskey will temper my aggravation.

As I'm leaving the dance floor, the guitarist strings a few chords together that tug at my memory. And as he sings the opening lines of Coldplay's "Yellow," my breath catches, and I turn back toward Cat's table.

Maybe the author of this narrative has a surprise for us. Maybe our story isn't over yet. Maybe we're just gearing up for a second act.

31

TURNING PAGE BY SLEEPING AT LAST

Cat

The world stopped tonight. My brother chased after Grace, Vanessa whined about being ditched, Tessa tried to comfort her, and Carter disappeared to the bar. But my soul stood on the dance floor.

I haven't felt this alone since I was a little girl. Since I sat at my mother's funeral, surrounded by people and yet without the one person who made me whole. And that's saying a lot, because I've suffered alone in the last thirteen years more than any one person should.

For a short time, Jay pushed away the loneliness for me.

But seeing him with her tonight cut me open. The pain I felt watching them dance was almost as potent as that day I cradled my swollen belly and stared at the photo of the two of them in *Jolie* magazine all those years ago.

As the band serenades the crowd with "Yellow," I push back from the table. And despite how desperately exhausted I am from running, I do just that.

I dart from the tent, smacking into a server on my way out. I gasp out an apology before bolting into the yard. Away from the music. Away from the memories.

But he's faster. He's always been faster.

Jay loops an arm around me and pulls me into his chest, cradling my head with one hand. "Shh, I got you," he murmurs softly, kissing my head and rubbing soothing circles on my back.

Of course he knew I needed him. He knows precisely how to fix me. How to make me feel whole again. Every damn time he breaks me.

Exhausted, I lean against him while he sways to the song. Out here, the music seems louder, and the stars shine brighter than they have in years. Likely because I'm in his arms.

Everything is better when I'm in his arms.

"Do you know how many times I called you?" I whisper into the night, wincing at the pain that lances through me. "How often I worried about you…prayed for you…*begged* for you?" A tear skitters down my cheek, and I swipe at it angrily. Fuck. The dam has officially broken.

"And then, after months of radio silence, of wondering if we were real, doubting my own mind and heart, I see you with *her*. Announcing a damn relationship."

Jay places his palms flat against my cheeks and pulls back so I'm forced to make eye contact. "No, Kitten," he urges, his voice rough, and anguish marring the lines on his face. "I wasn't announcing a relationship…I was protecting you."

"From what?" I shout in a strangled cry. "Did you think ghosting me would hurt less than being honest about not wanting me? I called and called…"

Jay grimaces, and his shoulders sag. "I can't tell you everything…"

I push against his chest. Fuck him and the lies he's still holding on to.

Grasping me tighter so I can't escape, he groans. "It's not my secret to tell, Cat. It's your grandfather's."

"*What?*" I whisper, shock stealing my voice. "What does my grandfather have to do with this?"

Jay sighs. "I can't…" He drops his head, and his blond hair falls forward. He's devastatingly handsome in his tux tonight. But his hair is the perfect mess I love. My hands itch to swipe it back, to reveal the blue eyes that always give him away. At least to me. "I didn't ignore your phone calls, Cat. I was in a coma." With those words, he finally looks up.

The air is sucked from my lungs, like I'm hurtling into an abyss, clutching at anything to keep myself from falling. "*What?*"

"When my father was killed—" He sucks in a deep breath and lets it out slowly. This must be so painful for him. "The people that came for him, they beat me to within an inch of my life. I was in a coma for months."

I can't grasp the facts he's laying out for me. His voice is muffled, and the world around me is fuzzy. I can't comprehend a word he's saying, but I need to touch him. The need to hold him as he speaks is so overwhelming, I may shatter if I don't get my hands on him. Tenderly, I brush my fingers across his forehead, pushing the hair from his eyes.

He leans into my touch. "I would have done anything to change how that night went, Cat. *Anything.* But what happened couldn't be undone. I won't apologize for staying away. I was protecting you. Dating Grace? That was protecting you. Not getting on the first flight to Paris? That was protecting you. And staying away from you for the last thirteen years—until I was sure the threat was gone—*that* was protecting you."

A sensation warms the backs of my eyes, and tears threaten to spill over my lashes. "From what? Who? What were you protecting me from?"

He squeezes his eyes squeeze shut and lets out a frustrated sigh. "The men who put me into a coma."

Nothing makes sense. It's like he's speaking a foreign language. Jay in a coma. A threat to my life. What is he talking about?

"But my messages…" Even if he was in a coma, at some point, he had to have gotten them. He had to have gotten the news about our daughter.

"I never got them," he says softly. "Your grandfather had my phone. He was fielding my calls. It's how I knew you planned to come back. Your grandfather told me you were desperate. That if I didn't do something drastic, you would come back to Boston, and we both knew it wasn't safe. So I started dating. I contacted the magazine to do a spread on Grace and me because I knew if you saw it, you would stay away…"

The tears fall freely, and the pieces of my heart he shattered so long ago ache. "So you never heard my messages?"

He shakes his head. "It would have killed me to hear you begging, Cat. I was already dead inside without you. Hearing your voice, seeing you…it would have been too much. So your grandfather kept them from me. I assumed he told me the things I needed to know. But Cat, please know if I had any choice in the matter, I would have moved fucking heaven and earth to get to you."

He doesn't know about Chloe.

He doesn't know about Chloe, and he didn't willingly leave me.

"Why are you here with Grace tonight?" I ask. Is it because I asked him to be seen with her, or is it because he wants her?

He studies me openly. "Because you don't want her with Cash. I've been trying to break them up like you asked. I know how much it hurts when you see her with him, baby. And I don't want you to hurt anymore. I want you to feel nothing but love for the rest of your life. And I want to be the one to provide that to you."

"Because you love me?" I whisper, still unsure.

"Yes, Catherine. I'm in love with you. Irrevocably. Completely. Head over *fucking* heels in love with you. I fell in love with you thirteen years ago when you broke my nose at the train station," he says softly, "and I never stopped."

I can't help the laugh that sneaks out along with another sob.

Jay brushes the tears from my cheeks while valiantly fighting back his own.

"I love you too," I breathe, the quiet words punching hard into the air between us.

Jay's shock can't be hidden. It's evident in the way his eyes widen and how his jaw drops. "You do?"

I nod as another tear falls. "I fell in love with you on a perfect fall day while we ate waffles at the farmers' market"—I suck in a breath—"and I never stopped."

He smirks now, cocky and beautiful. "Thought you hated me, Kitten."

I push against his chest. "Don't tease me."

He snatches my hand before I can pull it back and brings it to his lips. "But it's my favorite thing to do."

"I need you," I say desperately, grasping at his shirt with my free hand.

He chuckles. "It's about fucking time you admit it." He scans the garden, and then his eyes light up. "Come with me."

He pulls me down the path, the chiffon of my dress flying up as we run.

"Where are we going?" I laugh, feeling lighter than I have in years.

Jay looks at me over his shoulder, his blue eyes brighter than I've seen them since our trip to New York so many years ago. "It's not where we're going; it's where we're returning to…"

32

FALLING LIKE THE STARS BY JAMES ARTHUR

Jay

Hand in hand, we run wildly toward the greenhouse I noticed earlier. I press the door open and push Cat into the warm room, taking in every inch of her.

"Fuck, you're gorgeous," I whisper. And it's the goddamn truth. I think it's possible she's even more beautiful now than she was when she was twenty-two.

She's smiling brightly when I angle in and kiss her until we're both breathless.

"Say it again," I beg against her lips. No one's spoken those words to me in over a decade, and she's the only person I've ever wanted to hear them from.

Her brown eyes warm like caramelized sugar, and she sighs up at me. "What?"

"Tell me you love me, Kitten. Please, say it again."

"I love you." She grins and presses her hand against my heart. The warmth and weight of her palm alone ground me to this moment. Her hands glide over my shoulders and around my neck. "And I need you, Jay." She tugs at my hair in emphasis. "I need you so fucking bad. Make love to me."

I lift her up and set her on a table that stands in the middle of the room. The stars shine on us through the panels in the walls, though the greenhouse remains dark. The moonlight reflects in her eyes as I lift up her skirt and pull down her panties. The second they hit the ground, she grabs for my belt and quickly frees me from my pants, her eyes glowing as she finds me hard and straining for her.

"Fuck," I mutter.

She's almost desperate as she grips me. "What?"

"Condoms. I don't have any. *Fuck.*" I drop my head back in aggravation.

"Oh," she breathes, bringing my attention back to her gorgeous mouth. She bites her lip and peers up at me through her lashes. "I—uh—well, I mean, I'm on the pill, and I've never…"

When she doesn't continue after several seconds, I ask, "You've never gone bare with anyone else?" I hate that this is a necessary conversation. It should only have ever been the two of us.

She shakes her head. "I've never *been* with anyone else."

I choke. "Cat, I saw you with Frank."

"We only…well, we didn't do that. You're the only person who's ever been inside me…like that," she whispers, looking away.

I'm catapulted back to years ago, when she nervously told me she was a virgin. Like that wasn't the greatest thing I'd ever heard.

"Wait…you've never been with anyone else?" I say, shocked stupid.

She shakes her head and sighs. "I know it's not the same for you, so if you want to wait—"

"I haven't slept with anyone in years," I rush out.

Cat's eyes widen. "What?"

I run my hands through my hair and swallow thickly. "I wish I could say I haven't been with anyone at all. I wish I'd never touched another woman after you, but I honestly didn't believe we could ever be together. For a while, I tried—miserably, I might add—to move on. But the second I realized there was a chance, as soon as I put my plan in place to remove all the threats, that ended. I've been celibate for over ten years."

"Oh my God," Cat mutters. By now, her eyes are as big as saucers.

I chuckle and cock one brow. Despite the serious topic, I'm still hard, and I want her more than ever.

"So—"

That's all I manage to get out before Cat grips the front of my tux shirt and pulls me to her, taking my lips with hers and stealing my words.

She wraps her legs around my waist and pulls me to her as she slides her body to the end of the table and lines me up against her.

"Wait," I say before she pulls me all the way in. "We've been in the dark for too long. I want you to watch as I sink into you, Kitten. Look down and watch me take back what's mine."

She nods, her lip trapped between her teeth, as I slide between her lips, coating myself in her desire. The moment my tip enters her and her warmth engulfs me, we both hiss.

"Shit," she mutters.

I push in slowly, alternating between witnessing the way our bodies become one after so long and watching her expression as she remains transfixed by our connection. As each inch disappears, my heart pounds faster and my breaths grow more ragged.

"Oh my God, Jay, it's—" She holds her breath and grimaces.

I cup her face, pulling her lips to mine.

Just like the first time, I'm stretching her, breaking her, molding myself inside her. She cries through it, but as I sink fully inside her and our breaths mingle together, she lets out a sigh.

"God, I missed you," she whispers as a tear tracks down her cheek.

"No crying, Kitten. No more tears," I say, swiping it away, consumed by her beauty.

She's so fucking beautiful. And so fucking mine.

"Then make me feel good, Jay. You owe me thirteen years of orgasms, and I'm ready to collect."

I chuckle and kiss her. "Fuck, I love you."

Her eyes soften. "I love you too. Now, please, make love to me."

I pull out slowly and then slam back inside her. "Lie back, baby."

When she settles back against the table, I pull her leg up onto my shoulder, desperate to be seated as deeply as I can.

"Look at us, Kitten." I wave to where our reflections dance in the mirrored greenhouse glass. The stars shine brightly, as if just for us. "This is how it was always supposed to be. Just you and me."

She lets out a strangled sigh and watches our movements from every angle. "You should see how beautiful the stars are right now."

"I'm looking at the only thing that I wanna look at, Kitten. The most beautiful thing I've ever seen." I thrust inside her and pull out again. "For years, I stared at the stars and thought of you. Imagined you were looking at that same night sky. And in those few moments, I felt the smallest sliver of relief."

Cat twines her fingers with mine and gasps when I push into her harder once again. She's gripping me so tightly, and it's been so long for both of us. There's no way we'll last much longer.

"My life was darkness without you. I understand why your grandfather called you sunshine. Although even the brightest star in the sky doesn't hold a candle to you. You're more like a shooting star, Cat. You're magic. *My magic.*"

She whimpers as I pick up the pace and find her clit with my thumb. It's torture each time I pull away from her, but with each thrust, she squeezes me tighter.

"I'm so close," she whispers. "But I want to feel you come with me, Jay. Fill me. I've been so fucking empty without you."

Looming over her, I wrap one hand around her throat and hold her in place while I lick her lips and kiss her through the tidal wave of our simultaneous orgasms. "I love you," I whisper as I collapse on top of her.

"Take me home, Jay." Her erratic heartbeat matches mine. "And don't ever let me go."

33

SOMETHING JUST LIKE THIS BY THE CHAINSMOKERS AND COLDPLAY

Cat

My reflection in the computer screen is almost comical. The song Jay just sent me makes me smile wider than I think I ever have.

After all this time, we're finally getting a second chance.

And he didn't abandon his child. He never knew about Chloe. He still doesn't.

Chloe. My heart constricts at the thought of her. Next week, Cynthia is leaving her in my care. She's taking her to New York City for a few days before school starts, but then it's just Chloe and me.

I need to tell Jay.

He needs to know he has a daughter.

And I need to talk to Cynthia. Twelve years ago, she gave up more than she ever should have to take on my daughter. To help me when I needed it most. She deserves to control the narrative as much as we do.

I hate the secrets, the lies, the plotting.

But this isn't a magazine article or a book. This is real life. I have to approach it with thought. As much as I wanted to, I couldn't just blurt out the truth to Jay last night.

Every one of us deserves better than that.

I close out the document I've been working on all summer and beeline for Cynthia's office. The office buzzes around me. In the corner, Dexter is flipping through a rack of clothes. He groans when he comes across an orange number that I'm pretty sure he just called the most hideous piece of clothing to ever be created. I stifle a laugh and look to my left, where Rose is guiding a group of interns around the office. I study each one of them, wondering who will actually make it through the year. In the middle of the pack are two girls who look as awestruck as I felt on my first day.

I may be nervous about Cynthia's departure next week, and I may feel unprepared to do this parenting thing on my own, but that look right there reminds me that I've been striving to be her since the first day I walked into this office. From the moment I laid eyes on her.

And here I am, likely the next editor in chief of *Jolie*. That reminder alone is all I need to be sure that I can handle whatever life throws at me.

I'll be someone my daughter will be proud of. Someone she can look up to. And all of that starts with telling her and Jay the truth.

At Cynthia's door, I knock twice before entering. When she sees me, she smiles and motions for me to sit as she finishes up a call. I pick up the photograph on her desk and smile. Chloe looks so damn much like Jay. She's even been blessed with the confident air he has. And she's a natural negotiator. Whether she's trying to talk me into taking her to her favorite restaurant every night of the week or convincing us to take her to fashion shows that don't even start until after her bedtime.

She's going to give me a run for my money over the next few years. And I can't help but smile when I think of how she'll likely wrap Jay right around her finger the moment she meets him.

"Where's Chlo?" I ask as she hangs up the phone. I want to have this conversation before they leave for New York, but I don't want Chloe hearing it. Not yet, at least.

"Oh, Sophie took her back to see Dexter. They're going through outfits for the November edition and asked for Chloe's opinion."

I snicker. "Oh my God. That will *so* go to her head."

"You look good," Cynthia says. She's got her head tilted as she studies me.

I place the picture back on her desk, fold my hands across my knees, and clear my throat. "Jay doesn't know about Chloe."

Her eyes go wide. "What?"

I swallow and search for the best way to explain. "It's a whole story, but the bare bones are that when his father was killed, he was attacked too—Cyn, my grandfather had his phone all these years. He never got my messages."

Cynthia leans back in her chair and closes her eyes. "Fuck," she whispers.

"Obviously, I need to tell him," I rush out. "He deserves to know he has a daughter."

She nods but remains silent.

"But once I do, I have no idea how he'll react. He'll probably lose his mind."

She bites her lip and sits up straight again. "We never made it legal for a reason, Cat," she reminds me. "I think you and I always knew this day would come."

"No," I counter. "You will always be her mother."

She stands and rounds her desk, then drops into the chair beside me. "So will you. It's different, *yes*. But that doesn't make it any less beautiful. The more people who love Chloe, the more she has in her corner, the better. That's all we could ever want, right?" she asks, squeezing my hand.

How this woman manages to maintain her calm even in a situation like this is beyond me. This is why I chose her all those years ago. She's fearless in a storm. Since the beginning, she's had my back, and that gives me the strength to believe that we can make this work.

I nod, my throat growing thick.

"And for the record, you have that too. You have me. You have Soph and Dex. Your brothers, Chloe. And I think you know in your heart of hearts that you have Jay too."

"I'm scared, Cyn. I'm scared to want it. To even believe that it could be possible," I whisper.

"Well, buckle up, because whether you're scared or not, it's happening. You have to tell Jay the truth and trust that he'll do the right thing."

"And you're okay with that? Him being a father to her? If that's what he and Chloe want?"

She smiles wide and lets out a long breath. "God, yes. I stepped in when you needed me, and I'll always do that. I love Chloe, and I love you. Always will. And I'll always be a part of your lives. But if Jay wants to be a father, if Chloe wants to call him Dad and she wants to call you Mom, I'm 100 percent okay with it all. Like I've told you time and again, she's already got two moms. *She's always had two moms.* More parents are good. More love is good. Let her have that, baby."

Tears well in my eyes. It appears that last night's waterworks weren't a one-time thing.

"I really appreciate you," I whisper.

Cynthia has been like a mother to me for most of my adult life. If I can't have my own mother, then this woman is the next best thing.

She smiles as she pulls me in for a hug. "I really appreciate you too. I'm glad you'll have the weekend to talk to Jay. And I'm looking forward to spending some time in New York with Chloe. I think she is too."

"Oh, she definitely is. She hasn't stopped talking about how you're taking her to Sienna Langfield's shop."

Sienna came on to the fashion scene last year. Her designs are absolutely flawless, and quite frankly, I'm jealous that Chloe and Cynthia are meeting her without me.

"Yeah, I'm looking forward to that visit too. Maybe I'll see if we can get a few of the designs from her spring collection in our Christmas preview."

"Are you going to miss doing the Christmas edition?" I tease, needing a change in topic to ease the burn behind my eyes.

Cynthia gives a knowing smile. "I have a feeling the new editor and chief will do a wonderful job."

"Oh yeah. When's that announcement going to be made?"

"Just worry about this weekend. Everything will happen when it's meant to."

As I stand to leave, Chloe appears in the door with a Balenciaga scarf in her hand.

Cynthia tips her head back and huffs at the ceiling. "What is that?"

Chloe smiles. "Aunt Soph gave it to me. Dexter said the color works marvelously with my eyes." She bats her lashes at us dramatically, sending us into a fit of girlish giggles.

"Oh my God. We've created a monster," I tease.

"Can I have a snack before we leave?" Chloe asks.

"Yeah, I'll find something in the staff room. Want to watch something on my computer until your mom is ready to go?" I ask.

"I'm wrapping things up. I shouldn't be more than half an hour," Cynthia says, making her way around her desk again. "Then we can get going."

Back in my office, I get the computer set up with something Chloe will like. Then I wave her over to me. "Do you know how much I love you?"

She throws her arms around my neck and squeezes. "I do. And I love you too. I'm so excited to have sleepovers with you for the next year."

My stomach twists. Does she think this arrangement has an end date? Is that all she wants?

"And you're sure you're okay with staying here? If you've changed your mind and want to go back to Paris with your mom, that's okay."

"Honestly?" she asks, her voice soft, reminding me that, although she sometimes acts as mature as I feel, she's barely more than a little girl.

"Always, Bug. I always want your honesty."

"I feel bad because I *don't* feel bad." She cringes. "I know I'm going to miss Mom, but…" She looks away quickly, then glances back to me, but she doesn't make eye contact.

"Chlo, you can tell me anything," I remind her.

She takes a deep breath. "I'd rather be with you. It's nothing against her, it's just… I know we don't say it, and I know we don't talk about it, but you're also my mom."

"I am." I smile. "We both are."

Thankfully, Cynthia's pep talk has helped me realize that it's okay for Chloe to want us all. Sure, it's unconventional, but millions of people co-parent all the time. This isn't all that different from blended families and stepparents. We both love Chloe. We've both always been part of her life. Who she lives with doesn't change that. "I couldn't have done anything without Cynthia's help," I tell Chloe. She's old enough to understand things like this now. "She gave you something that I couldn't when you were born."

"But you can now, right?" Chloe asks, wringing her hands and peeking up at me.

This girl. She is so wise. "Yeah, Chlo," I say, looking into her deep, soulful eyes and pushing back the brown bangs that are forever falling forward, just like her dad's. "I can be that person now. You can stay here as long as you want, or you can go back home."

"But w-what if," she stutters, "what if my home is with you?"

I pull her in for a big hug. "Nothing would make me happier. We okay?" I ask softly.

Chloe smiles. "Yeah, we're good."

34

EASY ON ME BY ADELE

Jay

Whistling, I stroll into the building that houses *Jolie* and greet Remi, who mans the front desk.

"You back, boss?" he asks with a grin.

"That I am," I say, a lightness to my step.

This morning, I told Garreth that I'm stepping back from Hanson Liquors completely. I'd rather spend my time here, working with Cat, day in and day out.

This place is what brought us together all those years ago. The whiskey company is what tore us apart. I want no part of anything that reminds me of all the time we've lost.

Cat invited me over for dinner tonight. She said it would be easier for us to talk if we weren't in a restaurant. I couldn't agree more. Obviously, I'd like to do other things as well, but just fucking talking to her is enough for me. Being where we are now is more than I expected.

"Those for me?" Remi points to the yellow roses in my hand.

I choke out a laugh. "No, these are for my girl."

He smiles as he waves me on. "She's a lucky one."

"Believe me," I call over my shoulder, "I'm the lucky one."

I probably look like a lunatic, standing near the back of the elevator, smelling the damn yellow roses in my hand. But I don't care. I told her years ago that if she were a color, she'd be yellow. I made so many promises the day I slipped that necklace with the yellow diamond around her neck. Without a doubt, I'll have to replace it. Knowing Cat, she probably tossed it when she thought I betrayed her. I chuckle as I imagine my feisty girl doing something rash. I'm going to have fun with that temper for the rest of my life.

Pushing her buttons is literally my favorite thing.

As the doors open to the twelfth floor, I nod at people as I walk through the office. I'm met with smiles, raised eyebrows, and a quiet buzz that fills the office when the boss enters. I can guarantee that before I arrived, the place was loud. Now every employee here is busying themselves, pretending they're in the middle of a project. "That's right, friends, Daddy's back," I mutter to myself, unable to wipe the smile from my face.

I head straight to Cat's office, wondering if she'll be pissed or excited when I tell her the news. Probably a little of both.

She'll think I'm micromanaging, that I don't trust her as editor in chief. And I might tease her relentlessly, but I know without a doubt the magazine will be in the best hands with her at the helm. As soon as Cynthia gives me the okay, I'll let her know the job is hers.

I'm temporarily distracted from my mission when Dex wraps his arms around Sophie and pulls her into an unoccupied office. I chuckle and turn back to Cat's office. But instead of the woman I love, her desk chair is occupied by someone much smaller. I look down the hall, but when I don't spot Cat, I peek into the office. Maybe she's in the corner, out of sight.

"Oh, hi, are you looking for my mom?" the little girl asks.

She has long dark hair with bangs that cut straight across her forehead, rosy cheeks, a button nose, and a rounded chin which is tipped up as she sizes me up. She looks oddly familiar.

I take another step in and rub the back of my neck, unsure of what

248

to say. I'm never really around kids. They're definitely something I want with Cat one day, but I just…well, I don't actually know how to talk to them.

"Um, I don't think so." I don't know who her mom is, but I'm looking for the woman who normally occupies this office. Unless… "Did Cynthia promote her already?"

The little girl tilts her head to the side, as if she's trying to figure me out. "Are you all right, mister?"

I nod. I think I am. But…something nags at the back of my mind. Why does she look familiar?

"What are you watching?" I ask absently, still trying to figure out what's bothering me.

She studies me for another moment, her pale blue eyes serious in their inquisition. "*America's Next Top Model.*"

I laugh. "I don't know why, but I didn't expect that."

"My Uncle Dex says that Tyra Banks is legendary. Personally, I prefer Heidi Klum."

Uncle Dex? Who the hell is this kid?

"Do you have an opinion?" she asks, dropping a hand to her necklace and pulling the pendant from side to side. It takes me a minute to snap back to reality, and when I see the frown on her face, I feel like an ass for staring at her like a complete creep.

See? I knew I was bad with kids.

"I—uh—" I stammer.

Before I can form a coherent sentence, the sun catches on the yellow diamond pendent she's playing with, sending rays of light scattering through the room and snaring my attention.

A lump lodges itself in my throat, but I manage to rasp out, "Where'd you get that?"

She lifts the pendant and smiles at the yellow diamond. The look on her face is nothing but pure joy. "Oh this? My mom. Well, actually my dad gave it to her, and she gave it to me because I never met him and she knew I'd want something from him."

"Hey, Chlo, I got Twizzlers, but don't tell your mom I let you have them before you had lunch." Cat waltzes into the office without a care in the world, holding a small red package.

I swallow hard and look from her to the little girl, my mind going a million miles per minute. For a moment, I decide I'm nuts for thinking anything so crazy. Cat just referred to someone else as this little girl's mom, didn't she? But then Cat sees me, and her eyes go wide. And though we only just reconnected, I know her every expression. That look was not one of surprise. It's outright fear.

She's terrified that I know the truth.

She's petrified that I just met our daughter.

I have no doubt that's exactly what happened. That's why this little girl—Chlo?—is so familiar. She looks just like Cat in the pictures I've seen at her grandfather's house. They're identical in every way but one. Her eyes. The girl sitting in Cat's chair is studying me with piercing blue eyes, categorizing my every thought as if she can hear them, as if she's putting the pieces together just as I am.

Cat shakes her head. It's a slight movement, but I see the desperation. The pleading in her eyes. She's silently begging me not to freak out, not to scream about how she's hidden my daughter from me for thirteen fucking years.

I turn back to the little girl—*my daughter*—and I use every muscle in my face to force a smile. "I agree with you. Heidi Klum is much better than Tyra. I'll let you get to your snack, though. It was nice meeting you…"

She smiles the most beautiful smile at me. "Chloe. Chloe Bouvier Caldwell," she says, pulling her shoulders back and looking at Cat. *Her mother.*

Cat's face is ghostly white, and she stands stock-still. "Jay," she chokes out. "I'll walk you out." To Chloe, she says, "Here, Bug. You can have your snacks. I'll be back in a minute." She drops the Twizzlers onto the desk and follows me out of the office.

I stomp down the hall, desperate to get as far away from the room as possible. I don't want Chloe to hear me lose it.

"Jay, wait," Cat whisper-shouts, trailing behind me.

I spin. The roses I'm still clutching whip in the air, and a few petals fall to the ground. "Is she my daughter?"

Cat's eyes plead with me to understand. But I don't even know what I'm supposed to understand.

"Answer me," I demand.

"Yes," she whispers, tears filling her eyes. "Yes, she's our daughter."

My heart beats wildly in my chest and my vision tunnels. Cat reaches out for me, but I yank my arm back.

"Don't touch me," I hiss. "Were you ever going to tell me?"

Tears fall down Cat's face. I don't reach to wipe them away. I'm too blinded by my anger to comfort her.

We have a child. A daughter. I've missed out on everything.

"Tonight. I was going to tell you tonight," she sobs.

I nod. That's all the information I need. I push the flowers toward her, unable to bear looking at them.

They're too happy. Too bright. *Too her.*

And then I run.

KITTEN'S SONGS

It takes me over an hour, but I don't remember a minute of the drive. My mind blanked the second I pulled out of the lot, and I relived every moment of my time with Cat thirteen years ago.

The first time I laid eyes on her in the coffee shop. Our train rides. The day she punched me in the face. Our first kiss, when the world simply stopped around us, and I knew that nothing would ever matter more to me than her.

Teaching her how to give a blowjob in the library, where she literally schooled me.

The first time we made love. The first time I'd *ever* made love to anyone.

Since that first day, she's been it. My constant. The only thing that mattered…*until now.*

I have a daughter.

My head spins.

I asked Theo for one thing when he came to the hospital. One thing only.

"You'll let me know if she ever needs me, though, right? If she's in danger, or…" I don't even know what I'm asking. The only danger she'd face would come from being with me. If I let her go, if I let her believe it was all a lie, she'll be safe.

Theo watches me for a long time, taking in my deteriorated state. The atrophied muscles and the sallow skin. Spending a month in a coma can wreak havoc on even the strongest people. His jaw is tight, but his eyes are filled with the pain he knows we're both going to inflict on his granddaughter, the woman I love. But I force him to agree. I force him to promise that he'll keep her from me. That he'll keep her safe.

He places his hand on my forearm and squeezes lightly. "You're nothing like your father," he says, his eyes glossy with tears. "Nothing. And one day"—his voice cracks—"one day, son, I hope she knows that."

I bang on the front door like I have a right to be here. Like I have a right to my anger.

The only person to blame for this mess is me. But that doesn't stop me from banging. *From screaming.* From yelling at the top of my lungs. Catherine's grandmother opens the door with a glare that could cut ice.

"Jonathan Hanson, calm the hell down!" she scolds.

"Where's the phone?" I shout, darting past her into the house, my focus trained on one thing and one thing only.

She chases after me, hollering, but I ignore her as I make my way through the office door and to his desk. Over the years, I watched him, studied him every time we played chess. We spent hours together, talking about business, talking about life, talking about anything but the one thing that mattered.

He knew.

It's all I keep thinking.

He. Knew.

Because the alternative, one in which Cat never called, never attempted to tell me we were going to have a baby, is a reality I refuse to acknowledge.

"Where is it?" I scream, opening one drawer after another.

She closes her eyes and shakes her head. "If it's anything of value, it's likely in the safe," she says, as if she thinks I'm here to steal from them.

I'm not surprised. She likely views me as a fraud. A liar. A deceiver.

I doubt she knows about my friendship with her husband.

And I'd bet money she doesn't know about Chloe.

"You never gave a damn about her," I sneer.

"Who?" she asks, bringing a hand to her chest.

"*Cat.* You don't see her. You don't get her. She's hidden herself from all of you because she knows you'd just judge her. You're the reason she's closed off. The reason she's broken—"

She scoffs. "You think I don't know about the two of you? It's about time you look in the mirror, Mr. Hanson. The reason my granddaughter is cold and detached? You'll find him in that reflection. Now either take what you came for or get the hell out of my house."

"My phone," I rasp, my voice gravel, and my heart hammering in my chest. "He had my phone."

She sighs, then pulls her shoulders back and tips her chin up. The amount of self-control this woman must have is astonishing. She's like a robot. "Let me check the safe." She shuffles toward the wall safe, glaring at me and pointing. "You stay over there. If you come near me, I'll grab the gun instead."

I laugh at the absurdity of this conversation. It all started with a goddamn gun. Maybe if I'd just walked out of my dad's penthouse that day, if I'd called the cops or run away with Cat myself...

But maybes can't change things now. Maybes are good for nothing but regrets.

I nod in defeat and kick at the hardwood floor beneath me as I wait for her to check the safe.

"Is this it?" she asks, holding up an older model iPhone. The key to everything.

Once I turn it on, I can't go back. Either way, it will hurt. I'll either suffer through painful, desperate messages from Cat, or there will be nothing. The alternative is something so awful, I can't even fathom.

"Yes," I rasp, holding out my hand. I have no choice.

"I love my granddaughter, Mr. Hanson." Mrs. James eyes me and places the device in my palm. "Whatever has you this desperate, whatever has broken you like this, she's feeling ten times worse. So get the information you need and get your act together. Do you hear me?"

Taking a deep breath and closing my eyes, I give her a grim nod.

"And don't you ever walk into this house hollering again."

"He cost me everything. Your son and your husband, they've taken *everything* that mattered from me. I'll never forgive them."

I step outside holding all the power. This phone was the only thing I needed from them. Theo's had my silence for years. The dirty truths no one wanted exposed.

I think back to that day in the office when I pleaded with him to tell me the truth. And then he hit me with something I never expected.

Truths about his son.

My mother.

And we can't forget Carter's secret child. And Chase's mom.

So many secrets.

I always thought he kept them to protect the people he loves. He kept Mia out of Carter's life, which God knows was a good thing. But how would Carter feel if he found out he has a child? Probably like me. Blindsided.

Theo made all these decisions for us. Without our input. Without our knowledge.

Maybe it's time I undo them. Maybe it's time for the truth to come out.

35

GIVE ME SOMETHING BY SEAFRET

Jay

The light of the moon reflects off the screen of my ancient iPhone as I sit in my office, a whiskey glass in one hand and a finger dangling precariously over the Play button on the first of Cat's thirty-two messages.

Thirty-two.

Huffing out a sigh, I scroll to the last one. The pain in my chest is so acute, I worry I won't survive this. But I have to know how she sounded when she finally said goodbye. What it took for her to give up.

So, although sliding a knife repeatedly into my heart would be easier than listening to this, I hit Play. I fucking deserve the agony. If she endured what I think she did, I deserve so much worse.

The wails of a baby echo from the phone's speaker. Then heavy breathing and a desperate sob. "I can't do this, Jay. I can't…I've tried. I've waited. I've called. I didn't want to believe you could walk away like this. That I meant nothing to you. For so long, I've held out hope that you'd walk through the door and tell me it was all a misunderstanding. But—" Her voice breaks on another sob, and the baby cries again.

"Shh, it's okay Chlo, shh."

I bite my lip so hard I taste blood.

"I can't do this on my own, Jay," she says. This time, her voice is clearer, more sure.

And damn it, I can't help but feel a swell of pride at her change in tone. Our daughter needed her, and she did what she had to do.

I pause the recording, close my eyes, take a deep breath, and then hit Play again.

"I'm giving her up for adoption. It's what's best for her. For months, I've left you messages. I called you while I was in labor, begged you to come. But it's time for me to accept that you aren't interested in being her father. That we don't matter to you…" Another broken sob escapes her throat, and she sucks in a harsh breath just as I do the same. "I won't bother you again. I just thought you should know that we're not your problem anymore."

The phone goes silent, and I stare at the screen, willing the message to change. Wishing I could jump through time, go back to that moment, and cradle her in my arms. Cradle my daughter in my arms.

She thought I didn't care.

She thought I got her messages, then chose to ignore her.

She thought I let her *give up our daughter*.

And it's all my fault.

The sound of heels clacking on the marble floor startles me. When I sit up straight, Vanessa Simpson, Cash's date from the ball, is watching me from my office door. I have no fucking idea how she got in. The office has been closed for hours, and the building should be locked up. I came here because I didn't want to see anyone.

"I don't know why you're here, but it's not a good time," I grumble, dropping the phone onto the desk and taking a deep breath.

"Oh, you want to make time for me." She ignores the death stare I'm throwing at her and saunters farther into my office. "Ya know, I really like Cat. It'd be a shame if she got hurt because of what you've done."

A coldness settles over the room, and the sliver of light from the moon highlights the hatred in her eyes.

I grab for the gun I keep stashed in my top drawer.

But just as my palm lands on the grip, Vanessa hisses. "I wouldn't do that."

I arch a brow in her direction. "You're threatening one of very few people who mean anything to me in this whole world. Why the fuck shouldn't I kill you?"

"I'm not threatening her," she says primly. She's far too calm for someone who's standing within shooting range. "I'm trying to protect her. Because as I said, I *like* Cat."

"How are you trying to protect her?"

"Use your manners, Mr. Hanson. Invite me to sit down."

I close my eyes and squeeze the bridge of my nose as I point to the chair in front of me. "Sit." When she glares in response, I add, "*Please.*"

With more poise than I'd expect from anyone in this position, she takes a seat and crosses one leg over the other. "Now, as I was saying, I like Cat. But I don't like her enough to die protecting her."

"Why would you die?" I ask, even as I consider whether I should shoot her.

She doesn't have much time. Quite frankly, I'm trigger happy right now. I'd love nothing more than to take out my anger on someone deserving.

Throwing her head back, she lets out a haughty laugh. "You didn't really think Evan would let you ride off into the sunset without monitoring you, did you?"

Ice courses through my veins at the name, but I maintain an even tone, as if I don't have the faintest idea who she's referring to. "Evan?"

She smirks. "Please don't play dumb. We don't have much time."

My tongue feels thick, and my mouth goes dry as fear threatens to crack the façade I'm maintaining. If Evan knows about Cat…fuck, if he knows about Chloe, he'll know everything.

"What do you want?" I ask, resigned to doing whatever she asks.

"One million."

I let out a relieved breath. That's simple.

"A year for the rest of my life," she finishes.

I drop my head back and glare at the ceiling.

"Or I could shoot you right now, and I won't have to pay a dime," I reply, bringing my focus back to her.

"Do that, and the information I have will be emailed to Evan. My sisters have been given strict instructions about what to do if anything happens to me."

What information? Does she know about Chloe?

Keeping my cool, I counter, "I could kill them too."

She glares at me. "You're awfully greedy, Mr. Hanson. You have more money than you could spend in a lifetime. You can have your precious Kitten, and in return, all you have to do is share the wealth."

Internally, I breathe a sigh of relief. She doesn't know about Chloe. Regardless, she has me. I'll do anything to protect Cat. Which she knows since she's aware of my goddamn nickname for her.

"How do I know you won't go back to Evan as soon as I hand over the money?"

She laughs. "Because I'm going to disappear. If I don't, he'll kill me for betraying him."

My mind races at that comment, and I squint in confusion. "Why are you betraying him?"

She focuses on something just over my shoulder, and when she looks back, she smiles. "Because, like I said before, I like Cat. She's a good person. And if Evan finds out her family took the money, that the funds were funneled into her account…" She closes her eyes.

She doesn't need to finish the sentence. It's the reason I stayed away for so many years. I thought Evan would be appeased when I put him in his position. I thought I could go back to my life. But I should have known better. Mobsters only know one thing, and that's greed. Being in

260

charge wasn't enough. To him, I hold too much power. Which means he needs to have something to hold over my head in order to guarantee my silence.

Fuck. I should have thought of this before.

Why didn't I think of this before?

And now I have more to lose. Now, Cat and I aren't the only ones who would suffer. Now I have a daughter to protect.

"We need to make it believable," I say, accepting my new reality.

Once again, I have a role to play. And despite popular belief, playing the villain has never been something I relished.

KITTEN'S SONGS

The next afternoon, I sit in the studio with a whiskey in my hand, knowing precisely what I'm about to take part in. What I've orchestrated. No matter how many times I justify it in my head, I know the truth. I'm destroying one woman to save Cat and my daughter.

And I'd make the same decision over and over again if I had to. Nothing matters to me more than Catherine and Chloe.

Unfortunately, Grace is about to pay the price for that.

"Send the text," I whisper.

Vanessa cocks a brow. "Transfer the funds."

The last time someone tried to blackmail me, I didn't take the bait. And because of that, I lost Catherine. I lost the privilege of knowing and raising my child. Mia took the money from my father instead, and my life went up in smoke. I'm not taking the chance that something will go wrong this time.

I run my tongue over my teeth and take another sip of whiskey. "It's done."

She smiles and snatches her phone from the end table to confirm that she's received the money. "I'll send the text, and then I need you to have the plane ready."

I glower at her. "*Obviously*. There's a suitcase by the door. It has your new identity. News about your firing and being run out of town will surface tomorrow so you'll have time to get settled."

"Thank you, Jay," she says with a sincerity that shocks me. I have no idea how she got involved with a man like Evan McCabe, but better her than someone who has no morals.

At least she can be bought.

And she protected my girls.

That's the only reason I didn't put a bullet in her head. Not many would risk their lives by coming to me like Vanessa did, even if she did it for money.

I watch the footage play out on the screen. We've been in the editing room since she finished her interview with Grace. An interview we'll manipulate to destroy the James family.

It's payback for all Theo took from me. Vanessa's timing couldn't have been more perfect. Not only will I get rid of her, but I'll also enact the perfect revenge.

Theo hid Cat's pleas from me. He hid *my child*. And in return, I'll spill all of his secrets.

But I'll give them a way out.

No one can ever accuse me of not being fair.

There's a way for all of us to walk away unscathed. And I'll make sure they have no other option than to take what I offer them.

In the interview, Grace told Vanessa she wanted to start over. Her company is notorious for catering to wealthy men, but she wants to change that by taking on women as clients.

I already know who her first client will be. I'll destroy Grace's reputation and save it in a matter of days.

And hopefully that will clear my conscience. Absolve me for what I'm about to do.

I've killed men and felt less guilt than I do right now.

"Send the text," I direct again.

We watch the video again, and I imagine Cat is doing the same right now.

An image of Grace and Vanessa appears on the screen of Vanessa's phone, and a voice plays over them. "Tonight at six, Grace Kensington, the new owner of The Happily Ever After Makers matchmaking service, discusses her latest client, Cassius James, and the reason she's no longer catering to billionaire men."

Grace's voice cuts in. "If I've learned anything through my own experiences, it's that women deserve the chance to find a man. I mean, what does money matter if a man has secrets, or fetishes, or God forbid, a criminal background? Or if he cheats. Women deserve to know this ahead of time, and that's what we do."

The voice-over continues. "Listen tonight to find out what she learned about the James family and how her interaction with them led her to literally switch sides and represent only women."

"I'm excited for this new chapter in my business and in my life," Grace says. "After my divorce, when I was finally single and coming out of an unhappy marriage, well, let's just say I've learned how easy it is for a man to hide things. Hopefully, I'll be able to use my experience to spot the liars."

"Send the next text," I demand.

Vanessa types out the message containing the link to a gossip article suggesting that one of the James brothers has an illegitimate child. It promises to disclose the identity of Chase's mom and bring to light Cash James's affair with a married woman.

Payback is a fucking bitch named Vanessa, and I'm the one pulling the strings.

Cat will remain unscathed, and our daughter will remain hidden. But I know what she'll do to protect her brothers. All I have to do is wait by the phone.

36

BREATHE BY ANNA NALICK

Cat

I've spent the past twenty-four hours hiding in my apartment. I can't even face Sophie. After Jay stormed off yesterday, I somehow managed to go to the bathroom and make myself presentable so I could say goodbye to Chloe without drawing any attention.

I don't even blame him. I should call him. I should do something, *anything, but sit here feeling sorry for myself,* but I'm too lost to formulate a plan.

We were so close to having it all.

My mind can't help but replay every moment Jay and I shared over the last few months. I'm seeing everything through new eyes. The lengths he went to in order to win me back. The songs, the waffles, the sex club, buying the fucking magazine. The way he looked at me, like it physically hurt not to press closer to me.

I stopped trusting myself years ago when it came to his actions, interpreting his thoughts, believing his words, and so I didn't recognize the truth, which was plain as day for everyone else to see. It wasn't a game to him. Jay showed his love through actions. He always has.

God, what have I done?

To top it all off, Carter confirmed that Cash has moved Grace into the penthouse. It shouldn't bother me. Jay told me she meant nothing to him all those years ago. *Means* nothing to him now.

That should be the least of my worries after the way Jay stumbled upon Chloe and then stormed out.

And it would be, if not for the text message that just popped up on my phone.

> Vanessa: Your brother really should vet the women he dates first. But I guess it's no surprise. Like father, like son.

What the hell does that mean? None of my brothers are anything like my father. Every one of us loathes that man.

A link pops up in the text thread. It's a video clip of Grace and Vanessa sitting on a couch. They're angled toward one another, interview style. The link is from Channel eight, the station Vanessa works for. My stomach drops.

Please God, do not let them know about Chloe.

I reread the text and watch the video. Then I click back to the article she sent after it. My mind spins. Once I've scanned it a second time, I dial Frank. I need him to bring me to Cash immediately.

It's no secret I've never liked Grace, but this goes beyond anything I imagined she could do. And my idiot of a brother told her all our family secrets? Not to mention the pregnancy. How is Cash stupid enough to get her pregnant?

But part of me can't help but sag in relief at the knowledge that Chloe's parentage hasn't been revealed. Not that I'm surprised. Cash doesn't know she's mine, so he couldn't have told that media-hungry whore about her.

My next call is to Cynthia. She needs to know so she can keep Chloe out of town until I figure out how to deal with this.

"I saw," she says in a low voice without saying hello.

"I can't believe this," I hiss.

Frank is studying me in the rear-view mirror. He doesn't know what I've seen. I don't want him to give Cash a heads-up. No, I want to see my brother's face when I show him this.

"You know who could fix this," she says.

"Who?"

I'll do anything to keep this from airing.

"The magazine and channel eight are owned by the same company. They're part of the same media conglomerate."

As quickly as a sliver of relief was dangled in front of me, it's snatched back.

Would Jay really work with Vanessa and Grace to take down my family? He's upset about Chloe, but this is insane.

When we pull up to the James building, I fling the SUV door open and rush inside. My blood pressure rises as I ride in the elevator, my eyes darting to the penthouse button. My stomach rolls as I think of everything that led us to this moment. To the many times Jay and I rode in this space, our hands itching to touch one another, our bodies only inches apart. To the desperation I felt when he almost walked away before we even started.

God, please don't let him be behind this.

Stalking past the receptionist who yells after me, I burst into Cash's office, the last bit of my control gone. If Jay is behind this, we may have to add murder to the laundry list of James scandals hitting the media today.

"Did you get Grace pregnant?"

He lets out a surprised guffaw. "What? *No.* What are you talking about?"

Anxious about what I have to do, I bite the inside of my cheek and stare at my phone. I hate that I'm about to hurt my brother, but I don't have a choice. I need to confirm it's Cash's child and not Chloe they're referring to.

"What's wrong, Kit Cat?" Cash asks, his caring tone breaking me.

I shake my head. My newly healed heart splinters. Because I'm the one who put him in this position. I should have minded my own business rather than pushing Vanessa on him. And I never should have trusted Jay.

Fuck.

"I don't even know how to say this. I think I fucked up." Shit. I can't even look at him.

The tension in the room is so thick I can taste it.

"What did you do to Grace, Cat?" he grits out.

My temper flares at the insinuation that Grace is the innocent one here. "I didn't do anything to that media whore." Taking another step toward my brother, I fling the phone at him.

And before my eyes, my brother's heart crumbles as he watches footage of Grace betraying him in the worst way possible, spilling all of our family secrets in order to boost her business.

I bite my lip. "It gets worse."

"How could it get worse, Cat?"

"The tell-all involves the story about our family. But she hinted that it involved a hidden baby. If that's not yours and Grace's, whose is it?"

The door to the office swings open and crashes into the wall behind it. "*Motherfucker!*" Carter shouts as he barrels into the room. "Motherfucker, motherfucker, motherfucker."

His face is beet-red, and his hair is a mess, like he's been raking his hands through it.

"What's wrong?" Cash asks.

"I've got a fucking kid! *A fucking kid*! And they're doing a story about it, as if I'm some deadbeat dad."

Cash's face is like stone. "What are you talking about?"

He throws his phone at Cash. It bounces off his chest and clatters

270

to the floor. He crouches to retrieve the phone, and once he's upright again, he studies its screen. "Who is this?"

"My friend who works at channel eight. She sent me a heads-up. They're running a tell-all on our family tonight. Apparently, they have inside information on our family, and someone we know is going to verify it all on air."

"You don't have a kid." That statement comes from Cash.

"You're damn right, I don't. Or at least I don't know that I do. But according to my friend, they have DNA proof. I have a fucking kid, and I had no idea."

While Carter paces the room, I shoot Cash a sad smile. "Okay, at least it's not your kid."

Chase storms in next. His hands are balled into fists at his sides, and he's silently fuming.

Oh no.

"Chase, what's going on?" Cash asks. It feels like we're piling into a clown car of nightmares.

"Is it true?" He stomps straight up to Cash's desk and plants his hands on the top, bracing himself so he's looming over our brother.

Cash frowns in confusion. "Is what true?"

"Did our father take advantage of your nanny who was underage?"

Oh fuck. This is so bad. "Chase," I soothe, reaching for his arm, "why don't you sit down?"

He shakes off my touch without acknowledging me. "You're the head of this family now," he growls at Cash. "Answer me. Did our father *rape* my mother?"

Cash nods, affirming the horrible truth.

Chase turns without looking at Carter or me, then storms out without another word.

"Someone needs to go after him," Cash says, looking from me to Carter with so much pain in his eyes that it almost drops me to my knees.

271

The room spins around me, but I already know what I have to do. I snatch the phone from Cash's desk. We're out of options. I won't let my family be destroyed.

"Who are you calling?" Cash demands.

I shake my head as I swallow my pride.

He picks up after one ring. "I've been expecting your call."

I close my eyes. That was all the confirmation I needed. Somehow, I manage to choke out, "Jay, I need your help."

"Consider it done," he says with no preamble.

Of course he doesn't need me to elaborate. He orchestrated the entire thing.

"Name your terms," I say, my voice somehow calm, while inside, I fall apart.

"Marry me, and we merge the companies," he says immediately. He knew what he was doing.

His every play has already been carefully calculated—*plotted*—for how long, I'll never know.

And to think only an hour ago, I was beating myself up over not trusting him at his word. Not believing my heart.

"Nothing comes out?" I ask, using all my strength to keep my voice from shaking.

"I have them prepared to quash everything. Vanessa will be discredited and gone within the hour," he murmurs into the phone.

"How long?"

"How long what?" he asks.

"How long do we remain married? You're doing this because you want control of James Liquors, right? So how long do we keep up the marriage charade?"

He laughs darkly into the phone. "Oh Kitten, I couldn't give two fucks about either liquor company. But you and Chloe? You're mine forever."

"Why are you doing this?" I whisper, desperate to get through to him. We were already his. He's the one who walked away from me when he learned about our daughter.

"I've only ever wanted one thing. And your family took it from me."

I swallow thickly. I have no idea what he's getting at. "What's that?"

"A family. First your father took my mother from me, and it killed her. Then your grandfather hid my daughter from me. I'm not letting it happen again. I'm taking back what's mine."

My father and his mother?

"Jay, please. This is *my family*. You're mad at me. *Punish me*."

"I'm your goddamn family, Cat! *Me*! You, me, and Chloe. *We're* the family. And I'm not mad at you," he hisses. "I fucking love you. You're all that matters to me. Everything I do is for you. You and Chloe are what I want. But that's not enough, Kitten. That doesn't right the wrongs. That doesn't give me back the last thirteen years or any of the moments of *my daughter's life* I missed. I want your grandfather to feel what I've felt. I thought he loved me. I thought he cared about me. But he betrayed me."

"Jay, please, just…what can I do to make this better? I can't change the past, but destroying my brothers? We won't survive this. *Don't* do this."

"Agree to the merger. Say you'll marry me. Then I'll kill the story. I protect my family, Cat. Make your family mine, and I'll protect everyone."

I drop my head back and focus on the ceiling to keep the tears at bay. If I thought he actually cared about me, that he understood what love was, then maybe I'd think he was doing this because he wanted us. That he was moving mountains to be with me. But I'm not that naïve. To him, I'm nothing more than a chess piece.

Closing my eyes, I let out a long sigh. I'm out of options. I put my family in this position by allowing Jay into our lives all those years ago. By believing that anyone could fall for me the way he did. I've known it for years. That kind of love truly doesn't exist.

"Kill the story," I grit out. Accepting my fate, I hang up without waiting for a response.

"Who are you talking to?" Cash asks.

I turn to him, giving myself a few silent seconds to absorb the enormity of what I've just agreed to—an arranged marriage, a life *without* love, a life with Jonathan Hanson.

What was once a dream is now a nightmare.

Carter shuffles over to Cash. "What's going on, Cat? What did you do?"

I take a deep breath and hold my head high. "I fixed everything. They'll kill the story."

"What? How?" Cash stutters.

"Jay is going to handle it. He owns the building that channel eight leases. He'll make sure it doesn't air."

Cash's eyes flare. "So you didn't handle it. You are *trying* to handle it, but we all know Hanson will benefit from our family being destroyed. So in the end, that story will come out."

Isn't that the fucking truth. But I shake my head, refusing to let them see the way my heart is breaking. "He won't."

"Why, Cat? Why would Hanson suddenly care about covering up our family's secrets when they've been trying to spill them for years?"

I look out the window to garner strength. When I feel like I can finally say it without breaking down, I turn back to my brothers. "Because we're going to be family. Hanson Liquors and James Spirits will be merging."

"The fuck they will!" Carter shouts.

"Jay and I are getting married. Our companies will merge just like our families."

"Are you nuts?" This from Cash. When I don't reply, he grits out, "Over my dead body."

I settle in the chair opposite his desk and cross my legs, exuding all the tranquility and assuredness I can muster. I grasp for any kind of façade that will keep me from losing my shit.

"I did what I had to do. And now you guys will too. We'll sign the documents, we'll become family, and we'll take this company in the right direction."

Cash's brow is furrowed, but his eyes are still wide. He's looking at me like I'm nuts. And he's right. "You can't do this, Cat."

But here's the thing about me. When I'm told I can't do something, that's when I dig in. So I stare down my brother, determined to make this right. "It's done."

Cash swipes a stack of papers off his desk and growls. "Stop acting like you can decide this."

I've had enough of his anger for today. "I'm not an idiot, Cash. I can see it written all over your face. You told Grace about Chase, didn't you? You're the loose lip. So don't fucking tell me what I can and can't do." I plant both feet on the floor and drag myself to the edge of my chair. "I told you to stay away from her, and you didn't listen. Now we have to clean up this mess. I won't let this information come to light. It will destroy Chase if this is made public. Let alone Carter's unidentified child. Jesus Christ, we're a fucking disaster of a family; it's pathetic. What will Pa say? I'm doing what has to be done," I grit out, pointing a finger at him, "and you'll let me, because it's your fucking fault we're in this mess."

Cash's silence confirms my theory. The devastated look on his face brings my anger down a few notches, but before I can apologize for jumping down his throat, he stalks out of the office, and I'm left staring at my hands, wondering what the hell I've done.

37

ATLANTIS BY SEAFRET

Jay

F rank is the last person I thought I'd hear from after the fallout. But he didn't know who else to call, and after what I did to Grace, I have no choice but to show up.

Cash didn't even give her a chance to explain. He tore her apart and left her, crying and confused, in a puddle on the floor.

Riding the elevator up to the penthouse for the first time in thirteen years hurts more than I expected it would. So many things that happened today were set in motion the first time Cat brought me here. When she told me who she was. When she begged me not to walk away. When I almost did just that.

But then I won her back and fell so fucking hard for her. And I'll never regret a moment of it. Because being loved by Cat is the only thing I want out of this life. She's the reason behind everything I've done since the day I put her on a plane to Paris and told her I'd meet her there.

It's the reason I destroyed this woman. The one curled into a ball on the floor in front of me.

I recognize her symptoms. I know them well. The haunted eyes. The distress.

Heartbreak.

There is no cure.

Time doesn't heal.

Words won't help.

Losing a love like what she and Cash shared, like Cat and I share, doesn't just destroy a person. It eviscerates every fiber of their being. It makes it so that merely standing hurts. Living is a chore. I wouldn't wish this feeling on my worst enemy, yet I did it to someone as undeserving as Grace Kensington.

I snake my arms under her and pull her against my body. "Shh, Grace, I got you. I'll make this all better, I promise," I say as her tears soak my shirt.

Frank watches on, his fists clenched and his jaw tight. Pure hatred radiates from him. He has no idea. What he knows doesn't even come close to scratching the surface.

I hate myself for what I'm doing, but in the end, my girls are all that matter. And one day, Cat will understand. One day, she'll love me again.

I hope.

With Grace in my arms, I pass the security guards in the lobby and the tourists on the street who turn and stare. Frank holds open the SUV door, and I climb inside and silently settle Grace on my lap, knowing nothing I say will make this better.

38

YOUNG AND BEAUTIFUL BY LANA DEL REY

Cat

I don't take the car back to my office. Instead, I aimlessly wander around the city for hours. Turning down streets I don't recognize, getting lost in the crowds of people who go about their days happily, or distractedly, or without their hearts shattered into a million pieces.

Somehow, hours later, I end up back at the James building, with my finger pressed on the elevator button for the roof. Because of course that's where my body takes me. Where my soul leads me. Back to the start.

I shouldn't be here. This is Cash's place now. But I need the space. I need to return to the place where I spent so many nights falling in love with Jay. I need to somehow make sense of how we got to where we are now.

But there's no making sense of it.

Jay hates my family. That much is obvious.

But why?

The sky is almost black. Even the stars are hiding from Jay's wrath. As I search the vast emptiness above, a flash of lightning in the distance has me mesmerized, struck stupid by its sight.

"You can't marry him," a voice echoes from behind me.

I turn around and spot Carter stumbling toward me. His hair is a mess, and his eyes are bloodshot. At his side, he swings a half-full whiskey bottle.

"Sleep it off. We can't resolve any of this tonight." I'm so damn tired of justifying myself to my brothers.

If the idiots would have kept their damn dicks in their pants, we wouldn't be in this mess.

"I know what he did," he snarls, his eyes glistening.

"Enlighten me, please." I hold out both hands to signal that he has the floor.

Being the only sister of these three boys is exhausting.

He holds up the bottle and uses one finger to point at me. "You fucked him back then. I know it."

I let out a sarcastic laugh and search the damn heavens for patience. "Big deal. You fucked anything with legs."

"Yeah, and it cost me my freedom," he bellows.

Scoffing, I shake my head at his idiocy. "You are *so* dramatic."

"Really?" he asks, moving closer. "Because whatever happened between you and Jay is what led Pa to force me to join the military. Threatened that if I didn't, he'd cut me out of the business. I served over-fucking-seas for years because of him!"

"Watch your mouth!" Jay shouts from the door.

I'm seriously starting to wonder if I've been equipped with a tracker I know nothing about. Why are they here? Why can't everyone just let me fall apart in peace?

"Oh, fuck you!" Carter screams. "This is between me and my sister. You know, the girl you fucked when you were supposed to be my best friend?"

"I said *watch* your mouth." Jay's voice is dangerously low as he steps in front of me, blocking my brother from my view.

"Jay, it's fine," I say, placing my hand on his shoulder.

But he ignores me. "That's the future Mrs. Hanson you're talking about. Apologize."

Carter laughs and stumbles over his own feet. When he rights himself, he takes another sip and points at us again. "Was this the plan all along? Use her for revenge?"

Stepping around Jay, I glare at Carter. "Enough. I get that you're freaking out about potentially having a child—"

Jay barks out a laugh. "Oh, there's no potentially. He's got a child, all right."

I spin and pin Jay with a glare. "What?"

Jay closes his eyes and lets out a long breath, like he's working to compose himself. "Don't you think it's time we got everything out in the open? Finding out you're a dad years later fucking sucks. I'll tell you that."

My hands shake. This is further confirmation that Jay planted all that information. He fed it all to Vanessa and Grace so they could destroy us.

"Why?" I rasp, my voice as tired as my heart.

"Because he hates us, Cat!" Carter hollers. "Fuck it. If you don't want to listen, I can't help you." He stumbles back and glares at us, then he turns and disappears through the door to the stairwell.

Tension slices through the night air as I regard Jay. "I still don't get what happened between you two all those years ago. Why does he hate you so much?"

Jay sticks his hands in his pockets and stares at something over my shoulder. "It doesn't matter."

"Who's the mother of his child?" I ask, moving closer so he's forced to look at me.

Closing his eyes, he rubs his forehead. "It's been a long day. A long fucking week. Just get Cash on board with the merger and let me know when you and Chloe are moving in."

I can't hold back a sardonic laugh. "Are you *insane*?"

His jaw tics. "Don't push me, Cat. I'll give you time to figure out how to sell this to Chloe, but you *will* sell it to her. I've lost twelve years with my daughter," he says, his voice cracking as he turns toward the horizon. After a long moment, his steely eyes lock on me again. "Your family cost me twelve years with her. You should hate them as much as I do for what they took from us."

"But why, Jay? What aren't you telling me? *Why* did my grandfather interfere?"

Eyes wild, he yells, "Because the Mob would have killed you!"

What? Try as I may, I can't comprehend a scenario where that could be true. "Why would the Mob come after me?"

"Because you had their money," he whispers, all the while scowling like he's angry with me for having to explain.

"What money?"

"The money I planted there."

I suck in a breath through my teeth, and black dots dance across my vision. "What?"

Jay rakes both hands through his hair viciously, like he's holding himself together. "I was ten when I found them. Your father and my mother." It's barely a whisper when it comes out. A rasp. A plea for me to stay rooted in place. To force myself not to run. Because he knows that's what the mention of my father does.

As if I could move after the revelation he just handed me.

"From that moment on, my sole focus in life was to destroy your father." The words send a cold shiver down my spine. "Revenge. That's what you were."

The admission is like a punch to the stomach, leaving me gasping for air.

"Until I met you," he says, his words laced with pain, "and I fell so fucking in love with you, I couldn't see straight. Or maybe I finally could. But I was too far gone. Too involved. Too beholden to the past to untangle it."

"What did you do?" I whisper as tears blur my vision. I've known from the beginning that Jay hates my father. I've always assumed it's because of business. But love makes so much more sense. Love is always the root of the most heinous crimes. But Jay was truly capable of this one? Stealing my heart, my virginity, my soul...for revenge?

I was nothing but revenge.

Unlike moments ago, his face is devoid of emotion as he tells the story. Like he's rushing through it to get it over with as quickly as possible. "At my father's request—ha, more like demand—I planted an SD card on Carter's computer. I thought it would only implicate your father, but I was wrong." His eyes dart to mine. "The money my father stole was in your account. When everything went down, they'd go after you. Yours was the name on my father's lips when I shot him in the head to keep him quiet."

A sob rattles through my chest. I break for the ten-year-old who witnessed something horrible and whose life was destroyed so quickly. I cry over the death of the illusion I never let go of, the hope I held on to—that Jay and I were soulmates, that we were something *more*. That he really loved me.

And I cry because in some sick way, he did. He *killed* his father to protect me.

But if this is what love is, I don't want it.

I've always convinced myself that Chloe was the product of love. That she was the best parts of us, the reason we were meant to spend those months together. The reason I endured *everything else.*

But I was nothing more than a plot in his revenge. A part of his scheme. And he let me go. In the end, his revenge was more important.

I can't take much more, but I need to make sure Chloe is safe before I end this conversation. "Why did you come back after all this time?"

Jay startles at the question. As if he thought I'd fall to the ground and thank him for coming back to me.

"I thought you were safe. Because all those who threatened you are dead," he says, his eyes boring into me, asking me to understand. "Because it's our time. We were supposed to be together, Cat. I know this is a lot, and I'm sure you have more questions—"

I hold up a hand to cut him off. "No, Jay. We're done. Finally." Incredibly, all I feel is relief at that admission. "I finally understand your obsession. Your"—I choke over the lump in my throat—"*devotion*. It never made sense to me. For years it burned me. How easily you went from *loving* me to nothing. How you chased after me, how you refused to take no for an answer..." I shake my head and pull my shoulders back. "You weren't dedicated to me. You were *dedicated* to revenge."

Revenge is one thing I understand completely. I have been dedicated to it too. For the last few months, it's all I've thought about. But now? I realize it was all a waste. I don't want revenge. I want him to cease to exist. Instead, he'll be my husband.

Jay shakes his head fiercely. "No, Cat. You aren't listening. Nothing was about revenge once I met you. Once I fell for you, my vengeance became a subplot in my life. A secondary storyline. And when you told me who you were? It became the thing I had to overcome so I could have you." He steps closer, ducking so I'm forced to look at him. "But I did, Cat. I gave it all up. I told my father I was done with his plans, done with it all."

"And then what happened?" I ask, tearing my gaze from him. "Because obviously you didn't give it all up. You're still Jonathan Hanson, CEO of Hanson Liquors, and now you own a controlling stake in James Whiskey too. Looks like it all worked out."

"Mia happened."

My blood runs cold as I remember what my grandfather said so many years ago. Jay cheated on me with Mia. She also has his child.

"The pregnancy. Right. I'm sure knocking up your girlfriend's best friend put a wrinkle in your plans."

God, how did I get myself into this mess?

"*What?*" Jay sputters.

Weighed down by years of bitterness, I can't find the enthusiasm for a reply. Not even a sarcastic one. I slump and study the ground below me, ready to make a hasty retreat.

He presses so close I can feel the heat radiating from him, but I refuse to look at him. He grasps my hand. The simple touch slices through me. "I never touched Mia. Carter did," he sneers.

My heart squeezes, and I have to blink several times to make sense of that statement.

My brother and Mia. Bile coats my throat at the thought.

"I needed the SD card from your brother's computer. I had to figure out what my father planned so I could stop it." His voice softens as his eyes plead with me. "Baby, I was trying to fix it. I know I screwed up. I know what I did was awful. But all my life, I'd been told that my mother killed herself after her affair with your father. And my father fed my hatred for years. I never could have imagined it would turn out how it did."

"Jay," I whisper, my heart cracking right down the middle.

He shakes his head. "She didn't kill herself. But I found that out too late. I found out everything too late. All I wanted was to make it all right."

"What did Mia do?"

He coughs out a bitter laugh and drags his hand down his face. "What she always does. She poisoned everything. When Carter showed up and found her in his room, she seduced him. Then she tried to sell the SD card back to me when she found out she was pregnant."

My gasp slices through the night air. "*Mia* is the mother of Carter's child?"

The lightning reflecting in Jay's eyes as he regards me sends a chill through me. He doesn't need to respond. That look alone tells me all I need to know.

"Fuck." I swallow thickly. "And he never knew?"

Jay presses his lips together and shakes his head.

"But my grandfather did?"

"Yes." Jay drops his shoulders in defeat.

Pain, thick and forceful, threatens to drown me. "You told me my grandfather had secrets that weren't yours to tell. Was that it? Mia's baby?"

Moistening his lips, he shakes his head.

God, he looks even more terrified than before.

"Just tell me," I urge. "I can't live in the dark anymore."

"After I left you in New York. I went to see your grandfather. To figure out how to protect you. But what he told me shocked me stupid."

"I met your mother, you know?" Theo said, studying my reaction.

I cleared my throat. "Did you?"

He shook his head and smiled. "Your mother was a lot of things, but suicidal wasn't one of them." He closed his eyes for a long moment, and when he opened them again, a war waged within them. Then he pointed to a photograph on his desk. "And she didn't kill herself when she was pregnant. That's your brother right there. He's very much alive. Just as he was when she left him with me so she could go back for you."

"You're Chase's brother?" I whisper, shell-shocked.

I'm set to marry my brother's brother?

This nightmare just keeps getting worse.

And my brothers are going to lose their minds.

"Yes," Jay says, his voice low.

"If I hadn't agreed to marry you, would you have exposed that information?" I seethe.

Jay gulps, but he doesn't look away. "I knew you'd never let that happen."

Fury sends my heart rate racing. "Answer the question, Jay. Were you willing to take that chance?"

"I'd do anything to make you mine. So yes, I was willing to take the risk. I would take any risk necessary, including one that could cost me my life, because you and Chloe are all that matter. I love you, Catherine. Everything I've done is because of that. If you know nothing else, *please* know that."

His confession is so fervent and his expression so distraught that it hurts to listen to him. But I don't know if I believe him. There have been too many lies between us. Too many secrets.

"What kind of guy falls for a girl he barely knows? It's a convenient lie you're telling yourself. Maybe you've changed, maybe you did protect me, but you can't change how we started. You said it yourself. I was nothing more than revenge when we began. *That*. That's something I don't think I'll ever move past. Now please, Jay, just go."

"You were the first thing in my life that *wasn't* about revenge. It was selfish, yeah. But I couldn't let you go. I knew the risks. And I knew it couldn't end well. And I took you anyway. I couldn't *not* have you."

He heaves a heavy breath, and thunder in the background rumbles as his eyes plead with me. "And letting you go…" His voice drops off with a wistfulness that almost chokes me. "Letting you go was the most selfless thing I've ever done. You couldn't have me *and* your family. And I never wanted you to have to make that choice."

I shake my head as lightning streaks across the sky. "You have no idea what I would have done had you told me the truth."

His smile is sad. Patronizing. As if he thinks he has me all figured out. And maybe he did back then. But I'm not that girl anymore.

"You would have chosen me, Kitten. Just like I chose you."

"You didn't choose me." My voice wobbles, the vulnerability I've been staving off for so long making me weepy. "You *never* chose me."

His jaw hardens and he narrows his eyes. "I've chosen you every goddamn day since I walked away from you."

"You have a funny way of showing it. Sleeping with Grace, announcing your relationship with her in the society pages." I choke back a sob and blink back my tears. "I was still waiting for you."

Jay brushes at the rogue tear that slips down my cheek. And for a second, I find myself wanting to lean into his touch, to fall apart in his arms. But I pull back.

"No. You don't get to rewrite history. I know what happened. And I won't let you do this. Was Grace conning my brother? Was that your plan? String us along, then break our hearts? Then what? Is this where the two of you stroll off hand in hand, laughing about the fools you left in your wake?"

Jay's eyes ice over. "You have no idea what you're talking about. I destroyed her for you."

I laugh but it hurts. Everything hurts where Jay is concerned.

"Just go," I beg, turning away from him. I won't cry in front of him anymore. He doesn't get to see how utterly lost I feel knowing the only person I ever thought truly loved me *didn't*.

"It's not that easy, Kitten. They're back. I thought you were safe, but…Cat, I need you to listen to me. I'm the only one who can keep you and Chloe safe."

A shocked laugh escapes me, and I round on him. "*Safe? You?*" I scoff. "You're the one who put me in this position!" I cross my arms over my chest and pull myself up to my full height. "No, thank you. I'll go to my brothers."

Jay takes two big steps so we're chest to chest. "The fuck you will. You aren't listening to me, Cat. You and Chloe aren't safe unless you're with me."

My heart pounds so loudly it's hard to hear over it, but I stand my ground and glare. I need to call Cynthia and beg her to keep Chloe away until I can figure out what's true and what's not. I refuse to let Jay see the way I'm caving under the weight of all he's told me, but inside, I'm falling apart.

I turn away from him. "Please go. I can't do this right now."

Jay grabs my chin and tilts it until I'm forced to look into his eyes. Their depths are so full of longing I can't understand. "You are and always will be the love of my life, Catherine. Our parents stole so much from us. Don't let them steal that too. You and Chloe are everything to me, and I'll spend the rest of my life proving it."

"I don't really have a choice but to spend the rest of my life with you, now do I?" I yank myself out of his grasp.

Jay's eyes cloud as he wars with himself. Then he presses close to me, his breaths mingling with my own. I suck in my breath to keep from cracking. It'd be so easy to fall for his charm. To believe his words. But doing that will only end in heartache for me.

The thunder rumbles closer. The warm air from the impending storm sticks to my skin as the sky lights up with another crack of lightning, making Jay almost glow as his pained voice glides into the space between us. "I may be the villain of their story, but I'm the hero of yours, Kitten. You just don't know it yet. One day, you'll realize everything I did was for you."

39

WHEN WE WERE YOUNG BY ADELE

Cat

> Jay: Meet me at your brother's office tomorrow morning at nine.

I turn the screen to Sophie, who pours another shot of tequila for me. It's the last thing I need, but she said that since tequila was our drink of choice when she got engaged, it's tradition. I think she's rewriting history, because I was very pregnant when Dexter proposed, but I'm just glad she drove into the city to be with me the minute she got my call.

We're seated on my cozy black chenille couches, a splurge of mine when I first purchased this apartment. To this day, I've relied upon my own income to do everything. My apartment is smaller than what any of my brothers would own, but it's mine, and right now, I'm thankful for this safe space.

Tears flowed down my cheeks when I explained how I was nothing more than revenge to the man I thought was my entire world. And now that I've started, I can't stop. It's really freaking annoying.

"Your face is leaking," Sophie teases, but even that doesn't help.

"I know," I wail. "Make it stop!" It's like a decade worth of tears are escaping.

She pulls me in for a hug, and I let go of the gray blanket that I have draped around me to accept it.

"You're going to be okay."

"How? For one beautiful day. No, not even a goddamn day. More like fifteen hours. For fifteen beautiful hours, I got to live in an alternate reality where Jay and I were happy. And now I'm back in hell again," I whisper through another sob.

I pull the blanket around my body again and tilt my head back in hopes that it will make my eyes stop leaking.

Sophie rubs circles across my back. "I know you said you could never forgive him, but—"

I cut her off with a glare. "There is no *but*. What he did was unforgivable."

"Is it, though?" she asks.

Traitor.

I bite my lip to keep from screaming. "Yes. Yes, it's unforgivable. I was revenge. What we had wasn't real!"

"That isn't exactly what he said," she counters, throwing her hands up when I shoot figurative daggers her way. But she doesn't stop. "He told you his revenge ended the minute he met you. That he tried to stop the plan."

"Then he actively plotted to hurt my family. He put us in danger. Not just me, but my daughter."

Sophie's voice is far too calm. "He didn't know about her, babe. He was in a coma. He didn't ignore your phone calls. And he didn't actively hurt you, Cat. He tried to protect you. I can only imagine that he's devastated now that he knows about her. That's what this is. He's hurting and acting out…"

"I don't believe him," I huff.

She tilts her head and studies me in silence for a moment. "You really think he knew about Chloe?"

I blow out a breath and give the only answer I can. "No, I don't believe he knew about her. Yes, I believe he was in a coma. But...I don't trust that his feelings were real."

With a sigh, Sophie hits me straight in the solar plexus. "That's because you don't believe people can love you."

Breathing through the pain that comes with that accusation, I shake my head. "That's not true."

In response, all she does is hiss.

"You think that's true?" I level her with a glare. "You said I couldn't love anyone else because of my emotional turmoil over Jay. Now you're saying I can't *accept* love either?"

Sophie tilts her head one way, then the other, as if she's weighing her words. "I think that your family has done a number on you." She licks her lips and shifts on the couch beside me. "And losing Jay in the way you did, believing that the man you thought loved you so desperately had conned you? I think it affected you deeply. But Cat, take a deep breath and think it all through. Because what he's telling you is that none of that happened. He didn't just walk away. He didn't ghost you. He was *kept* from you. And he's trying now. *Let* him try."

"I-I can't," I admit, and the waterworks start all over again.

Sophie's face says it all. I *can't*. Because I can't accept love.

"Sweetie, I say this with all the love in the world, but if you have a shot at happiness, any chance at all, it's with that man. Give him a chance."

My chest shudders with another sob. That's all I wanted for so long. But now that I know the truth, I have no freaking idea how I'll ever trust him again.

"I know we hate him—"

I hold my shot glass up to stop her from adding a *but* to that statement. I'm tired of crying. "Please do not qualify that statement." I down the shot while keeping my eyes trained on her. "What do I tell Chlo?" I ask as the tequila burns my throat.

How am I going to tell her I'm marrying her father? God knows I can't tell her he forced me into it. Or that the only reason she exists is because of some sick revenge he concocted years ago.

"What will Chloe think of me?" I whisper my fear into the room.

Sophie sits up and loops her arms around me. "Aw, babe. She'll think you're a badass woman who did what she had to do to protect the ones she loved. Like you've always done."

I shudder. Because the truth is that I'm out of time. I have to tell Chloe about Jay soon. And all I can do is hope that she knows I'll do everything I can to make this right.

Cassius James @CashJames · · ·

Grace Kensington is a con artist. Her mother was correct when she said all Grace cares about is money and fame.

Cassius James @CashJames · · ·

She took advantage of me as her client. I was unaware of her marriage and am deeply sorry to have caused my family embarrassment.

EXTRA DIRTY

I groan at the text from Frank that wakes me. Two screen shots. Both of Cash's tweets from the night before. What a fucking asshat.

Did you not think to take the phone away???

Frank: I couldn't get close enough. The guy is unhinged. What time will you be here?

Give me an hour.

KITTEN'S SONGS

Standing outside the James building, I suck in a breath and summon the courage to call Chloe.

"Oh my gosh, Cat, you'll never believe the outfit that Sienna let me try on!" she screeches without even saying hello.

At the sound of her voice, I find myself smiling for the first time in days. "Oh yeah? I can't wait to see it."

"Mom and I went to dinner and had the crème brûlée. It was even better than L'Etoile's!"

I laugh at her excitement, and slowly, a sliver of my sanity seeps back into me as I listen to her rave. "Oh, we should plan a weekend there soon."

"Really?" she chirps.

"Yeah, let me get through this merger, and then we'll go."

"Oh my gosh, that would be amazing!"

"Listen, Chlo, you and I need to talk later. Things are going to change a bit, but I want you to know that no matter what, you always have me."

"You're scaring me," she whispers. The fear in her voice sends my heart plummeting.

I drop my head and pinch the bridge of my nose. I'm screwing this up. "Don't be scared. It's all going to be fine, okay? I love you."

"Love you too," she murmurs, but the excitement she was so filled with has been sucked right out of her.

I tell her goodbye and end the call because I don't know what else to say. Cynthia and I need to come up with a plan for telling Chloe about Jay.

And I hope like hell he doesn't make this harder than it has to be. He may have used me to get what he wanted, but I'll be damned if he hurts Chloe. She'll never know anything other than love. If he can't honor that, then maybe I'll take those vows to heart. The *till death do us part* ones.

40

HEAL BY TOM ODELL

Jay

I stand mere feet from Cat, wishing more than anything that I could take her into my arms. But the anxiety etched into her every move and the way her shoulders are hunched as she speaks into her phone keep me in place. It doesn't stop me from straining to hear her side of the conversation, though.

"Listen, Chlo, you and I need to talk later. Things are going to change a bit, but I want you to know that no matter what, you always have me."

I shuffle closer and swallow thickly when she drops her chin to her chest.

"Don't be scared. It's all going to be fine, okay? I love you."

What the hell is she telling our daughter? If she's making her hate me before I even have a chance to get to know her, I'll lose it.

My heart beats hard in my chest, and without thinking, I grab her arm and yank so she spins my way. She startles when she recognizes me, and the phone clatters to the ground.

I stare her down as she quickly bends to grab her phone and pockets it.

"What did you say to her?" I ask, feeling desperate.

"That's not—" She looks away from me. "I don't want to talk about that right now."

I let out a haughty laugh. "You made it sound like you're dying. She's going to hate me."

She holds her head high and glares. "I agreed to your terms. What more do you want from me?"

My patience snaps. "I fucking did this *for you*, Cat."

"Don't," she scoffs darkly. "Don't you fucking dare pin what you did to my family on me, you selfish prick."

It's like a slap. I grasp her arm, desperate to get our connection back. To show her I'm still the man she made love to only days ago. "Don't do this, Cat. Don't shut me out. I swear to God, I did what I had to do for our family."

Her jaw is locked so tight I'm afraid she'll crack a tooth. "As did I. You can dictate where I live and what I do on a daily basis. Hell, you can fuck me whenever you want. I've given up everything to protect my family," she fumes. "But you can't force me to respect you. To trust you. To *love* you." She screams the last few words, garnering attention from passersby. "You wouldn't know love if it smacked you in the face."

My stomach sinks. *What did I do?*

I'd give my life for this woman. Everything I've done has been for her. I've clearly fucked up royally, and I have no idea how to make it right.

But she's wrong.

I love her. I know love. Maybe the way I love isn't enough. Maybe it's not right. Because she's correct about one thing: it's an obsession. Consuming. My love for her dictates my entire life. At times, I can't even see straight, can't think, because of it.

But if she keeps our daughter from me, I'll never forgive her.

I don't know how to make sense of it. I don't know how to see reason. I'm so fucking angry.

We stare at one another, chests heaving, neither of us willing to back down, until Frank interrupts.

"You two going to come inside or stare at the building all day?"

Without a word, we turn and step inside. I'm not sure how this meeting will go. All I know is that I'm holding on by a thread. And I'm fucking pissed.

41

SET FIRE TO THE RAIN BY ADELE

Cat

Beside me, Cash's leg bounces as he signs the papers Jay presented moments ago. Few words have been spoken. We've communicated in grunts and glares for the most part. For my brother's sake, I'm doing my best to hide behind a mask of tranquility. He needs to think that I'm happy about this wedding, even though I'm anything but. Inside, I'm shaking. Scared shitless.

When I take in the man across the table, the man I've dreamed about for almost half my life, I can almost convince myself that he's hurting. That he'll reconsider what he's done when he's had time to think. When he gets to know Chloe. But his nonchalance over the merger and the way he barely glances at me remind me of the truth. Jay cares about no one and nothing but himself.

"This is going to be great," he says after Cash slides the final paper across the table. "We will plan the announcement in a few weeks."

Cash glares in response. "You aren't really going through with this sham of a marriage? I signed the papers—it's unnecessary."

Jay smirks. "Sintac wants a family business. What's better than two family businesses joined together in holy matrimony? This is a happy time, Cash; get on board."

Beside my brother, I hold my breath.

"You don't have to do this," he mutters.

I fake a smile. "We are doing this, Cash. We're friends. Jay and I are happy. It's what's best for both of our companies."

Across from us, Jay's smile grows, although, like me, he's putting on a front. "See? A family affair. It's going to be great. So will Grace be there?"

His words are like a slap to the face.

Beside me, my brother seethes. "I know what you did. I know you and Grace planned this. I'll figure out how to prove it, and then I'll get my company back."

Hoping to keep the peace, I sigh. "Jay had nothing to do with Grace's tell-all. He stopped it from being aired." The words taste hollow on my tongue, but I force them out anyway. Though I make sure to narrow my eyes at the man across the table. "Jay, stop bringing her up. I told you, we're done with her."

His cold stare makes me shiver, but it's nothing compared to his frigid words. "And I told you, she's my friend. She *didn't* do this. And you don't need your company back, Cash, because I didn't take it. We are merging—you will still have management of your side, and Cat will handle the expansion. This is a win-win."

Cash snaps, "If you want this to work, I'd suggest you don't mention Grace to me again. We're done. I don't deal with liars and cheats or people I can't trust, and Grace is, unfortunately, all of those."

Taunting my brother, Jay laughs. "You're a bigger fucking fool than I thought. That woman gave you everything, and she would have given up even more for you. She practically did. You were off-limits in the interview, Cash. Vanessa played her. And nothing came out. All the secrets remain under wraps. *Nothing* is coming out. Forgive her, or you'll regret losing her."

That's rich coming from the biggest scam artist around.

Cash pushes his chair back. "Let's just stick to talking about business.

Stay out of my personal life, and I'll stay out of whatever fake marriage bullshit you guys are doing."

"Sit down," Jay barks, halting my brother on the spot.

"Don't tell me what to do."

"Sit the fuck down, *please*," he says in the most condescending voice I've ever heard.

I meet my brother's eyes, silently begging him to make this easier on all of us. I'm barely holding on, and I just want to get this meeting over with.

With tense shoulders and a clenched jaw, he obeys.

"Now, you are going to have your publicist put out this statement. And if you get asked anything about Grace, you will refer to the statement or give nothing but a glowing review of her. Do I make myself clear?"

Cash doesn't even look at the paper. "Not going to happen."

Sick of their childish bullshit, I grab the paper and read it aloud. "Several weeks ago, I engaged Grace Kensington to help me in my pursuit of a wife. During that time, I was introduced to Vanessa. Although I did not see it going anywhere past the first date, she apparently did not feel the same way. After our date, and after I learned of Grace's pending divorce, I pursued a relationship with Grace. When Vanessa found out about this, she was apparently angry and somehow hacked my account last night to make those slanderous allegations against Grace."

I scoff and glare at Jay. When he meets my eyes with his steely gaze, I continue. "At this time, I want to make clear that Grace Kensington was an utmost professional when I was a client. She did not pursue me. She did not introduce me to anyone after I made it clear that I was only interested in her, and she is a victim of Vanessa's lies. I am profoundly sorry for how she has been affected and hope that Vanessa is brought to justice for her crimes."

I throw the paper at Jay. "This is shit and you know it."

Though Jay's next words are for my brother, his focus never leaves me. "This only works if you make that statement. If not, let's rip up the contract. I'll go to Sintac, get the deal myself, and move on. You all seem to forget that I don't need you. *You* need me."

As much as I hate to admit it, he's right. My brother's stupid tweets last night made everything worse. It gave credence to the previews the news channel ran before Jay shut them down. All of Boston is probably speculating about what we're trying to cover up.

Carter's child, the identity of Chase's mother, her age. And God forbid they find out about Chloe.

Cash won't let it go, though. "Why are you doing this? I get why it makes sense for us. I fucked up with the tweets, yeah. But you're right. You could just go to Landry and take the deal with him yourself. Why are you helping us? What do *you* get out of this?"

I hold my breath, waiting for an answer that doesn't come. Pleading that he'll be the man I believed him to be years ago and tell us it's because he loves me.

"Because Grace doesn't deserve what you did. I may not be a man who *loves* many people," he says with a glare in my direction, "but I love her."

In that moment, the world around me goes fuzzy. The image of Jay and Grace on the magazine cover flashes in my mind. The memory of crying out for a man who never loved me as I gave birth to our daughter stabs me so sharply, I'm surprised I'm not bleeding out.

When my vision finally clears and I can breathe through the pain, I realize I've missed part of the conversation.

Jay is midsentence when I tune back in. "I won't have her lose everything because of you."

Cash slams his fists into his thighs. "Fine."

I jump to my feet. "You can't be serious! Both of you. You can't be serious. Jay, I won't stand by and let you do this. We can fix everything with our relationship. We don't need to fix things for her."

308

He barely looks at me. "Oh, you have a part too," he spits. "Don't you worry. After we leave this office with Cash's signed statement, you and I have an appointment with Grace Kensington."

The pain in my chest ratchets up another notch. "You've lost your damn mind."

The sound of Jay's palms landing on the table makes me jump. "This is the last time I am going to say this. I care about you, Cat, but don't make me choose."

I blink back the tears that threaten to fall at the threat in his words. *Don't make me choose between my family and yours.* He'll take Chloe if I don't agree to his damn terms. He'll let the world know what my grandfather did, what my father did, what my brothers have done, if I don't agree to his damn terms. He's got all the power, and we both know it. "No surprise there." I take a deep breath and turn to Cash. "We good?"

My brother is silent, and he doesn't bother to even glance in my direction as he stands and heads toward the door. But as he passes Jay, he moves in close and mutters in Jay's ear. I can't be sure, but it sounds like, "Does she know?"

My darling husband-to-be doesn't even look at me. "Walk it off, Cash. Don't ruin more than you already have today," he warns.

"What's he talking about?" I ask. Does Cash know about Jay and me all those years ago?

"Don't worry, Kitten," he says. He uses the once-sacred name in the cruelest way. He wants to show Cash that he has power over me. That he's in control.

Dropping my shoulders, I resign myself to my future. As the woman Jonathan Hanson will use—over and over—for the rest of his life.

42

THE NIGHT WE MET BY LORD HURON

Cat

"Why are you doing this?" I whisper as we leave Grace's office. Unsurprisingly, the meeting didn't go great. Grace and I don't get along. On that, we could agree. Anything else? Not gonna happen.

"Why am I doing what?" Jay asks, his eyebrows knitting together. He's wearing a navy suit, and his blond hair is gelled perfectly in place. He looks like a robot. Not like my Jay. The one whose hair is always haphazardly styled so it falls over his eyes. The one who used to smile at me so easily. Who teased me constantly. This *isn't* that man.

And maybe he never was.

"Why do you want me to date other people?" I ask when we're alone in the elevator and headed to the ground floor.

Jay asked Grace to take me on as her new client. Her *first* female client. But why? What's his motive? Is it only to help Grace? Is he really willing to watch me date other people in order to save her career?

The man is a conundrum. One moment, he's pledging his undying love, telling me he's been trying to come back to me for thirteen years, and the next, he's cold and detached, angry even.

I believed the lies he sold me once, and the scars from being burned then still hurt. I need to go into this marriage with open eyes.

He raises his brow as we step off the elevator. "What did you tell Chloe about me?"

I grunt and stride for the front doors. "*Nothing*. I haven't said a word about you to her yet."

He snags my wrist, forcing me to stop. "I don't want her to hate me."

"She won't hate you." It's not even a lie. Chloe isn't like that. "Now tell me," I say as the doorman ushers us out of the building, "why did you ask Grace to set me up on dates?"

When we're on the sidewalk, Jay sighs and rubs the back of his neck. When he ducks his head, his hair falls forward slightly. It's just enough to undo the perfection that almost moments before made him seem unhuman. As if the cold façade he's worn all morning is slipping away before my eyes.

"You're in danger. I told you that." He holds out a hand, gesturing for me to slide into the waiting car ahead of him. Once he's seated beside me, he continues. "I don't want the Mob to know you're the one I've been protecting all along. If you're seen dating other men, and then we end up together as one of Grace's matches, we can spin things so it looks like we just started dating."

I close my eyes and slump back against the soft leather. I'm so tired. Emotionally and physically. "Fine."

He squeezes my leg, but I don't move. "No snarky comeback? No fight?" he says, a teasing tone to his voice. The man is giving me severe whiplash today.

His touch alone burns me in a way that makes me hate myself. How is it possible to hate him and yet love the feel of his hand on my body? Crave it, even.

I blow out a breath. "Just take me home, please."

"I know you're angry with me—"

"Angry?" I ask, finally opening my eyes so I can glare at him.

"Catherine, everything I've done has been for you."

I laugh. Not this again. "You've got a funny way of showing it."

"Just—*fuck*. Trust me, this is not the way I wanted you to agree to marry me, but please believe that everything I have to do over the next few weeks is to keep you safe. Because you're the first thought I have when I wake up and the last thought I have at night. It's been that way since the moment I met you."

"Grace destroyed my family," I whisper, trying so hard to ignore the desperate tone he constantly hits me with when we're alone.

Jay runs his fingers over his forehead, rubbing aggressively. "She didn't. Just trust me. You've got it all wrong."

"Trust you?" I ask weakly. "Trust you? Jay, every time I trust you, I get burned. You told me you loved me and then you weaponized what Vanessa and Grace did to my family so you could take our business and force me into a marriage. Why the hell should I trust you?"

Jay's face turns red. "Because you wouldn't listen to me. You still aren't. I didn't *want* to do it. But you're not safe. I need you to be safe. I seriously could give a fuck about the company."

He clears his throat and pulls his hand away from my leg. The loss of his touch sends a chill through me the moment it's gone. I hate how much I want that small touch. If I'm not careful, I'll fall for his lies again. Falling for my future husband feels far more dangerous than taking on the Mob. He can worry about them, and I'll work on protecting my heart.

"I want you to move in with me."

I cough. "Excuse me? You just told me you want us to pretend we don't know one another. There's no way we can keep up this ruse if we live together."

He sighs. "Fine. But you and Chloe need security."

"I'll call Frank," I say, closing my eyes once again.

"The fuck you will," he bites out. "You'll end it."

"End what?" I ask with a sigh. This conversation is going in circles.

"I won't be made to look like a fool, Catherine. You'll be my wife, and you won't even look in the direction of another person. End your relationship with Frank."

"What relationship?" I scoff, shifting in my seat to glare at him.

Jay presses so close I can feel his hot breath on me as his face reddens. "Any relationship you have. You're mine going forward. Understood?"

When I don't reply, his jaw tics. "Let's be very clear, Catherine. The dates you go on? They are *fake*. You don't look at another man. Or woman. Allow another man to touch you, Kitten, and he will die. Touch another person, and they will die. I've killed more than enough people during my life for you. I have no problem adding one more."

43

KEEPING YOUR HEAD UP BY BIRDY

Cat

O nce I agreed that he could have security parked outside the building at all times, Jay finally acquiesced and let me return to my apartment.

He's ridiculous.

But also, his words in the car? That he'd kill for me? Well, they were hot.

"How are you?" Sophie asks over the phone.

"My head is spinning. And Cash is a disaster."

"Have you spoken to him?"

I sigh. "Not since he signed the merger documents. He won't talk to anyone. But Frank is with him. Said he isn't handling this well."

"What about Carter and Chase?"

God, I've been so worried about myself and Chloe that I haven't even checked in on my other brothers. Though I have no interest in speaking to Carter anytime soon. He owes me an apology. Asshole.

"I don't know," I admit. "Chase disappeared after the article broke." I've yet to wrap my head around the truth that Chase is Jay's brother as well. My grandfather has a lot of explaining to do when he's feeling stronger.

"God, Cat, I don't know how you've kept this bottled up for all these years. Are you okay?" she asks softly.

I shrug, even though she can't see me. "I will be." Ready to move on from all things James Liquor and Hanson Liquors and the handful of difficult men in my life, I change the subject. "Could Chloe stay with you guys when she gets back from New York? It won't be for long. Just until I figure out how real this threat is."

"Of course, babe. She can room with Del. You know how much they love each other, and it's been too long since they spent real time together."

I hum. Time is slipping by quickly.

The thought of living with Jay is insane enough, but the idea of bringing Chloe into that world makes it almost impossible to breathe.

It's this vision I never allowed myself to conjure. Raising our daughter together.

Even if I'm being forced into this domesticity, even if it's not real, a tiny part of me has yearned to give this to Chloe since I discovered I was pregnant.

And if my daughter can have it all? Her mother and her father, *a family*, something neither Jay nor I ever had? The possibility makes every choice I've made until this point worth it. Even the forced marriage. I'll never let her worry, even for a moment, that she isn't wanted, that she isn't perfect and loved.

And I know for a fact that Jay will do the same.

The marriage will be far from perfect, I have no doubt, but I'll make sure Chloe thinks it is.

Will she hate me when I break the news? Will she think I kept her from him? The truth is hurtling forward like a freight train, and I'm out of time.

"I just want to get through this farce of a dating disaster Jay coerced me into."

"What?" Sophie asks.

"Guess I didn't get to that part. Jay says in order to protect me, we need to make it look like Grace Kensington introduced us."

She sucks in a breath. "No fucking way!"

"Exactly what I said. But unfortunately, I don't get much say in the matter, because Jay controls how I breathe from now on."

Sophie laughs softly. "Please. You've had that man by the balls since he first saw you. He may have the upper hand right now, but you'll always be the one in control."

"I wish," I whine. "Seriously, Soph, I don't get him. One moment, he's glaring at me, and the next, he's telling me if I so much as look at another man, he'll kill him."

"Oh, that's hot."

I groan. Damn it. "Tell me about it."

"Poor Cat," she sings. "You have to marry a hot billionaire who loves giving you orgasms and would kill for you. And as a bonus, he's the father of your daughter. I mean, how will you survive?"

I cough out a laugh. "When you put it like that…"

Despite all that, I'm still terrified of getting closer. Of giving him the chance to wreck me again.

"It's going to be okay, babe," she comforts.

"I know, I'm Catherine James. I bounce," I say with false assurance. "I just need to get through lunch with Grace tomorrow without killing her for hurting my brother. Wish me luck."

Her cackle is so loud I have to pull the phone away from my ear. "That poor woman has no idea who she's dealing with."

I smile. I'm counting on it.

KITTEN'S SONGS

I figured meeting Grace in public would force us to be on our best behavior. Besides, there's no way I'm stepping foot in her office again.

I'm not surprised at all, though, when I walk in and see her best friend Tessa sitting beside her. I met her the night of the ball at Blithewold, when Carter showed up with her as his date.

It feels like a lifetime ago, but in reality, it's only been a week.

At the time, I thought Tessa could be good for my brother. She didn't take shit from anyone, least of all Carter, and to my absolute shock, she had him eating out of the palm of her hand. That's something I've never witnessed when it comes to him.

Right now, though, she's wearing a tight expression as she watches me approach. She's here for Grace. God, the woman sure knows how to fool the people around her.

"You couldn't handle me on your own, Grace?" I quip as I reach the table.

She shrugs. "I just don't really *like* you, Cat. I figure if I have to share a meal with you, I might as well have my best friend along for the free lunch."

Tessa's eyes dart from her friend to me and then back again. "Down, girls. Down."

I take a deep breath and sit. "Well, at least you're not being fake. *Anymore.*"

Grace laughs. "Seriously, you are the one who needs help finding a man."

Flames erupt in my belly at her words. "Do you really think *I* need help finding someone to spend time with me?"

"Why else would Jonathan be begging me to take you on as a client?"

"To help *you.* Believe me, I'm not doing this of my own free will. I'm doing this because I had to cover up your bullshit lies that almost destroyed my family and *did* destroy Cash. Do you know how much you hurt him? Do you have any idea what you've done?"

Grace's cheeks redden and she remains silent. *Finally*, the woman shows the smallest hint of remorse.

But her best friend picks up where she left off. "You have no idea what you're talking about."

I roll my eyes. "I don't expect you to back me up, Tessa. She's your friend. I get it. But even you have to admit that what she did was pretty shitty."

The tension at the table eases momentarily when the server appears to take our drink orders. "I'll have a dirty martini," Grace says.

I almost smile. "I'll have the same. But make it extra dirty."

"As I was saying," Tessa says after she places her order and the server leaves us, "you have it all wrong."

Cocking my head to the side, I sit silently, waiting for her to get her little spiel over with. She's like a tiny dog barking at me, demanding an audience.

Tessa breathes out a long breath. "It was me. I'm the one to blame. Vanessa was upset at the party because she found out about Grace and Cash. She thought they were playing her the whole time."

"Well, *she* was," I say, tipping my chin toward Grace. "My brother would never do that, though."

Grace lets out a "ha!" in response, which only makes the fire smoldering inside me burn hotter.

Tessa jumps in again. "You and I both know that your brother was head over heels for Grace and that Grace continued to push him away. Let's not rewrite history."

Has this girl been brainwashed? Grace conned Cash. He had no idea she was married until after he fell for her. I open my mouth to speak, but Tessa holds up her hand.

"Can you please just let me get through this?"

I nod in acquiescence, ready to hear what other bullshit she's come up with.

Tessa exhales and pulls her shoulders back. "She was going on about how she was going to destroy your brother. The press would know what a player he was. Cat, she was acting crazy." Rolling her eyes, Tessa shakes her head and brushes a few loose strands of hair from her face. "I *thought* I was helping. I thought she was *your* friend."

"Yeah, me too," I mutter. I really can't believe yet another person I let into my life has betrayed me. My track record is shit.

"I thought if I told her *why* Grace stayed away from Cash for so long, she would understand. I explained that your brothers were all screwed up over your father's actions. I told her how Grace wanted to protect him from any bad press or any attention at all because he had enough on his plate. I never thought Vanessa would use what I told her to destroy your family *or* Grace. You have to believe me; if I thought for even a second that she would have done what she did…" Tessa stops and studies her clasped hands on the tabletop. "If I had a clue this would be the outcome, I never would have opened my mouth." Watching me with what looks like genuine remorse, she goes on. "I am so very sorry that your family has suffered because Carter trusted me. And I am so sorry that Grace has been the one to pay for my big mouth."

Cash isn't the only one spilling secrets, I guess. Thank God my brothers don't know my biggest one. It seems like I'm the only member of the James family who knows how to keep her mouth shut.

When our drinks arrive, I stare at my martini, twirling the olives through the liquid as I try to figure out what to say. How to move forward. Debate with myself about whether I believe them. Whether I should trust them.

"Listen," Grace says, breaking my train of thought, "you and I obviously got off on the wrong foot."

I tilt my head and take her in. That's the understatement of the century. Little does she know I've known about her for far longer than she's known about me.

She shifts in her chair. "I would really like to keep my word to Jonathan and help you. Or maybe we are just both helping Jonathan—I have no idea. But either way, if you can move on from the past now that you know there is no chance of your brother and me dating, we can work together. What do you say?"

I take a deep breath. I told Jay I was going to give this a chance. And while promises rarely mean anything these days, especially his, when I give my word, I mean it. So I hold out my hand to the woman who may still be my undoing. "Hello, Grace, my name is Cat James. It's nice to meet you."

Her eyes widen in surprise, and then she smiles and takes my hand. "It's nice to meet you too. Now, if you were looking for a man, what exactly would you be looking for?"

44

LABYRINTH BY TAYLOR SWIFT

Cat

Days later, I'm still angry with Jay and unwilling to rely upon his assurances that he'll take care of the threat against Chloe and me. I'm taking matters into my own hands. I know exactly who to call to get to the bottom of the threats. Jay wouldn't approve, but since he's the one who got us into this mess in the first place, I'm not giving him a say in the matter.

My daughter should be at home with me, and the only way I'll allow her anywhere near me is if I know with absolute certainty that she's safe. Jay said he took care of the threats, that the men who were after him remain clueless about my connection to him, but I don't trust a word out of his mouth.

So I called the one man I do trust. The one person who has been by my family's side no matter what it has cost him.

"I can't tell you how much I appreciate you looking into this," I say to Frank as his large frame settles in the chair in front of me.

He runs his hand against his lip. "Been a while since I've been in this office, Princess," he grates out.

"We're not going there," I say with a nervous laugh.

He smirks. "No shit. Your fiancé would kill me."

"You have *no* idea."

Tipping his head to the side, he examines me for a long moment. "Actually, I do. From what I've heard, the pretty boy is a lot more dangerous than either of us gave him credit for."

I laugh at the pretty boy comment. He *so* is. "He'd also kill you if you called him that."

Frank shrugs. "Pretty sure I could take him."

I laugh but tap my foot under my desk nervously. "So…what are we looking at? Is this a real threat?"

Frank leans forward and drops his elbows to his knees. "Yes. My brother was looking for information to hold over Jay. He still wants to know who stole from the Mob. He knows it wasn't Hanson. But I think his plan will work."

My breath catches. I'd always had my suspicions that Frank's family was involved with the Mob, but I didn't expect him to be so forthcoming about it. Nor did I understand just how involved his family was. "You're sure?"

He nods and leans back. "Yeah. They'll believe that Grace introduced you and Jay if that's what you sell to the press. Just fucking sell it. And since he owns a media company and you run the biggest magazine in the country—"

I stop him there. "I don't. I'm just an editor."

With a tip of his chin, he smirks. "You and I both know that Cynthia and Jay will make you editor in chief."

Anxiety swirls in my stomach at the thought. The announcement should be coming soon. What the hell are they waiting for?

"Maybe," I admit. "So you think I'll be safe? That Chloe will be?"

Frank studies me. "One day you'll tell me that story, right?"

I lick my lips and nod. Yes, one day soon they'll all know the truth.

"Yeah, I think you're both safe. And for extra protection, I let it slip that you and I were sleeping together until recently. Doubt my brother will suspect you've been involved with Jay."

"My brother won't take it nearly as well as yours if he ever finds out about you and me."

Frank coughs out a laugh. "No. He won't. Let's leave that as our little secret. It's over anyway, right?"

"Yeah, I think I'm really going to give it a shot with Jay."

His green eyes light up, and he claps his hand to his knee. "Fuck, that makes me happy."

"It does?" I ask. I can't hold back my surprise at his excitement.

"It really does. If anyone deserves to be happy, it's you, Cat."

"Not Princess?" I tease.

"Doesn't feel right anymore." He shrugs. "You're his now."

His.

Despite how angry I still am at Jay, the words don't feel wrong. I've always been his. I'm just not sure he's ever been mine.

"Yeah," I whisper. "Maybe."

"Now if only your brother would get out of his own damn way, he could be happy too."

My chest squeezes at the thought. I tried to talk to Cash after I met with Grace. I told him I made a mistake, that I jumped to the wrong conclusions, but he won't hear it.

He loves her, and the guilt I harbor over the role I played in their demise eats at me a little more every day. Now that I'm removed from it, now that I know Jay was never interested in her…now that I know the truth…I can see how happy she made my brother. I realize now that she isn't the horrible person I made her out to be.

And unfortunately, it may just be too late.

KITTEN'S SONGS

The next night, comforted by the information Frank provided, I sit across from my daughter. The bewildered expression as she silently works through all the information I've spewed at her is one I've seen on Jay's face so many times. Cynthia met us at my apartment after I picked up Chloe from Sophie's, and once dinner was over, I forced myself to open up about Jay.

"That was my father? In your office last week?" Her brows knit together and she nibbles on her lip nervously as she puts the pieces together.

I explained how her father came back into my life recently. That we've reconnected, but that's as far as we've gotten.

Gulping down my fears, I nod. "That was your father."

She picks at an invisible speck on the couch beside her leg and peers up at me. "That day…in your office…did he leave because of me?"

"No, Bug, absolutely not," I rush to assure her. "He left because of *me*." I squeeze my hands into fists to fight off the way they shake.

"Because he didn't know about me?" Her voice cracks on the last word.

I take another deep breath. "He didn't know about you, no. But not because I didn't want to tell him. I was going to tell him that night."

In my periphery, Cynthia shifts and folds her hands in her lap, but I keep my focus on Chloe.

"And he was upset?" she asks in the tiniest voice.

"He was upset that he didn't know you. He was *not* upset about you being here. Only that he's missed out on so much of your life."

"But I thought he didn't want to be part of my life," she says in a rush. She looks from me to Cynthia and then back again, wearing a frown. "Don't take the blame for him."

I glance at Cynthia. "There's no easy way to explain it. Yes, I told him about you, but he never got my messages. He had been in an accident, and when he recovered, he didn't have access to his phone. All this time, I thought he just left me. No one is to blame, Bug. It's just…a bad situation."

"And now? Does he want to know me?"

The crack in her voice has me dropping to my knees in front of her and resting my palms on her thighs. "*Yes*. He wants to know you and be a parent to you. How we go about this is up to you, and we can take it at whatever speed you want. But he absolutely wants to be a part of your life."

She inspects me for a moment, then lifts her gaze to Cynthia for reassurance.

"Chlo," she says in a soothing tone, "your father is a good man. Bad things happen sometimes, and people make mistakes, but I would never let you stay with him if I had even the slightest inkling that he would hurt you. You know that."

My girl nods, but she tucks her chin to her chest and twists the pendant that hangs around her neck, just like she always does when she's uncertain. We sit for a few moments in silence, and when she looks up, her blue eyes are swimming with tears. "I always wanted to meet him. I don't know why, but I just always did. Is that wrong?"

I have to blink the tears from my eyes and clear my throat before I can respond. "Not at all. It's natural to be curious about him, and I'm so relieved that the two of you have the chance to meet."

"And you'll be there?" Her eyes are huge. The unshed tears still shining in them make the blue of her irises glimmer more brightly. Her expression is a perfect mix of hope and fear. In this moment, she looks so young.

"Bug, you won't be able to get rid of me." I laugh, swiping at the tears that spill from my eyes.

"And you?" she asks Cynthia, who's moved to her side.

She squeezes Chloe's hand. "If you want me there, then yes. But I really think you and Cat should do this together."

With a nod, she glances at me, then focuses on Cynthia again. "You're still my mom, right?"

Cynthia wraps her arms around Chloe tightly and pulls her in for a hug. Tears shine in her eyes now too.

I drop to the floor and watch the interaction. Years ago, I made an impossible decision. One that has only grown more difficult with each passing year. But I'd make it again in a heartbeat. Because what Cynthia gave my daughter, what she continues to give her, is something so utterly beautiful in its complexity that it makes all of this worth it.

"Always, Chlo, always."

KITTEN'S SONGS

Hours later, I tuck Chloe in for the night. As I shuffle to her bedroom door, she calls for me. "Can you tell me about him?"

I take a minute to compose myself, sucking in a breath and fixing a smile to my face, then I turn back to her. "Of course. What do you wanna know?" I settle on the bed next to her and stroke her hair.

"How did you meet?"

Laughing, I poke her in the belly. "Well, you know how I've never been good at making a cup of coffee?"

"You're not very good at making anything in the kitchen," she replies far too quickly.

"Hey, that's mean!" I tease, although she's 100 percent right. "Anyway," I say when her giggles die down, "your dad owned a coffee shop."

Chloe sits up against the headboard and burrows into my side. She has no idea how much comfort she brings me. Just her proximity allows me to settle into the memories with a fondness I haven't felt in years.

"Like I said, I didn't know how to make a cup of coffee, but my friend asked me to watch over the coffee shop while she went to run an errand. While she was gone, a line a mile deep formed."

Chloe giggles. "A mile deep? *Right*."

I smile down at her and tug her closer. "Work with me here. So there was this big line, and this really aggravated girl who kept tapping her fingers against the counter. The guy at the front of the line was starting to get loud too. And it felt like every person in the shop was giving me attitude."

Chloe grins and shifts so she's looking at me.

"Yes, it was deserved, because I had no business being there. But still, I was freaking out."

"Until you saw my dad?" she chirps. Somehow, my girl is imagining my first run-in with Jay as a romance novel–worthy meet-cute.

"Um, no, I was still freaking out when I saw him, but he had this look." I pause, trying to put my finger on it, trying to remember precisely what I thought the moment I saw him all those years ago. Wondering if I knew even then that the moment would become such a turning point in my life.

"He was entranced," I say when the full memory takes shape in my mind. "Even though I was a disaster and had no idea what I was doing, he looked at me like my every move and my every word were charming."

"I love this story," Chloe says with a yawn. "So then what happened?"

"He asked for my name and number." I chuckle. "And I told him no."

Chloe's eyes go wide, and her mouth drops open. "Why?"

"Told him he had to earn it." I shrug. I can't help but grin when I remember his shocked expression. It matches the look on our daughter's face right now. God, she really does remind me of him. Those intelligent, soulful eyes light up, as if she's just as enchanted by me as her father was.

And it's in that moment that I know. There is no way I was revenge. The truth behind Jay's pleading is right there in my daughter's gaze.

Our story began that day. When a boy walked into a coffee shop and what he saw stole his attention. Reminded him that life was about more than revenge. The day a girl stood at the counter and locked eyes with her future. When she met a man who made her question so much while also giving her the space to find the answers herself.

Our parents had nothing to do with how we were brought together. No, that was the stars. And if I allow our parents to tear us apart, if I allow their tortured history to destroy what that couple from the coffee shop fought so hard for, then I'll be fighting against the stars.

45

LOVE ME AGAIN BY JOHN NEWMAN

Jay

I run my hands through my hair and groan as I look over the numbers again. Something doesn't add up. After the merger with the Jameses, I volunteered to go through the financials, since I'm familiar with both companies.

But I can't find any evidence of the things Theo was supposed to put in place or the plans we made. Either Cash has run this company into the ground in mere months, or we have a much bigger problem.

The truth, though, is that I'm using this as a distraction. I've been waiting for Cat to call me and tell me how her conversation went with Chloe. Will my daughter want to meet me? Will she allow me to get to know her?

I don't even know how to talk to a kid, let alone one who likely hates me.

Cat hasn't spoken to me since we left Grace's office. I told her I'd let her stay in her apartment if she allowed security to monitor her building. I didn't tell her that I'm the security. I sit outside with my security guard every night, just waiting for the moment she finally gives in. My neck hurts from sleeping in the car. Hopefully, she comes around sooner rather than later.

"Mr. Hanson," Elyse says through the intercom.

"Yes," I reply, thankful for the interruption. My thoughts are spiraling again.

"Ms. James is here to see you. Shall I send her in?"

My heart jumps at the sound of her name. "Yes, send her back." While I wait, I clear my desk and run a hand through my hair. I can only imagine what a mess it is. I've probably tugged on it a hundred times today. Then I blow my breath into my hand, checking that I smell okay.

I grab a mint just in case.

As the door to my office opens, I snatch the first thing I can find on my desk to make myself look busy and grimace when I realize I've picked up the stapler. I squeeze it a few times, because what the fuck else am I going to do?

"You okay over there?" she says, zeroing in on my hand.

I squeeze it a few more times and smirk. "Just working out my hands. I was getting a cramp. Don't you do this? If not, you should. It's totally good for your fingers…and you know how I need to keep my fingers strong."

Her face contorts as she scrutinizes me. "Are you okay?"

No.

"Who me? I'm fine. Why are you acting so weird?"

She lets out a nervous laugh and points to the chair. "Can I sit, or should I leave you alone to finish your workout?"

I drop the stapler like it's got rabies and the staples I've needlessly set free scatter across my desk. "All done." I turn my attention to her. "So, uh, to what do I owe the pleasure?"

She clears her throat, crosses her legs, and places her hands flat against her knee. "Well, um, I came to say that I think I was wrong."

"About?"

"Grace."

Surprised by the topic, I lean back in my chair and observe her for a moment. I want to ask her about Chloe, but maybe she's trying to let me down easy. Maybe Chloe wants nothing to do with me, and Cat is buttering me up with this. I rub my hand over my face and silence my racing thoughts. When I focus on Cat again, she's looking at me like I'm insane.

"Really? Why do you say that?"

She licks her lips, and my eyes track her tongue before it darts back. "I had lunch with her and Tessa. They told me everything. I'm...I'm sorry I didn't listen."

"That's hard for you, huh?" I tease, feigning a levity I don't feel. Hoping she can't see how I'm dying inside and silently begging her to get to what I really want to know.

She rolls her eyes. "I admit I didn't handle everything well. But to be fair, you sprang a lot of shit on me."

I blow out a breath and steeple my hands below my chin. "I did. And for the record, Kitten, I'm sorry too. I wish I could change the past."

She nods. "I know. My point is...maybe we could start over?"

"I'm not following."

"We're going to be married," she says, swallowing thickly. "If that's still what you want." She looks out the window before meeting my eyes. "I mean, if you just wanted the company, I understand."

"I want you," I blurt with far less finesse than I'm known for. Then I swallow my fears and put my heart on the line. "You're it for me, Cat. You are the only thing I want. You and Chloe...if she's open to meeting me, that is."

Cat drops her gaze to the floor, and my stomach plummets. But then she drags her focus back to me, and I'm hit with a look I wasn't ready for. Happiness. Maybe even relief. As if, maybe, just maybe, I said the right thing for once.

"She'd like to meet you."

"She would?" I practically shout in disbelief, bolting upright in my chair, which causes it to roll away from the desk.

She shakes her head, but her eyes remain bright. "Yes, but you have to play it cool."

"I'm cool." With a scoff, I give her the coolest look I have and hit her with a smolder.

She laughs and shuts her eyes. "No. No, you are not. But it's okay. I'm not cool when it comes to her either."

My chest squeezes at the smile on her face as I settle into easy banter with my favorite person. It's like coming home. A soft blanket that's worn in all the right places. "You're not?"

She shakes her head. "Not at all. Just don't go demanding we move in with you right away," she taunts.

I lean back in my chair and lace my fingers behind my head. "Not *right* away. But eventually, yes, you'll move in with me."

She puffs out a tedious breath. "We aren't uprooting Chloe any more than she already has been."

"Cat, my place is huge. She'll have her pick of rooms, a pool on the roof, *the hot tub*." I waggle my brows. Okay, maybe that incentive is more for my fiancée. She always did love the hot tub.

Her exhale is harsh instead of airy like I hoped. "I could have all those things too, Jay. I'm not marrying you for your money."

I chuckle softly. At least she's dropped the being forced into marriage bit. She's almost got me convinced that she wants it too—that she wants *us* too.

"I'm aware, Kitten. Fuck, am I aware. I just..." I scrub a hand through my hair. "I want to give Chloe everything. I've missed out on so much."

She gives me a soft smile, her lip tipping up as if she's in on her own joke. "I'd like to say all she wants is your time, but she does like the finer things in life..." She laughs and gets this far-off look. "Last week, Cynthia took her to Sienna Langfield's shop, and she hasn't stopped talking about it."

"She likes fashion?" I'm desperate for any information she'll give me about our daughter.

Cat's smile grows. It's full of pride, and she wears it so fucking well. I love seeing her like this. Easy. It all comes so damn easy to her. There's something so beautiful about that. Cat has struggled her entire life trying to figure out who she is, what she is, who she wants to be, but there is no struggle when it comes to her role as a mother.

"She loves fashion. And music…" She peeks up at me through her black lashes, and a moment passes between us. *Music*. It's always been our thing.

"I can work with that." I rub my hand over my mouth and blow out a steady breath, then add, "Thank you, Cat."

"For what?" Her brows knit together.

I ache to smooth out those lines, to kiss that very spot.

"For sharing. I know this isn't easy, and I know it's not the life you envisioned…" I study the wood grain of my desk. I can't look at her, or I'll lose my nerve. "But I hope you'll give us a chance. Give *me* a chance." True hope ignites in me for the first time. Not just a spark, but a real flame, small as it may be. I risk a look at her to gauge her reaction, hope daring to peek out after a decade in hiding.

She holds my gaze, her eyes more amber than their usual whiskey color, and I get lost in a dream that life could be different for us. That she and Chloe and I can be a real family. She clears her throat and finally speaks. All my focus is fixed on her lips as the words form. "I'd like that. But if I'm being honest, I'm still not sure I trust you."

"But you're open to trying? To letting this be something more than just an arrangement?"

"Yes." Her answer is quick but quiet. Like she couldn't keep it from slipping out. She appears almost surprised by it.

"Fuck, why can't you two just move in with me? God, I want to skip all the awkward parts and get to the good."

"Jay," she laughs, "I said I'd try. We aren't even dating yet."

I smirk. "You're my fiancée, Kitten. I think we're past the dating."

"But that's my point," she murmurs, pushing her hair behind her ear. "We never got to date. Not even back then. I was always your dirty little secret."

I fling myself back in my chair and ball my hands into fists on the armrests. "*No, you weren't.* We may have liked things dirty, Cat, and I know for a fact you still do," I growl, "but make no mistake, I told the people who mattered."

She arches a brow. "Not my brother, who was allegedly your best friend."

I blow out a breath. This won't be easy. "I really did like Carter. At times it put me at war with myself, but I was dedicated to my father. To our revenge."

Her chin stiffens. "And me?"

"You were everything. You *are* everything. And I know it will take a long time to prove it to you, and I know I've made millions of mistakes and will likely make more, but trust me when I say that I'm going to make it right. I'll give you the future you deserve. One you both deserve."

Her eyes glisten with unshed tears as she gives me a slight nod.

Giving in to the need to be closer, I stand and settle myself in front of my desk with one ankle crossed over the other.

In the chair in front of me, Cat runs her tongue along her lips and gives me a thorough once-over. Every inch of me her eyes rake over ignites until I'm afraid I'll burn the building down.

"Better stop looking at me like that if you don't want me to bend you over this desk right now."

A surprised laugh escapes her. "And how am I looking at you?"

"Like you *want* me to bend you over this desk and do dirty things to you with these fingers I've been working so hard on." I wiggle my fingers.

340

She guffaws but quickly schools her expression. "There will be no bending anyone over any desks."

"Oh yeah?" I challenge.

"We're dating, Jay. Getting to know one another. Building a foundation." She lectures me like she's the teacher, and I'm the wayward student.

Fuck, she's hot when she bosses me around.

"When can I meet her? Tonight?" I ask, dropping my palms to my desk and angling closer to her.

She shakes her head, but she's smiling the whole time, her eyes sparkling with humor. "Can't. I'm going out with Grace to discuss my dates."

I groan and run my hand over my face. "I take it back. That's the worst idea I've ever had. I don't want you dating anyone but me. Even if it's fake."

She laughs and stands. And then suddenly she's pressing her body to mine. With one hand planted on my chest, she brushes her lips against my cheek and whispers, *"Petit à petit, l'oiseau fait son nid."*

It's so surprising I don't even have a chance to wrap my arms around her before she's pulling away.

"What does that mean?"

Her eyes dance. "Literally? Little by little, the bird makes its nest."

I bark out a laugh. "Why the hell did you say it? I mean it was sexy as fuck."

She smirks. "It means slowly but surely, Mr. Hanson. Patience."

"The only French I know is ménage à trois."

She giggles. "This is going to be so much fun, Mr. Hanson."

My heart stutters, and a bolt of desire races through me. "Let the games begin, future Mrs. Hanson."

KITTEN'S SONGS

From my spot at the bar, I have an unobstructed view of the entrance, allowing me to monitor every person who enters the restaurant. But it's Kevin who spots them. "Kitten. Five o'clock," he practically shouts, nudging me in the ribs.

Garreth swirls the liquid in his rocks glass, the ice inside clanking. "You aren't a fucking spy. Just say you see Cat sitting in the corner."

"And don't ever use that fucking nickname again," I say, shooting him a warning glare.

Kevin downs his drink. "Well, aren't you two a good time? Why am I here again?"

Garreth sips his drink, watching me over the rim. "The same reason we've all become puppets for my little brother. Because of her." He nods in Cat's direction.

Despite my brother's annoyance with me, I can't help but smile at the woman across the room. Her lips are painted a deep red and her cheeks are highlighted by bronzer, but tonight her hair is what draws my attention. She cut it.

And it's drastic.

She's always had long, dark hair that sways as she walks. But the woman I can't take my eyes off sits at a small table with Grace, martini in hand, with hair cut to her chin. The new style highlights her long neck, tempting me to march over there and press a kiss up every inch.

"Fucking gorgeous," I mutter, mesmerized, before taking another sip of my drink and leaving the men at the bar.

I don't miss the good-natured grumble Garreth lets out. Yeah, he's right. I'm fucking gone for her. Have been for a long, long time.

No point in denying it. My brother knows the truth, anyhow. Every single decision we've made over the last decade has been in preparation for this moment.

The moment I finally take back what's mine.

They haven't spotted me yet, so I pause nearby when Grace asks Cat what she's looking for in a man.

Cat peruses the patrons around her, focused and determined, and when she's found what she's looking for, her eyes light up. But fuck, it's not me she's pointing at. It's a couple engrossed in conversation at the bar.

"Him," she says.

The fuck?

He's good-looking, sure, in that dark, broody way, I suppose. But he looks like an uptight asshole to me.

"Why him?" Grace asks.

Yeah. Why him? What's she got against hot blond men with a sense of humor and impeccable taste in fashion?

Cat's red lips turn up in a smile. "He's looking at her like my brother looked at you. Not a woman in this room could tear his gaze away. I want to be that for someone. I want someone to *feel* that way about me. But I want him to almost lose control in his thirst for me. I want him hungry. Desperate for me. Find me that, Grace. Anything less isn't worth my time."

My heart pounds in my chest. Yeah, she's ready.

"Got it. One insanely hot, narcissistic asshole coming up," Grace teases.

I can't help but laugh. Loudly. "Did someone summon me?"

Cat's eyes dart to mine, and she shakes her head, but the smile remains on her face. That's right, baby, I'm here. I'm the one you've been looking for. And I swear to God her eyes are saying the exact same thing. She knows it, and I know it. Fucking finally, we're both on the same damn page.

"You ladies enjoying dinner?" I ask as I squeeze Grace's shoulder. I lean down and kiss her cheek and whisper in her ear. "Is she playing nice?"

She laughs and motions to the chair beside her. "We're fine. Join us for dinner? Or do you have a date tonight?"

Before replying, I move to the object of my desire and press a kiss to the spot just below her ear. "Completely. Irrevocably. Head over fucking heels. Our life begins tomorrow, Kitten. You own me," I whisper.

She bites her lip and shakes her head, but her eyes are wide and filled with wonder.

Turning back to Grace, I reply, "Can't. Just wanted to stop and say hi to my two favorite girls. Make sure you're playing nice." I wink at Grace and then look back at Cat, because honestly, I can't take my damn eyes off her. "I'd ask you to join us for a drink after dinner, but I don't want my friends looking at either of you the way I know they will."

Grace pouts. "After all I've been through, you'd deny me a fun night of no strings attached?"

"Don't even think about it, Gracie. You deserve better than all of them. You deserve better than everyone in this damn restaurant."

"Thanks, Jay. Enjoy your drinks."

Before I walk away, I pin Cat with a look and mouth, "Only you."

Then I stride back to the guys, because tonight is the last night before my life begins again. And I'm going to enjoy it.

46

CARDIGAN BY TAYLOR SWIFT

Cat

"**I** need you to dress me," I shout as I walk into the models' closet. Inside, Dexter has Sophie pressed up against the wall. One hand is splayed across her breast, and the other grips her hip tightly.

I roll my eyes. They never stop. "Guys, focus!"

Dexter groans as Sophie pulls away and rights her shirt.

But my best friend ignores his protests. "Oh my God, Cat," she says, eyes wide. "Your hair looks fucking amazing."

I finger the ends nervously. "You think?"

Dex nods. "You look hot."

"You're like a mom but hotter," Sophie teases.

I snort. "You goof. But seriously, I need help. What does one wear when introducing her daughter to her long-lost father who until recently was thought to be the devil incarnate but is actually quite likable and she maybe sort of likes him but wants him to suffer a bit longer before putting him out of his misery?"

Dex blinks a few times and Sophie bursts out laughing.

"Oh, I love this version of you." Without another word, she whips around and sifts through the racks of clothes. "Dex, where is that red sweater with the slouchy neck and the open shoulder?"

Dex blinks again and then mutters, "With the flat black boot, right?"

"And the jeans with the buttons instead of zippers."

"Fuck, Soph, you're hot when you talk fashion with me."

All I can do is grin at the two of them as they move around the closet in synchronization, each grabbing items as they go. In a matter of minutes, they've collected five outfits and are shooing me toward the closet. "The others are for any upcoming outings, but start with the sweater. I think that will be perfect for tonight." Sophie winks.

Dex mumbles something about giving us privacy, then he grasps the back of Sophie's neck and gives her a searing kiss before disappearing out the door with a nod in my direction.

"*God*," I breathe, "how do you get anything done with that around all the time?"

Her eyes are still on the door, and her jaw is a little slack. After a moment, she blinks and licks her lips. "We like to keep it interesting."

"You make marriage look easy." I sigh. Will my marriage to Jay be like that? Easy? Or will I always harbor these insecurities?

Sophie cocks a hip and raises her brows. "You wanna know what marriage is? Last night, I'm giving Dex a blowjob, and I'm really getting into it, you know?" She pauses, seriously waiting for me to acknowledge the idea of her giving her husband head.

All I can do is smile and nod. My best friend is ridiculous.

Seemingly satisfied that I'm listening, she continues. "In the middle of it, he cups my chin, and I'm feeling myself, loving the way his thumb brushes against my cheek so damn reverently. I feel like one of those girls in a romance novel. So cherished...or so I think. Suddenly, there's a tug on my chin, so I look up, thinking he's going to hit me with some dirty talk. Call me his dirty little slut or something. Nope. The fucking guy is yanking on a damn hair on my chin. He smiles and says, 'Sorry. That was distracting me.'"

I squeal in laughter, but Sophie doesn't stop. "A fucking hair was distracting him during a blowjob."

"Did you stop?" I say between broken breaths.

"No. I let him come on my face, but that is totally not the point of the story."

"Okay, I'll bite. What's the point of the story?"

She takes a deep breath. "Marriage is about friendship. Laughing at the absurd moments. Together. Because, of course, after he gave me a facial, we laid in bed and giggled over it. It's stealing those special moments, especially when you've got kids. And I'm so fucking excited for you to experience it, Cat. I have a feeling tonight is going to be the first step in your happily ever after."

Fighting back tears, I pull Sophie in for a hug. "You're a good friend," I whisper.

"I'd be a better friend if I told you that facials are really good for your skin." She tilts closer so I can inspect the smooth skin on her face.

She *does* look radiant today, and now I'm a teensy bit concerned she's serious.

I take my time trying on all the outfits, saving the red sweater for last so I don't have to change when I get home. Dex and Sophie were right; it's perfect. It shows off a hint of skin on my shoulders, and the slouchy neck highlights my new haircut.

"What are you guys having for dinner?" Sophie asks as we head toward the elevators.

I trip over my own foot—the black boots Dexter suggested fit perfectly—because I haven't even thought about food for tonight. "Shit, Soph, I didn't get that far. I have no idea." Panic claws at my chest.

"Calm down, drama queen. Pizza should work." She furrows her brow and inspects me like I've lost my mind.

"He's a billionaire, Soph. Do billionaires eat pizza?"

Sophie cackles. "He eats waffles from a street vendor; I'm sure pizza is fine."

"Don't you *dare* diss Ivan's waffles. Those things are spectacular."

"Cat." My best friend shakes her head, clearly fighting back a grin. "Do your brothers eat pizza?"

I shrug. "Yeah."

"Do *you* eat pizza?"

"Um, yeah."

"Then I think it's safe to say Jay does too, you weirdo. Seriously, get out of your head."

"What if she hates him?" My chest aches at the mere thought. Because how could we possibly make this work if Chloe isn't on board?

Sophie tilts her head and searches my face. "Jay can be an ass, for sure, and he's done some pretty stupid things, but in general, he's a loveable guy. I mean, even when you hated him, you still couldn't resist him."

I blow out a breath. "You're right. He is so freaking annoying in that way. She'll probably like him more than she likes me."

47

DANDELIONS BY RUTH B.

Jay

"How are you feeling?" Hayden asks the second I accept his video call request.

"Nervous as fuck," I admit.

Garreth and Hayden may be twins, but they're easy to differentiate. Garreth's golden hair and beard are always perfectly groomed, and his blue eyes are piercing in a cold way. Hayden, on the other hand, has long, unruly hair that hangs to his shoulders, though he usually keeps it back in a bun of some sort, like it is right now. His shoulders are broad, and he's more cut than his twin, since he spends all his free time playing one sport or another. And he has laugh lines around his eyes and mouth because the guy is never not smiling.

"Maybe bring a gift?" he suggests. "Any idea what she likes?"

I point at the screen of my phone. "You are fucking brilliant. Of course I should bring a gift. Cat said she's into fashion."

Hayden chuckles and runs his hands over his mouth, eyeing my suit as he does. "Of course she is."

Yes, I like nice things. I own that.

"She went to Sienna Langfield's shop last week and loved everything. I need her number."

My brother scoffs. "I meant get her flowers or something, not a fucking commissioned outfit from a famous designer."

I laugh as I type out a text to Elyse, asking her to get me Sienna's information. "*An* outfit? As if I'd get her just one."

Hayden drops his head back and lets out a groan. "Jay," he says when he rights himself again, "you've barely met her and she's already got you wrapped around her finger."

"She's part Cat, part me. The two people I like most in the world. Obviously, she's going to be awesome."

"Oh my God, you are so full of yourself. Just get her flowers."

"Of course. She wears the yellow diamond necklace I gave Cat years ago, so I'll pick up yellow flowers. Definitely not yellow roses, though. That's what I was holding the first time we met, and I'd rather not relive that moment."

"You'll do fine. Just be yourself." He grins. "Strike that. Maybe be a little less yourself. More humble, less cocky."

I smirk. "Don't worry. I'll save all the cocky for Cat."

Hayden rolls his eyes. "Can't wait to meet her. Think I can when I come next week?"

"Hope so. We'll see how it goes. I'm letting her and Cat guide how fast or slow we take this. If it were up to me, Cat and I would head down to city hall and make it official, and I'd have them both living with me by the end of the day."

I sigh. Somehow that feels like it's a pipe dream.

My brother smiles his signature smile, his eyes crinkling. "I'm happy for you, Jay. You deserve it."

"Thanks." Sitting back in my chair, I run a hand through my hair. "I'm not sure I do, but I'm taking my shot anyway."

KITTEN'S SONGS

I step out of the elevator holding a bouquet of yellow daisies for Chloe and a fall bouquet for Cat. The arrangement is Cat in flower form. All burnt oranges, yellows, and hints of red berries mixed throughout. At the door, my girl is cradling a pizza box and digging through her purse to pay the delivery man.

"I've got it," I say, pulling out my wallet as I hustle to the door.

Cat looks up like a deer in headlights, all wide eyes and nervousness. Her shoulder is peeking out of her red sweater, temping me to drop a kiss there to ease the tension. But instead, I drag my attention away from her and deal with the pizza guy. Once he's headed to the elevator, I turn back to a speechless Cat. With wild eyes and heaving panicked breaths, she takes a step out of her apartment and slams the door behind her.

"Fucking stunning," I whisper as I lean in and kiss her cheek, enjoying how she instantly turns pink at my words. "We gonna go in there, Kitten, or are we eating in the hall?"

That snaps her out of her stupor, and with an eye roll, she sighs. "I just thought we should talk—make a plan—before going back in there." She nods toward the door.

I tangle my fingers in her shorter hair and tug gently before I push it behind her ear. "I thought *I* was freaking out, but you're putting me to shame right now." Hoping to ease the tension she's carrying, I give her one of my devastating smiles.

She leans against the door, settling a bit. "I ordered pizza," she says weakly, holding up the box.

Chuckling, I nod. "Is that what that is?"

"You like pizza, right?"

I bark out a laugh. "Cat, pretty sure we ate pizza in bed all those years ago. Like every other night."

She blows out a breath, but she avoids my gaze. Instead, she focuses on something behind me. "Right."

"What's wrong, Kitten?"

She sighs, but she still won't look at me. "I don't cook."

"I don't need a chef."

"No, like, I don't cook, period. I'm not good at this mom thing...and I'll probably be terrible at the wife thing."

Crouching low, I gently set both bouquets on the floor. Then I take the pizza box from her hands and place it next to them. When I straighten, I angle in close to her and lift her chin with my thumb, forcing her to finally look at me so she hears my every word.

"I haven't had the honor of witnessing you as a mother, but just hearing you talk about her? And seeing all you've done for her over the last twelve years? The choices you've made..." I cup her cheek and swipe the pad of my thumb back and forth. "I'm in awe of you, Kitten." Taking a step closer, I ghost my lips across her mouth. "And as for being a wife..." I chuff out a dark laugh. "Food is the last thing I want from you, Catherine."

The gold flecks in her eyes meld together, and tears threaten to spill over her lashes. "What do you want from me, Jay?" she whispers, her lips brushing against mine with her every word.

"All of you." I pull back an inch or two. "These lips," I say as her tongue darts out to moisten them. "This heart." I press my free hand flat against her chest, relishing the wild way it beats against my fingertips. Sliding my hand around her neck, I drop my forehead to hers and pull her so her mouth meets mine. "This body. Fuck, baby, you own me, and I'll take anything you're willing to give me. But I promise, the last thing you should ever feel is insecure as a mother or as a wife. Because to me, you're perfect."

Her eyes soften, and she swallows thickly. "I like you like this," she whispers.

I dig my fingers into the back of her neck, barely holding myself back. "And how am I, Cat?"

Her tongue darts out again. "Unhinged, sweet, devoted. Maybe a tiny bit mine."

I can't help but laugh. "I'm 100 percent yours. And those other things? For you, yeah, I'm all of those."

She stares at me for what feels like forever, her eyes never leaving mine, but she doesn't respond.

I kiss the tip of her nose and release her, knowing that if I take her lips the way I want to right now, I'll be inside of her in less than a minute, and that's not what this night is about.

Releasing her neck, I lean down to grab the pizza and the flowers. But I don't miss the disappointed look that crosses her beautiful features.

"And Cat," I say as I open the door to her apartment, "I'm glad you like me." I pause and smirk in her direction. "Because I'm fucking obsessed with you."

48

MESS IS MINE BY VANCE JOY

Cat

Two seconds. That's all I allow myself. Two seconds to lean against the wall and smile so big my cheeks hurt. Then I take a deep breath, square my shoulders, and follow Jay inside.

Tonight is not about us. There's a little girl here who needs to know that this man is interested in getting to know *her*. That he's not just coming around because of me.

It's not even a concern in my mind. I know Jay. I've always known him, even when I wouldn't acknowledge it. It's why I struggled to trust what my grandfather said about him all those years ago. Because this Jay, *my Jay*, would never turn his back on his daughter.

He didn't willingly turn his back on me.

And after almost thirteen years of suffering for the both of us, it's time to focus on the good. It's okay for me to move forward. Because I want the man who's standing in the center of my living room, taking in each detail as if he's cataloging it for later and waiting for the moment he lays his eyes on Chloe again.

If he's nervous, he doesn't let it show. Steady hands slide the pizza box onto the stove top and set the two bouquets on the kitchen counter. Then warm blue eyes are tracking the space, searching for our missing puzzle piece.

"Chlo," I holler. "Jay's here." In a lower voice, I say to him, "She likes listening to music while she does her homework."

He nods in acknowledgment, but his gaze remains focused on the hallway where faint strains of music are floating through the air.

"Want a glass of wine? Beer? Or whiskey?" I offer. "I only have James Whiskey, though," I tease.

Jay grimaces. "Soon it will be one and the same, beautiful. You ready to tell your brothers we're switching grains so that their whiskey can get on par with Hanson?"

Rolling my eyes, I mutter under my breath, "Cocky bastard."

At the sound of a door opening, we both dart glances at the hallway. Then Chloe is standing at the edge of the kitchen, swaying back and forth awkwardly.

Taking a deep breath, I jump in to introduce them. "Chlo, you remember Jay from my office? Jay, this is Chloe. Our...*daughter*." The last words are whispered as the enormity of the moment settles on all of us. It's like a fog lifts, making everything around us more clear.

Two sets of matching bright blue eyes blink at one another, and then Jay is moving in her direction.

My heart stops at the sight, and I hold my breath in anticipation of what he'll do.

"It's good to see you again, Chloe," he says, holding out his hand to greet her.

I have to bite down on my bottom lip to hide my smile as I watch the adorable train wreck. It's not his fault he doesn't know how to talk to kids, but shaking her hand? Oof.

Chloe blinks at his outstretched hand, then looks past him to me. For a split second, her eyes are filled with humor. I lift my chin and smile, encouraging her.

She presses her lips together and slides her hand into his. "Nice to see you too," she says. Her tone is all awkward and slightly teasing.

360

"I ordered pizza," I say, breaking the tension in the room.

"Yeah," Jay chirps, "your mom was afraid that billionaires don't eat pizza."

Chloe laughs. "Considering she doesn't cook, you better get used to it."

Struck by the way Jay referred to me as *mom* and Chloe didn't correct him, I'm left gaping at them.

Chloe tilts her head sheepishly and says, "Come on, we still love you," as if she believes I'm upset by their teasing.

What she doesn't know is that this moment—the easy way Jay referred to me as her mom and how the two of them instantly ganged up to tease me—is probably the greatest moment of my life. And this is only the beginning.

KITTEN'S SONGS

"And you got to go backstage?" Chloe asks, her eyes wide.

Jay eats up her excitement, a boyish grin falling across his face. "Even better." He nods. "Afterward, I went out with them and sang karaoke."

"Shut up. Cat, did you hear that?" Chloe asks, like I'm not sitting at the table with them. "Jay sang with Harry Styles."

Jay holds a slice of pizza up and winks at me across the table. Every cell in my body screams *we love this man*.

Turning to Chloe, I avoid blurting that out and reply, "Yeah, I heard him." I grin and turn back to my fiancé. "Harry must have been drunk to agree to sing with the likes of you."

Jay smirks. "I happen to remember you loving my voice, Kitten."

The blush that burns my cheeks is instantaneous.

"Kitten?" Chloe asks, her nose scrunching.

A breathy laugh leaves my throat, and I shake my head at Jay. He's sporting a grin and wiping his hands with his napkin in satisfaction.

"Your mom never told you that's her nickname?"

The way he continues to call me her mom and the way he smiles at me *and* our daughter shreds all my defenses. I'm putty in this man's hands, and he knows it.

She shakes her head. "She *did* tell me she refused to give you her name the first time you met."

Jay throws his head back and guffaws. "Pretty sure that's the moment I fell in love," he says. His irises glitter, pulling me under his spell.

Chloe's smile says it all. She's enjoying herself.

"And when I finally caught her name, I told her I thought she seemed more like a Kitten than a Cat."

I laugh. "And the name stuck."

Jay cocks a brow. "Don't act like you don't like it."

Shaking my head, I try to fight back a grin, but it's no use. "You told me you fell in love with me when I punched you."

Chloe cackles at that. "*What?*"

In response, Jay only shrugs. "What can I say? I'm a glutton for punishment."

"But why did you punch him?" Chloe asks with a mouth full of pizza.

"Because he grabbed me as I was walking off the train, and I didn't know it was him."

Chloe purses her lips and nods like that makes complete sense. Good, at least she knows what to do if a stranger approaches.

"Frappadingue," she whispers.

All I can do is laugh in agreement.

"Wait, what did she say?" Jay asks.

Chloe giggles as I reply, "She called you crazy. Or, more accurately, a nutcase."

Jay glowers at us, and we both giggle.

362

"How'd you get her to talk to you?" she asks.

He rubs his thumb over his lip and smirks. "I gave her a song."

"No," I retort. "You *stole* my iPod. *Then* you gave me a song."

Chloe gasps and drops her crust onto her plate. "You stole her iPod?"

"And wiped her entire playlist. The only songs she could listen to were the ones I put on there."

We smile at one another across the table. They're soft and goofy and probably cheesy as hell. But the comfort of returning to the past in this way is like finding a favorite teddy bear to cuddle with in bed.

I want to be cheesy with him. I want to be cheesy with them both.

"Which song did you give her?" Chloe asks.

"'Poker Face' by Lady Gaga," I tell her. "I still don't know why you picked that."

Jay licks his lips. "I think you do." He laughs softly to himself. "I think you know exactly why."

Twisting my lips, I acknowledge that he's probably right. He was trying to get to know me, but I hid myself well. And maybe I still do. Sophie says I don't let people in. That I make people work for my affection. But Jay knew precisely how to get it. I'm not sure he even had to try that hard.

Then or now.

No one else saw me back then. It always felt like no one really tried. Not even my brothers. But Jay did. And he told me I was beautiful.

I hum. "Maybe," I whisper. Before I let the past swamp me with emotion, I stand and collect our plates. "It's getting late, Chlo. You should say good night and get in the shower."

Jay stands as well and tucks a hand in his pocket. "I—uh—got you something," he hedges, his attention on Chloe.

She peers up at him, then darts a glance at me. When I nod, she turns back. "Oh yeah?"

He pulls his hand from his pocket and holds out a silver device.

Tears well in my eyes the instant I see it. *This man.* He knows precisely what he's doing.

"Like I said before, I used music to get to know your mom. You and I have a lot of time to make up for, and since I can't see you every day…" He trails off and looks to me, silently pleading for my help, like he thinks he's screwing up.

Lips squeezed tight so I don't sob, I nod in encouragement.

He closes his eyes for a second, like he's searching for strength. Then he looks back at our daughter. "I got you an iPod. Would it be okay to send you a song every day?"

Chloe beams. "Really? Can I see it?"

I turn toward the sink and swipe a tear from my cheek while the two of them chatter about the playlist he's created. My focus remains on the dishes until I feel Jay's breath against my neck.

Banding one arm around my waist, he takes the dish that I've been furiously scrubbing and places it in the sink. "I think this one's clean, Kitten," he whispers. Then he drops a kiss below my ear, eliciting a moan from me. "Now spin around and tell me why you're hiding from me."

Jay gives me space to turn, but as soon as I do, I bury myself in his chest and grip the front of his shirt. "Not hiding," I murmur.

His chest shakes with silent laughter. "Oh yeah? Coulda fooled me." He cups my jaw and tilts my head so that I'm forced to meet his beautiful blue eyes. "Hi," he whispers.

"Hi," I murmur back, lost in euphoria. Because tonight far surpassed my expectations.

"Can I kiss you?"

His focus dips to my lips. When I nod, he presses a hand to the small of my back and pulls me so close our bodies are flush against one another. Then his mouth is finally on mine.

It's a quick kiss, just our lips fused together. No groping, no tongues.

364

Just a softness, as if he needed to breathe in a little of me, much like I did him, though I didn't realize it until now.

But that's how Jay has always been. Giving me things before I even ask. Before I even know I need them.

"Tu m'as manqué," I whisper against his lips.

His brows pinch together. "You said that the first time I kissed you again. What does it mean?"

"*I missed you.*" And no truer words have ever been spoken. I missed this man so much it feels like I'm finally coming up for air after a lifetime without it.

He smiles and presses another soft kiss against my mouth. "Do you think it went okay?" he asks, his eyes swimming with vulnerability and his hold on me tightening.

Smiling, I nod. "You knocked it out of the park."

He glances over his shoulder to the hallway, and when he turns back to me, a smile pulls at his lips. "She's amazing. You've done a really good job with her."

Leaning back against the counter, I give us both some space. "It was all Cynthia."

From below his ever-falling lock of hair, Jay peeks at me in that shy way I rarely see these days. "No, Catherine, it was you too. I'm not denying what Cynthia did for our daughter, but don't discount what you did either. I just hope she gives me a chance to get to be something to her as well."

I swallow, at a loss for words, unsure whether the right ones even exist. But I know Chloe, so the right answer slips out anyway. "She will. The iPod idea was sweet, by the way."

"You two have your own little language. I want something like that."

I can't help the laugh that slips out at his despondent expression. "It's not our own little language, Jay. It's French. An entire country speaks it along with us, as do the Canadians."

365

He laughs and turns shyly toward the hallway again. "You know what I mean."

I smile. "I do."

Jay studies me before slipping his hands back into his pockets. "I'll let you get to bed. When can I see her again?"

"Whenever you want. You're her father, Jay. I'm not going to stand between the two of you. I want you to get to know one another."

He gives me that boyish grin again. "And what about her mother? When can I finally take you on a date?"

I shrug. "My calendar is pretty full right now. Lots of dates coming up, so I'm not sure."

Jay lunges for me and grasps me around the middle, tickling me. "Fake dates," he reminds me.

"Oh, I know. Wouldn't want you to have to hurt anyone else," I tease, but we both sober at my words.

Jay palms my cheeks and then kisses each one. "How many bedrooms does this place have anyway?" he asks.

Surprised by the question, I squint at him. "Two, why?"

Jay pulls me in for a hug, and his laughter tickles my ear. "Just figuring out where I'll stay when we finally announce our engagement," he teases, pulling back and waggling his brows. "*Roomie.*"

I roll my eyes and guide him to the door.

"One-bed tropes are my favorite, Kitten."

"Go home, you fool." I laugh as I push him out the door.

Before I can shut it, he hauls me into the hall, presses me against the wall, and kisses me. He licks at my lips until I let him in with a moan, then grinds against me. "Soon, Kitten," he mutters against my lips, "soon *this* will be my home."

49

YOUR SONG BY ELTON JOHN

Cat

I'm still getting used to being responsible for getting another human up and moving in the morning. Every day is a mad rush to shower, get dressed, make sure Chloe's dressed, pack lunches, and somehow find time to gulp down a liberal dose of caffeine before we're out the door. I don't know how anyone does this with more than one child. Or smaller children.

I'm still blow drying my hair five minutes before we have to leave to get her on the bus. She rushes into the bathroom, iPod in hand, shrieking, but I can't understand a word because of the hair dryer.

With a toothbrush in her mouth, she pushes it toward me. "He sent me a song" is what I think she says.

Turning the hair dryer off, I give her my attention. "Oh yeah?"

She presses one earbud into my ear and the other into hers and hits Play. Looking down at the iPod screen, she narrows her gaze. "Elton John?"

Smiling, with tears in my eyes, I take her hand and watch as she listens to the words of "Your Song."

KITTEN'S SONGS

Sophie appears at my door at nine a.m. with two cups of coffee in hand. Holding one high, she struts inside, her eyes glittering with excitement. "This is all yours if you spill how last night went."

Huffing a laugh, I hold out a hand, motioning to the chair opposite my desk.

She slides one cup of coffee onto my desk and plops down, bouncing in anticipation.

I, on the other hand, take a long sip before replying, enjoying the way she surveys me while she waits for the details.

When she lets out an exaggerated sigh and taps an imaginary watch on her wrist, I laugh.

"It was good."

"Girl, I did not get up early and take my fat ass to your favorite coffee shop only to hear that *it was good*." She gives me a withering look. "Tell me *everything*."

"So dramatic." I giggle.

Her eyes bulge and her chin dips in exasperation.

"It was…" I sigh, remembering the way Jay and Chloe got on yesterday. The way he held me in the kitchen. The way he kissed me against the door. How he affirmed my role as a mother and told me he's obsessed with me, that one day he hopes our home will be his. "Perfect."

Sophie wears a knowing smile. "Oh, you are so falling for him again."

I push my tongue against my teeth, but my smile can't be hidden. "Shut up."

"You're falling for your future husband."

"I should fucking hope so," Jay rasps from the door. The cocky grin he sports when my eyes snap to him has me full-on beaming.

"Morning," I say, hiding behind my coffee cup and drinking up the delicious way he looks today.

He watches my perusal of him, smiling like the smug bastard he is.

He's in a navy blue suit today. The color makes his eyes glow, and that blond hair that drives me wild is already falling forward. He makes his way into my office with two take-out boxes in hand. "Thought maybe we could have breakfast together," he says, pressing a soft kiss against my lips. The way he approaches me, as if he has every right to, as if this is the new normal, makes my heart skip a beat.

My eyes find his as he pulls back, and I savor his soft smile. "Good morning."

The skin around his eyes crinkles. "It's a great morning if I start it like this, beautiful." He kisses me softly again and only pulls away when Sophie clears her throat.

"I'll give you two some privacy," she teases. "But you owe me lunch, Cat." She points at me and stands, smoothing her skirt as she does.

"Sounds good. Thanks for the coffee," I add, holding it up.

"Oh," she says, turning in the doorway, "do you want Dexter to pick up Chloe from school and bring her right to our house so you don't have to go back and forth before your date?"

The growl that rumbles through Jay's chest is hard to miss. I press my hand to his cheek and massage away the scowl but keep my attention on Sophie. "Yeah, that works. Thanks."

"And what are the plans for her birthday this weekend?"

Sucking in a breath, I glare at my best friend, but she looks on innocently while Jay's piercing eyes burn a hole in my face.

"It's her birthday this weekend?" His voice is all gravel. "Fuck," he mutters under his breath and takes a step back. "I don't even know when my own daughter was born."

"September fifteenth," I whisper. "She was overdue."

"I'll just—" Soph points to the hall and then disappears.

Jay slumps into the chair, still holding the boxes in his lap. He's wearing the saddest frown I've ever seen and looks so lost. "I've missed so much."

Biting the inside of my cheek, I give him a minute to come to terms with it all.

He clears his throat. "Can I—" But he doesn't finish the sentence.

"Can you what?"

"Can I celebrate with you?"

Warmth spreads in my belly, and I smile. "Yeah, I think she'll like that."

Jay nods, but his eyes flit back and forth like his mind is working overtime. Pushing my chair back, I stand and round my desk. I take the boxes from him and place them down, then settle on his lap. His heartbroken expression makes my heart pinch. Running my hands against his clean-shaven face, I smooth away the tension in his jaw.

"What did Sophie mean when she asked about your date tonight?"

"Your plan," I chide.

Dropping his forehead to mine, he closes his eyes. "Fuck," he mutters.

I flatten my palms against his cheeks and pull his head back so I can kiss him softly. "It's *fake*."

"Doesn't make it any easier," he grumbles. "But the sooner we get it over with, the quicker I can have breakfast in the kitchen with my family every morning instead of having to bring it to the office, right?" He eyes me hopefully.

Family. Squeezing my eyes shut, I make a wish that this will last forever. The way he looks at me. Our easy banter. His openness. The joy I feel now that I have the two most important people back in my life. "Right."

Once his expression relaxes, I settle in the seat beside him and dig into my waffle.

"Did Chloe say anything about the song this morning?" Jay's voice is soft, unsure.

"It was perfect."

"Had a chance to listen to yours yet?"

"You sent me a song?" My heart skitters at the thought.

His forehead creases, and he mutters something unintelligible under his breath. "Is your iPod there?" he asks, nodding to my desk.

"Left it at home."

With a humph, he slides his phone from his pocket and unlocks the screen. After a moment, he settles it between us as Coldplay's "Clocks" plays quietly.

I watch him and he watches me. Neither of us speaks, but we say so much. Music. Jay gives me music. And in this moment, I realize that I've been living in silence for years.

He sings along softly, the gravel in his voice stealing another piece of my heart. As much as I want to close my eyes and feel everything, I'm mesmerized by the way his lips move. With nothing but honesty in his expression, he sings about how nothing compares to us, and he tells me I'm his home. Confesses that he wants to come home.

The song ends, but our song continues. The music still plays vividly between us.

Our story.

Our future plays out in front of me. I can picture every second of it. Like him, I want to skip past the fake dates. I yearn for the day I can tell the world that this man is mine. That I'm his and I always have been.

"Isn't this cozy?" A harsh voice snaps me from my daydream.

When I turn, I find Carter standing at my door, wearing a scowl.

"Already perfecting the act, I see," he sneers. "Having breakfast together? What's next, waking up in her apartment?"

Jay doesn't turn around. He keeps his focus locked on me as he smiles. "Probably."

I huff. "Carter, what are you doing here?"

"I thought maybe I could talk to my sister, but considering you're hanging out with the enemy by choice, I suppose that means you're against us now."

Dropping my fork, I glare at my brother. But before I can respond to his tantrum, Carter pushes in and grabs Jay's shoulder. "Where's my child?"

Jay runs his tongue over his lip slowly. "Apologize to your sister, and I'll tell you whatever you want to know."

Carter grunts. "Get over yourself. You don't care about her. You don't care about anything except your dick, so she must be fucking you again."

Jay's chair scrapes against the floor as he hauls himself to his feet. The sound is jarring, but it's the sound of Carter's head smacking the brick wall when Jay slams him against it that makes my stomach drop.

"Jay, stop," I cry.

"That's my fucking life you're talking about," Jay grits out, pointing at me. His face is red, and his expression murderous. "The love of my fucking life. My future wife. So do me a favor; don't even look at her until you can show her some goddamn respect."

Carter gives a disgruntled laugh. "Fuck you." Then his eyes find mine. "And fuck you too. You make me sick. You're destroying our family."

I sob when Jay pushes him again. At the sound, he lets go of my brother and strides over to me. With a comforting *shh*, he holds me in a strong embrace.

My ability to cry has returned since Jay came back into my life. It's like I'd frozen into an icicle and lived that way for years, but now that the warmth of the man who loves me has returned, I'm slowly melting. While I hate feeling weak, it's better than feeling nothing.

I suck in a harsh breath and borrow courage from the man holding me tight. Over his shoulder, I meet my brother's cold stare. "For thirty years, I've given you grace because I know you're hurt. Maybe

374

more than any of us. But she would be devastated to see what you've become. Change, Carter. Or stay out of my life. The choice is yours, but I'm done being your punching bag. *I'm done.*" I bury my face in Jay's chest and loop my arms around his waist, knowing full well that I may have to choose between him and my brothers. But the truth is, it's not a choice. Jay and Chloe are my family. These arms are my home.

50

EVERYTHING HAS CHANGED BY TAYLOR SWIFT AND ED SHEERAN

Jay

I glide across the ice fast, zigzagging past Kevin. Beside me, Hayden keeps pace, ready for me to line up the shot. As Beckett barrels toward me, I shoot the puck to the side, and Hayden slices his stick hard against the ice, sending the puck spiraling straight at the goal. Gavin tries to stop it, but as the puck hits the net with a whoosh, both Hayden and I throw our hands up in the air and whoop in excitement.

"Fuck yeah!" I scream, adrenaline coursing through my body. Everything seems to be going my way lately.

Beckett grumps as he skates up to me, but he offers me his glove. "Nice play," he says as I bump my glove with his.

Amid a little friendly gloating and grumbles, we head toward the sidelines and make quick work of taking off our gear.

"How'd last night go?" Gavin asks as he grabs waters from the cooler next to the bench.

I smile and accept the one he holds out to me. "Couldn't have gone better." I squeeze a stream of water into my mouth and grin. "And my daughter, fuck, she's smart. And pretty. God, the kid is perfect."

Garreth gives me a rare smile. "When do we get to meet her?"

I sigh. I'm ready to move to the next step. Hell, I'm ready for everything, but I can't push. "Who knows. It's her birthday this weekend. She's going to be twelve."

"Fuck, almost a teenager. Damn, we're old," Beckett mutters. "I can't imagine having a kid."

"Yeah," Gavin grunts. "No one can imagine you having a kid."

"Fuck you. I like kids," Beckett grumbles, slamming the back of his hand against Gavin's chest.

All five of us stare at him.

"What? I'm not any worse with kids than the rest of you. Hell, maybe I have a kid out there somewhere too."

Gavin laughs. "You are not pleading your case, bro. Just stop."

Beckett grumbles under his breath and drops to the bench to unlace his skates.

Beside me, Hayden nudges me. "What are you going to do for her birthday?"

Garreth smirks again. Odd, he hasn't even met my daughter yet, and she's already made him smile more than any other woman. "He'll probably buy her a fucking fashion line."

Hayden laughs. "Or a music label."

"Those James women do have him wrapped around their little fingers," Kevin hollers.

"She's not a fucking James," my brothers and I say at the same time.

Kevin holds up his hands. "You guys need to cool it. Hate to break it to ya, but the kid is half James, and your enemies are her uncles."

Garreth crosses his arms. "Fuck it. I'll buy her a fashion line. No way are the Jameses going to be the favorite uncles. They've already had years with her. Beckett, your sister can help us out, right?"

"She like music?" Gavin asks.

"She's my kid. Of course she likes music."

He glances at Beckett and smirks. "I happen to know the owner of a certain stadium hosting the biggest concert of the year. And it's this weekend."

Beckett shakes his head and sighs. "Fucking A. If you guys embarrass me, I'll have your asses."

"Harry Styles loved me," I defend.

With a scoff, Beckett glares. "You told him your favorite song of his was 'Sorry.'"

Gavin fucking giggles. "'*Sorry*.' Fucking Justin Bieber's song. The best part was he actually sang it with you."

That sends all of us bursting into laughter, and even Beckett cracks a smile.

"So who's performing this weekend?" I ask.

KITTEN'S SONGS

"You got tickets to see Taylor Swift?" Chloe screeches.

I smirk when Cat whips around and stares at me with wide eyes. "You didn't."

I shrug. "True. I didn't get tickets."

Chloe's face falls, but I put her out of her misery quickly. I hold up the tickets in my hand and grin. "I got backstage passes."

51

ONLY YOU BY PARMALEE

Cat

Last year, I spent Chloe's birthday in Paris with her and Cynthia. We started it out at a café, eating chocolate-stuffed croissants. Then we went in and out of tiny boutiques, all three of us finding outfits from unknown designers—one of which ended up featured in the April edition of *Jolie*—and then we dressed and went to dinner with Peter, the sparkling Eiffel Tower the backdrop.

This year, we woke up early, ate waffles on Styrofoam plates in the park with Jay, FaceTimed Cynthia and Peter, and then donned matching shirts with Taylor Swift's face on them for what Chloe deemed the best night of her life.

Yes, Jay and Dexter wore Taylor Swift T-shirts, and I'm pretty sure Jay knew more of the words to Taylor's songs than Chloe and Del, which he scream-sang out of the top of the limo down the streets of Boston after the concert. Chloe's smile was wider than anything I'd ever seen, and her joy was blinding. Sophie kept squeezing my hand and pointing at her and Jay. It really was beautiful watching how quickly they had bonded.

We ended it with ice cream cones. We stuck a candle in Chloe's, then broke out in a rowdy rendition of "Happy Birthday."

It wasn't just the best night of Chloe's life. It was one of the greatest of mine.

Since then, every day like clockwork, Jay sends a song to Chloe, and then he and I share a cup of coffee while we listen to the one he's selected for me for the day. We talk about business. About the merger. Ideas I have for the whiskey company as well as the magazine. Jay listens thoughtfully to every word. He advises when something is too far-fetched, and stares at me in awe when I come up with something he hadn't thought of yet.

And I do the same when he points out something that would be good for the magazine. Ideas Cynthia and I never came close to even dreaming of.

We're good for one another. At work and personally.

And slowly, he joins Chloe and me for dinner a few times a week. We don't want to push it all on her too quickly, but I'm impressed by how well she's handled the changes. Every time I watch her chatter with Jay over dinner, I fall a little more in love with him.

Which is probably dangerous.

But I can't seem to make myself care.

I haven't spoken to any of my brothers since the encounter with Carter in my office. Cash has been a complete tyrant since losing Grace. He refuses to listen to anyone when we tell him she's not to blame for what happened. And until Carter gets on his damn knees and apologizes, I won't be speaking to him. As for Chase, he's been missing for weeks. I love them all, but every one of them is acting like a child these days. I've spent my life worrying about them, but for once, I'm focusing on me.

"Cat, you need to hear the song Jay sent today," Chloe says as she settles herself on the counter while I do my hair. This is another new normal. She comes in while I'm getting ready, and we listen to Jay's song. When it's over, we chat about what she has going on for the day.

I never thought I'd care about what Lyla is wearing to the school dance or why Alana shouldn't wear white when she has her period.

I never thought I'd be discussing periods with Chloe at all.

But here we are. And my daughter opens up to me more every day. Our relationship grows in an organic way. It almost feels easy. Normal. How it was meant to be.

"What song, Bug?"

She rolls her eyes and laughs, then she hits Play. Taylor Swift's "Never Grow Up" comes on, making me blink back the prickle of tears. "He's so embarrassing, Cat. But I can't wait to hear him sing this one tonight."

I clear my throat. "You're actually going to Sophie's tonight. I have that date."

Her face falls. "Oh, I thought Jay mentioned Chinese food and watching *America's Got Talent.*"

Swallowing hard, I busy myself putting my makeup away. "I'll record it, and we can watch it tomorrow, okay?"

"Yeah," Chloe says, but her tone is full of disappointment. She slides off the counter and heads for the door but stops when she reaches it. Looking back, she meets my eyes in the mirror. "Do you like Jay?"

I can't help the laugh that escapes. We are so past like. Turning around and giving her my full attention, I reply, "Of course I do."

"Then why are you dating other people?" she asks, her frown marring her face.

I sigh. "That's not an easy answer, Chlo."

While I believe in honesty, there are things I just can't share with her. I'll never tell her all the details about what happened between Jay and me because I would never want to jeopardize her relationship with her father.

"He likes you," she counters.

"I know." Scanning her face, I sigh. "It's complicated."

She bites at her nail, still watching me in the mirror. She's working through her thoughts, and all I can do is be patient. None of this is easy for any of us. "I like it when he's here."

"He's not going anywhere."

She blows out a breath and nods. "Yeah, okay. I'm going to finish getting ready."

As she leaves, the heaviness of the conversation hits me. We've been trying to give her time to catch up to what we feel, but if her comments this morning are any indication, she's more than ready for the next step.

My little girl wants her family.

KITTEN'S SONGS

"What does a lemon say when it answers the phone?" Jay asks, sauntering into my office with breakfast in hand.

I quirk a brow. "Huh?"

"*Yellow*!" he sings, a cheeky smile pulling at his lips.

I snort a laugh. "Are you insane?"

He doesn't reply. Instead, he sets the box down and rounds my desk. "Morning, beautiful," he murmurs and presses his lips to mine.

"Morning, baby," I hum before stealing another kiss.

Like every morning, I follow him to the other side of my desk so we can sit beside one another. We share one waffle now. Two seemed a bit overboard for the frequency with which we eat them, but I can't seem to get myself to tell him to stop picking them up on his way in. These few minutes we share in the morning have become some of my favorites. Bringing a strawberry slice to my mouth, I study him while he cuts a piece of waffle for me.

"Have you heard about the chocolate record player?" he asks, holding his fork to my lips.

I shake my head and take his proffered bite.

"It sounds pretty sweet."

I chuckle. "What are you talking about?"

"Testing out my dad jokes," he says, then he takes a bite of his own. "Do you think Chloe will laugh? She'll get them, right? She's smart." He shakes his head. "Of course she'll get them."

Placing my hand on his knee, I lean forward so he's forced to look at me. "Jay," I say softly, "Chloe's crazy about you. She doesn't need jokes."

He drops his chin to his chest. His hair falls over his eyes, making him look so much younger than he is as he peeks up at me. "Really?"

I squeeze his knee. "Yes, just like me. We're both crazy about you."

He latches on to the armrests of my chair and drags me closer, spreading his legs so I'm tucked between them. With his hands on my cheeks, he looks at me with so much reverence that my breath catches.

"What do you call cheese that isn't yours?"

The air trapped in my lungs forces its way out, and I push him away. "Jay!"

He grins. "Nacho cheese!"

The man is ridiculous, but I can't help but laugh.

"She really likes me?" he whispers against my hair.

I nod into his chest. "She's sad that you're not coming over tonight."

He pushes back and peers down at me. "I thought we were having Chinese?"

My shoulders sag as the weight of his disappointment is added to Chloe's. "I have a date."

"Fuck," he growls. "This is the last one, Cat. I'm done with this shit."

"It was your idea." I pull back. "And I didn't put us in this position."

Jay looks away, his jaw ticking.

"I'm sorry." I blow out a breath. "Jay," I plead, begging him to look at me.

He shakes his head. "You're right. It's my fault. Keeping you and Chloe safe is all that matters. Not my fucking ego and the bruising it takes when you're out with someone else."

Palming his face, I force him to look at me. "It's like a business meeting. That's it. You and Chloe, you're my world. *Only you.*"

He leans in to my touch, his lashes fluttering as he settles into my confession.

When the phone on my desk rings, we both jolt at the sound, and Jay pulls back.

With a sigh, I pick it up. "Catherine James, how can I help you?"

"Hi, Ms. James, this is Mrs. McCormick. I'm the nurse at St. Luke's Middle School. Chloe is in my office complaining of a stomachache."

"Oh, okay. Does she need to come home?"

Jay's eyes dart to mine, and worry etches itself in every line on his face.

"Do you want your mom to pick you up?" Mrs. McCormick asks, her voice quieter, like she's pulled the phone away.

I listen for Chloe's muffled response, and then she's on the line. "Hi, Cat. It's okay. You don't have to pick me up if you're busy."

"I'm never too busy for you."

Jay stands and looms over me with his hands on his hips.

"I think I can make it through the day, but do you think Jay could pick me up and stay with me tonight so I don't have to go to Sophie's? I don't want to get anyone else sick."

I have to fight to keep a grin from splitting my face in two. "You want Jay to pick you up?"

I lose my battle when surprise flashes across Jay's face, and I full-on beam at him.

"If-if he's free," she hedges.

The man before me would cancel a meeting with the president for his daughter. I have no doubt. "I'm sure he'll work it out," I assure her.

"You sure you can make it through the day?" I tease.

"Yeah, I'm feeling a little better, but I don't want to risk it with all the kids."

I hum. "Probably a good idea."

"So he'll pick me up?"

I smile. "Yeah, I'll let the school know. Give me a call if things change and you want to come home sooner."

When I hang up, Jay is laser focused on me and practically holding his breath, waiting for information.

"She wants you to pick her up and spend the evening with her."

That shy grin hits me right in the heart. "Yeah?"

I laugh. "Yeah, she doesn't like you at all," I tease.

He settles in the chair beside me again and goes back to the waffle. Then he turns to me with a smile. "Bacon and eggs walk into a bar…"

I palm my face. "Oh my God."

"The bartender says, 'Get out of here! We don't serve breakfast!'"

52

MAKING MEMORIES OF US BY KEITH URBAN

Jay

Armed with soup from my favorite bistro, ginger ale, crackers, and about sixteen different medicines, I picked Chloe up from school. When she got into the car, she peeked inside the bags at her feet and gave me a small smile, then turned to watch out the window. She was silent the entire way home, so I followed her lead, unsure of whether she really didn't feel well or whether she was feeling as nervous as I was.

In the lobby of Cat's building, I shake hands with Fred, the security guard on duty. "How's Beth feeling?"

He gives me a big smile. "Due any day now, and *cranky*."

I clap him on the back. "You're a lucky man."

"Don't I know it." We say our goodbyes, then I continue toward the elevator. Chloe's eyes are on me the entire time.

"How are you feeling?" I ask once we're inside.

"Who's Beth?" she asks, tilting her head and squinting at me.

"Fred's wife. But you didn't answer my question. How are you feeling?"

She quietly regards me for a long time, and damn if her intense scrutiny doesn't feel exactly like her mother's. She's so fucking smart. I have to work hard not to squirm under her inspection.

When the elevator stops on Cat's floor, she still hasn't answered, so I give in and step out into the hallway. When we make it inside, I set the bags on the table. "Soup okay?" I ask.

But Chloe is already retreating down the hall.

I sigh and slump against the counter. *What did I say wrong?*

KITTEN'S SONGS

I tap on Chloe's door a little while later. "Soup's ready." I may not know much about raising a daughter, but I know better than to enter a bedroom without being invited. No idea what the heck she's doing in there.

She opens the door and brushes past me. "Mom lets me have ice cream when I'm sick," she grumbles.

I follow her to the kitchen, at a loss as to what I'm supposed to do. Silently, we settle at the table and eat.

"Feeling any better?" I try.

She glances up at me, then back to her bowl. "Cat's on a date."

I choke on my soup and cough obnoxiously. Watching my daughter, who's looking at me with a suspicious amount of innocence, I take a slow sip of water. I swear she's more Cat in this moment than she's ever been.

I can do this. I've had dinner with a president. I've conned mobsters out of their life savings. I've killed people. Having a conversation with my twelve-year-old daughter should be a walk in the park.

"You don't seem sick," I comment, searching her face for a reaction.

She looks down into her soup again.

"Is there a reason you didn't want to go to Sophie and Dexter's? Did something happen with their kids?"

She narrows her eyes at me. "How come you know the name of our security guard's wife?"

Suddenly sweltering, I pull on my shirt. "Because I wanted him to watch out for you."

She raises her eyebrow. "Me? Or Cat?"

"You. *Both* of you."

Chloe bites the inside of her cheek but doesn't look up. "There's a dance at school coming up," she says so quietly I have to strain to hear her.

I clear my throat. "Okay. Do you want to go?"

"It's a daddy-daughter dance." Her voice trembles and her lip wobbles as she finally brings her gaze to mine. She looks every bit her age in this moment, despite her earlier attitude.

"Was someone rude about you having two moms? Because if they were, I'll kill them," I grit out. The idea of anyone making Chloe feel unworthy sends rage coursing through me.

She laughs and eyes me, her dark hair swaying as she shakes her head. "No. It's 2022, Jay. People don't care about that. Besides, my moms are Cynthia Caldwell and Catherine James. The most iconic woman in the fashion world and her protégé. People are begging to be friends with me."

Damn, she's smart. And as sassy as her mom. All I can do is nod in agreement. But I still can't figure out why she's shut down. "Then why are you upset, Chlo?"

She pulls her bottom lip between her teeth and studies me. Her blue eyes are so full of emotion, so fucking vulnerable, it takes all my self-control not to reach across the table and pull her into my lap. "Because it's a daddy-daughter dance, and I've never had a dad."

The words are like a knife to the chest, but I keep my voice steady. "I understand."

Her head shoots up. "You do?"

391

"Yeah, it's okay that you don't feel comfortable. This is going to take time. I'll be here when you want me to be. And if you want space, I'll give you that—"

"I don't want space," she rushes out.

"You don't?" I swear my heart feels like it's going to explode.

"No." She picks at the napkin beside her bowl, avoiding my gaze. "I wanted to ask you to come, but I thought maybe it was too soon. Or maybe it would be too much for you."

"I'd fucking love to take you to the dance, Chloe," I practically shout. "Don't tell your mom I cursed. *Either of them.*"

Her face lights up, and she wiggles in her seat. "You really want to go to the daddy-daughter dance with me?"

My heart pinches. "Chlo." I take a risk and pull her chair closer to mine and wrap my arms around her. "There is nowhere else I'd rather be."

"Not even on a date with Cat?"

I huff out a laugh. She's got me there.

"Is that something you want? Your mom and me to date?"

She tilts her chin and examines me with a pensive frown. "Is that what you want?"

"Yeah, I've wanted your mother since I first met her. There's never been another woman who held a candle to her…"

Her face falls.

"What? What did I say wrong? You've got to communicate with me, or I don't stand a chance here."

She shrugs. "Is that why you're here? Because you're trying to win her back?"

I sigh. "If you'd let me finish, I was going to say that no one has compared to her *until you*. The two of you are everything to me. So honestly, I'd take a date with you over her because you and I have never had that chance. So will you do me the honor of being my date for the dance?"

She smiles. "Yeah, I'd like that."

I couldn't wipe the smile from my face if I tried. "Now, about that ice cream…"

KITTEN'S SONGS

I've just closed Chloe's door, having indulged her in a story before bed, per her request, when the front door closes quietly. Hidden in the dark hallway, I take the opportunity to examine Cat as she slips off her heels, leans her head back against the front door, and exhales like she's releasing a month's worth of stress.

She looks utterly exhausted.

In just a few strides, I'm in front of her and pulling her toward the couch.

Her eyes fly open, and she breathes my name as she stumbles to follow me.

I drop to the cushion and pull her on top of me. It only takes her a few seconds to catch up, and then her lips are tipping up in a smile as she adjusts herself so she's straddling me.

"Hi," she whispers.

Squeezing her hips, I press a soft kiss against her mouth. "Hi, Kitten."

She sighs. It's soft, and as her breath mixes with mine, I can't help but close my eyes and revel in her proximity. In the ease with which she settled with me. I may not be getting everything right, and I'll likely continue to stumble, but possessing the ability to calm this wild one, when only moments earlier, she was carrying the weight of the world, will never get old.

"How was your night?"

"It was really good."

"Chloe feeling okay?"

I chuckle. "She's just fine."

"What's so funny?" she asks, brushing at a speck on my shirt.

Unsure if Chloe wants me to share our earlier conversation, I just shake my head. "I'll let her fill you in. So tell me, how was your date with Gavin Langfield?"

I despise this ruse, but Gavin did me a solid by taking her out. This way, I knew she was in good hands with a man who would be respectful and keep his distance.

Cat licks her lips. "I mean, he wasn't hard on the eyes," she teases.

My hands tense on her hips, and I pin her with a pointed look. "Yeah?" I ask dangerously.

Her face remains expressionless. "And there's just something about hockey players," she hums.

"Good thing your future husband knows how to play, then," I counter.

Cat's eyes light up. "You do?"

I laugh and rest my head on her chest. I love surprising this girl. Leaning back against the couch, I get comfortable and look up at her. "Yeah. Gavin and I met after—" My voice catches, but I push forward. "I needed a distraction after everything happened. Garreth, my brother," I explain, unsure if she remembers, "he saw all the anger I'd bottled up and told me to find a hobby." I laugh. I looked like such an ass on the ice that first year. "I could barely skate when I started."

Cat shakes her head, but she's smiling. "Why not pick a sport that's a little less difficult?"

I give her hips another squeeze, grounding myself to this moment. Reminding myself that I can talk about those dark years, because the light has returned.

"Nothing else could shut my mind down. Basketball was second nature. I could do it without thinking. And boxing…" I shrug. She can probably guess why I stopped boxing. It was something Carter and I did together. It's what all her brothers did. They still do.

"So you learned how to ice skate."

"I wasn't fucking twirling around," I banter, picking up on where her mind is going.

She giggles. "I love ice skating."

The one and only time I had Cat on the ice was at Rockefeller Center thirteen years ago. Memories flash in my mind and threaten to choke me. A yellow diamond necklace. Promises of forever. Our goodbye.

"Maybe we could take Chloe sometime," she says quietly, her melancholy expression matching the way I feel.

I have no doubt her thoughts are right there with mine. On that cold December day.

"I'd like that."

"You know what else I'd like?" she says, rolling her hips over me in a seductive manner.

I slide my palms up her thighs. "What?"

"A night alone. Just you and me. Bottle of wine. Lots of sex."

Then she's taking my lips with hers. Her kiss is hungry, desperate, needy. Her tits are pressed against me, and her heart beats wildly against mine as she grinds against me.

It's been over a month since I've had her. And fuck, I want her. I want her so desperately, my cock is ready to burst through my pants.

But with a groan, I pull her to me and hug her tightly. "I can't believe I'm going to say this," I mutter.

Cat stills. "Is something wrong?"

I don't answer immediately. I breathe deeply and just enjoy the way she feels in my arms.

"Jay?"

"Chloe thinks the only reason I'm sticking around is because I'm trying to win you back."

Cat's face falls. "Fuck."

Cupping her cheeks, I rake my gaze over every inch of her face. "I want you so fucking badly, but I need to show her that she matters. She needs to know she comes first."

"Of course she does," Cat says quickly, pushing at my chest.

I don't let her move, though. "You both do. I'm not here for her alone, and I'm not here just for you. I'm here for you both. You are my family, and I want to reassure her of that."

Her eyes soften. "You don't have to explain it to me, Jay. I feel the same way."

"But that doesn't mean we can't spend time together, Kitten," I whisper and drop a soft kiss to her lips.

"It doesn't?" she asks, a little breathless.

"Just means you need to learn how to be quiet," I tease.

Her eyes light in challenge.

"Can you be quiet, Kitten?"

She practically purrs against me as I lift her in my arms. "I can try," she says, nibbling along my jaw as I carry her toward the bedroom.

53

STILL FALLING FOR YOU BY ELLIE GOULDING

Cat

It's not until Jay flicks on the bedroom light that the nerves hit me. We've had sex in public. We've played in the club. And we've certainly flirted a whole lot over the last few months. But this is so much different.

Not just because we're parents. And not because we have to be quiet.

This time, we're going into it with eyes wide open.

He hasn't touched me since he learned I had a baby. He hasn't seen me in the light, scars and all.

But I don't want anything between us anymore. I want him to see all of me and still *choose* me. There's an innate need for him to want me even when things aren't sexy, because lord knows life will be filled with plenty of unsexy moments. But if we're doing this—if we're really going to make this work—then I need to know that even when I'm ordinary, he'll still be desperate for me.

And Jay doesn't disappoint.

Spinning, he presses me against the wall. His presence hovers above me, and in the bright light of my bedroom, every detail of his face is on display. The five o'clock shadow, the thick black lashes that flutter subtly as he studies me, the sexy black glasses that frame his piercing blue eyes. When I shuffled into my apartment, I was dead on my feet. But when he stepped out of the shadows, I couldn't help but clench my thighs at the sight of him in those damn glasses. For the first time in my life, I understand the appeal of Clark Kent. Damn.

"This is what I've been looking forward to most," he says, his lips skating up my neck.

"What?" I practically pant.

"*You*. In the light. Seeing every inch of you. Fuck, Cat, I love our games, you know that, but I've missed this the most."

Softly, I ask, "You've missed what the most?"

"A simple Wednesday night with you. Anticipating the way I'm about to explore your body, kiss every inch, worship you. And it's just us. It's not about anything or anyone else."

My heart beats wildly in my chest. "Only you." There are no truer words. We'll always put Chloe first, but when it comes to anyone else, he's the only person who matters. The one my body craves and who makes my soul complete.

His warm breath mixes with mine as he dips close, then his lips are on mine, possessing me. His hands slide down my ribs and disappear under my shirt. Fingers graze against the underside of my breast, then slowly make their way under my bra until he has my nipple in his grasp. Tweaking and teasing, he kisses me until I'm almost desperate and grinding against him.

"Can I see you, Kitten? Will you let me see every inch of this body?"

Whimpering, I nod, even as my apprehension skyrockets.

With more reverence than should be given to such a simple task, he guides my top over my head. Then his gaze is on my chest, and he kisses every area he sears with his eyes, as if he's reacquainting himself with every inch.

"So beautiful," he murmurs against my skin.

With two hands, he finds the zipper at the side of my skirt and lowers it. As he slides it down my legs, he takes my stockings with it. When he reaches my feet, I flatten my palms on his shoulders to steady myself.

From his position crouched before me, he hits me with a look filled with potent desire and licks his lips. "No panties?"

I run my thumb across his cheek, hoping to ease the silent war waging behind his eyes when he takes note of my lack of undergarments and pairs it with the knowledge that I was out on a date with his friend. "I never wear panties with stockings."

His Adam's apple bobs. "I'll have to remember that." He sets my clothes on the floor, and then he's between my legs again, ghosting his palms up the outer edges as he stares up at me.

It's an awkward angle, but I try not to squirm as his attention finally lands on the scar from my c-section. The line I've hidden from the world with one-piece bathing suits, high-waisted underwear, and a closed-off demeanor that meant I never gave myself completely to another human.

I've never been so happy with a decision in my life.

There wasn't a moment in the last decade where I didn't belong to this man.

Others saw it as an inability to love or to be loved, but the reality is that I'd given all my love to him. There was nothing left to give to another. And I know now that no other person could love me like this man does.

He presses his lips gently against the scar, and from under that messy blond hair, he looks up and shatters me. "Thank you," he says firmly, his grip on my heart almost as tight as the one on my hips. "I love you so much."

I drop my head back against the wall as he kisses a hot trail down my pubic bone. The moment his tongue slides between my lips, I buck against him and cry out.

He stills in response. "If you make a sound, I stop," he warns. Then he kisses away the sting of his words and starts again.

With my lips folded in on themselves, I strain to stay quiet as he takes me slowly, drawing out my pleasure. Licking, teasing, fingering. Every touch undoes me, breaks down my walls, leaving me completely bare to him.

My legs tremble as my orgasm takes over. Without stopping, Jay looks up at me from his spot on the floor with a wicked glint in his eye as he silently dares me to stay quiet through it. Not wanting the pleasure to end, I squeeze my eyes shut as my orgasm rips through me. Jay's soft chuckle vibrates against my clit, and he presses another soft kiss to it before sucking it into his mouth and moaning. "Such a fucking good girl tonight. Proud of you."

Boneless, I practically fall when he stands and kisses my mouth, his tongue delving in, possessing me. I press back, needing a moment to breathe. To think. To remember what I want. "Baby, I need to see you. Please," I beg.

Jay smirks. "You never have to beg, but I love when you do."

I grip his shirt and pull it over his head quickly, gasping when I catch sight of his bare chest. "What is this?" I whisper, tracing the three stars tattooed across his ribs with my fingers. Two of the stars are black, but the one in the center is a pale yellow.

"A reminder of the only thing that has ever mattered to me. Star-crossed lovers. Written in the stars. Opposing ideas, obviously. Fated to love? Fated to hate? The truth is, Catherine, none of it mattered the moment I met you. One way or another, I always intended to rewrite the stars so I could make you the center of my universe."

"That's why the one in the middle is yellow?" I breathe, tracing it with my fingers. "Why are there three?"

Jay shrugs. "I have no idea why I chose three at the time. Maybe somehow my heart knew what my brain didn't. That it was always meant to be the three of us."

Like Jay, I have an innate need to drop my lips to his skin. To the place where he branded himself with our memory.

With quiet determination, I help him undress. Then we stumble to the bed and kiss lazily for what could be minutes or hours, I don't know. And then he shifts his hips, dragging his hard erection between my legs, bringing forth a gasp he swallows as he sinks inside me.

Slowly, he moves in and out of my body, his focus trained on my face the entire time. Holding our connection. Telling me with every punishing thrust how he loves me, that this is it. *This is forever.* This is what we were always meant to be.

And when my body convulses around him, squeezing him tightly, he kisses me through it, keeping me quiet. Then he pulls out quickly and paints my stomach with his own pleasure.

From: <JHanson@jolie.com>

To: <CJames@jolie.com>

Subject: Last night

September 25, 2022

Kitten,

I can't get thoughts of you covered in me last night out of my head. I need you. My office, fifteen minutes.

Love,

Jay

From: <CJames@Jolie.com>

To: <JHanson@jolie.com>

Subject: Re: Last night

September 25, 2022

I can't believe Rose walked in on us. I'm going to kill you.

From: <JHanson@jolie.com>

To: <CJames@jolie.com>

Subject: Dinner

October 1, 2022

I'm picking up Chloe from choir practice, and then we'll pick up dinner from Lucia's. I'll keep your food in the oven. Don't work too late.

Love you.

54

ONLY YOU BY HARRY CONNICK, JR.

Cat

As fall arrives, our days only get busier. While I haven't actually been named editor in chief, I've somehow slipped into the role while also helping Jay with plans for the merger.

No matter how hard I try to work with Cash, though, he pushes me away. Since we started the fake dating ruse, I've gotten to know Grace and have realized how wrong I was about her.

She is genuinely kind, and she's everything my brother deserves. I just wish I'd recognized it before I worked so hard to break them up.

My brother spends his days drinking and falling further and further into depression. Out of desperation to fix things, I brought Grace to his club. I really believed that if he saw her again, he'd realize how wrong he was.

Boy, did I misjudge that.

The night turned into a disaster. And now Grace won't speak to me either.

"What's the best band to listen to in autumn?" Jay asks as he walks into my office with his phone in his hand.

I smile, waiting for the punchline.

"The Spice Girls." He grins and shimmies his hips as "Wannabe" plays through his phone.

I let out a loud laugh as he dances around my office, completely unconcerned about the growing number of people who have paused what they're doing to stare at him.

"You're insane," I whisper as he continues to sing his way toward me. He drops a kiss on my lips before he goes right back to Sporty Spice's line, planting one hand on his waist and cocking a hip.

He's such a diva.

"Why do you look so stressed, Kitten?" Jay asks when he gets a good look at me. He turns off the music and crouches beside me, smoothing a thumb over my brow.

I sigh. "I'm just so happy."

He laughs and moves to stroke my cheek reverently. "And that's making you unhappy?"

I lean in to his touch. "I destroyed them, Jay," I whisper.

"Who, baby?"

"Cash and Grace. They should be together. They should be as happy as we are."

His brows knit together. "That's not on you, Cat."

"It is, though," I huff. "Cash was my best friend. For so many years, he was my favorite person in the world. Now I don't even recognize him. All he does is drink. And hang out at his stupid club," I say with a groan. Chase as a club owner? That I can see. But Cash? All he's ever cared about is James Liquors. Until now. Now that he's lost control of it, he's spiraling.

"What can I do?" Jay asks.

"Nothing," I sigh. We tried to get them back together, and it backfired. At this point, I have to step back and let my brother figure this out himself.

"I know something that will make you smile," Jay whispers.

"What's that?"

"Google our names, Kitten," he says, wearing a sly grin.

Pursing my lips, I narrow my eyes at him. "What did you do, Mr. Hanson?"

Though his efforts are valiant, I know him well enough to see the slight crack in his façade, the nervousness over whatever he's done.

Wiggling my mouse to wake up my computer, I watch the black screen light up to a picture of Chloe and me in Paris. It's from the last trip I took before my grandfather got ill. God, that feels like a lifetime ago. Six months ago, if someone had told me I'd be sitting in my office with Jay Hanson right now, I'd have laughed my ass off. Then I would have raged and probably thrown a thing or two.

I *never* would have believed I'd be spending my weekends with this man and our daughter.

Flicking my eyes to him, I smile, then type our names into the search bar. I suck in a breath as I read the headline out loud. "Jonathan Hanson Confirms Relationship with Catherine James."

When I turn to him, he's studying me, waiting for my reaction. "Oh my God," I whisper.

"No going back now, Kitten," he says softly, his features still pensive.

Nibbling at my bottom lip, I turn back to the screen and read the press release.

Cat and I have been friends for years, but it wasn't until Cat started working with Grace Kensington that I was able to see her in a different light. Grace has a tried-and-true method that leads to a real connection, and Cat and I are so grateful to her for helping us realize what has always been right in front of us.

I let out a soft laugh. "That's one way to spin it."

"We'll do some press. A talk show or two. Really beat the story into everyone's heads so Frank's brother doesn't suspect a thing."

I blow out a breath. "And Chloe?"

He scrubs his hand over his face. "They can't know she's mine, baby. I fucking hate it more than anything, but if they know she's mine? Fuck, it puts you both in danger."

"More secrets," I mutter. Though there's no other option. "I hate this."

"Let's just focus on the good. You're done with fake dating other men. You and Chloe are safe. And we're together. Who cares what the rest of the world thinks? What matters is our family. From here on out, it's the three of us, and that's all I care about."

"I just wish…" I break off, scanning the barren shoreline outside my window. Fall really is here. It makes me want to take a blanket and picnic basket down there and lose myself in the season.

"What do you wish, baby?"

I shake my head. No more wishing, no more sadness. "Let's go for a picnic. Let's pick Chloe up from school, grab waffles, and celebrate."

Jay's eyes light up. "Yeah?"

"Yeah, let's tell her we're doing this. Let's show her exactly what that means."

55

MY GIRL BY THE TEMPTATIONS

Jay

Chloe steps into the living room, her brown hair curled into ringlets and a bright smile lighting up her face. The navy dress I had custom designed by Sienna Langfield is simple and elegant. The only adornments are the ruffled hem at the knee and a bow on one side of the neck.

"Stunning." I hold out the corsage I brought for her with a smile. I'm not sure if these are still a thing, but fuck if I wasn't getting my little girl flowers. Cat appears behind her, wearing black drawstring sweats and a sweater that falls off one shoulder, exposing one of my favorite spots.

"This dress is gorgeous," Cat says, twirling Chloe to face her.

My daughter peers back at me, her eyes darting to the flowers. "I still can't believe Sienna designed this. The girls are going to flip!"

Smirking, I kiss her on the cheek first and slide the corsage onto her wrist. When she grabs her phone so she can text "the girls," I finally give Cat the attention she deserves.

"How is it possible that you look more beautiful in sweats than most women look on the runway?"

She gives me a coy smile and loops her arms around my neck. Instead of responding, she pops up onto her toes and kisses me. It's a quick one since Chloe is nearby, but she's getting more comfortable with affection around her. Every time she catches us, there's a glint in her eye. She doesn't fully trust it yet, which I understand, but along with her concern, there's a glimmer of hope. And tonight, I plan to let her in on a little secret that I hope will help her trust my intentions. I want her to see that Cat and I aren't just trying things out. She needs to understand that we're building a life together and she's at the center of it.

Holding Cat in my arms, I spin so we're facing our daughter. "Hey, Chlo, what's the best dance to pair with chips?"

Cat groans beside me, but Chloe's eyes light up. She's loving my jokes. Not going to lie, I'm kind of awesome at the dad thing.

"*Salsa*," I say as I spin Cat out. I curl my wrist and pop my hip, doing my best salsa impression. "*Olé!*"

Chloe giggles, and despite her best efforts, Cat beams.

Yeah, I'm awesome.

KITTEN'S SONGS

"Del hasn't stopped talking about Chloe's Sienna Langfield dress," Dexter says, arching an accusatory brow in my direction.

I chuckle and hold up my hands. "Sorry, man. I have over a decade to make up for."

He slaps my shoulder and gives it a squeeze. "It's good to see them both so happy."

"What was it like—" I cut myself off and shake my head. I'm not sure why I'm going there.

Dexter scans the crowd until he spots our daughters dancing in the middle of the gym. We've been relegated to the outskirts of the space with the rest of the dads. "I'm not going to sugarcoat it. Watching Cat struggle when she found out she was pregnant and you just up and vanished…it was brutal," he says gruffly.

I blink back the emotion that pricks at the backs of my eyes at the memory of Cat's voice mails. All thirty-two of them.

He clears his throat. "I'm not sure what happened back then, and it's none of my business, but I can see that you're trying. *Hard.* And in the end, that's all that matters."

I close my eyes. "I'll never stop trying."

"Good."

Giggles draw our attention to the girls bouncing in front of us. "Dad," Del says, "will you dance with me?"

Dexter brings his hand to his heart and smiles. It's obvious he's a great dad. "Never thought you'd ask," he says, holding out his hand to his daughter. They weave their way to the dance floor, where dozens of daddy-daughter duos awkwardly shuffle in circles.

Holding out my hand, I look at my daughter. "What do you say, kiddo? Shall we show them how it's done?"

Chloe's eyes light up and she giggles. When she takes my hand, I spin her into my chest, garnering a delighted laugh that makes my chest feel tight. I may have missed the first twelve years of her life, but from here on out, she'll never wonder how I feel. Through actions, words, and time, I'll give her everything she deserves.

I let her lead me to the center of the dance floor, and when we're in place, I nod to the DJ I made sure to chat up when the night began, and mid-song, the music changes. The familiar Temptations song echoes through the cavernous space, and I swear every dad in the place is smiling and every girl is giggling as they dance along to "My Girl." I dance like a goofball and tug Chloe into my chest. As we sway, I tell her exactly how I feel—like my life is finally brighter—by singing the lyrics to my girl.

56

FEELS LIKE BY GRACIE ABRAMS

Cat

"I think my ovaries might burst," I chirp with a smile permanently plastered to my face.

Sophie holds her phone so we can both watch the video Dexter sent moments ago. Front and center, Jay dances and sings to our daughter. It's seriously doing things to me.

"Told you Daddies were hot," Sophie teases.

I don't even have it in me to fight her. "That really wasn't what I thought you meant, Soph. But yeah, you were right. I've been missing out."

Watching Jay tackle fatherhood like he would tackle any other project, including winning me over—with determination, a smile, and confidence that he'll get what he wants—has been amazing. Every day, he shows up for us both.

Songs sent to our iPods. Breakfast in the office. Afternoons with Chloe, where they do God only knows what while I finish the day at work. Evenings spent making dinner—Jay, not me; I still haven't mastered the art of cooking—dancing in the kitchen, then snuggled on the couch with Chloe tucked between us, watching *America's Next Top Model* or *America's Got Talent*. Sometimes *Jeopardy*.

Stolen kisses, quiet, excruciatingly perfect sex, followed by so kisses as Jay leaves me wanting forever to start now.

I never anticipated being the one to beg to make this all official, but all I want is for him to move in so we can move forward. I'm not sure what's holding us back now. The fake dating is over, and we've publicly announced our relationship, but he's yet to mention the next step.

And now he's at a daddy-daughter dance with Chloe, wearing a damn suit that makes my thighs clench and a smile so full of love as he gazes at our daughter. That alone has my heart doing somersaults.

"It's good to see you so happy," Sophie murmurs.

I blow out a breath. "I just wish my brothers weren't suffering." Guilt eats at me, because while I'm experiencing so much joy, they continue to spiral.

I've been working on rolling out ideas for the merger, but Cash is sinking further into depression. Jay and I met with him this week to tell him about my idea to throw a party to announce the merger, and for a moment, pride flashed in my brother's eyes as he looked at me. We've never worked together, and therefore, I've never experienced how it feels to have his approval.

But as soon as he caught Jay squeezing my thigh, the light left his eyes, and the pride was replaced by hatred.

My brother, my best friend, despises me. He believes I'm an idiot for falling for Jay.

He doesn't know him, and I'm partly to blame for that. I hid what Jay meant to me back then, and now it's almost impossible to explain our connection.

Too many years have passed.

Too many secrets remain.

And it's the only thing that keeps me from being truly happy.

How can I feel such joy when my brothers are all falling apart?

"They'll come around when they see who Jay really is," she comforts.

And that's what ultimately allows me to sink into my joy. I can trust

Jay. Sophie sees who he really is too. As does Cynthia. If she didn't, she'd never allow him near our daughter, no matter that he's her father.

The people who really know Jay see how real our love is.

As for Cash, all I can do is wait for him to dig himself out of his depression. He needs to see Grace for who she really is, or he needs to move on. I can't do those things for him any more than Sophie or Cynthia could have healed my heart all those years ago.

There's a reason I never moved on, and that reason is holding our daughter close and dancing before me on the tiny screen, lighting a fire in my belly and easing the ache in my heart.

From: <CJames@Jolie.com>
To: <JHanson@jolie.com>
Subject: I miss you
October 24, 2022

Jay,

I wish you and Chloe could have come to Fashion Week. I miss you both so much. Show her these pictures of Sienna's latest designs. God, that woman is a freaking genius. And Lucy Montgomery even made an appearance. Her designs are to die for. I want her in our spring edition.

I love you.

Cat

From: JHanson@jolie.com
To: CJames@jolie.com
Subject: Re: I miss you
October 25, 2022

Kitten,

Come outside. I brought you a surprise.

Love you.

KITTEN'S SONGS

Hovering over the mockup for next month's edition, I comb through page after page, racking my brain for what's missing. My mind is still buzzing with ideas days after Fashion Week. And they aren't all work-related ones. Spending a few days away from Chloe and Jay was much harder than I anticipated. I've spent the better part of the last decade alone, but after only a few weeks with Chloe full time and dinners with Jay most nights—and quality time in bed at night—I've gotten used to the noise. The quiet was impossibly lonely.

Then Jay went and stole another piece of my heart when he flew Chloe to New York to surprise me for the weekend. Sitting at a fashion show with her, hearing her thoughts on every design, will never get old. And Jay's take on every outfit never disappointed. He had both of us giggling as he told us how the lines of a design were *so amazing* or later at night when he walked the "catwalk" of our hotel room, proving that he could model better than what we'd witnessed hours earlier.

We ate at an upscale restaurant and clinked glasses of champagne while Chloe gave us her critique of every dessert. The following night, we went from one pizza place to the next, trying a slice at every stop until we declared a winner. It was the perfect weekend with my two favorite people.

"Maybe we could get a few quotes from Sienna," I suggest to one of our copy editors. "The story is missing heart. Her designs are gorgeous, but our readers want to know why she became a designer rather than going into the family business. They'd be more interested in what she had to give up and whether the sacrifice was worth it."

Her story speaks to me at a cellular level. There aren't many women who have done what she's done. Who have forgone the easy path and forged their own. Sienna could have had any position she wanted in her family business, but sports didn't interest her.

And she didn't use her family's money to build her career like many suspect. Yet her business skyrocketed anyway. There's a story there. What did Sienna have to do to get to where she is?

"You're right. Although I'm not sure how quickly we can get an interview scheduled on such short notice."

"Pretty sure she'll agree if the editor in chief of *Jolie* calls her," Jay says from where he's propped himself up in the doorway. His arms are folded across his chest and his expression is unreadable. In his black suit with the white shirt unbuttoned at the collar, he looks like sin.

"I can have Cynthia call," I agree.

Jay shakes his head. "She's not the editor in chief any longer. I'm sure Sienna would much rather hear from the newly appointed one."

I frown, confused. Cynthia hasn't mentioned the change, and nothing official has been announced.

Jay holds out his phone. "I saved her contact information when I had her design Chloe's dress. Why don't you give her a call?"

I swear my heart stops. "Me?" I squeak, pressing my hand to my chest.

Jay wears the widest grin I think I've ever seen. "Yes, Catherine. *You,* our new editor in chief. Effective today."

"Really?" I ask, breathless. I have to plant a hand on the table to keep myself upright.

"Really," Cynthia says, peeking out from behind Jay.

Screeching, I run at her, shocked to see her. At her appearance, the truth finally seeps in. I'm really editor in chief. All these years—all the hard work, the late nights spent studying fabrics and colors, weekends lost to fashion shows, sore feet from stalking around in heels all day— my dreams have finally come to fruition.

"You did it," Sophie says from the hall.

I squeeze Cynthia once more and book it toward my best friend.

"We did it," I tell her as she pulls me against her.

"Little girls all over are going to want to be you," she whispers.

"Us," I remind her. "Without you, I never would have stayed." I swipe away a rogue tear.

"You're right," she laughs. "I really do deserve a raise."

"Done," Jay says from behind me. When I turn around, he holds out his arms. "Congratulations, Kitten," he murmurs when I lean into his embrace. He smells of coffee and waffles and all my dreams coming true.

"Is this real?" I whisper, burying my face in the crook of his neck.

I don't just mean the job. Becoming editor in chief is such a small part of this moment, but it's a symbol of everything I wanted. The day I walked into *Jolie* for the first time, I knew I wanted to be Cynthia, but at the time, I had no idea what that entailed.

Years ago, I wanted people to fear me. But the way the people around me look at me is so much better. Their expressions emanate reverence. Love. Adoration.

Being feared has always been a powerful aphrodisiac, but being loved has set me free.

Free to step down from the burdens I've put upon myself to be perfect. Free to accept my flaws. Free to walk around in flats or even barefoot rather than the sky-high heels required to keep up with a persona I've created that really isn't me.

Jay cradles my face. "It's a dream, beautiful. *Your dream*. But yeah, it's all real. And it's all because of you. Now go make that phone call, because I have a celebration planned."

I peck his lips and snatch his phone from his hand. As I saunter from the room, I shoot over my shoulder, "I'll see if I can schedule you in. I'm a very busy woman."

He smacks my ass, causing a round of gasps from all those watching our exchange. "You have an hour, Chief."

My steps falter and my jaw drops. That might be my favorite nickname yet.

57

SAY YOU WON'T LET GO BY JAMES ARTHUR

Jay

'm nervous. It's not something I can hide. It's uncontrollable, really. I may have forced Catherine to agree to this marriage, and I know she'll go through with it for her family, but ultimately, I don't want her to recite her vows out of obligation.

Pacing the length of the roof, I wonder if I made a mistake. The fact that there were only two rooms in her apartment meant she would eventually be forced to share a bed with me. Now, she'll have all the space in the world.

If she even agrees to my plan.

Fuck, what if she doesn't agree?

What if she isn't ready to move Chloe again?

What if she says no to *everything*?

I press my hand to my heart and take a steadying breath. Cat cannot see me squirming like this. But the sweat dotting my forehead is a clear giveaway to my current state. It's almost November, and I'm on a rooftop in Boston. Even with the space heaters set up to warm the area, it's still chilly.

But *fuck*, I'm nervous.

Today, Catherine's dreams came true. She's wanted to be editor in chief of *Jolie* since well before the moment I first set eyes on her.

The only thing I've ever wanted is for her to be mine.

And today, I hope I can make both our dreams come true.

I check the time on my phone again and frown. She's late. I scroll the list of songs on the playlist to distract myself from the panic bubbling up inside me. Years' worth of music. It's been a while since I've pulled it up. For a long time, the only way I could get through the day was by listening to the songs from the beginning of our relationship. Those were the moments where I didn't know if I could go on breathing if we weren't sharing the same air.

I survived on these songs and hope.

Hope that one day I'd do exactly this.

Hope that Catherine James would one day willingly become my wife.

58

MARRY ME BY TRAIN

Cat

By some kind of miracle, Sienna Langfield happened to be in Boston today and agreed to meet me at her brother's brownstone. I had to cancel my plans with Jay, but I couldn't miss this opportunity. And if anyone knows that business waits for no one, it's him.

Standing on the sidewalk in front of the tall red-brick building, I'm taken aback by just how gorgeous it is. It sits across from a park dotted with trees whose leaves are every shade of fall. And its proximity to the water means there must be one hell of a view from the rooftop.

Like most brownstones, this one has almost no yard, so I imagine it has a decorated roof.

A place like this would be incredible for Chloe. The wide-open park we'd enjoy for at least three of the seasons, with running trails that would help ease my anxiety.

I can almost picture it. Walking hand in hand with Jay on the meandering paths while Chloe fills us in on her day. Maybe pushing a stroller or teaching a child to ride a bike.

I've never given myself the permission to think like this. Never wondered what it would be like to have more children. To have a partner to share my life with.

There was no point, because I never allowed myself to consider a life with anyone but Jay.

But standing in front of this brownstone has all those thoughts flooding my mind.

I dig through my bag and pull out my phone.

"Aren't you supposed to be in a meeting?" Sophie answers.

"Do you think Jay will want more kids?" I rush out, my breath uneven.

"Cat," she says softly.

"What if we have a baby and then I get sick?" I ask, admitting my worst fear. I refuse to let it suck me down, but that doesn't keep me from blinking back tears. "I can't do it, Soph. I can't lose them again. I just got them back."

"You aren't losing anyone. And they aren't losing you. Let Jay in. Tell him your fears. Go to the fucking doctor and deal with it."

"But what if…" I whisper into the wind.

The leaves above my head swirl, almost as though they'll carry my worries away if I let them. Tipping my head back, I watch them, immediately catching sight of the one person who has always had the ability to calm me. And he's standing on the roof of this house, dressed in a tuxedo and frowning into the distance. "Soph," I whisper.

"Yeah?"

"Why is Jay standing on the roof?"

She sucks in a breath. "Go get your happily ever after, Cat. Life isn't guaranteed. For any of us. We're given moments. Moments that are interrupted by the everyday, by kids and orthodontist appointments, by disappointments and work failures and mundane Monday sex. By too many nights having chicken for dinner and fights we don't remember the next day. It's not all beautiful, but the man up there on that roof wants to do all of that *with you.* And if you only get a few years with your soulmate, isn't that better than no time at all?"

"Well, fuck. Now I'm crying," I mutter, swiping at my cheeks.

Her laugh crackles down the line. "Yeah, me too. But it's because my best friend is about to get everything she's ever dreamed of, but instead of seizing the opportunity, she's on the phone with me."

Jay is up there, and I'm not stupid enough to leave him waiting any longer. We've both waited for far too long for this moment.

And he never gave up.

I shake my head in pure wonder. Because despite all life's challenges, I somehow found a man with that kind of dedication. "Holy shit, Soph"—I look down at my black coat—"am I dressed okay?"

She laughs. "You thought you were meeting with Sienna Langfield. Of course you are. Dexter made sure of it."

And I'm in yellow.

I shake my head. "You all set me up."

"You're late," she cries. "Go!"

KITTEN'S SONGS

Unsurprisingly, the person who opens the door greets me and leads me to the roof. With a smile, I follow, playing along with Jay's plan.

The inside of the house is everything one could ever want. An open floor plan downstairs, with a beautiful kitchen that would be wasted on a terrible cook like me. A fireplace, already lit and crackling, sits opposite the kitchen, leaving the house smelling cozy and woodsy. On the floor before it is a pile of blankets and throw pillows and several vases filled with roses. My heart leaps, and anticipation for what Jay has planned sends butterflies fluttering in my stomach. The man doesn't slow his pace through the house, so I rush to catch up, my heart melting at the sight of flickering candles lining the steps as we make our way to the rooftop.

I don't get the opportunity to check out the second floor, but as we pass, I count several doors down the hallway. Rounding our way up another level, we pass the most gorgeous stained-glass window, but again, my guide doesn't give me time to study it. The third floor is open and empty, just dark wood and natural light filtering through the windows.

"This way," the man says, leading me toward another door.

When I reach the top of this flight of stairs, I find myself blinking into the sunlight. It takes a moment for my eyes to adjust, but when they do, I suck in a sharp breath.

It's like I've stepped foot inside a magical garden. Greenery everywhere, with pops of yellow. Daffodils, daisies, and calla lilies wind around the entire space.

Candles of varying sizes glitter across the rooftop.

And across from me, Jay stands under a pergola, wearing the shit out of a black Tom Ford tuxedo, his hair blowing in the breeze and his lips parting, as if I've stolen his words.

Fortunately, the roof is warmed by heating lamps, so I drop my coat to the ground. And in a yellow chiffon dress that hugs my curves perfectly and feathers out midcalf, I take one step, then another, toward the love of my life.

"How did I get so lucky?" Jay breathes as he holds his hand out to me, wearing an awestruck smile.

I blow out a shaky breath. "What are you doing here?"

"Forgot to give you your song today," he says, his voice stronger now, easier.

"Oh yeah? I just figured you didn't have one."

Jay shakes his head and lets out a soft chuckle. "No, Kitten, I always have one. Haven't gone a day since we met without picking out a song for you."

"What?"

Jay holds out his phone. "Here. Take a look."

I survey him for a minute, trying to wrap my mind around what he's saying. When he doesn't elaborate, I take the phone and scroll through what looks like a never-ending playlist.

"Go to the first one," he says.

I stare at him stupidly.

"The first thing I noticed when I saw you in the café were the gold flecks in your eyes. You *calmed* me. I have no idea why." He chuckles. "You were frazzled. And you were completely destroying my business with your inability to work a damn coffee pot.

"I was evil. Completely uncaring about anyone but myself. Focused on nothing but my task—to destroy your family. And then I saw you, looked into your eyes, and that damn song started to play on repeat."

"There are hundreds of songs here," I mutter.

"Four thousand, seven hundred and fifty-three, to be exact."

"What?"

"A song for every day since I met you."

"But…" I shake my head, at a loss for words.

"There wasn't a day while we were apart that I didn't pick out a song. An inordinate number of them are titled 'Only you.' You'd be amazed by how many there are. My favorite is by Parmalee. Actually, I take that back. I love Harry Connick Jr.'s too. That's a classic."

My heart stutters in my chest and my head spins at his admission.

"Honestly," he continues, taking a step closer, "it kept you close. Even when my heart was breaking without you. They're not all sad, though. I got glimpses into your life. I'd see your smiling face in a magazine, and it would turn my week around. Even while we were apart, you'd give me enough light to make it through the next dark spell. To keep me going. Because, Cat, many days, I wondered why I was still alive. What my purpose was, when the only person I've ever loved hated me."

"I didn't hate you," I croak.

He chuckles as he wipes a tear from my cheek. The gentleness of his touch is a contradiction to the rough pad of his thumb. "You hated me, Kitten, and I deserved it."

I shake my head. "Even then, I knew there was a reason. I didn't understand it…and it broke me…but I never hated you. Swear it."

Another piece of my heart rights itself when, hair falling over his eyes, he ducks so we're eye to eye and gives me that shy smile, the real one that he saves for only Chloe and me.

"Almost five thousand songs on the playlist. It will take me an eternity to get through this," I say with a breathy laugh.

"My goal is to make sure you never do."

"Why?" My heart pounds wildly at the reverence I see in his expression.

"Because I plan to give you one a day for the rest of our lives. For as long as I'm alive, Cat, my heart is yours. Until my last breath, you'll have music in your life."

"Jay," I whisper, stunned. All I can do is breathe through the emotions coursing through me.

"Go to the first song, Kitten."

Tears blur my vision as I swipe aggressively.

But when I reach the first song, the air burns in my chest. It's not "Poker Face."

"How?" I ask, sure he changed it.

"Even then, I knew."

My heart beats wildly as I stare at the title.

"Marry Me" by Train.

"That day, I wanted to blurt out those words. Marry me. I wanted to drop to my knees and beg you to spend your life with me, but I barely got up the nerve to ask your name. And when I did, you told me to earn it." He chuckles.

While I brush at the tears cascading down my face, he hits Play.

Then he gently takes the phone from my shaking hand and sets it on the ledge beside us.

And before I know it, he's on his knee, the blue of his eyes shimmering like a glacier under a clear, sunny sky as he gazes up at me. "Marry me, Kitten. Grow old with me. Give me the opportunity to give you a song every day for the rest of your life. Because I love you. I'm *hopelessly* in love with you," he says with an almost exasperated laugh. "Completely. Irrevocably. Head over fucking heels in love with you," he murmurs. "I know I don't deserve you, but I'm begging you to marry me anyway."

His expression falls when I shake my head, but I'm quick to explain. "You are everything I deserve, Jay. *Only you*," I whisper.

"Is that a yes?" Chloe shouts from behind me, making me jump.

I crane my neck, spotting our daughter standing at the door with Cynthia and Sophie. Every one of them is grinning at us.

"You did good," I whisper, turning back to him. With a nod, I hold my hand out, motioning for him to stand. "It's a heck yes!" I shout with a laugh.

Jay lets out a loud whoop and jumps to his feet. Then he's pulling me into his arms and spinning me. We're a whirlwind of energy, and just like in that moment I first pressed my lips to his, the season wraps around us. The air changes, and the fallen leaves on the rooftop kick up and flutter as we spin.

He presses his lips to mine, lighting me up from the tips of my fingers to my toes. When he pulls away slightly, I go in for one more.

"May I?" He holds out his hand, palm up, showing me the underside of a ring he has on his pinky finger.

I nod and giggle. The ring hadn't even crossed my mind. My man on his knees before me was more than enough. He grabs my hand and slides the ring onto my finger so all I can see is the band. I gasp as the yellow diamond comes into view when he spins it over.

"Jay, this thing is probably visible from the moon," I tease.

He smirks. "Good. Then everyone will know you're mine."

I press a kiss to Jay's jaw, then spin in his arms and holler, "Okay, guys, you can come here now."

The three most important women in my life rush out and immediately fawn over the ring. Cynthia and Sophie take turns hugging me and wiping away their own tears, and Chloe's got hearts in her eyes as she hugs her father.

Champagne and sparkling cider appear, courtesy of the man from downstairs, and we toast.

"Will you dance with me, Kitten?"

"Of course. Chlo, pick a song. There are, like, five thousand to choose from," I tease. "Jay, give her your phone."

Jay's chuckle sends the fine hairs at my neck fluttering as he whispers, "I think I can do one better."

He nods to the guide-slash-server who's waiting by the door to the roof. When he pulls it open, a man with a guitar steps out into the sunlight.

"Holy fucking shit, Jay. That's Chris Martin!" My hands tremble as I spin around to look at my fiancé.

He smiles so damn casually and kisses my cheek. I'm dumbfounded and maybe a little woozy as he steps away to say a few words to Chris fucking Martin.

"Soph!" I whisper shout, unable to keep my cool.

She tilts her head at me in response, and beside her, Chloe is beaming.

"Did you all know about this?"

Silently, the three women who became my family when I lived in a world of utter darkness all nod.

Jay guides the lead singer of Coldplay over and introduces us. "Chris, this is Catherine, *my fiancée*," he says with a glint in his eye. "And Cat, this is Chris."

This is Chris. Oh sure, just Chris.

He holds out his hand, but instead of reciprocating, I giggle and nod like a bobble-headed fool. "I'm so sorry…is this real?" I whisper to Jay.

Chris laughs, and I finally take his outstretched hand. "This man loves you a lot."

Jay gets him settled on a bar stool he pulled from behind some greenery, and then he stalks toward me, takes my hand, and pulls me against his chest as Chris Martin sings "A Sky Full of Stars."

As I lean into Jay's embrace, our hearts beat as one, and I feel contentment like I've never known.

"I can't believe you did this," I whisper as the song ends.

"I'd do anything for you." The adoration in his tone and in the way he looks at me makes my stomach flip.

"You ready?" Chris asks, propping his guitar against the wall near the stairway.

"For what?" I scrunch my nose, watching the Grammy winner make his way to the pergola instead of bolting like I expected he'd do after he completed a favor for a random billionaire like Jay.

"To get married, Kitten." Jay loops his arms around my waist from behind and nuzzles my neck. "I don't want to wait another day to make you my wife. Marry me tonight. Move into this house with me. Let's give Chloe everything we never had. A family full of love. That laughs together, dances together, *sings* together."

My heart rate ramps up again as I spin to stare at him. "You're serious? You bought this house for us? You hired Chris Martin to marry us?"

He chuckles. "I hired him to sing you a song to convince you to marry me. In case you said no."

This man is ridiculous. And the most romantic person I've ever met. With a small smile, I place a hand on his cheek and just soak in his warmth. He leans into my touch, inhaling and closing his eyes as if he's memorizing this moment, as if he really doesn't believe it will last.

The truth is, I plan on touching him like this for the rest of our lives.

"And besides," he says, his eyes fluttering open and that smirk dancing across his face, "I'm Jay Hanson. Of course I hired Chris Martin to sing to you. And to officiate our wedding. What kind of billionaire would I be if I didn't?"

Laughter skitters into the night air, and pure joy vibrates around us.

"And this house?" I squeak. "It's really ours?"

He swallows thickly, his Adam's apple bobbing. "If you like it."

I throw my arms around him, pulling him close. "I love it," I whisper. "Yes…yes I'll marry you."

And then, as the sun sets over the park, with our daughter by Jay's side as his best person, and Sophie and Cynthia by mine, my soulmate and I say our vows. And Chris Martin, the goddamn lead singer of Coldplay, pronounces us husband and wife.

And when we hold tight to each other under the stars on the rooftop of our new home, sharing our first dance as husband and wife, he sings "Yellow."

59

A SKY FULL OF STARS BY COLDPLAY

Cat

We walk our guests out through the front door and say goodbye. Sophie shoots me a saucy wink as she leaves, and Cynthia takes Chloe with her for the night. When we're finally alone on the sidewalk in front of our new home, Jay turns to me with blue flames dancing in his eyes. "C'mere, wife."

Wife. Holy shit. Is there a hotter word in the English language?

When I stare up at him, still stunned stupid, he slides his hands beneath my knees and my back and cradles me against his chest. With a kiss to the temple, he strides for the door, then carries me over the threshold of our home.

"Say it again," I whisper.

Jay licks his lips as he meets my gaze. "Wife."

The word is uttered with such reverence. Such appreciation. So much love and unwavering devotion.

Wife.

"Need you now," I pant as he sets me on my feet in front of the fire next to the makeshift bed and a bottle of champagne in a bucket of ice.

We make quick work of undressing one another. The tuxedo, which stretched perfectly against his broad shoulders, is quickly forgotten, along with my yellow dress. Then his lips are on mine, and we kneel together, more desperate for one another than ever before.

There will be no long, slow worshipping of bodies. This is about connection. About sealing our vows. Becoming one.

Jay lies back and pulls me on top of him. I lift my hips, more than ready for him, and then, in one thrust, he slides home.

And in that moment, I close my eyes and memorize the feel of him. The fullness.

The sheer perfection that is this moment with my husband.

"*Husband,*" I whisper, opening my eyes and gazing down at the man who will forever hold that title.

"Fuck, I've never wanted a name more." He slides his hands to my hips and drags me against him, knowing precisely how to maneuver my body. To play me like an instrument. "Now ride my cock, wife."

Together, we chase our orgasms, our bodies moving in sync. Words of love are whispered, curses are uttered.

Legs trembling, I ride my husband, relishing every spark, every hit of desire that works its way through me as he sucks one nipple while he tweaks the other between his fingers. "Oh, Jay…" I breathe, feeling the telltale tingles building in my core.

He bites down on my nipple. "No."

Startled, I pause my movements and frown down at him.

"Call me husband when you come."

I give him a wicked smile and work myself over him again. "As you wish, *husband.*"

Our slick bodies move erotically as I fuck my husband slowly.

And in no time, we're right on the brink again. My release builds, and his cock swells. And as he sucks hard on my nipple once again, I shatter, convulsing around him as he twitches inside me and then fills me completely.

Breathless, I fall against his chest. With our hearts beating in rhythm, we lie that way in silence. When our breathing has evened out, Jay smooths a hand over my hair and kisses my forehead. And when I attempt to shift so I can clean myself up, he locks his arms around me and pulls me to his chest, keeping us joined as one. "Are you on birth control?"

Shifting so I can face him, I answer, "Yes."

"Throw it away. I want to fill my wife up with only me, and I want to see my wife pregnant."

My eyes widen. "You what?"

Jay's eyes show such warmth as he studies me. "I missed out on your pregnancy. And God, I can only imagine how beautiful you were."

I snuggle into his chest. "I've got pictures stashed somewhere. I'll show you."

Jay lifts my chin with his forefinger. "I would love to see them. But I'd love to see another baby in that belly even more. Give Chloe a sibling or two."

Unease tugs at me. I should have done this before. Told him my concerns. He should have had all the facts before we said I do.

"Jay," I whisper.

His brows pinch together. "What's the matter, Kitten? If you don't want more kids, that's okay." The sadness in his expression belies that sentiment, but like everything else, he'd give that up for me. He'd give up everything for our life together.

Tears pool in my eyes at that realization. "It's not that I don't. It's that…" I take a deep breath for courage. "My mom was diagnosed with cervical cancer when she was thirty-five. She was dead two years later."

"And tomorrow, you turn thirty-five," he murmurs.

I close my eyes to keep the tears at bay. "Yeah. There are screenings. But I've been putting them off."

"So you're scared," he says quietly. "I can work with that, baby." He kisses my forehead as if he's got this under control.

"All the money in the world won't stop cancer, Jay."

Watching me with a look of pure certainty, he runs his thumb against his lips. "I know that, baby, but neither will fear." He pulls me close. His heart beats wildly against his rib cage. "Give me your fears. *Always.* I can't protect you from everything, even I know that, but I'll never stop trying. If it's just you, me, and Chloe for the rest of our lives, that's enough for me. But avoiding the doctor, avoiding answers and screenings, that only gives cancer a chance to take you away from us. So please, baby, don't live in fear. We'll face this, just like we do everything else. *Together.*"

"But what if…" My voice cracks. I'm terrified that all I have will slip through my fingers. Just as I finally have it all figured out. "What if the doctor tells me I have it? I don't want to have more babies and then leave you all."

Jay shakes his head. "Then we fight."

"You make it seem so simple."

He rubs my cheek with his thumb. "Because it is. We can't predict the future. But I'll fight every day for you, and I need you to do the same for Chloe and me. Can you do that? Can you trust that I'll be by your side no matter what the outcome is? If we have six months together or sixty years, I'll be by your side until my last breath."

"I love you," I whisper, in absolute awe of my new husband.

He leans down and captures my lips. "I love you too," he says between kisses, already hardening inside me again. "Now let's practice making a baby, wife."

60

BROWN EYES BABY BY KEITH URBAN

Jay

Knowing the importance of family to Cat, I arranged our birthday dinner at a hibachi restaurant with the intention of including her brothers, my brothers, Sophie's family, Cynthia, and, of course, Chloe. While the rest of the world can't know that I'm Chloe's dad, the people attending the party all have the right to know. I was hoping that honoring their family tradition of always spending birthdays at a hibachi restaurant would garner affection from her brothers.

If not affection, then at least not downright hostility. As of last night, we're family, and I'll be damned if my wife loses her brothers due to our marriage.

"Morning, husband," Cat coos, running gentle circles against the tattoos on my chest.

Fuck, I love hearing her call me that.

"Happy birthday, wife." Tipping her chin up in my direction, I kiss my bride.

She hums as I pull back. "Happy birthday, baby. I could get used to waking up like this."

Tickling her side, I roll on top of her. "You should get used to waking up like *this*," I growl. Then I slide down her body and settle myself between her legs.

"Oh yeah, okay, that works too," she says on a gasp as I lap at her pussy.

When her phone rings beside her, she groans and huffs at the display. The call is coming from her brother's office.

"Pick it up," I murmur into her flesh. "Like old times."

She swats at my head and grasps my hair to guide me where she wants me.

But I pull back and watch her with a smirk. "Want to play a little game, wife?"

She grunts. "It already went to voice mail."

The second the words are out of her mouth, it rings again, and I can't hold back a guffaw.

She rolls her eyes and picks it up, smiling at the display this time. "Go on now," she whispers, bucking her hips into me.

I chuckle as I settle back between her thighs. I fucking love the taste of her. The feel of her legs wrapped around my neck, pulling me closer. The way she grips my hair when I hit her in a spot she doesn't want me to leave.

"Hey, Soph," Cat says when she hits the speaker phone icon, still maintaining her cool.

Determined to throw her off, I thrust two fingers inside her, pumping in and out quickly.

"Happy birthday, gorgeous! How was your wedding night? Is our sweet Cat no longer a virgin?"

My wife's laughter is husky as she bites her lip. "Uh—yeah, Jay took that quite a long time ago."

Caught off guard by their insane conversation, I have to press my face to Cat's thigh to stifle a laugh. She takes the opportunity to regain control by wrapping her ankles tighter around me.

Oh, my sweet Kitten. That won't do. I slide a thumb closer to her ass, and in response, she clenches, trying to keep me at bay. I suck hard on her clit, and as she loses herself in the sensation, I press my thumb inside her, forcing a gasp from her lips.

"I'm sure Jay has all sorts of plans today, but just wanted to say I'm so proud of you both, and I couldn't be happier for you. The two of you have overcome so much—"

Cat moans as I work her ass and pussy at the same time.

"Oh my God. He's totally going down on you right now, isn't he?" Sophie's tone is filled with mock horror.

Cat bucks her hips against my face, and, breathless, she says, "You did call the morning after we got married."

This time, I can't hold back my laughter. Her desperation makes me giddy.

"Oh fuck, I'm totally hanging up," Sophie mutters at the same time Cat cries out, "Oh fuck, I'm coming."

And ten minutes later, so was I.

KITTEN'S SONGS

With my heart in my throat, I stare at the clock on my phone, silently begging her brothers to show. I asked them to arrive thirty minutes early so I could talk to them before Cat got here. But the party starts in five minutes, and none of them have shown.

They're not my biggest fans, and I can handle that, but Cat has always been there for them. To not show up for her birthday is low. When Cat walks in with Chloe and Cynthia, I paint on a smile, refusing to allow her brothers to steal any more of my thoughts.

Chloe darts toward me and throws her arms around my waist.

"Happy birthday, Daddy," she says, looking up at me with wide eyes and her lip caught between her teeth. She's never called me Dad before. At least not to my face.

My heart squeezes, making it impossible to breathe as I get lost in a pair of blue eyes that match my own. I kneel so I'm eye level with Chloe and band my arms around her. "Best birthday ever," I whisper into her hair.

She squeezes tighter, and when she lets go, we both wipe at our eyes.

Cat gives me a knowing smile, then steps closer and pulls us both in. For a minute, the three of us just hold one another.

"I never thought I'd see the day," Cynthia murmurs when I let go of my girls and kiss her hello.

"Wouldn't have been possible if not for you," I say, a gravel to my voice.

She frowns and shakes her head. "They're the best thing to ever happen to me."

"Me too."

"Her brothers?" Cynthia says in a low tone, her lips barely moving.

Shoulders slumping, I meet her gaze.

That's all the answer she needs. She sighs and reaches for Chloe. "Come on, Bug. Let's go pick a seat."

Cat and I greet our guests one by one as they come in.

Garreth surprises us with an actual smile when we tell him he's going to meet his niece tonight and that we actually tied the knot. "Fuck, I'm happy for you," he says, clapping me on the back.

Hayden tugs Cat to his chest. "Welcome to the family, sis. Try keeping this guy smiling. He's been much easier to block on the ice since you came back into the picture."

Cat's eyes light up as she looks past him to me, but I don't miss the way they dart to the door when I hold out my hand to lead her into the party. "I'm guessing you didn't invite my brothers," she murmurs as we

450

walk into the dining room.

Cracking my neck, I lie to my wife for the first time. "Sorry, wife. I should have thought of that. We'll plan something with them soon, I promise."

She squeezes my hand and leans her head against my shoulder. "Probably better you didn't. They might not have shown anyway, and that would have been worse."

Pausing at the door before we enter and determined to put a smile on her face, I tug her against me. "Hey, Kitten, can I show you something?"

Before me, she takes a deep breath, her chest heaving, and closes her eyes, resetting herself and letting go of the things she can't change. For now, at least. "Yeah, please."

I slide my fingers against her left hand, over the yellow diamond on her ring finger. "I know we can't announce to the world that we're married, and I would give anything to see a wedding band along with this ring—"

Cat squeezes my hand and shakes her head, but I continue.

"And it kills me that I can't wear a wedding band either. I want the world to know that I'm yours." I flip my left hand over and show her the inside of my ring finger and the new *C* tattoo there.

A small gasp slips past her red pout, lifting my spirits a little.

"But for the rest of my life, Catherine, I'm yours and you're mine."

She lifts my hand up and pulls it closer to her, studying it. Then her brown eyes meet mine. "I want one."

I chuckle. "Yeah?"

She smiles. "Yeah. After dinner. *Please.* I want your name on my body, Jay. We may not be able to tell the world, but I've been yours since we first met, and I want the proof of that etched on my skin, the same way you're tattooed on my heart. You and Chlo are the only family I need."

"Fuck, I love you." I pull her into me and press my lips to hers.

"I love you too, *husband*."

Later that night, wearing matching smiles, Cat and I sneak into a tattoo shop and meet with the artist I've known for years.

Dinner was fun. And celebrating our birthdays with Chloe, watching her interact with my brothers and hearing her call me Daddy throughout dinner made this the best birthday of my life.

As Cat sits in the chair, she holds out her hand to me. I bring it to my mouth and lick my lips, then suck her finger into my mouth and drag her engagement ring off by my teeth for safe keeping.

"Could you get any hotter?" she purrs.

Then we both watch as the tattoo artist stains her skin with my name.

61

UNCONDITIONALLY BY KATY PERRY

Cat

Between preparing for the Christmas List for *Jolie* and dealing with the merger of the whiskey companies, November flies by. Cash and I still aren't in a great place, but we're on speaking terms again. It still hurts that my brothers didn't reach out on my birthday. But I don't let myself dwell. Because while one part of my life may be falling apart, the other parts are so full. We've officially moved into the house across the street from the park. My workdays are long as editor in chief, but every night, I come home to find Chloe and Jay hanging in the living room. Sometimes they're watching television, and other times they're listening to music. I've even found them cuddled up on the couch sleeping a few times. I snuck a picture, and when I shared it with Jay, I'm pretty sure he swiped a tear or two, even if he tried to play it off like he had something in his eye.

The way Jay has fallen into fatherhood with such grace has been the silver lining of my life. There's no doubt he was meant to be a father. And when the time comes for the doctor's appointment Jay scheduled, we'll hopefully find out if that's a possibility.

Or, like Jay said, I'll prepare for the biggest fight of my life.

Either way, we'll do it together.

To top it all off, I have an engagement party to plan. Jay got it into his head that we should make a big show of it and somehow convinced my grandmother to allow us to use the house in Bristol.

I have an inkling that he's using the celebration to bring my brothers and me back together. But his motives aren't completely altruistic. Because my husband is a diva and probably wants to show us off as well.

And secretly, I love that about him.

I'm approving photos for the January issue when the door to my office swings open and Carter appears, looking disheveled. His hair is a mess, and his suit is rumpled. "You married him."

I jump up from my chair and usher him into the room. "Shh," I hiss, shutting the door. "Keep your voice down."

Carter glares at me. "You married Hanson."

Searching the ceiling for patience, I count to ten. It's been weeks since I've seen my brother, and he's yet to apologize for the way he spoke to me last time. "It's really none of your business. Is that all you came for?"

"Fuck, Cat." Carter slumps in his chair and drops his head in his hands. "Chloe's your daughter, isn't she?"

My heart drops to the floor, and I sway. In all the years my brothers have known Chloe, they've never asked. Honestly, they'd have to be blind not to realize. She looks more and more like our mother every day.

Jaw tight, I nod.

"And Hanson's her father."

"You can't tell anyone," I plead.

"Why? Why all the secrets? And why did you marry him? Is he blackmailing you? Has he threatened to take Chloe away? Because we'll fight him, Cat. We'll protect you both." Carter pulls at his hair.

The look of desperation on his face has my walls crumbling around my feet. I settle in the seat next to him and pull on his knee, forcing him to face me. "No. I love Jay, and he loves me. And Chloe. We're happy, Carter. Happier than I ever thought possible."

Carter's face pinches like he's in pain. "But how? He's…fuck, Cat, you don't know what he did back then."

I settle back in my chair. "I do. I know everything."

"So then you know he used you. That he got Mia pregnant and threatened to—."

Shaking my head, I let out a loud sigh. "He didn't do those things. Carter, Mia had *your* baby. Her child is your mystery child."

My brother's mouth drops open, and his eyes go wide. "I—fuck—seriously? You've known?"

Biting my cheek, I rack my brain for a way to explain who Mia was to me. And why it's taken me so long to come to terms with the knowledge that my brother had sex with her. Even if he didn't know who she was to me.

There's no delicate way to word the truth, so I jump in with both feet. "Mia…well, she was my Mia before she was yours."

Carter scowls. "She was never *my* Mia. We hooked up once." He drops his chin and shakes his head. "And we have a kid," he whispers. "Fuck. Do you know where my child is?"

"I'm sure Jay can find out." I shrug. "That's not really the point."

Carter glares at me. "I've got a kid out there—"

I hold up my hand. "I get it. You want to know your child. And learning about him or her years later has been painful. Jay and I went through the same thing. So I'm not discounting that. But can you let me get through this?"

Carter huffs, but he sits back quietly, signaling for me to continue.

"Mia was my best friend in high school—"

"She was *that* Mia?"

"Yeah."

"Fuck," he mutters, running his hand through his hair again. "Cat, I

455

never would have—"

"I know. I just…it took me a minute to wrap my brain around what she did. Back then, she was a user. She was great at manipulating people. And I have no idea what went down between you two. But I'm sorry I didn't tell you as soon as I found out. I was just—"

"Pissed," my brother answers for me.

I let out a bitter laugh. "Yeah, pissed."

"I was an asshole. I'm really sorry, Cat. I just—*fuck*, I fucked up."

"Yeah, you did," I admit, my voice cracking as a tear slips down my face. I swipe at it, but my brother doesn't miss the movement.

"Shit, Cat, I'm so sorry. I—this isn't me. I hate who I've become."

I shrug. "I haven't been so fond of that person either."

Sitting up straight, he clutches my hand. "I'll do better. Swear it."

All I can do is nod in response. For his sake, as well as mine, I hope he does.

"That's not actually why I came, though. I got distracted when I walked by Hanson's office and heard him talking about his wife."

I huff a laugh. Jay does love talking about me. And that word. He's obsessed. All day long, he murmurs that one syllable. His emails are filled with the term. He whispers it to me when we're in a crowd and shouts it when we're alone. I swear if he could legally change my name to wife, he would.

I temper my smile. "Okay, then why did you come?"

"Grace is pregnant."

The information knocks me back a bit, and I suck in a sharp breath. I didn't expect him to talk about her, period. Honestly, since the night at the club when we tried to get her and Cash back together—which ended abysmally; he was an ass, and she stormed out, then refused to speak to me—I've tried not to think too hard about how her life was destroyed to save mine.

I've been selfish and so self-absorbed that I pushed her pain to the back of my mind. And now history is repeating itself. Except this time, it's not my child who is suffering from the lies, it's Cash's.

I rub at my forehead, willing the headache that's building to abate. "Does he know?"

Carter nods. "He overheard her talking to Hayden."

Grace and Hayden have become close friends recently, and he's one of her newest matchmaking clients. "Ugh," I groan. "I'm guessing he didn't take it well."

Carter chuckles. "Yeah, he's losing his mind."

"Maybe this will get him to talk to her. And then maybe he'll stop being a gigantic ass."

"I really am sorry, Cat. We've all been awful. It's just—Pa had us all so certain that Jay betrayed you."

I hold up my hand. "Jay isn't blameless in all of this. I know that and he knows that. But he loves Chloe and me. Really loves us. And everything he's done has been because of that."

Leaving it at that, I look away from my brother. Right now, at least, he doesn't need to know that the only reason Mia slept with him was to get information for Jay.

But even then, he was trying to save me.

"None of this is easy. But rather than holding a grudge over things that took place so long ago, I want to move on and enjoy life with the only person I've ever loved. One action doesn't make a person. It's how we act throughout our lives that matters. And for the most part, Jay is good."

Carter squeezes my hand. "It's going to take me a minute to get there. Forgiveness, that is. But if you can find out where my child is, that would be a great start."

I nod. "On it."

"Thanks." Carter stands, but he doesn't move for the door. "And maybe you could talk to Grace. Get her to tell Cash."

I sigh, dropping my shoulders in exhaustion. "She wants nothing to do with me."

"He deserves to know the truth, Cat."

"Okay. I'll try. Thanks for coming by."

Carter strides to the door but turns back at the threshold. "Kit Cat?"

My heart warms at the term, and I smile. No one calls me that but Cash. And Cash doesn't know it, but it's the nickname my mother used for me. Carter remembers, though. And hearing it from his lips means more than he could ever know. "I know Cash has always been your guy, but I'm here if you need me. Always."

I launch myself from my seat and rush into my brother's arms. "She wouldn't be disappointed in you, Carter," I whisper, looping my arms around him. "She didn't judge. She loved. Let's do a better job of emulating that."

To my surprise, my brother shakes in my arms, and when a sob rips from his chest, I cradle him tighter.

The truth is, we're all just trying our best.

62

US BY JAMES BAY

Jay

"Now just slip it under. Yeah, just like that. And twist—"

"Oh, like this?" I ask.

"Yeah, that's good. And then over—"

"What in God's name are the two of you doing?" Cat asks, appearing out of nowhere.

I drop the hair and meet Dexter's eyes.

"We were just—" Dexter starts.

I smack him in the chest to shut him up. "You promised!"

With a hand to his chest, he barks out a laugh. "Chloe asked Jay to do her hair this morning. Now he's freaking out because he only knows how to do a normal braid. I'm showing him a few new techniques."

"Fuck," I grumble, swiping the mannequin's head off the edge of my desk.

Cat leans against the door wearing a small smile. But this smile is a sad one. I can feel it from over here.

Dexter stiffens as he spots the strain on Cat's face as well. "I'll just, uh, I'm sure Sophie needs me for something." Dexter snatches the disembodied head off the floor. "Find me later. We can practice some more."

He squeezes Cat's shoulder as he walks by, and she smiles softly at him. Even sad, she looks incredible in a black sweater dress that hugs every one of her curves.

Aching for her, I pat my lap, urging her to come to me. "What's wrong, Kitten?"

Like the dutiful wife she is, she obeys. She shuts my office door, then drops herself into my lap with a sigh. "Hi, husband," she murmurs against my lips. It feels like she needs the kiss. The connection. The reminder that she's not alone in this world. That we face everything together.

Pulling away, I cup her face and drag my thumb against her bottom lip. "Why the frown?"

"I went to see Grace."

"How did that go?"

She blows out a breath. "Not well." A sad laugh leaves her lips, and she looks away from me. "She told me our mothers used to be friends. That *we* used to be friends."

Pressing her lips together, she looks back at me, searching my face for an answer. Like she wonders whether this is information I'm already privy to. It's not. The coincidence is almost insane.

"Really?" I ask, squeezing her hip.

She relaxes against me, then. She believes my genuine confusion. "I was awful to her, Jay. Awful. And now I find out we used to play together when we were kids. What are the chances?"

"Not fucking high." I laugh and pull her closer, cradling her body and running my hand through her hair. "Baby, you can't change the past, but you're trying to make it right. You've *tried* to make it right."

"Is that enough?" she murmurs, her eyes so full of pain.

I hate that I can't fix this. She's reconnected with Carter, and he's even reached out to me to apologize for how he spoke to her the last time I saw him. But she and Cash are still not in a great place, and that weighs heavily on her. Especially now that we know that he and

Grace are going to have a baby and that they're still not speaking. It's a fucked-up situation, and no one is more at fault than me. It kills me that my wife is taking any of the blame.

"You've done everything you can. The ball is in Cash's court now."

"I told her she has to tell him."

"Of course she does," I say. The words are harsher than I intend, but I'm still bitter about the time I missed out on with Chloe.

"But what if that isn't enough?" Cat asks, oblivious to my turmoil. "I just want them to be as happy as we are. It feels wrong."

"I know, sweetheart." I brush her hair behind her ear. "You have the most beautiful heart. But in the end, it's up to them to choose happiness and move past the anger."

When I pushed aside the hurt and clung to what I had, it made all the difference. And I hope one day they can find that peace too.

"If they'd just talk—"

"Always easier to say from the outside." I give her a sad smile. "If I had talked to you years ago…"

She sighs, leaning into me. "You were protecting me."

"Yeah, but we lost so much time."

This time, she's the one to brush my hair from my eyes. "We're together now, though, and things are amazing."

"Yeah?" I ask, hope lighting a fire inside me.

"More than amazing," she says as she sinks to her knees in front of me.

"What are you doing, Kitten?"

"Showing you just how amazing we are," she says, working the button and zipper of my pants, then pulling my stiffening cock into her hands.

"Holy fuck," I grunt as she wastes no time deep-throating me.

Her mouth is hot, her grip is tight, and her tongue works over the vein that makes me growl. Then she peers up at me and smiles around my dick.

I drop my head back and laugh. "Don't do that, Kitten."

Her smile only grows. Her eyes flash with challenge, and in return, I wrap my hand around her throat. She gags as I hold her still and fuck her mouth.

The door to my office opens without a knock, and Sophie appears. "Have you seen Cat?"

Cat doesn't stop, even after I grip her neck tight, trying to keep her still. Instead, she sucks harder.

And despite my best efforts, a grunt slips from my throat in response.

"Oh my god. She's totally under your desk blowing you, isn't she?" Sophie asks. Her eyes are huge with shock, but her smile is wide.

"Could you please leave and shut the fucking door on your way out?" I growl.

Sophie cackles and grabs the doorknob. As she's pulling it shut, she cheers, "Good job, Cat. Don't forget to swallow!"

From: <JHanson@Jolie.com>
To: <CJames@jolie.com>
Subject: I love you
December 8, 2022

Wife,

Only one more day until I get to dance with you at our party.

P.S. You did an incredible job on these invitations.

You are cordially invited to the engagement party to celebrate the marriage of Jonathan Hanson and Catherine James.

Date: December 9, 2022
Time: Six p.m.

Completely. Irrevocably. Head over fucking heels in love with you,

Your husband

From: <CJames@Jolie.com>
To: <JHanson@jolie.com>
December 8, 2022
Subject: Re: I love you

Husband,

You're just trying to butter me up since you left your laundry on the floor in front of the washer after your hockey game this morning. It stinks. Do better.

Love,
Your exhausted wife

From: <CJames@Jolie.com>
To: <JHanson@jolie.com>
Subject: Re: Re: I love you
December 8, 2022

Husband,

I'm sorry. Your message was really sweet. I'm looking forward to tomorrow too.

Don't forget, Chloe and I are leaving early for our hair appointments. Make sure you arrange a driver for yourself.

Still head over heels in love with you despite your disgusting laundry,
Your wife

63

NOT ABOUT ANGELS BY BIRDY

Cat

In my robe and sweats, I sit in the garden my mother designed and read the words on her headstone for the thousandth time in my life. I wanted to celebrate our engagement here, because I knew it would make me feel closer to her. Like we're including her in some way.

"Hey, Mom," I whisper, the cold December air leaving me almost breathless. "I got married."

Maybe it's foolish talking to a piece of stone. If she's watching over me like I believe, then she already knows about my wedding. But saying it somehow makes it more real.

"I got married to the most amazing man I've ever met. He makes me so incredibly happy. Makes me feel loved, accepted…makes me feel whole." I swipe at a tear. "And he wants babies, Mom. He wants more children, and he's the best father ever. But I'm scared. I'm so freaking scared to leave them." The image on her grave, the silhouette of a woman and her three children held tightly in her arms, comforts me. "But I feel like you didn't regret it. I don't remember much, but what I do remember is the way your arms felt when you held us. And the sound of your laugh. God, you had the best laugh. I'd do anything to hear it again." A sob ripples through my chest, and I drop my head and press my hand against the image, wishing for warmth when all I feel is cold, hard stone.

"Mom," Chloe says as she approaches me. Her voice is quiet, shaky.

I spin around and pull my daughter into my arms, cradling her how my mother once cradled me.

"Are you okay?" she asks, looking up at me with wide, concerned eyes.

I drop my head to hers and nod as I allow the tears to fall. "Yeah, just...I was just telling your grandmother about your father."

Chloe snuggles into me. "I wish I had met her."

I cry harder as I reply, "Me too."

64

YELLOW BY COLDPLAY

Jay

I'll never understand how the company that thrived for years under Theo's stead has so quickly declined under Cash's. Shaking my head over another email from a concerned supplier, I slip my phone into the pocket of my Armani tux. Now is not the time to worry about business. In an hour, guests will start arriving, and I've yet to even see Cat.

I considered going to see Theo this afternoon, but I'm still so damn angry at the man. And though he's lucid and speaking, according to Cat, he's still bed bound, so I'd have to get through Carolyn to see him. It's unlikely that she'll let me anywhere near him after our last interaction.

For now, I'll have to be content with the knowledge that she consented to throwing the engagement party on their property. Cat misses her brothers desperately, and I'll do anything to get them back to a good place. Things with Carter have improved, but Cash is still cold and angry. And the possibility that being with me could cost her a relationship with her brother eats at me a little more every day.

As I step into the living room in hopes of finding Cat, a voice startles me.

"Heard congratulations are in order." He's facing the fireplace with his back to me. He's tall and broad shouldered, and he's wearing a black button-down and slacks.

It's an all-white party, and this man is clearly not dressed for the occasion.

"Thank you," I say, tucking my hands into my pockets and waiting for him to turn around.

His dark chuckle grates on me. "Oh, I'm not doling out congratulations. Nor will I allow you to marry my daughter."

My jaw tics when I realize who the mystery guest is. It's been almost thirty years since his affair with my mother set me on a path toward revenge, yet I'm still not prepared for this moment.

"It's a good thing we aren't looking for your blessing, then," I mutter, choking back the rage that rolls through me.

Edward James spins around, glass in hand, and scowls. The man looks shockingly like his oldest son, though his face is weathered and his eyes are glassy. And even from across the room, the one similarity between him and his daughter is blatant. They have the same whiskey-colored eyes. And his are glowing amber just like hers do when she's angry. "You going to tell her you share a sibling?"

My heart drops, and my stony exterior falters for a moment. Refusing to let him see how shocked I am at his candor, I straighten my shoulders and lock the mask back in place. "So you admit that Chase is my brother?"

Without a reply, he brings his rocks glass to his lips and watches me silently.

"You ever going to tell him? The kid is spiraling. He deserves answers."

"You think we're so different," he sneers. "You screwed my daughter's best friend."

I pinch the bridge of my nose. "No. I didn't. That was your other son. But none of it matters. You know what's worse than being hated by your family, Edward? Being nothing. You are inconsequential to Cat, and therefore, you are inconsequential to me. You have no power over me. What you did with my mother? What you and my father did? None of it matters, because in the end, I have her. And everything else—well, it all is just shit, right?"

Tipping the glass slightly, he stumbles forward. "Your mother hated living in that house. You think I don't matter? She picked me over both of you. She was willing to give it all up to be with me."

His words stab violently at my heart, even if he's giving me information I already have. Even if I always questioned my mother's feelings regarding my father and me. Obviously, we weren't enough. But in the end, that's on her.

"Do you know what he did to my mother because of you?" I grit out.

"From what I've heard, they never found a body, so I'm afraid I don't," Edward replies with zero emotion.

He's a fucking monster. He had a child with her, yet he acts like her death doesn't concern him in the slightest.

"Father!" Cat snarls, appearing out of thin air. Truth is, I'm so stunned by his presence, I don't have any idea how long she's been in the room.

Cat slips her hand into mine and squeezes. "I'm so sorry," she whispers.

At her touch, her proximity, my heart rate slows and my strength returns.

"You are not marrying him." The low growl rumbles through the room.

Cat doesn't even give him a moment's attention. The strongest woman I've ever met tugs at my hand and keeps her eyes locked on me. "I need help zipping up my dress. Let's go."

It's only then that I realize she's standing in a white robe. Still stunned, I nod. And with that, she pulls me away from the man who nearly unraveled my entire life.

"You aren't merging the companies, and you sure as hell aren't going to be a Hanson."

Cat turns around and smiles at her father. "Watch me."

KITTEN'S SONGS

"You okay?" she asks when we're shut in her room.

"I wanted today to be perfect for you," I rasp. Those are the only words I can come up with after that encounter.

"*Jay*." Cat scans my face. Her eyes are full of compassion and love. They speak of her loyalty and her heart. This woman has willingly taken on her family over and over again for me. Always choosing me.

No one has ever chosen me.

Until her.

I grasp the back of her neck and pull her close to me. "I'm fucking perfect because I have you," I whisper against her lips. "Thank you, Kitten. I love you."

Her soft breath tickles my lips as we study one another. "Baby, you always have me. We don't have to talk about it." Her eyes dance back and forth between mine. "But know that you don't have to be perfect for me, right? You're allowed to fall apart. Especially over something like that." She throws her arm out, pointing at her closed door.

Tipping my forehead to hers, I close my eyes and hold myself in this moment. I memorize exactly how it feels to have my wife in my arms this way. Our lips barely touching, our breaths mingling, our heartbeats in sync. Every moment I have with her is better than the last. And I intend to make this a night she won't forget.

KITTEN'S SONGS

EXTRA DIRTY

As requested, our guests all arrive wearing white. The only pops of color come from the greenery and cascading wisteria around the outdoor tent. The silk fabric is so thin the stars are visible above and the twinkling lights and chandeliers give the entire space an ethereal feel.

The designer had strict instructions to create a space where the stars above would be the main focus, and she knocked it out of the park. Cat is a vision in her long white dress. The nude-colored layer beneath it is pure torture for me, making it appear like she's walking around in just lace.

No one can keep their eyes off her, least of all me. I'm smiling like a damn fool.

"You put on one hell of a show," Cash mutters under his breath beside me.

I quirk a brow in his direction. "Pardon?"

"You've got everyone fooled, but not me. I know you really want Grace. Just let my sister go."

Despite my determination to work out a truce with Cash, I laugh. He's delusional. As if on cue, Cat walks toward us before we can exchange any more barbs, likely knowing her brother is being an ass. It's par for the course lately. Unbothered by his insanity, I hold my hand out to Cat and pull her against my chest. When she tips her chin up to smile at me, I kiss her hard. I'll probably be covered in her red lipstick, and tonight, I'll gladly accept the evidence of her love for me.

When I pull back, she's breathless, but she doesn't pull away. She simply uses a finger to brush the hair off my forehead, then swipes at my lips.

"The only woman I want is standing right in front of me, Cash. Why don't you pay less attention to our love life and more attention to your company? Forester emailed me today."

He glares at me as I take my wife's hand and walk away.

KITTEN'S SONGS

With over a hundred guests in attendance, I'm kept busy for the majority of the night. I try not to let Cat stray too much and keep my focus on her and Chloe. While Cash may not be on board with the wedding, Carter is a lot less hostile. He took Cat for a spin around the dance floor, and he even asked Chloe for a dance. Cat and I laughed at Hayden and Garreth as they argued over which of them was next. Chloe made us all crack up when she asked what each of them would give her if she chose one over the other. Hayden offered to pay for college, but my girl was more interested in the front-row seats to the next Taylor Swift concert Garreth offered up.

What can I say? My girl loves music as much as I do.

While teasing Hayden, I spot Cat once again in a heated argument with Cash. Fuck. It's time to take matters into my own hands. No one is going to upset my wife today.

Grabbing the microphone from the lead singer of the band, I bellow, "Will my wife please make her way to the dance floor?"

"She's your fiancée!" Hayden hollers as the crowd roars with laughter.

Cat cocks a wicked brow at me, then saunters toward me slowly.

"Semantics," I say into the microphone while pulling Cat to me with my free arm. Handing the mic back to the lead singer, I bring my mouth to Cat's ear and ask, "Dance with me, wife?"

Biting her lip, she presses into me, allowing me to sway her to the music. "Always putting on a show, husband."

"Having a good time?" I spin her out and then pull her back to my chest.

"The best. Thank you. I know it was a lot of work."

Looking down at her, I pull her closer and bring her hand to my chest and cover it with mine. "Nothing is work when it comes to you." I kiss her softly. Then I throw my head back and yell, "I love this woman!"

Embarrassed, she buries her face in my chest as the crowd cheers.

With a laugh, I grip her chin and force her to look at me. "It's only ever been you, wife."

It isn't until later that night, when we're discarding our clothes and ready to sink into bed, that I spot the bottle of James whiskey in the corner of our bedroom along with a card propped up against it. I scowl, almost sure it's from her father. But my stomach drops when instead I find a note from someone else.

Hanson,

Heard congrats are in order. How lucky that you found the love of your life so quickly. And a new company. How perfectly matched. Maybe I should try out this Grace Kensington. Although my friend Vanessa has nothing nice to say about her.

Enjoy the whiskey.

Slainte,

Evan McCabe

From: <CJames@jolie.com>
To: <JHanson@jolie.com>
Subject: Pleaseee
December 23, 2022

Husband,

Cash and Carter are coming for Christmas. Please, please, please be nice!

Love,

Your wife, who is going to fuck you so hard for being a good boy tomorrow

From: <JHanson@jolie.com>
To: <CJames@jolie.com>
Subject: Re: Pleaseeee
December 23, 2022

Wife,

I think I need a preview to see whether it's worth behaving. My office. Naked. Now.

Love,

Your husband, who has been dreaming of your hot mouth all day

65

I LIKE ME BETTER BY LAUV

Jay

"I can't wait to get to London so we can see Chloe. I miss her so damn much," Cat says with a sigh as we step onto the plane. Her eyes dart to me and a smirk crosses her lips before I can reply. "God, I never thought I'd be on a private plane with you again."

I can't help the loud chuckle that shakes my chest as I squeeze her hand. "Don't get any ideas, wife."

Her eyes dance, and she shoots me one of my favorite smiles. "But why? My ideas are always *hot*."

We're headed to London to spend the rest of Christmas vacation with my brothers and Chloe. We did the James family Christmas while Chloe spent the holiday with Cynthia in Paris. Although I wasn't thrilled about the idea of not spending Christmas morning with my daughter, I understood Cynthia's request to have her. She gets so little time with her now, and she's never spent a Christmas morning without her. It still amazes me that Cat was able to do this for all those years. Spend holidays with her family while someone else raised our daughter, all because she knew it was better for Chloe. Her determination to give Chloe everything, all while missing out on those big moments, is just another example of how unselfish she is. It's also the reason I want to give her everything. Why nothing she asks for will ever result in a *no* from me.

Cat deserves a lifetime of yesses.

"You're right, Kitten. Everything in that brain of yours is sexy. So tell me, what is it you want?"

Cat attempts to take a seat beside me, but I pull her onto my lap so I can look into her eyes for a few moments while the flight attendant and captains ready the plane for departure. This is a bigger jet than the one we took all those years ago. That one was fine for domestic travel, but this is the family plane we use for our back-and-forth travels to England.

Cat may not be impressed by money, but that doesn't mean she's immune to it either. And I don't miss the way she impressively scopes it out.

Just another thing I love about her. Honestly, the list would be exhausting, but coming up with reasons why I love Catherine is one of my new favorite hobbies.

Cat tugs on my hair and brushes her lips against mine. Fuck, we've only been on the plane for one minute, and I'm already hard for my wife.

"Keep doing that and you're going to get fucked," I warn.

She licks my lips. "Promise?"

My chest shakes as I laugh and pull her closer. She can never be close enough.

"We're almost ready for takeoff, Mr. Hanson. Is there anything I can get for you?" Lindsay, one of the flight attendants, offers. She and Cara have been working our flights for the past two years.

While she addresses me in the way she always does, she glances silently at Cat.

I press a soft kiss to Cat's cheek and slide her into the seat beside me. Before she can get herself situated, I reach for the belt and loop it over her lap, tucking her in.

She giggles as she swats at my hand. "I can buckle myself."

"*Mrs.* Hanson and I are fine," I say to Lindsay. "We'll have iced teas, though, when we're in the air."

Cat's lips fold over on themselves momentarily. But then her eyes go wide and she lets a bright smile take over, like she's realizing that she doesn't have to hide her joy.

"Of course, sir," Lindsay replies. "If you need anything, Mrs. Hanson, we're here to assist."

Cat shakes her head when Lindsay disappears from our view. "You're brutal, *Mr. Hanson.*"

The relief I feel is palpable. She didn't tense when I referred to her as Mrs. Hanson. I know she loves me. I know we're good. But my last name carries all sorts of baggage. But she didn't shy away from it, and that's just one more reason I love her.

"No one treats my wife as anything but royalty."

"I'm not an idiot, baby. She wants to fuck you. As does every other woman we come into contact with. If I got upset by that, I'd spend my entire life worrying."

"You're not even remotely jealous, are you?"

Her eyes light up as she smiles. "Not even a teensy bit."

Fuck, that's hot.

"Why?"

She licks her lips, pulling my attention to her mouth.

I track the movement, adjusting myself in the process, because every fucking thing she does is sexy.

She giggles and twirls her finger as she points at me. "Because of that right there. You would never do anything I didn't say you could do. Hell, you were loyal to me for a decade, and we weren't even together."

I lean back in my chair and close my eyes. "I am pretty great."

She giggles as she snuggles in closer. "No, you're in love. And I trust it. I trust *us*."

With my head still on the headrest, I open my eyes and drop my head to the side so I can look into her eyes. "I trust us too. And you're right. I am in love. Head over heels in love with my wife."

"You love saying that." Her tone is light, teasing. Her smile unbidden.

The plane accelerates as we stare at each other with stupid smiles on our faces. I love being stupid with this woman. It's an underrated emotion. Everyone wants to be intelligent, important. But being stupid with Cat is the best feeling in the world.

That's true wealth.

Not a private plane. Not the ability to purchase anything and everything.

Moments where I can just be silly and feel pure joy with the person I love the most.

And after years of living as the wealthiest poor man in existence, I'm going to revel in the stupid.

"If I were a jealous woman, right about now, I'd be sinking to my knees and making it clear who you belong to," Cat says as Lindsay and Cara dart glances in our direction again. It's a shame I'm going to have to fire them, but disrespecting my wife is an infraction too far.

"They don't deserve your attention, Kitten. But I'd definitely welcome your hot mouth wrapped around my cock right about now."

Her naughty laugh hits the skin on my neck as she sucks on my throat. "Please tell me there's a bedroom on this thing. I'm not about bathroom sex, even if it's with you."

I'm out of my seat with Cat in my arms before the last word leaves her mouth. The jealous stares follow us as I coast by. "And to think, if they had been nice, I would have let them play with you," I growl in her ear.

"They don't want me, baby."

I hit her with a pointed look. "Everyone wants you, Catherine. I am a jealous man, though, and I'm not embarrassed to admit it."

Cat presses her fingers against my face as I open the door to the bedroom, holding me in place. "You never have anything to be jealous of." Her voice is soft, pleading.

"I read your article, Kitten."

She bites her lip.

The article she wrote over the summer was edgy, smart, and honest. She interviewed couples, married for different lengths of time, all who made the choice to open up their marriages in different ways. Some only liked to watch others, and some actively participated.

Cat simply wrote about their experiences, but she didn't elaborate on her opinion. That's the beauty of her writing, though. She lets others shine. She's a storyteller.

But because of that, I have no idea what her impression was. Is it something she wants? More?

I'll never say no, but I'm not sure how I feel about saying yes.

"Give me your hands," I demand, slipping the tie off my neck slowly.

My wife squirms on the bed, rubbing her legs together as she watches my every move. With my tie in my hand, I stalk toward her. She holds out her palms to me.

I can't help but take her left hand in mine. I turn it over and kiss the spot where my name is permanently emblazoned on her finger. It's a reminder, a promise, that even when we're like this, dirty and wild, my heart beats only for her. The sight of the dark ink with my name on her skin settles me in a way nothing else ever could.

With her wrists in hand, I tie them tightly together. Then I push her back against the bed and guide her arms above her head. "Now make me a promise, baby."

Cat's face is flushed pink. Her lashes flutter and her breaths come out quickly. "Anything."

The word echoes softly between us.

Anything.

It's the reason I'm confident that nothing we could do with another person would ever change what we have. Her confidence in us. Her complete submission, when necessary, is all the proof I need.

"You don't stifle a single fucking moan. I want everyone on this plane to know who you belong to."

Her wicked smile betrays yet another one of my wife's kinks.

"Done."

I tease the buttons of her dress, slowly undressing her while she's unable to do anything but watch. As her soft skin peeks through, I kiss down her collarbone and watch as goose bumps dust across her chest. My tongue follows the trail as I open the navy fabric until I reach the pink lace of her panties. Below me, my wife lies still, the way her chest and her taut stomach heave the only indication that she's the least bit nervous. She giggles when I press another kiss to her pubic bone and blow hot air against her skin.

"Fuck," she hisses when I slide my tongue across her soft skin, so close to where she wants me but not quite there yet.

"I've never been jealous of anyone," I say as I slide her panties down. Then I tilt my chin and wait for her to meet my gaze. "Until I watched someone else touch you and you told me I couldn't."

"*Jay*," she murmurs softly, squeezing her hands into fists. She loves to touch me, loves to run her fingers through my hair. It's her way of comforting me, and I've taken that from her because I want her to hear my every word.

"Hear me out," I murmur against her skin as I push her legs wide and settle in my place. "I don't feel that way anymore. Because now I know that if someone else did touch you, it'd only be because I said they could. Right?"

Her whiskey eyes flare. "What?"

I lick up her slit and moan as her sweet taste coats my tongue. My hair falls into my eyes, and I don't bother pushing it out of the way as I look back at her. "I know you like games, Catherine. Our marriage doesn't have to mean the end of them so long as you remember one thing."

"And what's that?" she whispers.

"The games you play are with me, wife. *I* say who can touch you." I slide my tongue between her lips and spread her wide with two fingers. "*I* say when you come."

She grows wetter at my words. Rolling two fingers slowly over her clit, I wait for her response. When she doesn't provide it, I squeeze.

In response, all I get is a hiss.

"Say it."

"Say what?" she gasps, already delirious.

I suck on her clit, and her hips buck up as she cries out loudly, just like she promised she would.

"Tell me who you are."

"Catherine Hanson," she pants out between heavy breaths.

"And who controls all your orgasms?"

"My husband."

"Even who gives them," I say as I slip two fingers inside her.

Her eyes flare at that statement. Like she's finally catching on to the meaning. Understanding the games I'm willing to play. The rules I'm setting for our marriage.

"Yes. You. *Only you.*"

Smirking, I settle back between her legs, ready to enjoy our new game. "Good girl. Now fucking come for me and let me lick up the mess. And be loud, wife. Let them know who you belong to."

66

ODE TO A CONVERSATION BY DEL WATER GAP

Cat

Boxes and wrapping paper litter the wooden floor of our apartment as the London Eye sparkles outside the window. As incredible as the scene is, it's no match for the one playing out in front of me. The Christmas tree next to the window glitters almost as brightly as my husband's smile as he watches Chloe open another present.

"How many outfits did you buy her?" Garreth teases, although he has no room to talk. The man bought our daughter a car.

She's twelve.

He says it's for her driver to take her around in.

As if she needs her own driver.

I swear these Hanson men get more ridiculous by the minute.

"Like the apartment?" Hayden slides a wineglass toward me.

I greedily gulp half of its contents before replying. Because this isn't just an apartment. It's our apartment. As in, it belongs to Jay and me. A place he recently bought, sight unseen, so we'd have somewhere to spend Christmas.

It's ridiculous. One does not need their own apartment for a two-week vacation.

But now I realize it's about more than that. With both of his brothers here, Jay is getting something that he has never had. Christmas with his own family. Doesn't seem so ridiculous when he lights up at the rare smile Garreth offers him. Or how his expression fills with pride when Chloe wraps her arms around his neck. Or when he winks at me from across the room while I chat with his brother. The man has wanted and ached and worked his fingers to the bone to have a family for years, and he deserves every moment of this overly extravagant vacation.

He deserves everything.

"It's a very nice apartment."

Hayden chuckles. "He's just excited to finally have you both here."

I nod. "I know. And we're happy to be here."

"How was Christmas with your family?" A tender expression crosses his face while he waits for my response. During the time Grace and Cash were broken up, Hayden and Grace started up a friendship that I think he wished could be more. Now that Grace is pregnant and she and Cash are working through their issues, it leaves him on the outside.

I squeeze his hand. "It was good. Rough," I laugh softly and roll my eyes. "But good."

"Your brothers good to you?" he asks in a protective way that makes me feel like I can be honest.

I shrug and blow out a harsh breath. "It's hard because Cash has always been my best friend. And over these last few months, the man you've seen? That's not him." I have to hold back the tears as I face him directly. "I'm sorry if you got hurt."

Christmas was different from years past. Carter and Cash were on edge, and Chase is still missing. But since Grace joined us, it wasn't as awkward as it could have been.

Cash chose to focus on her pregnancy, and he was civil with Jay for once. My grandfather was able to join us for dinner, but he and Jay kept their distance. I know my husband is upset with him. Hell, I'm upset with him. But I hope in the future, things can change. That one day we can all sit in a room like this, warm and cozy with all the ones we love.

Hayden frowns. "Not hurt. Disappointed, maybe. Honestly, anyone could see she was hung up on your brother. I truly hope they work it out. She deserves to be happy."

"So do you."

Hayden's focus returns to the floor where Chloe and Jay are now lying together, both wearing looks of concentration as they study the screen of Jay's phone, picking out a song. I love that they bond over music just as much as Jay and I do.

Hayden swipes at his pants before he gets ready to stand. "Not sure that's in the cards for me."

"Jay says you have a best friend," I hedge, not really sure where I'm going but feeling like maybe he needs to talk about it.

Hayden pauses as he turns to me, his brows knitting together. "Yeah, Anna." The way he says her name, like the thought of her steals his breath, is reverent, devout. Like it's a one-word prayer.

I test out her name. "Anna." Hmm. I nod. "And where is Anna this week? Will I meet her?"

Hayden grimaces, but he quickly wipes the expression from his face and lets out another deep sigh. "She's with her fiancé. But yeah, I'm sure she'll be around."

The plot thickens.

"She's royalty," he says quietly, looking at Chloe and then back to me. "So is her fiancé."

"Ah," I mutter with more understanding.

"Yeah, ah," he grumbles. "I'd tell you he's a gigantic arse, but since I'm English and supposed to be better than that, and you're American, I'll tell you he's a dickhead and Anna could do better."

His British accent comes out thicker when he says arse, making me giggle.

Squeezing his hand, I give him a sad smile. "I happen to know the Hanson men can be quite persuasive. Just tell her how you feel."

His blue eyes pierce me with their intensity. "Princesses can't marry commoners."

"Even billionaires?" I tease, trying to lighten the mood. But when he just blinks at me, I realize he's serious.

"Wait, you aren't joking? She's really marrying him and not you because you're not royalty?"

Hayden runs his hands through his long blond hair and slumps against the back of the couch. "Something like that."

"Hayden," I say softly, palming his thigh and squeezing.

Like an alarm is blaring, my husband's eyes land on where my hand is.

All I can do is I roll my eyes at him.

Hayden laughs. Even broken over his best friend, he still can smile. I hope Jay was like that when we were apart.

"Jay and I should never have been together. Our families hate each other. But look at us. We made it work."

Hayden side eyes me and then looks back to my daughter. "Your families were against you, not an entire country." And then he leans over, kisses my cheek, and mutters a good night.

KITTEN'S SONGS

Hours later, Jay and I lie in bed, our naked bodies melded together. Knees wrapped around one another, pelvises aligned, hearts beating to the same rhythm. Always in sync now. The apartment is quiet. Garreth and Hayden are gone, and Chloe fell asleep likely thinking about all the stupidly extravagant gifts her uncles bought her.

"A car," I mutter into Jay's chest.

He smiles down at me and brushes a lock of hair behind my ear, then presses a kiss to my forehead. "They mean well."

I sigh. "They're amazing, Jay."

I'd give anything to see my brothers like this with Chloe. We'll get there. I have to believe it. And because my husband has always had the ability to read me, he snuggles me impossibly closer. "Yours are too, wife. Years ago, watching you together made me extremely jealous. Not of you, but of that relationship. I'd always wanted what you all had."

I laugh humorlessly. "My, how times have changed. Now I'd do anything to see my brothers with Chloe."

"Why didn't you ever tell them?" he asks quietly, running his fingers lightly up and down my arm.

I trace the tattoos on his chest. It's become a ritual. Jay lifts my left finger up and kisses the spot where his name is branded on my skin and then sets it back down so I can return to my task.

"Things changed after you disappeared."

Beneath me, Jay stills, as if his heart has shattered for me once again. I press my lips to the yellow star and wait for him to take a breath before I continue.

"They treated me differently. I don't know what my grandfather told them, but Cash looked at me like I might break, and Carter didn't look at me at all. I didn't want that to continue, and I didn't know how to fix it. I thought you had gotten Mia pregnant. Hell, maybe they thought you did too. But the idea that they pitied me? Well, you know I'm not someone to pity," I say fiercely, looking into the proud gaze of my husband.

Jay chuckles, and it's like the sunlight comes back into the room. The beams warm every inch of my body from deep within. "No, Kitten, you are not someone to pity." He kisses my forehead again. "And your father?"

Now I'm the one who turns to stone. The man is the devil himself.

"I don't ever want him to know about Chloe. He'd use it somehow. He'd use her."

Jay nods. "I think he might be behind what's going wrong at James Liquors."

My stomach sinks. "Something's wrong?"

Jay's fingernails circle my back, a light featherlike touch that eases me instantly. "You remember how you mentioned Forester being a problem months ago?"

I nod. "But I haven't heard anything more about him since."

"That's just the tip of the iceberg. There's no way your brother has this little knowledge when it comes to the business. Your grandfather groomed him for this position, but the company is in some serious shit."

I sigh as I lean further into Jay's chest and close my eyes. "What did he say to you before the engagement party?"

"Your father?"

I hum a yes.

"Nothing I didn't already know. I can't marry you. Chase is my brother. My mother wasn't happy."

The last words are tinged with a pain so acute, it slices through me.

I hate my father even more in this moment. He's evil. Pure and simple.

"My father wouldn't know love if it kicked him in the face. Don't believe a word he says about your mother."

"She left us, Cat. She disappeared after I caught her and your father. Her concern wasn't me or what I needed. She just…left."

"I thought she died," I whisper, utterly lost in how to comfort him.

"Not at that point. Obviously," he chuckles darkly. "She was pregnant and had a baby. *Our brother*."

"Right."

"Part of me always wondered if she saw the bright and shiny, perfect life—two perfectly behaved boys, a beautiful house on the water, *you*; the daughter she'd always wanted—and decided to start over."

I rest my chin on his chest, tears blurring his face. "I don't believe that for a minute."

"Why?" His tone is so bewildered, so lost, so not the happy-go-lucky, cocky, know-it-all. And yet the humility makes me love him even more.

"She was coming back, baby. I believe it in my soul. But also—" My voice breaks, because what I'm about to say is unthinkable.

Jay's attention is rivetted to me. He needs an explanation he can cling to.

"If she'd come back and brought you with her…"

Jay's mouth drops open. "We'd be siblings." He curses under his breath. "That's fucked up."

I shrug and give him a wobbly half smile. "I don't know what happened to your mom, and I don't know why my dad is so evil. But you and I are here—" I hold up my hand, and he mirrors the movement so our initials are pressed firmly together. "We were meant to be, Jay. Nothing else—*no one* else—matters."

"You really mean that?" He's watching me like I'm an apparition, a fantasy, like I'm spun from gold.

I crawl up his body so that our lips are only inches apart. "Yes, husband. You, me, and Chloe. If I only ever have you, I'll have everything I need.

From: <JHanson@jolie.com>
To: <CJames@jolie.com>
Subject: Lunch
January 10, 2023

Wife,

You look fucking edible right now. You and me…lunch at the club?

Love,

Your husband

From: <CJames@jolie.com>
To: <JHanson@jolie.com>
Subject: Re: Lunch
January 10, 2023

Husband,

We've spent the last two weeks on vacation. We don't have time to sneak out for lunch. But yes, I agree. I do look edible. As do you. Now stop looking at me with those glasses on. Pay attention to Rose's pitch.

Love,

Your wife

From: <JHanson@jolie.com>
To: <CJames@jolie.com>
Subject: Re: Re: Lunch
January 10, 2023

Wife,

You do realize I meant I want to have *you* for lunch, right? As in I'm going to lick that pussy until you beg me to stop. Spank that ass.

Fuck. I'm hard now.

Kitten, please. I'm not above begging.

Love,

Your very horny husband

From: <JHanson@jolie.com>
To: <CJames@jolie.com>
Subject: Tonight
Wednesday February 28, 2023

Wife,

I got tickets to the game tonight. You, me, and Chloe courtside.

Love

Your husband

From: CJames@jolie.com
To: JHanson@jolie.com
Subject: Hi
April 6, 2023

Husband,

Don't forget, Cynthia is picking Chloe up from school today. I'm heading to Bristol to help set up for Grace's baby shower, so you're on your own for dinner.

Also, the caterer needs an estimated head count for the wedding. Call them, please.

Love you,
Wife

From: JHanson@jolie.com
To: CJames@jolie.com
Subject: Re: Hi
April 6, 2023

Wife,

Can't believe I have to spend the entire weekend without you. Also, can't believe that in four months, the world will finally know you're my wife. I'll call the caterer. Make sure you stop by my office before you leave. I need a taste of you to hold me over for the next forty-eight hours.

Love you,
Your husband

67

ALL I WANT BY KODALINE

Jay

"Stop staring at your phone. That's the fourth time you've looked at it in the last hour, I swear," Gavin grumbles.

Guilty. I can't help it. My wife writes the dirtiest fucking emails, and I live for the chime that signals each arrival in my inbox. But I put down my phone because it's Saturday afternoon, and both of my brothers came to watch the Boston Bolts play hockey with me.

Gavin groans when Beckett's phone rings next. "You too."

"It's Liv." He shoots his brother a look.

"Who's Liv?" I ask.

"She works for me. And right now, she's pissed."

I nod. "Ah, sounds like my Elyse. Don't piss off the second in command, Beck. You'll be attending the wrong meetings and drinking cold coffee for a long time."

Gavin laughs, and his eyes dance. "She doesn't look like your Elyse."

Kevin's brows shoot up and he scoots to the edge of his seat. "Oh, she's hot? I can dig a secretary. Dirty sex in the office. Ask Jay. That shit is hot."

"Stop talking about my wife," I grit out.

"Stop talking about my Liv," Beckett growls.

"Your Liv?" I say, practically holding back a gasp.

Gavin laughs. "Calm down, Beck," he says to his brother. Then, to us, he mouths, "She's married."

"This just keeps getting better," I mutter.

"I meant Liv. Fuck. Not my Liv. *Just Liv*. Gavin, look what you started," Beckett grumbles as he pockets his phone.

Gavin's shoulders shake as he laughs. He turns his focus back to the game, dropping his elbows to his knees. "I didn't say anything."

"Why do you even know his secretary?" Kevin asks.

Gavin sits up straight again. "She's not his secretary. She's the head of HR. For *all* of Langfield's divisions. My baby brother here is just the one who needs her services the most."

I bark out a laugh. "It's because you're an asshole." I elbow Beckett.

"Fuck you guys," Beckett says, rising from his seat and stalking to the back of the box where Garreth is standing. They both turn to their phones.

More and more, especially when Garreth is around, I look back and wonder why I ever thought I wanted to run Hanson Liquors. I enjoy life too much to be all business, all the time like he is these days. Just glancing back in their direction makes my chest feel tight.

When we were in London, Garreth sat Hayden and me down to discuss just how bad the James merger was looking. It felt like a wildfire. Every time we'd deal with one problem, another one would pop up. I told them to look in the direction of Edward James.

It's clear he hasn't slunk off into the depths of hell like we'd all hoped. No, the man is using his father's poor health to mount a campaign to take over instead of Cash.

Not that I think it'll work.

I also filled my brothers in on the whiskey bottle I received from Evan McCabe. *The threat.*

He didn't give any indication that he knew about Cat's connection to the stolen money. But that he knows about her at all eats at me. He's like a scab. He won't go away. And he never will. We need something to hold over him. More than just the power I gave him. Something that has obviously gone to his head. What he doesn't understand is that I'm the one who put him into the position he occupies, and that I have no problem doing to him what I did to his predecessor.

Hayden told me not to be too hasty in my actions—murder is a last resort as far as he's concerned. Garreth just sipped his whiskey and nodded when my brother wasn't looking. If we have to take care of Evan McCabe, we will.

Moments later, Garreth was lighting up, though, when we told Chloe that we were taking her to Lucy Montgomery's store. She's a fashion designer based in London, and Garreth is friendly with her husband Elliot. His real estate company handled the acquisition of our London office, and although it was a much smaller purchase, he helped me find the apartment for Chloe, Cat, and me.

That night, Garreth surprised us all with the news that Sienna Langfield was joining us for dinner.

The look on my wife's face was priceless. She'd planned a cooking class for all of us—probably because of the incessant teasing about her lack of skills in the kitchen that Chloe and I subjected her to. If she'd had time to plan, she would have had dinner catered to help her convince one of her favorite designers to partner with Jolie for a project she'd been discussing with me.

It's a brilliant idea, and I knew Sienna would jump on it.

Except we didn't have a chance to discuss it, because Chloe accidentally flicked tomato paste in Hayden's eye, and he took the opportunity to yell "food fight," and moments later, the entire kitchen was covered in food, as were all of our guests, which included a fashion designer and a princess.

Smiling at the memories made with my family, I pocket my phone and turn back to the game.

"Thought you said you were trading Parker." The second the words are out of my mouth, the player in question gets slammed into the wall by an opponent, and the three of us grunt in unison.

"Seriously? You weren't listening to a word I said that night. Did a memory of that conversation magically float through your mind all these months later?" Gavin brings his old-fashioned to his lips.

I grimace at him. It drives me nuts that he doctors up my whiskey. Especially when he adds sugar. Whiskey is meant to be experienced all on its own.

I shrug. "I can multitask."

"Or is it all that magical pussy you're getting now?" Kevin elbows me. "Makes you smarter."

"The fuck?" Gavin grumbles, glaring at Kevin.

My response isn't so subtle. With far more force than I should, I knock my arm into Kevin's shoulder. "Watch your fucking mouth. It's not pussy."

Kevin smirks. "Oh, now that you're engaged, it magically transformed into something else."

"Doesn't matter. Fucking asshole. Point is, you don't talk about another man's wife that way. The hell is wrong with you?"

Gavin nods beside me. "You're an idiot, Kev. You obviously haven't been eating from the magical pussy," he says with a laugh.

"Jay," Garreth calls from behind us.

The tone of his voice has me turning, and when I catch sight of his concerned expression, my smile drops.

"Have you seen the news?"

"What news?"

"There was an explosion outside of James Liquors."

68

KARMA BY TAYLOR SWIFT

Cat

My father is dead.

And no matter how many times I utter the words, I still don't feel a thing.

My father is dead, Grace was injured, and my brother is a basket case who's shadowing Grace's every move. Not that I blame him. Jay is just as bad, and I wasn't anywhere near the explosion two weeks ago.

"Seriously, Jay, I'm fine," I huff. Again.

"Are you sure you don't want to talk about it?"

"Did you want to talk about your father after he died?" I counter.

His face falls, and immediately, I feel like shit.

"I'm sorry," I say, pressing my palm to his cheek. "That was horrible."

Shaking his head, he pulls me onto his lap. "I just want to be here for you. I know that I had a strained relationship with your father—"

"*I* had a strained relationship with my father," I remind him. "You hated the man." I let out a low laugh, although none of this is funny.

"He was still your father." Jay cuddles me closer. "No matter how much I hated him, you're in this world because of him."

I sigh. Nothing in life is truly uncomplicated, I suppose. "Honestly, I'm fine. Do I wish that I had spoken to my father more than that one time in the past ten years? That he had even tried to be a better human?

Yes. Obviously. But the last thing he ever did was try to kill my brother's pregnant girlfriend. He's not worth mourning."

The motives surrounding Grace's kidnapping and attempted murder are murky at best. None of it makes sense. Why would my father go after her? Outside of the night of my engagement party, none of us had seen or heard from him in years. What did Cash do to upset him so much?

Asking Cash is pointless. I won't get a straight answer. If he even has one.

All I can do is let go and move on.

"Can we do something?" I ask, perking up.

His lips quirk up in a smile. "Anything. What were you thinking?"

I stand and pull him off the couch. "Let's grab Chlo and go to the park. I want to ride on one of those swans."

Jay grimaces. "In the dirty pond full of bird feces?"

"You said anything, husband."

"Bird. Shit," he enunciates, as if I don't understand.

"Yes, and you can work on those calf muscles while you pedal around the pond. You know," I say, waggling my brows, "for all the kneeling you'll do later."

Jay's laughter echoes around us, and he pulls me into his chest, hugging me close. "Fuck, you're my favorite person. Okay, let's take our daughter to the shit pond, and I'll get my workout in."

KITTEN'S SONGS

An hour later, I wink at Chloe as I glide my hand over the water, then splash Jay's face. Her giggles are as loud as his shriek, and both are the balm my tender heart needed today. The park is filled with families paddling around the pond, lounging on the lawn, and biking along the trail that cuts through. I can't help but turn wistful when I compare today to what a typical day looked like a year ago. Last year, I stood in my office and looked down at a beach full of families doing just this and wondered if I'd ever get out from behind the glass and live again. Now I'm riding in a swan and laughing with my husband and daughter.

It's surreal.

"Can we have takeout tonight and a dance party?" Chloe asks as Jay grumps and wipes his face.

I cuddle closer to her. "Sounds like the perfect night."

KITTEN'S SONGS

We're just finishing dinner when Chase's name flashes on my phone's screen.

"Hey." I shoot a look at Jay, then make my way to the living room. Chase has been a wild card ever since the Vanessa articles, and I'd rather not upset Chloe if this conversation goes off the rails.

Not that I have any intention of broaching the subject tonight.

But his voice on the other end of the line is a painful reminder that we still haven't told him that he and Jay are brothers. My stomach is in knots at just the thought. If only we could avoid it forever.

"Hey, do you have a minute?"

"Yeah, just finished dinner. What's up?"

For several moments, all I hear are heavy breaths. I can imagine my brother pacing and raking a hand through his blond hair while he works out how to say whatever's on his mind.

"Everything okay?" I prompt.

Chase coughs out a laugh. "No. Nothing has been okay for a

while now."

Nervously, I pick at my sweater. Is it possible he's found out who his real mother is?

"I know things have been hard, Chase—"

"Hard?" He laughs again, the sound far from jovial. "I feel like I'm losing my damn mind. I don't even recognize our family anymore. You're marrying a Hanson, Carter has stopped dating, and Cash? Don't even get me started on him."

"Maybe we should all sit down. It's been a while since the four of us have been together. I miss you." As I say the words, I realize how true they are. I'm tired of fighting with my brothers. And I'm tired of hiding my family from them. "I think it's time we get some things out in the open."

Chase hums. "That's why I'm calling. Our family has harbored too many secrets. Too many lies. Before you marry Hanson, you need to know what Cash has done. Fuck, you don't even need to marry Hanson now."

My heart lurches at his insinuation. "What do you mean what Cash has done?"

"Oh, it's not just Cash. It's Pa too. They were both in on it."

Unease tugs at me in the same way I'm unraveling my sweater with my incessant pulling. "What are you talking about?"

"Cash started a new company. Bankrupted James Whiskey. The merger"—he lets out a breathy laugh—"will be one big dent in Hanson's portfolio."

My stomach drops and my mind spins. I blink a few times, sorting through my brother's words. "He *what*?"

"He and Pa started a new company. In Bristol. Cat, this is good news. It means you don't have to go through with the sham of a marriage."

The phone falls from my hand, and I sink into the couch, drowning in a pit of quicksand and lies.

EXTRA DIRTY

We should have been honest months ago.

I should have been honest *years* ago.

And because I wasn't, Jay's family is going to pay the price.

69

YELLOW BY VANCOUVER SLEEP CLINIC

Cat

Hand in hand, Jay and I walk into my brother's new office in Bristol. I dig my fingernails into his hand, willing him to stay with me. Jay didn't yell or rage when I broke the news. It was almost like he wasn't surprised. Like it made sense. And then he took me in his arms, kissed my forehead, and told me it'd be okay.

How, though?

The revelation led to a late-night phone call with his brothers and a vehement defense on my behalf. I can only imagine how much they must hate my family now. Will the feud ever end? Or are the Jameses and Hansons destined to hate one another for the rest of eternity? And if so, where does that leave me? And more importantly, where does it leave my daughter?

But the man sitting at the head of the conference table is not my brother. A small gasp escapes me at the sight, though I'm not sure why I'm surprised. For years, my grandfather has apparently been playing puppeteer with my life. I always believed he was the one person who saw me for who I really was and accepted me. That he was my protector. Somehow, he's become the villain in my story.

"Theo," my husband says, pulling me out of my stupor.

"Take a seat." My grandfather nods at a chair to his right without greeting us.

Before we can sit, Cash strolls in wearing a smug smile. I don't even recognize him anymore. "You can let go of my sister's hand now." Cash reaches for me but keeps his eyes on Jay. "She's no longer your concern."

Jay goes rigid beside me, as if he thinks I'll abandon him at my brother's behest.

I pull my hand back from Cash and press it to Jay's heart. "Look at me," I whisper, ignoring my brother and my grandfather. "It's you and me. *Only you and me.* Got it?"

The surprise on his face breaks my heart. Does he not understand that no matter what, I'll choose him? That there has never been an actual choice.

"Please tell me you didn't actually fall for him." My brother groans, rounding the table.

My blood heats in my veins. "You don't even know him."

"I know enough—"

"Enough!" my grandfather growls, and for a moment, a flicker of hope that he's on our side ignites inside me. "Sit down and keep your mouths shut."

Jay pulls out my chair, and once I'm settled, he sits beside me and pulls me close so he can rest his palm on my thigh. He gives me a gentle squeeze, and then his attention returns to my grandfather. "I see you put our ideas into action."

I bolt up in my chair in response, and across from me, Cash gapes.

My grandfather's jaw tics. Despite being relegated to a wheelchair, he looks good. His color has come back, and the look in his eye is sharper than ever. "And you betrayed every one of them," he says, his voice hard and his gaze locked on Jay.

Jay squeezes my thigh and narrows his eyes at Cash before turning his attention back to my grandfather. "I kept your secrets for as long as I could."

"What secrets?" Cash scoffs.

I swallow over the lump in my throat as my grandfather and Jay stare one another down. The silence is excruciating, and hatred drips from them both, permeating the air with bitterness.

"I only did what you asked," my grandfather replies, doubling down.

"You kept my daughter from me. For twelve years. I missed twelve *years* of her life."

Cash's eyes go wide and lock on me. My heart shatters as a look of betrayal mars his features. "She's yours?" he whispers.

I nod.

"You had a baby and didn't tell us?" he says louder, angrier, as if this is his fight.

My grandfather holds up his hand, and like magic, all attention returns to him. "*You* put my family in danger. *You* begged me to fix your mistakes. *You* told me to keep her safe. How could I have done that if you knew she had a baby?"

This time it's my turn to break. "How could you? I *begged* you to tell me the truth. And my voice mails…if you heard them all, you knew. You knew how broken I was. How alone. And you let me believe he didn't care. That he'd gotten Mia pregnant. That I was nothing to him." A tear rolls down my cheek, and I swipe it away.

"Wait," Cash says, his face red with anger. "You told us that *he* got Mia pregnant." He points in Jay's direction, punctuating each word with a jab of his finger. "That he slept with her friend. You told us he betrayed them both!"

And suddenly, the final puzzle piece clicks into place. This is why my brothers hate Jay. Why Carter, his best friend, became his enemy. Why we're engaged in this damn war to begin with. A fucking lie that my grandfather told to keep us all apart.

To keep us…safe.

"I never touched Mia!" Jay bellows. "Your sister was everything to me. I gave up everything for her, and I'd do it again without a second thought. But what about you, Cash? You claim to love her. To care about her. Where the hell have you been for the last nine months? Your sister has been working herself to the bone for a company that you knew was going under. You told her you'd give her a seat at the table, and then you threw the goddamn wood in the fire and told her to watch it burn!"

My brother's eyes cut to me. He sees it now. That I've always told Jay everything. That this isn't and never was a marriage of convenience. That Jay is the love of my life.

Dropping his chin, he closes his eyes as shame ripples across his expression.

But is it me he's ashamed of? Or himself?

Cash's breaths are heavy. "Fuck you."

"No, fuck you and your lies." Jay pushes his chair back and holds his hand out to me.

I look between my brother and my husband, my heart splitting.

But Cash's lies, my grandfather's lies, are what brought us here. We could have had it all, but they only thought of themselves. And Jay is my family now—Jay and Chloe and me—so I slip my hand into his and stand.

"Please sit," my grandfather says, sounding less sure of himself.

Jay is red-faced and trembling with rage, but I tug on his hand, begging him to give me a few more minutes.

"We had an agreement," my grandfather starts, his eyes cold and set on Jay. "And when I got sick, you went behind my back, started going after the deal we'd discussed. *You* did this," he admonishes.

Jay's shoulders sag. "I would never have burned your family. I'd cut out my own eye before I hurt Cat again. But Cash didn't know about our agreements. He was angry. If I'd told him our plans, no one would have believed me."

Cash scoffs. "This is fucking unbelievable."

My grandfather clears his throat, garnering our attention again. "And then you used all the secrets I told you in confidence. The things I told you because you were a broken boy who needed the truth. And you used them to steal my company." His booming voice vibrates through the room.

Jay's heavy breaths beside me are like a drumroll, beating each of his words into my brain.

My father's affairs. Chase's birth mom. Even in death, Edward James's transgressions haunt us.

"I wasn't stealing your company. I was fucking honoring you by continuing with our merger plans."

Across from us, Cash gasps.

"The plans we made before you tried to destroy my company and force my granddaughter into a marriage she didn't want."

"He wasn't destroying our company." I squeeze Jay's hand and look into his eyes. "He was fighting for *his* family."

"Yeah," Cash scoffs. "He'll always put Hanson Liquors first. That's the point, Cat."

I turn to my brother, my heart pounding out of my chest. "No. *I* am his family. *Chloe* is his family. He was fighting for us. And it's time for me to return the favor. Do whatever you want with your new company, but I'll be working with Jay to fix the mess you've created. We're continuing forward with James/Hanson Whiskey. You want to destroy it? I'll build it back up piece by piece, and it'll be even better than before."

Jay peers down at me in surprise, his mouth slightly ajar.

"You were right, baby," I whisper to him, no longer caring about the audience before us. "You aren't the villain. Apparently, that role is dependent on who narrates the story. Now everyone will know the truth."

"I don't need anyone else to know, Kitten. Only you."

Jay looks at me with such love in his eyes, I can actually feel it warming me and giving me the strength to do what I just promised. I tug him up as I stand. "Now we leave," I whisper with a smile.

From: <CJames@Jolie.com>

To: <JHanson@jolie.com>

Subject: Dinner

September 20, 2023

I'm going to be late again. Can you feed Chloe?

From: <JHanson@jolie.com>

To: <CJames@jolie.com>

Subject: Re: Dinner

September 20, 2023

Wife,

Please come home. You're running yourself ragged.

I love you and I'm worried.

Still head over heels in love with you,

Your husband

70

UNSTEADY BY X AMBASSADORS

Cat

I swipe the tears from my face and pull up the next article waiting for my approval. It's been months since the explosion. Since my life changed so drastically. And I'm barely hanging on. The only bright spots in my life are Jay and Chloe. Even the magazine is a chore these days. I never imagined I could walk into this building feeling resentment. But every time someone asks for my opinion, I want to scream *can't you figure it out yourself?*

Night and day, I've been working to dig Hanson Liquors out of the debt my family put them in. Garreth and Hayden swear my family's deception barely made a dent in their portfolio, but I can't shake the guilt.

I learned a lot about the liquor industry and had some really great ideas before Cash drove James Liquors into the ground. Or so I thought. And I assumed Jay and I would work our magic there like we did at *Jolie*.

Instead, Jay shows virtually no interest in the liquor business and is constantly hovering over me, encouraging me to give up.

Doesn't he know me? Those words don't exist in my vocabulary.

"Hey, you're here late again," Sophie says as she taps on my door wearing a worried expression.

"So are you," I counter. I take a deep breath and bury the emotions threatening to escape.

"Dexter and I have a date tonight, so I'm waiting for him to finish up with a photo shoot." She walks into my office, studying me with a frown, and plops into the chair on the other side of my desk.

"Date? What's that like?" I ask, a sarcastic laugh bubbling up from my throat.

"*Cat*." Her tone is laced with disappointment. Or maybe it's pity. Either way, it has the tears escaping.

"How do you do it, Soph?"

"Do what?" She tilts her head in question.

"Balance everything. Work, motherhood, marriage." I choke on a sob. "You've got four kids. I only have one, and I feel like I'm drowning. I'm failing her. And Jay."

Sophie rushes over and kneels beside my chair. "You aren't failing them. And I don't have it all together. I schedule kinky sex with my husband. I rely on fast food far too often, and at least twice a week, I hide in the bathtub with a glass of wine while my kids scream for me."

"What?" I ask, my jaw slack. "Aren't you happy? I thought you were happy."

Sophie's smile is soft. "Of course I'm happy, but this is life."

"But why don't you ever talk about it? We should talk about it. I'm floundering and riddled with guilt. I feel awful because I have everything I ever wanted. Jay and I are together. Like *really* together. Chloe lives with us, and we have the family I've always dreamed of, and I just… shouldn't I be…I don't know, happier? Like I'm getting everything my mom didn't. Shouldn't it be enough?"

My throat burns as tears roll down my face.

"Breakfast for dinner," Sophie mutters.

"What?"

She clasps her hands in her lap. "Breakfast for dinner. It's my secret weapon."

"I don't understand."

"When I'm overwhelmed and feeling like a failure and need a small win to keep me going, we have breakfast for dinner. And it's like magic. Everyone smiles, and it changes the mood instantly. The kids think it's a special day, even though I'm at my worst."

"Breakfast for dinner," I mutter, "Fucking brilliant."

She smiles and stands. "Stick with me, kid. I've done this four times. But we're both still in it, and the battle never really ends. The men are great and all, and the orgasms are fantastic, but it's okay to vent when you're having a bad day. That's what I'm here for."

KITTEN'S SONGS

I'm not the least bit surprised when I walk into the spotless kitchen. There's a plate of food on the stove for me, and from the stillness of the house, I have no doubt Chloe is already asleep.

While I'm struggling with this parenting thing, Jay makes it look easy. Which leaves me irrationally annoyed.

Why is he so good at this?

When I step into the bathroom, I let out a sarcastic "Ha!" at the sight of his dirty boxers on the floor next to the laundry bin. I pick them up and toss them in, all the while cackling like I've lost my mind. "See, not so perfect now, is he?"

Feeling validated, I storm back into the kitchen, now donning my sweats, and warm up my food, then I take it into the dining room and settle at the table.

From the living room, Jay shouts, "You going to come say hello?"

I let out another haughty laugh and squint at him as I take a bite of my reheated pasta.

Without looking up, he says, "Why do I feel your dragon eyes on me? I swear I can feel the fire you're breathing."

"That's the third outfit you've worn today."

He finally looks up, then he slowly stands and shuffles over to me. With a peck to my forehead, he takes the seat beside me and rests his elbows on the table. "What?"

"This morning, you wore a T-shirt and gym shorts when you went for a run. Then you had your suit on for work. And now you're in a pair of sweats," I point out, as if I'm not the crazy one here.

Newsflash, I definitely am.

He quirks a brow. "And that's got you shooting daggers because…?"

"It's a lot of laundry. Add in Chloe's and mine, and I feel like I could do laundry every day and still not keep up."

Jay's eyes soften. "We'll hire help, Kitten."

With a firm shake of my head, I huff. "I can do it."

He doesn't get it.

"But why? You seem unhappy. And you have been for a while. Honestly, I'm nervous that you're having second thoughts about us."

My cheeks flame, and I drop my head. Damn it. I'm just picking a fight with him because I'm overwhelmed. He's not wrong. I am unhappy. I drop my fork and turn toward him. "Not about you. Never about you. Or Chloe. The two of you are everything to me."

I press my hand to his cheek, and he leans into my touch.

"Then what?"

"I don't think I can save the merger." I drop my hand to my lap. "I've cost you everything, and I'm drowning trying to balance that with *Jolie* and our family. And don't even get me started on *my* family." Pressing my lips together, I take in a long breath through my nose to keep my tears at bay. "My brother had a baby, and we haven't spoken. Hopie is a dream. Thank God I've had the chance to meet her. But my brother and

I have no relationship. I don't know how to wrap my head around it all."

Jay closes his eyes and rubs at his forehead. When he looks at me again, his irises are darker, almost gray, and angry.

"Have I not shown you over the last year and a half that everything I do is for you?" he whispers. "I killed my own father. You think I give a fuck about his company going under? I already handed it over to my brothers. I gave it up long ago. You should too."

"You what?"

"I refuse to spend the rest of my life fighting with your brothers," Jay says, as if the explanation is simple.

"But—"

"They're Chloe's uncles. They're *your family*. I'd do anything to give you the family we never had. Even give up my own," he says, his voice softer now.

"But they did this to you. To us…"

"And I'm doing this *for you*. For us. Don't you get it? Nothing in this world matters more to me than my two girls. *Nothing.* So give me your stress, wife. Give me your anxiety. Don't hold it all in and resent me. Don't stay at work late trying to fix the unfixable. Don't miss out on this life we've battled for because of a meaningless brick building and some alcohol. It's not worth it. *We* are worth it."

"Why are you so perfect?" I whisper as a tear slips down the stony mask I've been fighting to keep in place.

Jay gives me a soft smile. "I'm not perfect, baby. But I am perfect for you."

"You really gave up your interest in the company?"

Jay chuckles. "Don't worry, we're not going to be poor or anything."

"Oh no?" I tease. "Wouldn't want to lose out on that jet of yours."

Jay winks and takes my hand. "We'll still have plenty of trips on the jet. You're officially looking at the owner of one-half of Bouvier Media."

My heart stops at his words, and I lock my gaze on him. "What?"

"You heard me. We work so well together, and the magazine is just one facet. You can continue to run it and contribute ideas for other businesses we should acquire or create. Or you can appoint a new editor in chief for *Jolie* and take on more of a leadership role at Bouvier. Up to you."

He says it like he hasn't just stolen my breath like he stole my heart all those years ago.

Scanning his face, I ask, "You named it after my mother?"

One side of Jay's mouth kicks up. "I named it after the girl who brought me back to life. You still don't get it, Kitten." He shakes his head, causing his hair to fall over his eyes. "You were supposed to be my revenge, but you became my salvation. You are my fate. And every day from now until eternity, I'll thank you for that. This is just one small way. By honoring your mother. Besides, neither of our fathers deserves the honor."

Throwing my napkin to the table, I clap my hands to my husband's cheeks and plant my mouth on his. It's desperate and frantic. Beautiful and possessive. It's filled with promises and apologies. Years' worth of trauma. And happiness. So much fucking happiness. Because this man, he gives me the world and then asks what I want for dinner.

"Can we have waffles for dinner tomorrow?" I ask as I hold Jay's face.

He doesn't even question me. "We can have whatever makes you happy, wife."

From: <JHanson@jolie.com>
To: <CJames@jolie.com>
Subject: Black Label
September 21, 2023

Wife,

I have a surprise for you. Chloe is sleeping over at Sophie's tonight. Meet me at the club at seven.

Completely. Irrevocably. Head over heels,

Your husband

71

RIPTIDE BY VANCOUVER SLEEP CLINIC

Jay

Settling into the booth across from Frank, I nod toward the drink he's ordered for me. "Thanks. Sorry I'm late. I was doing laundry."

With a shake of his head, he smirks. "Oh, how times have changed."

I laugh. "You have no fucking idea." I take a sip of my drink and smile. "How are things in Bristol?"

"Not Boston," he grumbles. Then he shrugs and sits a little straighter. "But they're okay. The baby is cute, and Cash spends nearly half the day just staring at her."

I laugh. I can imagine I'd be the same way.

Frank and I started these lunches months back. Over the past year, I've come to trust him more than just about anyone. Vanessa's blackmail and Evan McCabe's threats made me realize I couldn't protect Cat alone. The stakes are too high. So I turned to the one man I know will protect her the way I do—who would pick her over his own damn family, just like me.

And he did. He's kept his ear to the ground. He's kept tabs on the Mob's activities and sifted through each threat to determine which are real in order to keep us two steps ahead. There is no one I trust more.

With Cat's well-being. And Chloe's. Along with the truth of who she is to me.

The man put himself through college, then went on to fight overseas all to earn a place outside his family. Asking him to return to that life wasn't something I took lightly. But he didn't bat an eye at the request. His only response was "just tell me what you need." That alone makes him one of the most honorable men I've ever met.

"Heard anything from your brother?"

Frank gives a quick shake of his head and scans the room. I imagine he's always doing that. Always checking to see whether his conversations are being overheard. Always looking for a threat. Being the son of a mobster surely comes with a lifetime of these ticks. But being in the Marines only added to it. "Has he sent any more friendly gifts?"

I cough out a dry laugh. "Not since the whiskey bottle the night of the engagement party."

Frank nods and blows out a breath, his leg bouncing as he drums his fingers against his drink. "Good. That's good. How's Cat?"

"She's…" My wife is working herself to death. But after our conversation last night, I'm optimistic that she'll take a step back. "Truthfully, she's struggling."

His forehead wrinkles as he studies me. And then he shakes his head. "I'm sorry. I really wish I could do something to fix this for them. Cash misses her, I know that. He just doesn't know how to make it right."

"He could start by apologizing," I grumble.

Frank tilts his glass toward me. "I agree. I'll talk to him again."

Resting my elbows on the table, I blow out a breath. "That's actually not why I asked you to meet me today."

"No?"

I run my tongue across my teeth, taking a second to prepare myself for what I'm about to ask. "Cat needs something."

"Anything. You know I'd do anything for her."

I smile as I settle back in my seat. "That's what I was hoping you'd say."

72

HANDS TO MYSELF BY SELENA GOMEZ

Cat

Smiling at the security guard, I step through the doors of Black Label. I wasn't exactly surprised when I received the invitation from Jay today.

He's nothing if not a man of his word. He promised he'd give me everything. That he'd be my partner as a parent and as a lover.

A night together, just the two of us, with a break from the responsibilities of parenting and the stress of being CEOs, is exactly what we need.

More specifically, a night of *play* is exactly what I need.

The erotic soundtrack that floats through the air in the hall that leads to Jay's office leaves me clenching. Unable to stop myself, I slow my steps and peek around the curtain that leads to the group activity room. As I take in the sight, I clamp down on my bottom lip and let the desire that warms my belly grow.

Hopefully Jay won't mind that I'm late.

Before me, two women are locked in a passionate kiss while their partners undress them slowly from behind.

One man slides the dress down his girlfriend's arms, causing her breasts to pop out. Her friend goes straight for her pebbled pink nipples, while her boyfriend claims her mouth. The way they move is choreographed like a ballet.

Pleasure drips down my thighs at the display, and the sensation is all the reminder I need. So I drop the cloth and head to Jay's office, needy and desperate.

I open the door and immediately stagger back. When I'm steady again, I blink several times, because my eyes must be deceiving me. Beside the bar, Frank stands with a shaker in hand, and his eyes are eating up every inch of me.

"Uh—" My mind goes blank. I literally can't form a coherent thought, let alone voice it. His shirt is unbuttoned at the collar, and his sleeves are rolled up to his elbows, exposing the tattoos that snake up his arms. His green eyes remain on me as he grips the shaker tightly, knocking the liquid inside back and forth.

It's only the sound of Jay's voice that breaks me from my stupor. "Hello, wife. Did you enjoy the show?"

My eyes dart to him next. He's sitting on the couch, legs spread wide, white shirt unbuttoned, smirk and come fuck me stare in place.

"What's going on?" I stammer, hovering in the doorway.

Jay lifts a hand and motions for me with his fingers as he speaks to Frank. "Pour my wife her drink and then join us."

Heart lurching, I look back to Frank. He's still focused on me, studying me, like he's gauging what I'll do.

Interesting. Because I haven't quite decided what the fuck I'll do. I have no idea what's going on. Has my husband lost his mind?

Cautiously, I shuffle toward Jay and stop a few feet in front of him. "Kiss me, Kitten. And say thank you for your present."

"What present?" I rasp as I lean down to kiss him.

When I'm within arm's reach, he pulls me onto his lap and takes my lips in a devastating kiss. His grip is hungry, and each nip of my lips is possessive.

Gaze sharp, intoxicating, he licks his lips and brings his mouth to my ear. "Frank is your present, baby. We're both going to fuck you tonight."

Oh.

My thighs clench, and I throb at the mental image of these two men with their hands on me.

As Frank appears beside us with my drink, Jay smirks. "He made it extra dirty, just like you like it."

Frank grasps my wrist and presses the drink into my hand. "You okay?" he asks far too gently.

My heart rate ticks up and my body heats at his proximity.

Jay squeezes my hips and forces me to my feet, causing my drink to slosh over the rim of the glass. "She's fucking perfect. Cat got your tongue, Kitten?" he asks, a teasing lilt to his voice. His eyes are almost silver as they roam over my features. "Soon it will be Frank that has your tongue. What do you think about that, baby? Can you handle us both?"

Need tugs at my core and desire pools in my panties.

Is he fucking serious right now?

"Take off her dress," Jay says. His attention is on me, but the command is for the man at my side.

Frank's nose finds my neck, and his breath tickles as he inhales. Goose bumps pebble my flesh, but my eyes remain on Jay, transfixed.

He's not angry. There isn't even the normal look of possession in his eyes. Instead, I find want, desire, and pleasure in the set of his jaw and the way his irises flicker as he watches my brother's best friend undress me.

Frank's fingers are gentle as they slip the neckline of my dress over my shoulder, much like the scene I witnessed only moments ago in the playroom.

As the fabric slides down my body and pools at my feet, Jay holds out a hand. I take it, and he steadies me so I can step out of my dress. When I've kicked the garment aside, I stand before him in a black bra and panty set. Both pieces are comprised of straps that crisscross my body. When I dressed for the evening, I imagined him pulling on each one while he fucked me.

"The fuck is this outfit, Kitten?" Jay growls, his eyes eating me up.

I clear my throat, finally gaining some semblance of control. "I had plans of my own tonight."

Frank chuckles as he kisses my neck. "Don't let us get in the way."

I shake my head fast. None of my plans hold a candle to the scene before me. I want this. *Them.*

"I think she likes my plan better," Jay pronounces with a knowing smirk.

I gulp down a niggle of discomfort.

Is this a test? Should I tell him I only want him? That he's enough?

If my husband is only doing this to please me, because he thinks I need it, then I will gladly step away.

My nerves must be written on my face, because Jay taps on my thigh, pulling my attention to him.

"I want this. I want you to have this. Nothing changes. I promise."

"Swear it?" I mumble. Because fuck, I want it. Maybe it's wrong, maybe I should only want my husband, but if he's offering me a night to escape *with him*, to play *with him,* I'll take it.

I'd do anything with him. And tonight, he's proving that he feels the same. The depth in which he understands me is what makes him the other half of my soul.

Jay nods and presses his face to my stomach, his nose skirting the line of my panties as he inhales. "I can smell how ready you are, baby. You want us both. Be honest."

Finally, with my lip caught between my teeth, I nod. I turn to Frank, whose hands have been lazily roaming up and down my arms. "Are you okay with this?" I don't want this to change our friendship.

He smiles that easy smile, and my body melts beneath his touch. "One last time," he says, his green eyes teasing as he slips a hand beneath my bra and tweaks my nipple.

Moaning, I arch into his touch.

Jay's laughter hits between my legs. "Already so needy for us."

The heat of his breath so near my core, mixed with the sting of Frank's fingers pinching my nipple, has my mind spinning. I'm going to pass out.

Frank pulls my face to his and devours my mouth.

My husband's low growl is all I hear as he tears my panties down. Then his tongue is sliding between my other lips.

Despite the moan that works its way from me and into Frank's mouth, my determination falters. Should I push him away or hold him closer? In the end, my tongue makes the decision and tangles with his, tasting him, spurring him on.

And as my hand finds Jay's head and I pull him closer, his laughter reverberates against my clit.

"You like his tongue inside you, wife?"

I pull back, breathless, and study Jay. He's running lazy circles around my clit, but he's watching me, studying me, looking at me like what he's doing right now is his favorite thing in the world.

"Yes," I pant.

"Naked. Now," he growls.

His words light an inferno in my core, and the flames lick higher when Frank pops the clasp of my bra and flings it across the room.

"Come here, Kitten." Jay angles himself so his back hits the armrest of the couch, then he pats the cushion beside him.

I don't hesitate, obeying my husband's every command.

"Lean back, baby," Jay murmurs, pulling me down until my head is on his lap. "Let him taste you. He's going to get you nice and wet for the both of us."

Swallowing hard, I look up at Frank. His eyes rake over me as he slowly unbuttons his shirt.

I groan when Frank's tattoo-covered muscles come into view. He's like a work of art.

"Show off," Jay grumbles.

Oh, husband. He's going to lose his fucking mind when he sees what lies beneath Frank's boxers.

The cocky Irish bastard doesn't smirk, he smolders. And the look he gives me as he settles between my legs makes me squirm. He's so fucking hot.

This is so fucking wrong.

And I'm going to enjoy every minute of it.

Jay forces my chin up and covers my mouth with his as Frank licks up my center.

"Holy fuck, Jay," I hiss against his lips. "Frank is licking me."

He chuckles darkly, his chest vibrating. "I see that, wife. Are you enjoying it?"

Oh God. Is he insane right now?

"Ye-yes," I stutter the words.

"You're going too easy on her. She can still speak," Jay deadpans, playing with my nipples as Frank eats me out.

"I've eaten your wife's pussy plenty of times," he grunts. "I know what she likes."

A laugh bursts from me, unbidden, and Jay growls, but his erection digs into my back more persistently.

"Just because of that, I'm going to stuff my cock down your throat," he says, dropping me against the cushion. He kneels on the couch, straddling my head, and fumbles with his fly.

When he finally frees himself, he places his stiff cock against my lips. "Open."

I smile, and for a moment, his eyes go soft. With a shake of his head, he looks away. "Fuck, I love you."

And that's when I know we'll be okay. The stress of the last few months, work, being a mom, becoming an us…through it all, it's still just him and me. Facing life together. Even now, we're doing this *together*.

"Love you too, husband," I murmur, "Now fuck my mouth while Frank does your job."

He chuckles and slides his cock between my lips slowly, watching me as he speaks to Frank. "I'll even let you have her mouth. But make her come first. I want to watch my wife come while your tongue is on her pussy and my cock is down her throat."

I have no control, and I relish every second of it.

Frank takes my legs over his shoulder, and then, with two fingers, he fucks me roughly while his tongue does wicked things to my clit and my husband holds my throat, keeping me in place while he thrusts into my mouth.

Our grunts and moans mingle, and all too soon, my first orgasm peaks. When my back arches off the couch, Jay pulls out of me and takes his cock in a vise grip, his eyes locked with mine. He's wearing a look of pure adoration that contradicts the obscene act we're taking part in. He pushes my hair out of my face as the wave hits, sending my body into convulsions.

"The most beautiful woman in the world," he murmurs. As my orgasm wanes, his mouth is on mine again, and he licks across the seam of my lips, seeking entrance.

In a daze, it takes me a moment to realize Frank has moved from the couch. Beside us, the sounds of Frank's zipper and the soft plop of his pants hitting the floor are barely audible over my heaving breaths.

Turning to the commotion, I open my eyes in time to watch him slide his boxers down his thighs, exposing his thick erection. I lick my lips as I stare at what can only be described as a beautiful penis.

Above me, Jay drops his head back and groans. "A fucking piercing. You've got to be kidding me."

I fold my lips in to contain my laughter, but when Frank chuckles, the giggles burst free, racking my body.

Jay presses his cheek to mine, and he tickles me and grumbles, "Wench."

"I still love your cock, baby."

He rolls his eyes. "Oh, now you're giving me a pity compliment. Fuck that." He holds his cock close to my face. "This thing is magnificent. Never heard you complain before."

I laugh and lick my lips, then drop a kiss to the head. "And you never will," I say, focused only on him, hoping he senses my sincerity. "Best husband ever."

"Fucking right I am. Now go suck Frank's cock so I can show you who fucks you better, wife."

I accept his help up, and then I follow Frank to the bed in the corner of Jay's office.

Frank settles against the headboard, his naked body a work of art I don't shy away from. Without hesitation, I crawl up the mattress and between his thighs, knowing my husband is right behind me.

"Ass up, baby," Jay directs.

I crane my neck and roll my eyes. "So bossy."

He lands a swift smack to my ass in reprimand, and I pulse in anticipation of the next one, knowing he's going to punish me for what I do next. With my hands planted on Frank's thighs, I tilt forward and tip my chin, motioning him to meet me halfway. When he complies, gifting me with a searing kiss, I savor the taste of myself and let out a long, loud moan. Another slap hits my opposite cheek, then another and another, disciplining me for kissing someone else.

When I finally pull away, Frank wipes his lips and chuckles. Then he puts his arms behind his head, awaiting my next move. "Your husband might lose his mind if you don't kiss him."

I wink at him and bring myself up on my knees, my back to Jay's front, and kiss him. He moans into my mouth as I bite down on his bottom lip and hold it between my teeth.

"Fuck," Jay mutters when I let go and drop down to face Frank again. With one hand, I circle him. The cool metal of his piercings is a contrast to his smooth, hot skin. Tentatively, I lick up his shaft, pulling a hiss from him. I look back at Jay once more, waiting for possessiveness to mar his face and take over. Waiting for him to stop me. But he watches me like I'm the most beautiful thing he's ever seen. Like he's enjoying this.

I swallow Frank's cock, sucking him deep and relishing the way they groan in unison. Frank's is full of pleasure, Jay's guttural. Almost like he can't bear to watch it, but he can't bear to stop me. His tongue prods my entrance, then presses inside me, and I moan around Frank's cock.

Our bodies move together. My hips buck as my husband fucks me with his tongue, and Frank's hips rise to thrust into my mouth. It's animalistic and wicked, and I love every second of it. The need inside me threatens to snap as Jay's thick head swipes between my lips and he digs his fingers into the flesh of my hips to hold me in place.

"I want to fuck you while you do that," he says, as if I'll say no.

I preen for him, pressing my ass into him, begging for it. Needing it more with every swallow.

I groan as he presses inside me, and Frank swells inside my mouth at the sound.

The bedding around us should be ablaze. This illicit encounter makes my body burn. "Fuck, baby. You're so tight. I'm beginning to wonder if you can handle what we have planned."

Jay's grunts are matched by Frank's laughter. "She can take it."

With another smack to my ass, Jay growls, "Straddle him, wife."

I still my mouth and my rocking hips at his words, suddenly

understanding with clarity what my husband meant when he said they were *both* going to fuck me.

Searching his gaze, I give a quick shake of my head. "No."

He grasps the back of my neck and pulls me back until his lips are on mine and he's kissing me languidly. Using his tongue, he eases me into the idea that he's somehow turned into a reality.

"Jay, I've never…"

He kisses the words from my mouth. "You've only ever been with me in that way. I know that. And that remains, Kitten. We're doing this together. I promised you everything."

I chuckle against his lips. "Most husbands buy their wives flowers when they have a bad day. You got me a pierced penis."

Frank barks out a laugh. "Don't mind me. The pierced penis over here is just relaxing."

"Don't get too relaxed," I purr as Jay finds my nipple and squeezes.

"There's my girl." He kisses me once more, then pushes me toward Frank. Pressing against my back, my husband leans forward and snags a condom from the bedside table, then tosses it onto the bare chest in front of me. And almost as if they've planned this, the guys switch positions.

When Jay is settled against the headboard, he crooks a finger, motioning for me to climb on top of him. "C'mere, wife."

I crawl up his body and settle over his hips. His thick erection presses against my clit as he positions me where he wants me.

"Have you ever?" I ask Jay as a hint of insecurity runs through me.

He shakes his head and leans up to kiss me. "Another first, Kitten."

I turn to Frank. "How 'bout you?"

He shakes his head, his emerald eyes dancing.

"Phew." I let out an exaggerated breath. "Guess I can't really fuck it up, then, huh?"

Frank barks out a laugh, and one side of Jay's mouth kicks up in a half smirk.

"You're about to take both our cocks in that perfect pussy, wife. Pretty sure you can't screw it up."

Right. I nod, doing my best to psych myself up for this. *Here's to burning.*

"Lift her up," Jay says.

Suddenly, Frank's hands are on my hips, and he's lifting me onto my husband's cock, and then, as Jay grips my thighs, Frank pushes me down. Pressed between the two, their heat surrounding me, I'm overcome by a hunger that's all consuming. And when Frank pinches my nipple and my husband arches up and sucks it into his mouth, I almost lose it.

"Come here, baby," Jay says, pulling me against his chest as Frank massages the globes of my ass.

"Oh my," I mutter.

Jay's lips find mine again, and at the same moment, I hear the cap pop and the telltale sign of lubricant being poured, then Frank slides a finger to the place where my husband is currently fucking me. The cool liquid on his finger adds another sensation that leaves me clenching around Jay. Then he swipes in a circle, stretching me, eliciting groans from Jay and me. Jay's tongue delves into my mouth, tasting, teasing. But it's not enough to distract me from the almost painful sensation when Frank's thick cock replaces his finger. Jay and I both tense, letting out simultaneous groans as he works himself inside me slowly.

"Oh fuck," I cry.

Jay bites down on my shoulder, and Frank runs gentle circles against my back, easing me into taking both of them.

The burn is so intense, I hold my breath in anticipation of pain.

"Breathe, Kitten," Jay whispers. He lays his palm on my cheek and pins me in place with those blue eyes, bringing me back to the moment.

I suck in more air when Frank's hips finally hit my ass and his cock is fully seated inside me.

"Fuck," Jay growls. "I can feel his piercing."

A burst of laughter explodes from me at the unexpected comment.

Frank silences me by digging his fingers into my hips. "Princess, you're squeezing our cocks so fucking tight. Fuck us before we both come."

Over my shoulder, I shoot him a wicked grin. "You do realize you're fucking your best friend's enemy, right?"

Frank smirks. "Pretty sure he'd be more upset about me fucking his sister. But yeah, I'm aware. Better make it worth it." And that's the last warning I get before he pulls back and fucks us both, his cock moving in and out of the tight space.

My body shudders with his every thrust. And when Jay bucks up into me, meeting him thrust for thrust, my eyes roll back and I convulse around them both. My orgasm rolls through me for what feels like hours. The feel of them both, their hands roaming my body—Frank's on my breasts, then on my ass, and Jay's on my thighs and hips—reignites the inferno inside me and sends sparks flying in all directions.

I'm not sure where one orgasm ends and another begins, but they swell inside me, and my husband fills me while Frank fills the condom, both cursing through their release. Frank scoots back, and without his body as support, I slump against Jay's chest.

He bands his arms around me tightly and kisses my forehead. "I love you, wife," he whispers.

"I love you too."

With my ear pressed to his beating heart, I give in to the tug of sleep, accepting its pull.

Just before I lose consciousness, another set of lips presses against my neck. "Thank you, Princess," Frank murmurs. Then, louder, he says, "Take care of her, Hanson."

Then the world goes dark.

From: <CJames@bouvier.com>
To: <JHanson@bouvier.com>
Subject: FWD: Langfield Deal
October 9, 2023

She said YES! She wants to do the show and she even agreed to film it in Paris! Is this real life?

From: <JHanson@bouvier.com>
To: <CJames@bouvier.com>
Subject: Re: FWD: Langfield Deal
October 9, 2023

Of course she said yes. Looks like we're finally going to get that trip to Paris. I'm so proud of you, Kitten.

Dinner tonight to celebrate. I'll make reservations and take my two favorite girls out. Have Dexter pick something out for both of you.

I love you,

Jay

From: <CJames@bouvier.com<
To: <JHanson@bouvier.com>
Subject: Re: Re: FWD: Langfield Deal
October 9, 2023

Only you.

73

MILLION REASONS BY LADY GAGA

Cat

"What's the French word for that?" Sophie asks with a smile as her gaze goes back and forth between the hockey rink and me.

I roll my eyes. "Ménage à trois, asshole."

She laughs. "I know. But seriously, look how far you've come. Not only do you talk like a big girl and use the proper terminology, you had two at once. Mama's proud."

I squeeze my lips shut to keep from laughing.

"So now what? Are you guys going to do it again? Is Frank going to be your boyfriend? Did Jay kiss him? Oh my God, I knew Jay wanted a man to spank him and call him a whore!"

I drop my head back and let out a loud laugh. "Shut up!" I hiss, looking around to make sure no one can hear her. Fortunately, there's no one to listen because the guys have the rink to themselves for their weekly Thursday morning skate. Sophie begged Jay to let us tag along since she's always wanted to, as she put it, "watch men dance on ice."

"Well, did he?"

"Oh my God, Soph, *no*."

"It's not that far-fetched, you know. Frank could definitely turn

I groan into my mitten-covered hands. "I don't know why I told you."

She grins. "Because how could you not? You're obviously freaking out."

I shrug. Surprisingly, I'm not. Things haven't been awkward with Jay. So we had sex with someone else. Honestly, I think it brought us closer. It's like he understands me in a way no one ever has. He knows what I need without my asking, and he willingly gives it because it brings him pleasure to do so.

"No, I asked you here to talk about the project with Sienna. And— wait, I didn't even ask you here. You begged Jay to come."

I'm still pinching myself. We're really going to film a show with *Sienna Langfield*. I'll continue to run *Jolie* from Paris, and Sophie is taking over the Boston office while we're gone. Knowing the magazine will be in her capable hands will allow me to work with Jay day in and day out on Bouvier's first television series. Already, the buzz around it is huge.

She laughs. "True. Okay, but seriously, we can talk about the Sienna thing after the game? Because right now, my girlie parts just want to focus on these men. I don't care if one happens to be your husband. There is just something about a man and a hockey stick."

I chuckle as I sip my coffee. She's not wrong. My husband is hot in a suit, and he's fucking gorgeous naked. But God, Jay suited up and on the ice, gliding smoothly across it with determination and ease with a hockey stick in his hand and in control of the puck? Fuck, I'd drop to my knees right now for him.

He slips past Kevin and passes the puck to Gavin, who shoots and scores on a grumpy Beckett. His resounding shout and then wink in my direction has me melting into a puddle on the floor. This man and the way I love him.

"Oh my gosh, Cat, look at the way he's slapping Gavin on the ass," Sophie teases.

I laugh as we stand, getting our stuff together. "Will you stop? My husband is not attracted to men!"

"Fuck, look who it is." Jay's voice carries through the rink, and Sophie and I watch as Rowan Parker enters the rink and skates up to Gavin and Jay.

Jay's eyes light up like Rowan is the greatest thing he's ever seen.

Sophie laughs. "Not into men, my ass."

I giggle and head down the bleachers. By the time we've reached the men, the rest of the players are heading to the ice, and I can't stop staring at them all. They're just so big. And powerful. I mean, watching my man on the ice was enjoyable, but this is something else. These men make Jay look small, and that's saying something.

"Remember how I said I was into daddies?" Sophie whispers, her focus never leaving the ice.

"Yeah, I hear you," I mutter, wiping at my chin to catch any drool.

The growl from behind us snaps me out of it, and I turn around just as my husband pulls me against his chest and brings his lips to my ear. "Mine."

I lean my head back against his chest and look up into his eyes. "One hundred percent yours."

"Well, I'm not," Sophie mutters, her focus still on the ice.

Jay's chest shakes with laughter. "Your best friend is a troublemaker."

Sophie doesn't even turn around. "Says the man who surprised his wife with a pierced penis."

"What the hell?" Kevin shouts.

Behind me, Jay growls and squeezes me tighter.

"Sophie!" I hiss.

She shakes her head like she's just come out of a daze. "Sorry. God, it's all the testosterone. It went to my head. Come on, Cat. Let's go eat donuts at the photo shoot. I need to reset."

"I need answers," Kevin says, his attention traveling down Jay's torso, which is hidden behind me.

"Take your eyes off my wife's body," he growls.

"If you'd move her, like, five inches to the left, I could get a look at what I'm trying to see."

"Kevin," Jay warns.

I can't help but laugh harder. Jay is going to kill him. Some things never change.

My purse vibrates, and I pull away from Jay to dig my phone out. When I realize it's his phone lighting up and not mine, I turn to hand it to him, but the name on the screen snags my attention, and before I can stop it, I've read the text notification.

> Vanessa: I need another million, or I'll have no choice but to tell all the secrets. Including who Chase's real mother is.

My stomach drops at the same time my mind takes off at a sprint. Why is Vanessa texting my husband? Why is she asking for *another* million? And *how* does she know about Chase? As far as I know, Jay and my grandfather and I are the only people who know his true paternity.

What the hell did Jay do?

74

WILD HORSES BY THE SUNDAYS

Cat

"**F**uck, we're late," I mutter, working the clasp of the necklace Jay left for me on our bedside table. It's a gold Irish cross, and while I wouldn't have picked it for this outfit, I can only assume my husband wanted me to have all the luck we can garner today.

From the bathroom, Jay calls, "We have over an hour."

He's right, but I can't help the nerves coursing through me. Today, my little brother is marrying the love of his life. Things are still tense between Cash and me, but he's trying. We've avoided topics that involve our businesses, but he's reached out multiple times to talk about Chloe. To apologize for how he handled things. And to invite me to spend time with his daughter.

It's not perfect, but it's a start.

And when he asked me to be his best woman, I knew we were heading in the right direction. Now that they're no longer business rivals, I hope that Cash will one day accept Jay as my husband. Because until that happens, I don't see any way to mend our relationship completely.

But that isn't what's causing this bout of anxiety.

No, I can attribute that almost solely to the roles we have to play today. The performance we'll have to give.

I think Vanessa is a conniving whore who wants more money, but Jay and Frank don't want to take any chances. They insist her message means that the Mob is onto us.

Which means we'll spend the day making it look like Jay and I are fighting. The entire plan makes me sick, but protecting Chloe will always be my top priority, so I'll go along with it. Because if Frank's brother discovers the truth about our past, we'll have a problem.

I'm just so tired of all the lies.

I'm tired of pretending Jay isn't the most important person on earth to me. I'm tired of pretending to be someone I'm not, period. For years, I've hidden my true self from every single person who knows me. I've given them bits and pieces of myself, but never my full truths.

Except Jay.

He's always pushed me to be my most authentic self. And he's loved every version of that person.

When he enters the bedroom, I can't help but gape at him. He's beautiful. It's stupid, really, how good-looking he is. How in love with him I am. His black tuxedo tugs across his broad shoulders as he stretches out his arm to fix the cuff on his left wrist. Immediately, I go to him, unable to fight the pull of his presence. His bowtie is draped around his neck, and he smiles down at me as I fasten it into place.

"You look beautiful, wife."

I sigh.

"Everything okay?" he asks, placing his hands over mine, stopping my work on his tie.

I choke back the nerves jumbling my mind. My little brother is getting married. Now is not the time.

"All's fine. But...maybe you shouldn't come today," I say, glancing away from him.

His shoulders sag. "*What*? What's going on?"

I shake my head, avoiding eye contact. "Today's about Grace and

Cash. I don't want my baggage to ruin their day."

"I'm baggage?" he says, his voice weaker.

My heart twists. "Baby, no. But I don't want to have to be mean to you. Or fight with you. I don't want to put on a show."

Jay's heavy breath breaks me and I pull him in close, pressing my heart against his.

When I showed him the text message from Vanessa, I was upset, of course. But it was the fear in his eyes that solidified it for me. Every lie Jay has ever told, every action he's taken, has always been for my benefit. Did he force this marriage originally? Yes. Did he use Vanessa to hurt my family? Also, yes.

Those are truths I have to live with.

But a single sentence doesn't tell an entire story. There are shades and sides and viewpoints. Like the way an object is turned, the way the light hits it, changes the appearance completely. The moon exists at all hours of the day, but it isn't until the sun's rays light it up that the rest of the world can see it.

I am Jay's sun. Without me, he looks like the villain. His actions make no sense, and only greed can explain what he's done.

But if my family had known the danger I was in all those years ago, if they could see the way Jay lights up when I'm around, if they would take the time to understand him, to see the beauty within all his darkness, they'd realize that I've been lighting him up all along.

They'd see what I see, the most beautiful man with the most tortured heart, who would quite literally live in darkness for the rest of his life if it meant that I continued to shine.

"We stick with the plan," I whisper against his chest.

Jay rests his hands on either side of my neck and angles me so that our mouths are only a breath apart. "I *can't* lose you."

"You won't," I rush out, then press my lips to his. Our kiss is frantic, filled with passion, begging, need. Every emotion we feel is filtered into this kiss, and soon I'm removing the tie I just fixed and he's slipping my dress off my body. And then my husband is sinking into me as we both plead with the universe to realign the moon and the sun so they can somehow find a way to shine at the same time.

KITTEN'S SONGS

"We'll fight, and you leave with Frank," Jay says as the limo pulls up to the wedding venue, which happens to be the place we reunited last year. The garden where Jay sank back into me for the first time and reclaimed what has always been his.

My smile is tight, and my heart beats wildly, but I nod. "I know the plan."

Squeezing my hand, he keeps me from reaching for the door. "If things don't go as discussed—"

I hold my finger to his lips. "No."

With a frown, Jay pulls my hand from his lips and flips it so that my palm is flat against his mouth and my tattoo is pressed against his lips. He keeps me locked in his gaze as he kisses my skin softly. "If things don't go as planned, I want you to be happy."

I shake my head as my throat tightens. "Stop it." It comes out as a raspy whisper.

"We fight. You leave with Frank. He'll know where to bring you." He studies me, ignoring my clear panic. "And if things don't go as planned, you will take care of our daughter, Cat. You'll continue to be the fiercest woman I've ever met. The love of my life. And promise me, Kitten, promise me, you'll be happy."

I swallow thickly. The sound of my heart beating in my ears drowns out everything but his voice. But he's right. I'm fierce. So I place my palms against his cheeks and demand the only outcome I can fathom.

"You listen to me, Mr. Hanson. We are going into that party. I'll pretend that I'm mad at you. We'll get in our fight. We'll make it clear to anyone who's watching that I'm lost as to why Vanessa is demanding money from you. If the Mob is watching, they'll believe I'm in the dark about all of it. And then we start fresh in Paris. You, me, and Chloe. *That* is the only result I'll allow. Promise me that, or we don't get out of this car."

Jay scrutinizes me, scanning my face, and then his lip lifts into that classic smirk I love. "Fuck, I love you, Kitten. You drive a hard bargain, but okay. Happily ever after, that's what you want?"

My heavy breath escapes. "It's what we've *earned*."

KITTEN'S SONGS

For a few moments while Grace walked down the aisle toward my brother, everything faded away. My guilt and stress ceased to exist as I watched the way my brother looked at his bride. It was exactly how Jay looked at me. With pride, affection, and overwhelming gratitude that she'd chosen him. That she'd *forgiven* him.

With the two of us standing side by side, our relationship slipped back into place. We'd both made mistakes. We'd both been selfish. But he's my brother. And despite how much he'd let me down in recent months, I knew he'd struggled with our rift as much as I did.

So when he asked me to dance, I accepted and followed him out onto the wooden floor.

"It's a beautiful wedding," I say, looking up at Cash.

He may be younger, but there is nothing smaller about him.

"It was all Grace." The smile he's worn all day somehow gets bigger and softer at the mention of his wife's name.

"Of course it was. She's perfect for you."

He chuckles. "She's too good for me."

I shake my head. "No. You're both perfect for one another. And for the record, I'm really sorry that it took me so long to come around to her."

Cash spins me out as the band plays "Wild Horses." When he brings me back to his chest, he squeezes me tighter. "I want you to be happy."

My smile is tight. "I am."

"But you and Jay—"

I stop him. He saw us fighting before, as he was meant to, but I don't want to talk badly about my husband. I don't want to extend this lie in private. Loudly, I'll make the scenes, but while dancing with my brother, I want truth. Not every moment of my life needs to be a lie. "It's complicated."

He raises his brow. "It's always complicated with you two."

I can't help the laugh that escapes as I rest my cheek against my brother's chest. "Ain't that the truth."

When I look back up, he smiles. Then his attention drifts to my necklace and his brows pinch together. "Where'd you get that?" he asks, lifting it from my skin.

"It was a gift."

Cash shakes his head. "Weird."

I study the cross. "I don't know. I think it's pretty."

Cash narrows his eyes. "It's almost identical to Frank's tattoo." His voice comes out strained. "Did Frank give this to you?"

"What? *No,*" I say, far too quickly. As if I have something to hide. And while I do, it has nothing to do with this necklace.

"It's his family crest. Why do you have it around your neck?"

Breathing becomes difficult as I put the pieces together. And, filled with a slew of new questions, I scan the reception for Jay or Frank.

Frank's family crest.

Fuck.

The McCabe family crest.

As if he can sense my need for him, Jay appears. "Dance with me, Kitten?"

I offer Cash a weak smile, praying he drops it. "Go enjoy your wedding. Thanks for the dance."

He nods but finally lets me go.

Jay presses me firmly against his chest and drops his lips to my ear. "Talk to me."

I peruse the dance floor, finding Grace and Tessa nearby, bobbing around with Hope in their arms. My niece smiles when Cash peeks his head around Grace's shoulder, taking her by surprise. Tessa moves back, a big smile on her face as my brother presses Hope between himself and Grace and moves to the beat.

Then Tessa's boyfriend, a giant of a man in comparison to her small frame, pulls her in close and rests his chin on her head as they sway.

Carter sits with a drink in his hand only a few feet away. His gaze hits Tessa for only a moment before he's standing and heading to the bar. It can't be easy seeing her so happy with someone else. One day, maybe he'll find someone like Cash and I have. I hope all my siblings are as happy as Cash is.

When I spot Frank in the corner, his focus locked on Jay and me, my mind returns to the task at hand.

"Don't look down, but did you buy a necklace for me?"

Jay's lips dip into a frown against my cheek and his steps falter. "No. Not today at least."

The sounds around me get louder and muffled as the room spins.

"Talk to me, Kitten," Jay murmurs, squeezing me tighter.

"It's a cross like the one on Frank's back. His family crest," I whisper.

The only indication that this information bothers Jay is how his fingers dig into my hips. "Where did you find it?"

"Our bedroom. Next to the bed. There was no note. I figured it was from you."

He blows out a hot breath against my neck. "Okay, I need you to listen to every word I say."

I nod but keep my gaze locked on Cash and Hope. He kisses her as the song ends, then heads toward Frank, who's still standing at the bar. Tessa tips her head up at her boyfriend and kisses his chin, then darts away to dance with Grace and Hope. He smiles brightly, watching her.

"You're going to push me away and start the fight. You need to be loud, Cat. Angry."

I close my eyes, hating every minute of this.

"And then you're going to leave. Go with Frank. Do not call me. Understand? His brother has to believe you're with him. That you're *back* with him. It's the only way this works."

"I hate this," I hiss.

Jay leans in close and inhales. Like he's memorizing me. Inhaling me. God, I'm doing the same thing. I made him promise that he'd come back to me. That we'd be together at the end of this story.

But I'm not fool enough to believe he has control over the outcome.

We know the risks. We know how this could all end. We've been here before. But last time, he was on his own. Last time, I didn't know we were saying goodbye.

Today I do.

So I close my eyes for one more moment and press my body as close as I can. "I love you, Jonathan Hanson. Completely. Irrevocably. Head over fucking heels."

Jay lets out a surprised breath, as if he'd been preparing for me to push him away. "Tu es l'amour de ma vie," he whispers.

You're the love of my life.

God, this man.

Jay lifts my hand, kisses the underside of my left ring finger, and then pins me with his gaze. *It's time*, he says with those heartbreakingly beautiful blue eyes of his.

"How could you?" I whisper loudly, drawing attention from those close to us as I push against Jay's chest.

His eyes fall shut at the loss. It takes everything in me to keep going. To look away from him. To run from my husband.

"Cat, wait!" he shouts, drawing the attention of a few other guests nearby as we speed walk from the center of the room.

In a voice barely above a whisper, I mutter, "Not today, Jay. Until you give me the answers I want, I have nothing to say to you."

"It's not what you think," he pleads, his voice taking on the desperation that I know he feels down to his core.

I get louder in response. "Then tell me what exactly it is. Why is Vanessa asking you for *another* million dollars? Why did you pay her the first million? What the fuck aren't you telling me?"

Cash's head snaps up, and he pierces Jay with a rage-filled look as he's surely piecing together our words. I hate watching the moment it all clicks. It's like the truth finally settles into place for him. The last puzzle piece he couldn't work out before. He's always accused Jay of working with Vanessa to set him up. We've always denied Jay was involved. Now he knows the truth. He and Grace missed out on so much time—he almost lost her—because of me. Because of what Jay forced Vanessa to do to protect *me*.

And here we are, doing it again. Making a scene at his wedding so Jay can protect me.

If rage was a picture, it would be the image of my brother in this moment. He's going to ruin his wedding to kill my husband.

Frank grabs Cash's shoulder and leans in close, muttering in his ear. When Cash continues shooting daggers and fire at Jay, Frank tugs on him harder. "I got this," he says loud enough for me to hear. "Go enjoy your wife."

Frank turns his hard glare on Jay and tilts his head toward the exit.

In my ear, Jay whispers, "You did perfectly, Kitten. Frank will meet you outside. Don't go anywhere without him."

My body begs to turn into him. To grab him and never let go. But we're being watched. This is what I have to do. So I pull my shoulders back and lift my chin without giving him another glance. So that the world only sees me storming away from my husband. But under my breath, I whisper, *"Only you."*

75

THE ROSE TATTOO BY DROPKICK MURPHYS

Frank

This really is like a fucking telenovela. When I was a kid, before my father sent me to boarding school, before I met Cash James and my entire life changed, I would spend my afternoons hiding in my best friend's kitchen, watching telenovelas on her grandmother's tiny portable television. The woman carried it back and forth between her bedroom, the living room, and the kitchen. She said having more than one television was wasteful.

She had a point.

The scene playing out in front of me now? I'm pretty sure I saw it on that little television.

God, life was simpler then.

I work my jaw and grab my best friend by the shoulder, trying to calm him down so he doesn't kill Jay in the middle of his own damn wedding reception.

Ellie would find this hysterical. She always had a sick sense of humor. Even when she was twelve.

I grab the back of my neck and squeeze. I need a good dose of calm right now too. I hadn't thought of Ellie in years. But since seeing a woman with the same electric green eyes as hers in the James building last year, I can't shake those early memories.

It's like she's haunting me.

Are her eyes still as bright as they once were? With baggage like ours, they've likely dulled like moss that's been trampled in the rain.

"I got this. Go enjoy your wife." I squeeze Cash's shoulder and press him forward. Once he sets his sights on Grace and Hope, his entire demeanor softens. She literally helps him shrug off his worries. It's amazing. And something I'll never have.

I turn to the next pain in the ass and sigh. It's not that I don't like Jay. Obviously, I like him well enough. But fuck if it isn't exhausting watching the people around me screw up constantly and then having to help them pick up the pieces. Or in Jay's case, obliterating everything we know because the only thing that matters to him is Cat.

Not that I blame him.

If there's one woman worth blowing a person's life up for, she's it.

Across the dance floor, she pushes past Jay and storms out of the reception.

"Hope you didn't go and fall in love with my wife," Jay says drolly as I meet him by the edge of the tent.

I merely stare at him.

I try not to think about Catherine too much. Or the hours inside that room with her. Or the many months we hid what we were doing from her brother. Or the first night I kissed her.

None of those thoughts serve me well.

"What's the plan?" I ask instead of replying to his ridiculous statement.

Jay studies me for a second longer, and then he runs his hand through his hair. "Your brother left a gift for my wife."

My jaw tics at that admission. "How do you know it was from him?"

"It was a gold cross with a claddagh inside it."

The McCabe family crest. Motherfucker.

"Fuck," I grit out. "Where did he leave it?"

"Next to her side of the bed." There's anger in every one of his words. And it's earned. My brother should never have been able to get into the brownstone. Jay hired security to watch Catherine's every move. To ensure she and Chloe were always safe. And we both vetted the security team.

"What do you want me to do?"

"Get Catherine to the cabin. If someone's following you, they'll think she's with you. That you're sneaking off to continue your affair."

I grunt.

Jay smirks. "Please. Like being in the presence of my wife is a hardship for you."

I run my hand across my jaw. No. Keeping my hands off his wife is the hard part.

"What are you going to do?" I ask, diverting the conversation.

He chuckles. "Like I thought. I'll see if it's really your brother or just Vanessa trying to scare me into paying her more money."

"Okay," I sigh.

Jay's expression sobers. "Listen, if something should happen—"

I hold my hand up. "No. You're going to be fine. Your wife and I will not go on to live happily without you, so just put that shit out of your head and go do what you need to do."

Jay places a hand on my shoulder. "You're a good man, Frank."

"You just like my piercing," I quip.

He lets out a loud laugh but sobers quickly. "Take care of my girl."

I plan on it. As I walk away from Jay, I pull my phone from my pocket and make a quick call.

It's a number I never thought I'd use. But that single call changes everything.

76

WILDFIRE BY SEAFRET

Cat

Storming out of the reception tent, I play the part of angry wife perfectly. When I hit the long gravel driveway, no doubt ruining my heels, I pay no mind to the gorgeous oak trees that tower above me or the caterers that stumble past carrying trays full of dessert selections.

"Great, now I'm going to miss the cake cutting," I grumble.

Before I can stop it, my foot slips on the gravel, and my ankle twists. But as my body flails forward, an arm wraps around me from behind, and a deep, familiar voice rumbles in my ear. "Careful, Princess."

For a moment, I'd hoped it was Jay. That he'd changed his mind. That he'd take me away from all of this himself.

I curse at the sky as Frank spins me around and pulls me against his chest. The faint smell of his soap tickles my nose and takes control of my senses. "Let's get out of here."

The familiar scent steals the fight from me, but I pull him to a stop. "You can't leave your best friend's wedding. Cash will never forgive you. Or me!"

But he doesn't stop. He only grips my hand firmly in his and drags me away from the wedding. "Pretty sure he'd kill me if anything happened to you, Princess. He won't even notice I'm gone. He only has eyes for two people right now, Grace and Hope."

I sag in acceptance. My brother is infatuated.

"All Jay told me was to wait for you. He didn't say we were leaving. Where are we going?"

"So many questions." He hits me with a rare smile.

Knowing he won't give in until he's ready to, I give up my inquiry and trudge along beside him, watching my step so I don't slip again.

When he stops beside a small black Aston Martin, I smirk. "Didn't peg you as the little car type, Irish."

The man smolders as he opens my door, but he blocks me from entering, forcing my body flush against his. "*Stop.*"

I shrug innocently. "No idea what you're talking about."

"You're flirting. You *can't* flirt with me."

Deflating, I drop my chin. "It's a defense mechanism. Sorry. But you should be used to it. I've been flirting with you for years."

"And now we've fucked. I know what it feels like to be inside you," he rumbles, his voice taking on a gravel that scrapes at me. He grips my hips and digs his fingers in. "I know what sounds you make when you come around my cock. I know what these lips taste like," he says quietly, closer, *too close.*

What the hell was my husband thinking, sending me away with Frank? This was a really bad idea.

He squeezes my hip to get my attention. "We played a dangerous game," he says when I finally turn back. "But it was just a game. I know it and so do you. You love that man, and he would give up the world for you. Get in the car. Let's make sure we get you to safety like I promised him."

KITTEN'S SONGS

As we cruise over the Mount Hope Bridge and away from Bristol, my mind reels. The glistening navy water below us is covered in a pink sheen from the setting sun. The silhouette of the lighthouse stands tall in the middle of the water, holding strong as waves crash against it almost ominously. The sun sinks deeper below the horizon, and with it, I sink farther into the leather seat.

Soon, the sun will disappear completely, and the moon will appear.

Seems appropriate. With me gone, Jay can do what he must. What exactly is he doing, though?

When the text came in from Vanessa, Jay told me how she'd been working with Frank's brother. How she essentially blackmailed him but also saved me in the process.

To say I'm conflicted over the entire thing would be putting it too lightly. Jay and Vanessa almost destroyed my brothers. While I understood Jay's reasoning, it was a hard thing to swallow. Up until an hour ago, we believed her text message was just a ploy to get more money. Now I'm not sure what to believe.

"Did Jay tell you about the necklace?"

Frank's knuckles whiten as he grips the steering wheel tightly and silently glances at the symbol hanging over my heart.

"Did you know that Jay and I share a brother?" I ask, going for shock value.

When Frank merely quirks a brow without taking his attention from the road, I realize he and my husband are a lot closer than I could have imagined. Apparently, sharing me isn't their only collective secret.

"Are you going to answer any of my questions?"

"If you ask me something that doesn't violate your husband's trust? Sure."

I fold my arms across my chest. "What's he doing right now?"

Frank huffs like it's the dumbest thing he's ever heard. "Talking to Vanessa. Probably paying her more money."

573

I groan. "Thought he was doing some type of spy thing."

A dry laugh escapes him, but it only lasts a second before his jaw is tight and he's sitting up straighter, his eyes darting from the rearview mirror to the side mirrors rapidly. My heart rate skyrockets as tension grows in the car and Frank begins weaving between lanes, going far too fast for these unlit back roads and kicking up dust as he does.

"Your seatbelt good?" he says, his tone giving nothing away, even if his driving leaves nothing to the imagination.

"Yup. What's going on?"

He accelerates again and moves around a green Toyota that blares its horn as we do. Looking in the mirror on my side, I watch as a black sedan maneuvers the same way we just did, gaining on us at an alarming speed.

Frank's phone rings, and he hits a button on the steering wheel. "Hello?"

"It's a setup. Get Cat to the house now," my husband barks, his voice echoing around the interior of the car.

"You okay?" I ask while I grip the door, trying to keep nervousness from my tone.

"I'm fine. Are you okay?" Jay asks, his tone gentler now.

"We've got two cars following us," Frank says calmly as he takes a wide left turn without warning.

My body hits the door, and I yelp in surprise.

"Talk to me. You okay?" a panicked Jay growls.

"We're fine," Frank replies, accelerating again.

"We are so not fine," I whisper.

This time, I spin my body so I can see if the other cars are following us. I only see one. I've only ever seen one. Not sure where Frank thinks the other one is.

"Eyes forward, Princess."

"What happened with Vanessa?" I ask, trying to distract myself from my inability to turn around. It feels like a weight is settling on my chest, and my entire body is wound tight.

"She didn't show. I shoulda known she wouldn't play games like that. She knew how to contact me, and it wasn't via text. Fuck, how did I miss the signs?" Jay's voice rises.

"Obviously, my brother used your distraction to his advantage," Frank replies as he weaves in and out of the lanes of traffic.

My focus remains on Frank, but when his eyes go to the rearview mirror again, I'm practically blinded by the car coming straight toward us.

"Frank!" I scream as I'm thrown forward. My head hits the glass of my window, and my screams mix with my husband's.

"Cat!" Jay shouts. "Cat, fucking answer me!"

The sound of metal hitting metal is the last thing I hear, and then I'm consumed by darkness.

77

SOMETHING IN THE ORANGE BY ZACH BRYAN

Jay

I stare at my phone, waiting to hear her voice. To hear Frank. To hear fucking anything. But after the blaring of horns, the sound of crunching metal, and Cat's screams, there's nothing.

"Fuck." I punch the steering wheel as I press down on the gas.

Begging for her to speak is pointless. The phone disconnected during the accident.

At least that's what I think it was. My gut twists. I know what McCabe's men are like. I've witnessed firsthand the way they take lives. Without mercy, without hesitation, and with extreme pain.

If he hurts Cat, I won't stop until every single person who works for him is dead.

I learned how to take a life the hard way. But after that, it only got easier. Right now, knowing that he's put my wife in danger has me fantasizing about all the ways I could end him.

Accelerating, I don't take a breath until I'm turning down the road that leads to my cabin. That's when I see it.

Smoke billows from two dark cars. Frank's tiny toy of a fucking car is sandwiched between them. The second my car is in park, I throw open my door and sprint toward the wreckage. The *ding, ding, ding* sound from my car, warning that the keys are in the ignition and the door has been left open, is the only sound that fills the night. As I reach the passenger side of Frank's Aston Martin, I stumble over a body. The man is slumped on the ground, and when I lift him up, I'm met by lifeless eyes and a gunshot wound to the head.

Cursing, I drop him back to his resting place and scan the area for Frank and Cat.

They aren't here.

I turn to the other cars for clues, and that's when I see the man slumped over in the driver's side of the car in the front.

It's clear Frank took care of both men. I just hope they were the only ones here. Neither of them is his brother. Then again, I have no doubt that Evan would hide behind his men. Send them out to do his dirty work.

Though my heart rate won't slow until I find my wife, I'm comforted knowing that Frank is with her. He'll protect her with his life.

And knowing Evan McCabe as well as I do, I know he cares about nothing but money. He won't hurt Cat. He's going to try to barter her.

Smart fucking man. I'd pay anything for her safety.

A sob breaks through the night, and I run down the long path toward my cabin. As it lights up and the door opens, I catch the silhouette of Frank carrying Cat through the entry. Sprinting faster and practically flying up the stairs with a jump, I make it into the cabin as Frank is settling Cat on the small bed that sits in the center of the room. In two steps, I'm in front of her and inspecting every inch of her body.

Blood coats her forehead, and she winces when I reach for her. "Who did this to you, baby?"

Cat's eyes fall shut, and tears stream down her face.

When she doesn't reply, I leer in Frank's direction. "What the fuck happened to her? Did someone touch her?"

Ignoring me, Frank shuffles to the bathroom.

I turn back to my wife. "Kitten, talk to me. Where does it hurt?" I inspect her body, checking for injuries, but her head seems to be the only thing bleeding. The cut must be hidden by her hair, which is matted and stiff.

"Her head hit the glass when they rammed us." Frank hands me a washcloth to tend to her wounds.

With a thumb under Cat's chin, I gently tilt her face up. "Baby, I think you're in shock. Talk to me."

Whiskey brown eyes full of tears dart back and forth, like she's finally realizing I'm right in front of her. She blows out a breath, and then another sob escapes. "Jay."

I settle next to her on the bed and pull her onto my lap, rocking her while she sobs.

"Any word from my brother?" Frank asks, his mood unaffected by Cat's hysterics.

I suppose that's the military training. Right now, I'm thankful for it. I, for one, am having a tough time remaining calm when my wife is shaking in my arms because she's so goddamn scared.

I did this. Once again, I put the one person I love most in danger.

Grinding my teeth, I give a curt nod and then turn my attention back to Cat. I rock her until the quiet sobs turn to steady breathing.

"She can't fall asleep," Frank urges.

As I kiss her forehead and murmur for her to wake up, a rhythmic pounding sounds against the door.

He's here.

"Fuck," I curse, dropping my attention to my wife. "I need you to listen to me, sweetheart," I say, my voice more urgent. "I need you to get in the closet. Stay as quiet as you can and don't come out. No matter what you hear. Can you do that? Stay hidden, no matter what. Promise me."

Sleep dogs her as she examines me with tired eyes. "*What?*"

"We don't have time," Frank says, snagging her around the waist.

She pushes back against him, clinging to me. "What's happening?"

"Frank's brother. He found us." I turn to the door as another round of pounding starts up. "I won't let anything happen to you."

Her eyes well with tears and she clutches my shirt. "I'm scared."

"I know, baby—"

The banging sounds again. This time followed by an Irish curse. "Get ye arse to the door!"

"Motherfucker," Frank mutters. "The man fakes a damn accent now, like he's a fucking leprechaun."

"Kitten, you need to hide. *Please*," I beg.

She finally seems to come to her senses, and fear plagues her eyes. With tears streaming down her cheeks, she grabs my face and kisses me. "Please don't die," she whispers.

Locking eyes with her, I brush my thumb over her cheek, then plant one last kiss to her lips. "I love you. Only you."

"Completely, irrevocably, head over fucking heels," she whispers.

Then Frank drags her off the bed and straight to the closet. Once the closet door shuts quietly behind them, I straighten my suit jacket, stand, and holler to the man who is once again banging on the door. "Hold your fucking horses. I'm coming!"

I swing the door open and have to jump back to avoid being trampled by the deranged Irishman with wild eyes who looks like he hasn't slept in days.

"Who the fuck do you think you are?" I growl, switching roles almost seamlessly.

The stench of whiskey wafts from him as he stomps past me, glowering. "You answer when I knock, Hanson."

"The fuck I do," I toss back. "Debt was paid, remember? I *made* you."

I should have put a hole in this asshole's head months ago.

He laughs. "Funny thing about that. Know what I heard? I heard you've been playing us all along. Catherine James is the one who stole the money." He cocks a brow and pauses for dramatic effect. "Oh. I forgot. She goes by Catherine Hanson now, right?"

"You know exactly who she is," I growl. "Say my wife's name again, and I'll kill you with my bare hands."

Evan holds up his palms. "Calm ye arse down. I'm sure there's a deal to be made here."

"Of course it's about money. It's always about money," I grumble.

He smirks.

I stalk toward the small table next to the bed. "How much will this cost me?"

No amount of money will ever be enough. If I allow a man like Evan McCabe to walk out of here alive, he'll always be a threat to my family.

The click of a bullet slipping into the chamber draws my attention back to the insane man.

"Not so quick," he mutters. "I'm not an idiot."

My heart pounds against my ribs, but I force out a laugh. "You really are," I say as I grip the weapon in the drawer, praying I can get a shot off before I drop.

This isn't about bargaining for my life. Mine is done. This is as far as I go. But protecting Cat? That will be the last thing I do.

When I spin, a deafening shot rings out, and pain almost as sharp as I felt the day I walked away from Cat radiates through my leg.

I fall to the floor but try like hell to stifle the groan that slips out. The second the sound rips from my lungs, I know my fierce Cat won't stay put.

And as if on cue, the door to the closet flies open. Gasping, she falls to the floor, still in her ballgown, and crawls to me as Frank rushes out behind her. Rather than going for Cat, though, Frank rushes his brother with a shout.

Cat falls on top of me, tears already cascading down her face.

"You've been shot!"

"Get in the closet, Cat," I grit, pushing her back so I can use my body to block her.

"Stop, Jay," she cries. "You're hurt."

I grab the gun from the floor beside me and point it to where Frank and his brother are wrestling across the room. Evan's gun sits halfway between them and where we lie near the bed. I try like hell to steady my hands and focus on my target, but the way they keep moving makes it impossible to get a clear shot of Evan without risking Frank.

Grunts fill the room as they fight, and Cat's sobs break me as she curls into my chest, begging me to live.

When Evan gets Frank on his back, straddling him and wrapping his hands around his throat, I know I have my last opportunity. If I don't take this shot, he'll have a chance to hurt my wife.

"Love you," I murmur as I aim the gun and fire.

The shots ring out in rapid succession. The first misses and draws Evan's attention. He eyes his gun on the floor a few feet from him, and releasing his brother, he pushes to stand, ready to defend himself. That's when I take my second shot, hitting him in the forehead. When he falls back with a loud thud, Cat clutches me and screams.

"You okay?" I holler to Frank as I grip my wife tightly.

He grunts and lifts his head up. "Yeah, good shot." Then he drops back to the floor and sprawls out. "You okay?"

I'm not sure.

Blood pools on the floor under me, and nausea rolls through my gut. "You gotta," I whisper. "Cat." I grasp her hand to get her attention, to break through her uncontrollable sobs and ground her. "Cat, you need to get me to the hospital," I rasp.

"Oh God," she cries, her eyes going wide at the puddle of blood we're lying in. "Fuck, Jay. I'll call an ambulance."

Frank shouts his disagreement as I shake my head.

He heaves himself off the floor and moves out of view. When he returns, he has a shirt in one hand, and he drops down beside me. With one quick tug, he rips the seam of my pants.

"I liked those," I grumble, a little woozy.

He smirks. "You can afford another pair."

Chills rack my body, and my teeth chatter.

Beside me, Cat sobs harder. "He's getting cold. We need to call an ambulance."

Frank gingerly moves my leg one way and then the other. "Thank fuck. It's a clean shot. We just need to get the bleeding to stop, and then you need to get him to the hospital."

"Why can't we call an ambulance?" she pleads, while Frank makes a tourniquet out of my shirt. His military training is coming in handy. Thank you, United States Marines.

"Remind me to buy you a car," I grit out.

With a grin, he ties the tourniquet tight, sending a burning pain searing through me. "I look good in red."

I grunt at the pain and take a few deep breaths. "You got it."

"Let's get you into the car." He squeezes my shoulder. "Don't die while your wife's driving, okay? She can't handle that."

"She can handle anything," I say with pride, my voice a bit breathy.

At that comment, she sobs louder and presses her face into the crook of my neck. "Why can't we call an ambulance?"

"Three bodies, baby. Frank needs to take care of the bodies."

She sighs against my neck and then nods, seemingly accepting the new plan.

It takes a bit of work, but Frank gets my car from the street where I left it and gets me to the car, helping me settle across the back seat. Before he shuts the door, he grasps Cat and pulls her to his chest. "You've got this" is what I think he says. "I'm so proud of you. Be happy. Be amazing. No more telenovelas for you or me, okay?"

"Why does it feel like you're saying goodbye?" she whispers through another sob.

He rocks her from side to side. "Because I am. I have to disappear after I clean up this mess. The people my brother worked with—"

"The Mob?" she asks on a sob.

He kisses her forehead, then tips her face up to his and kisses her softly on the lips.

I close my eyes, avoiding the moment he says his final goodbye.

"Yeah, Princess. Please. You need to get Jay to the hospital. Don't tell them how it happened. Tell them you found him like this. He'll know what to do."

I nod to myself as my brain gets fuzzy. *Yes. Encourage her to be strong.*

My beautiful Cat. The woman of my dreams. The love of my life.

He closes the back door and opens hers for her. When she's settled and the car is running, he knocks on the roof and walks back to the house.

She adjusts the mirrors and turns in her seat, a look of pure fear on her face. "You have to stay awake, baby, okay?"

I nod. "Tryin'."

She takes a deep breath and watches the backup camera as she reverses down the drive. My eyes fall shut, and I'm fighting sleep when a violent explosion rocks the car and Cat slams on the brakes. Adrenaline courses through me at the ear-splitting sound, but her screams are what jolt me into a sitting position.

In front of us, the house is engulfed in flames. Fire licks up the walls and smoke billows in thick clouds above it.

"Where's Frank?"

She doesn't respond. She only stares in horror at the house with her mouth open in an *O*.

"*Cat! Where's Frank?*"

In slow motion, she turns in her seat. Her eyes are filled with panic, and she gasps for air. "He...he walked in. He was in the house!" she screams.

78

PARIS BY THE CHAINSMOKERS

Cat

TWO MONTHS LATER

The days are harder now. Too often, I lie in bed, curled up into a ball, fighting back tears.

"Mom," Chloe calls from the doorway. When I turn, she's watching me with soft eyes and a frown. "You need to get up."

I swipe a tear away. "Yeah, I'll be right there."

The bed dips, and then her warmth hits my back. She snuggles in behind me like she does each time she finds me in this state. She's so strong. She's handled the whole situation so much better than I have. Which is pathetic. I'm the one who should be comforting her. But sometimes, I just can't.

Two months ago, my world was turned upside down, and I was rocked to the core. And I'm not sure I'll ever recover.

I don't know how to accept all we lost.

"Cat," Cynthia calls from the door.

I squeeze my eyes shut. "I know."

"We'll miss the flight if you don't get up."

Blowing out a breath, I focus on the picture on my nightstand. It's of

Jay and me on our wedding day. It feels like a lifetime ago. Two hopeful people standing under the stars, making promises of forever.

Another tear falls.

Cynthia sits on the corner of the bed and places a gentle hand on my hip. "Look at the two of you," she whispers with a soft smile. "You have to focus on the good, honey."

I nod again. It's been my go-to. Nod through the pain. Smile. Hold myself together.

But she's right. I promised Jay I would do this. Promised him I'd be there for our family. No matter what. His fierce Cat forever. So I press my fingers to my lips and touch my husband's picture. "I'll see you soon, baby."

KITTEN'S SONGS

The sight of the name *Bouvier* scrawled across the 787 makes my chest squeeze with pride, despite my blues. The James plane is far less ostentatious, but everything about this screams Jay, and that makes me smile.

He makes me smile.

He always has.

Garreth and Hayden are standing by the stairs when the limo drops us off. Hayden rushes over and pulls me in for a tight hug as soon as I step out of the vehicle. "You okay?"

I swallow my nerves. "Yeah, I just want to get there."

He nods and reaches for Chloe. "Come on, Chlo. Last one to the plane is a rotten egg!" The two of them take off at a run.

Garreth steps up and mutters, "Jesus Christ" under his breath.

"Hey, Gar."

"You ready?" he asks, his expression somber.

I wish everyone would stop coddling me. Of course I'm not ready. My brother's best friend died only a few dozen yards from me. One minute, he was kissing me, and in the next, he was gone.

Telling my brother that his best friend is gone was one of the hardest things I've ever done. He came back from his honeymoon excited to start his life with Grace, only to find out his best friend was dead.

Losing Frank devastated every single one of us.

But watching Chloe crumple at her father's hospital bed*? That* gutted me. Holding his hand while—

"Kitten, why are you staring at the plane like it's going to eat you?"

I suck in a breath as my husband saunters up beside me, his beautiful blue eyes lighting up at my shocked expression.

"I thought we were meeting you in Paris—"

Before I can chide him for not telling me he'd be here, he scoops me up and spins me around. When he sets me on my feet again, he says, "Wanted to fly with you guys."

"You flew home from Paris just so you could get on a plane *back* to Paris with us?"

His lips tip up in that gorgeous shy smile I've always loved.

"I'd ride the plane all day if I could spend just a few minutes sparring with you," he teases, reminding me of the words that swept me off my feet fifteen years ago.

Though back then, he was talking about a forty-minute commute from Providence to Boston. This time, he really will travel all day just to have more time with me.

"Jonathan Hanson, I love you," I say, sweeping my tongue across his lips.

He moans as he kisses me back. God, I've missed him.

Pulling away, he holds me at arm's length. "Fuck, wife. I'll go away more often if that's the welcome I get. *Je t'aimerai jusqu'à mon dernier souffle.*"

I will love you until my last breath.

I smile up at him. "I see you've been practicing. *Show off.*"

If losing Frank has taught me anything, it's that I don't want to live in the grief. I want to focus on the good. So when Jay suggested we spend Christmas in Paris with Cynthia and his brothers, it was a no-brainer. The Sienna Langfield show will start filming in the spring, but starting fresh in Paris as soon as possible feels like a necessity.

We put it off long enough. This trip has been years in the making.

My relationship with my brothers still hasn't completely recovered. I wish they were as close with my husband as I am with Jay's brothers, but it's possible that will never happen.

We're still trying to figure out how to tell Chase that he and Jay are brothers. But for now, we've decided to save that truth for another day. So many secrets have been exposed. So much loss. So much grief. And our hearts need time to heal.

I don't want to live under the weight of it all anymore. We deserve to be happy. And I've finally recognized that some relationships will never be the same. People change. We make mistakes. And that's okay.

Jay kisses my forehead once more and smiles down at me. "You ready, Kitten?"

Taking a deep breath, I close my eyes and let go of Boston.

79

RIPTIDE BY VANCE JOY

Jay

I can't get close enough to either of my girls. After finally reuniting with Cat and building a solid relationship with Chloe, only to come so close to losing everything all over again, when I say that I'd fly back and forth all day just to make sure that I'm traveling with them, I mean it. It may sound morbid or insane, but if anything were to happen, I want to go down with them. The idea of living even a day without them is too painful to bear.

Too many near-death experiences will do that to a person.

So will loss.

We've had too much of that in our lives. I couldn't be happier to say goodbye to Boston and set out on a new journey with my girls. Only a year and a half ago, Chloe lived half a world away from Cat and I had no idea she even existed. But now, she'll have all her parents in one place.

It's what's best for her. And I firmly believe it's what's best for Cat.

My wife needs this change. A fresh start. It's the adventure we should have had fourteen years ago.

"I can strap myself in, you know," Cat says with a smirk, though she doesn't fight me when I buckle her seat belt.

"I fucking missed you, Kitten," I growl, bringing her hand to my lips. "I'll never get enough of taking care of you, even if you are the strongest woman I know. So get used to it."

She rolls her eyes, but a smile lights her face. Turning her attention to our daughter, she asks, "What do you think of the plane, Chlo?"

"It's okay." She shrugs. "I think the James plane has softer leather, though."

"Excuse me?" I bark as my brothers and Cynthia groan.

Cynthia pokes our daughter, who has dissolved into a fit of giggles. "Don't tease him. I don't want to sit through an oration about why all things Hanson are better. I heard enough the first fifteen times."

Cat squeezes my hand when I glare at our daughter's other mother.

"It's a fact, Cyn," Garreth says as he settles into his seat on the opposite side of the plane.

Garreth and Hayden have been working tirelessly to rebuild Hanson Liquors. And they undoubtedly will. But that is no longer a part of my story. Bouvier Media is my sole focus—when I can tear myself away from Cat and Chloe. Because *they* are truly my world.

One day, we'll bring up the subject of having more children. But if Chloe is it for us, then I'm still the luckiest man on earth. Cat has been through more than most people can handle in the last few months, so forcing her to deal with the trauma of her mother's death and concerns over her own health is out of the question.

"What do you want to do first?" I tilt forward and eye my daughter across the aisle. She's created a list of the things she wants to show me, and I can't wait to learn more about the city she spent years traveling back and forth to.

"Duh. Obviously, I want to see the studio." Ah yes, she's most excited about spending time on the set of our show and rubbing elbows with Sienna Langfield.

Cat laughs, and the sound is like a balm to my soul.

KITTEN'S SONGS

Standing below the Eiffel Tower, I squeeze my wife's hand. "What do you think, Kitten? Should we sneak up there later tonight? I want to have you above the entire city."

She bumps her shoulder against me. "So dirty, Mr. Hanson."

"About that," I say, pulling her against my chest and bringing a hand to her chin. I brush my lips against hers, and then, because I can't help myself, I swipe my tongue across them, always craving her taste. "Chloe and I did a thing."

Cat's brows pinch together. "What kind of thing?"

Because I can't ever get enough, I press my lips to hers again. "We changed our last names," I murmur against her.

"You what?" she says, her voice raising an octave. She puts a hand to my chest and pulls back, scanning my face.

Above us, the stars sparkle and the lights of the Eiffel Tower glitter, but in this moment, there is nothing brighter than my wife's eyes. She glows as the meaning of my words sets in. "You changed your last name?"

"Yeah. But not to James," I tease with a smile.

Her lips tip up and she shakes her head. "God, you make me happy."

"Good. Because, Catherine Bouvier, I didn't know happiness until I met you. So what do you say? Can I have your last name?"

Cat purses her lips and gives me a teasing shrug. "I think that could be arranged."

"How 'bout right now?"

"Huh?" she asks, adorably confused.

"Marry me."

"But we're already married." Her smile makes my heart skip a beat.

"Yeah, but your family wasn't there."

"They're not here now either," she retorts.

"You sure about that?" I tilt my head and look at the crowd gathered behind her.

She spins so fast she almost trips over her heels.

There on the lawn in front of the Eiffel Tower, both our families have gathered. Bundled up and keeping warm on this cool December night, they watch on, wearing wide smiles.

Cat grabs for my hand, squeezing tight as she whispers, "What did you do?"

Theo, whose health has improved greatly since his stroke, is the first to approach. "He did what the rest of us should have done months ago. He brought your family back together. I'm so sorry, Sunshine." He holds out his arms, and Cat rushes into them.

While I'll never forget the hurt Theo caused by hiding Chloe from me, I understand his need to protect my wife and child. And because of that, I'll let the past go. And more importantly, I'll do everything I can to ensure Cat has what we both never did: both of our families.

Theo shakes my hand and pulls me in for a hug. "Really appreciate you arranging all of this. I know it wasn't easy."

"Easiest thing I've ever done is put Cat's happiness first," I say honestly.

When I turn, Cash is approaching Cat. "I'm so sorry, Kit Cat. I'll never forgive myself for how awful I've been to you."

My wife buries her face in his chest and squeezes him tight. "Let's let it all go. Please."

With a nod, he releases her and turns to me. "If not for you, we could have lost them both that day," Cash says, his voice breaking. On a sob, he doubles over and plants his hands on his knees. "Sorry," he says as Grace rubs his back. "I promised I wouldn't lose it…"

"Cash, it's okay. We all miss him," Cat murmurs.

Shaking his head, he swipes at his tears. "But he would want you to be happy. Cat, you have to know he loved you like a sister."

I can't help the scoff that falls from my lips.

Cat groans. "Now is so not the time."

Cash's eyes go wide, and he looks from me to Cat. "I fucking knew it," he says. And for the first time in who knows how long, he lets out a laugh. "Holy shit. You fucked my best friend," he whispers.

Cat eyes him, and then her face cracks, and she smiles as a tear slides down her cheek. "Yeah," her voice falters. "I fucked your best friend."

Shaking his head, Cash grabs her in a hug, and they both tremble with laughter and tears.

"As lovely as this has all been, we have a wedding to put on. And I'd rather not think about my bride with anyone else. Even if he was one of the best people I've ever known," I say, meeting Cash's gaze.

He nods and we clasp hands, and then I pull him in for a hug, patting him on the back.

"I really am sorry…for everything."

"My makeup!" Cat screeches as more tears cascade down her cheeks.

"Did someone say they need help with makeup?" Sophie says from the back of the group.

Cat gasps and claps a hand over her mouth when she spots her. "You brought my best friend?" she asks, peering up at me, then looking back to where Sophie, Dex, and their gaggle of kids step out of the crowd.

I smile at her. "Couldn't get married without her here, Kitten."

Another sob erupts from her. "I love you."

"I love you too. Now let's get rid of those tears, baby. The quicker I marry you again, the sooner we get another wedding night."

She smiles and pulls me close so that no one else can hear. "I have a surprise for you too."

I kiss her again. "Yeah?"

She smiles. "I went to the doctor this week."

"You did?" I raise my brows.

She takes a deep breath and slides a hand up my chest. "I did."

I place my palm against it and hold it tight over my heart. "And?"

"*Je veu avoir un bébé avec toi,*" she says softly, her eyes glowing.

I work the words over in my mind, trying to translate them, but they keep getting jumbled. Despite months of listening to nothing else in the car or at night before sleeping, I'm still not fluent in French. But I'm trying. I'll never stop trying when it comes to my family. "I don't think I know that one."

She smiles. "I want to have a baby with you."

"You got the test?"

She shakes her head. "Having a baby increases the odds that I'll get cancer, but so does half the stuff we put in our bodies. I won't let that dictate how we live our lives…" She bites her lip. "For too long, outside forces controlled every move I made. I want to try for a baby. I want to choose you. I want to choose joy and trust that you and I will figure out how to deal with whatever life throws at us. *Together.* No matter what. And if I get cancer, I'll fight."

Frozen, I stand in awe of the strongest woman I've ever met.

She holds her breath like she's waiting to see how I'll respond. All I can do is let the smile that pushes at my lips take over. It's the smile I've always saved for her. The real me. The man I became *because* of her.

"So what do you say, husband?"

I pull her against my chest and hold tight to the only woman I've ever loved. Ducking and bringing my lips to her ear, I rasp, "You're a dream come true, Kitten. Our life is a dream fucking come true."

"Swoony," she murmurs.

"And tonight, I'm going to fuck you so hard you'll forget both our last names."

She laughs. "Surprisingly, that didn't ruin the swoon. You've gotten better at this."

My hair falls over my eyes as I smile down at her. "Only for you."

"Head over heels," she whispers as I press my lips to her forehead.

Trailing lower, I pepper her face with kisses and cradle her cheeks. "Completely. Irrevocably. Head over fucking heels in love with you, *wife*."

THE END

EPILOGUE

MANY YEARS LATER

DIE FIRST BY NESSA BARRETT

Jay

"There's no fucking way my daughter is marrying a McCabe," I grumble as my wife tries to push me out our bedroom door.

"Shh, she'll hear you," Cat scolds. Her glare still heats me up in a way only she ever has.

I press her against the door, caging her in, and push my pelvis against her. "Let's just stay here. I don't want to do a meet the family dinner. I can make it worth your while."

Cat bites her lip to hide her smile. "Our only daughter is getting married. Keep it in your pants for once."

"Ha," I bark. "As if I'm the only dirty one here."

Her lashes flutter closed as she places her soft hands against my wildly beating heart. At forty-eight, my wife still takes my breath away. She's only gotten more stunning as her confidence has grown through the years.

We still play. Together and sometimes with others. But my favorite moments are when it's just the two of us, here, in our own little world.

She's all I've ever needed—all I've ever craved—and the smile on her face tells me she knows it.

Some couples spend their lives side by side yet living separate lives. Their friends interest them; strangers entertain them. I want nothing to do with them.

My wife is the most interesting person in the world to me. Her thoughts. Her expressions. Fuck, I could watch her for hours and never get enough. We don't live a life beside one another. We live a life *with* one another. She's my life. And I wouldn't have it any other way.

One year after our marriage in Paris, Catherine gave birth to our first son. Two years later, we welcomed our second. A year after that, my wife was diagnosed with cancer.

Because of her annual check-ups, we caught the cancer early, and as my wife always does, she used her experience to highlight the importance of annual screenings in an article she wrote for *Jolie*. She also started an editorial column online where she wrote about the treatments weekly.

While she was the epitome of grace under pressure, I was a ball of nerves. I told her we couldn't let fear dictate our lives, but the thought of losing her was so debilitating, there were times it was hard to let her go and get out of bed. But I did. We had children to raise and lives to lead. I promised Catherine she'd have my last breath, and I pray mine is before hers.

Finding Catherine all those years ago wasn't fate. It wasn't destined. It was fucking perfection. It was finding a needle in a damn haystack, and I worked hard for that fucking needle. I've worked hard for this life. But the work didn't stop years ago when I won her back. It didn't stop after we had kids, or after we found out she was in remission.

The work never stops. They say if you love someone, it isn't work. But that's fucking nonsense. Marriage is work. Love is work. If you don't have to fight for it, it's not worth it. But being her husband is the greatest job I've ever had. It's the experience of a lifetime.

I'd fight every day of my damn life for this woman, and she'd do the same for me.

I press my lips to hers and take her hand in mine, twining our fingers where our names are inscribed. I'll never get enough of my kitten. A quick kiss turns passionate, and of their own volition, my hands are in her hair, ready to undo the carefully curled tendrils secured in an updo that highlights my favorite spot. Right beneath her ear, where she shudders every time my lips meet her soft skin.

"*Dad*, they're here!" JJ calls. He goes by Jonathan Junior, even though we don't share the same middle name. The kid is my doppelganger. His younger brother, James, looks exactly like his mother. Right down to the whiskey eyes that have always been my undoing.

I growl into Cat's mouth as she tries to pull away from me.

"Jay." Her tone holds no scolding, though. It's all panting, want, and need.

I smirk as Cat pushes the hair out of my eyes and strokes *her* favorite place.

This is us. A little bit obsessed—okay, a lot obsessed—always slightly tousled, with swollen lips and big smiles.

A perfect life for two imperfect people who worked their asses off to get here.

"Please don't let her marry him," I beg.

There's no way Chloe could have found this with Evan McCabe's son. And how the fuck did my daughter—my literal pride and joy—end up dating someone in the Mob? It's insanity.

Cat grabs hold of the front of my shirt, drawing my attention. Not that she ever doesn't have it. "She's happy. And he's not part of the Mob. He's just related to them. He's an accountant, for fuck's sake."

I drop my head back. "Oh my sweet, naïve wife. He's an accountant *for* the Mob."

She tugs on my shirt, forcing my head up. "Stop. She's happy. And

I seem to remember another story involving a boy who most people believed didn't belong with the girl he loved. And look at how they turned out."

"Almost dead, Cat. *We almost died* to be together."

She coughs out a laugh. "So dramatic. And if I remember correctly, you'd say it was worth it."

I wrap my arms around my wife and pull her against my chest, pressing a kiss to her hair and inhaling that floral scent that first drove me crazy almost thirty years ago. "Always worth it. But are you trying to tell me he's her Romeo?"

Cat shrugs against me. "Maybe. Who are we to say?"

I groan. Of course she's right. Chloe is happy. Shane seems nice enough. Although, with all the tattoos, he's not fooling anyone. The man is most definitely working for the Mob. He's not just an accountant like my wife and daughter believe. But if I forbid it, I'll only push Chloe away. "Fine. Let's get this over with."

As we take the stairs down to greet our guests, I stare at my wife's ass in Chloe's latest design. "God, she's talented," I mutter, still in awe of our daughter.

At twenty-six, she's accomplished more than most fashion designers with *decades* of experience. And obviously, Cat has helped her. Being the daughter of a fashion icon who literally determines whether a designer's career lives or dies can never hurt.

But Cat, despite her love for our daughter, would never jeopardize the magazine's credibility if she didn't believe in Chloe's designs. If anything, she's harder on her than any other designer. But Chloe shines. Just like her mother, she makes people work for her affection. She's above the fray. Her cold blue stare brings everyone around her to their knees.

But fuck, her designs are gorgeous. Likely thanks to the mentorship she received from Sienna for all these years.

"She's got more talent in her pinky than most designers." Cat smiles as Chloe comes into view. She's relaxing with a glass of champagne in her hand while speaking with Cynthia and Peter, who look at her the same way we do—with complete pride and infatuation.

JJ and James stand beside the appetizer table, stuffing their faces like we didn't have lunch a few hours ago. Preteen boys never stop eating. I laugh as James catches my eye. The sight of the two of them beside one another always makes me smile. Our family is my entire world.

The chime of the doorbell has everyone falling silent.

"I'll get it," Chloe says, her eyes finding mine. "*Sois gentil, s'il-te-plait.*"

Be nice, please.

I grunt. "I'm nice. When have I not been nice to Shane?"

"It's not Shane I'm worried about. It's his uncle. Promise you'll keep an open mind."

"Because he's the head of the Mob?" I grumble.

Chloe rolls her eyes. "*Deviner chevre.*"

I turn to my wife and whisper, "What did she just say?"

"Literally?" Cat replies, her lips tipping up in a teasing smile. "She said don't have a goat."

JJ and James burst out laughing, and Chloe turns around and glares at her younger brothers. "It means don't be crazy." Then, under her breath, she mutters, "*Parler comme une vache espagnole.*"

Cat snorts.

"*Now* what did she say?" I growl as I pinch my wife's side. Even after years living in Paris, I haven't quite caught all the little sayings. I worry more about learning the sexy phrases my wife likes to utter while I make her come.

"She said you speak like a Spanish cow."

My daughter just shrugs. "I'm opening the door now. Remember, you're being good. Shane's not part of the Mob. His uncle is retired."

When I simply stare at her she sighs. "God, you're insane."

Right. And the Easter bunny is real. The fact that my wife and daughter believe his family isn't still involved is nuts.

But I puff up my chest and head to the door. "I'll be good."

Cat meets me in the entranceway and squeezes my hand. "*Je t'adore.*"

I adore you.

With a deep breath, I squeeze my wife's hand back and mutter, "you better adore my cock later" under my breath, then open the door.

Both Cat and I suck in air as we come face to face with the one man we never thought we'd see again.

"Heard we're going to be family," the Irish bastard says with a smile. "*Frank…*"

Read Frank's Epilogue NOW!
https://BookHip.com/MPAFTDD

PRE-ORDER IRISH TODAY
https://geni.us/irishfrank

ACKNOWLEDGEMENTS

I never thought a character would have a hold on me like Cash did and then Jay went and changed the entire script. I have loved going back in time to see all of these characters when they were younger and then to watch the growth of all of them.

I know you are all likely reeling from that final reveal. Frank is ALIVE! Did you really think I would kill him? He is a fan favorite and I know we all NEED his story. Irish is available to preorder now!

But before I move on, I just want to take a moment to say how much Cat's character really affected me. As a mother who is constantly running herself ragged trying to do all the things, it was so important for me to show just a little bit of realness with how Cat took on motherhood. This book is for every single one of us out there who wants everything… the spice, the love, the life, the career. I hope for a few hours you got to escape from the real world and you enjoyed yourself. Thank you from the bottom of my heart for loving these characters as much as me.

This book would not have been possible though if not for some really amazing people. Sara, Jay is still yours. You earned him with every tiktok, every instagram post, every song, every rant, every tear you let me cry and every time you read this book (quite a few) to help me make it the best it could be. I adore you. I love you. I praise you! Above everything else, I appreciate your friendship.

To my work wife Jenni who beta reads, listens to my random thoughts, deals with my insanity and agreed to start another business because obviously the universe told us to, thank you! It has been a joy working this author journey with you and I appreciate you immensely.

To my lovely editors, Beth and Brittni. You make my books better every single time. I will never stop singing your praises.

To Monique, my day one girl, as always another beautiful formatting job. I appreciate you.

To my Booktok Army and the Cocktail Club, my street team, you have made this year the most fun and the most rewarding. I am always in awe of your friendship and support.

To my OG crew, Amy, Amy and Anna, thank you for always taking the snippets that I send you. For loving my words and for always cheering me on.

A special thanks to my author besties, Daphne Elliot, Elyse Kelly, Jenni Bara (look you get two shout outs) and Swati M.H. I can't tell you how grateful I am that I met you ladies. Your support, your guidance and your friendship are unmatched. Also your books inspire me to become a better writer daily. Thank you!

And to my amazing readers, thank you for all of your messages, your Tiktoks, your dms, your posts and your rants. There is nothing I love more than hearing from each of you how a character affected you, or a storyline made you laugh. I love your reviews, your anecdotes, and the notes you send to me.

If you want to follow along on my writing journey and have sneak peeks into all the characters in Bristol, follow me on Instagram, join my awesome Facebook group, sign-up for my newsletter and follow me on TikTok.

OTHER BOOKS BY BRITTANÉE NICOLE

BRISTOL BAY SERIES

SHE LIKES PINA COLADAS
KISSES SWEET LIKE WINE
OVER THE RAINBOW
LOVE & TEQUILA MAKE HER CRAZY
A VERY MERRY MARGARITA MIX-UP

BOSTON BILLIONAIRES

WHISKEY LIES
LOVING WHISKEY
WISHING FOR CHAMPAGNE KISSES

DIRTY TRUTHS
EXTRA DIRTY

STAND ALONE ROMANTIC THRILLER

DEADLY GOSSIP

COMING SOON

IRISH